The Ravenell Dynasty Trilogy
Book Three
Double Promise to Love

written by
Kamrynn Bellary
Lenevar Publications

I0673822

Dedication

This book series is dedicated to all ladies on Earth, who endeavor a world of equality, diversity, and inclusion, and who believe in love and romance, and have taken a chance at love, only to have experienced heartbreak, and yet, maybe if even only deep down, still believe in the possibility of true love.

Double Promise to Love

. . . .

THIS FICTION STORY series is for adult readers/audiences, and contains elements of human life, including love, sex, violence, sexual assault, abuse, rape, suicide, death, grief, and spirituality.

"TW" is for trigger warning, and is placed at the beginning of each chapter where the author feels the reader may want a trigger alert warning for very emotional parts of the story that may deal with abuse, assault, sexual violence, or suicide. This courtesy is not a guarantee that every possible trauma trigger is alerted in this fiction work, however, it is with good intentions that this author places the alerts for the reader.

• • • •

AUTHOR ENCOURAGES ANYONE with suicidal thoughts, or any victims of sexual assault, physical assault, or domestic violence to reach out to your local community resources to receive help.

Chapter One

E ach of the Ravenell family members finds themselves in an extraordinary paradox. Being both day and night at the same time for each of them, is indeed, a paradox. The meaning of the word paradox for the Ravenells is the contradiction of impossible circumstances, which also turns out to be true.

Deirdre finds that as the night falls for her in Austin, Texas, with the clear blue sky and sparkling stars, it is yet daylight where her beloved Nicolaus is on the other side of the world trying to rescue his former father-in-law from a dangerous drug cartel. Though her mind is on her love, her man, her Nicolaus, with worry for his safety, and with love in her heart, she has endured a vicious attack from his brother, Niall. An attack full of lust, despite her being nine months pregnant.

Deirdre lays in bed, in the wing of the Ravenell mansion, which belongs to her and Nicolaus. She tries to rest as tears spill from her eyes as she thinks of the ruthless attack upon her person, while also thinking of her one and only love, her Nicolaus.

On the other side of the Ravenell mansion, Nigel recognizes in his thoughts that his sons are the future of the family. However, he is greatly perturbed by his younger son, Niall, not only by Niall's behavior towards Deirdre, he is also concerned about Niall's maladaptive behaviors in general, while at the same time being very proud of Nicolaus.

Nigel thinks about Nicolaus as he sits in bed, under the covers. He checks his watch, calculating the time zone changes in his mind, knowing it is the next day in the part of the world his son is trekking to rescue Niall's father-in-law.

As Ceil, the stern Ravenell matriarch, looks upon Nigel, sitting next to him in bed, she feels that her hatred for Nicolaus has softened a little after reading the beautiful love letter he had written

1

to Deirdre, at Deirdre's request. Ceil read the letter aloud for all present to hear. The letter made her see Nicolaus a little differently, yet again. She wonders why Nigel, her own husband of decades, had never written her a love letter. She wonders why he never spoke to her the way Nicolaus speaks to and regards Deirdre with such love.

Ceil feels bad for trying to break Nicolaus and Deirdre apart, though her mind has not changed about wanting Nicolaus banished from the family. She also worries about Niall. Why on earth if Niall is in love with Deirdre, why was he trying to drown her earlier? Ceil is certainly fearful that Niall will not get his head straight. How can he?

In a different part of the mansion, Elsa, Niall's wife, touches her pregnant belly with both hands, thinking of her new little one, as she lay in bed alone. She looks at Niall's side of the bed and wonders where he is. He said nothing to her, he just kind of disappeared. Elsa wants her husband near her as she wonders if he'd gone to the brothel, or to his old hangout on Red River Street. Would he enter the room drunk and mean? Did he have another woman in one of the other rooms in the mansion?

Elsa takes a deep breath and sighs it out, trying to relieve some of her stress. She thinks about her father and begins to cry. She prays that Nicolaus can get to her father and rescue him before a worse fate might happen to him. She prays for protection over Nicolaus.

Constance, Deirdre's sweet mother, drifts to sleep in a luxury room on Nicolaus' side of the mansion. Though she tries to stay awake to be vigilant, even with the door open, she is just too exhausted from the day. She is completely tuckered out by the excitement of the baby shower with all the guests and celebrities, then the excitement of seeing those beautiful flowers and hearing the words of the beautiful love letter from Nicolaus, and dealing with Deirdre's anxiety and worry. Then the horrid stress of finding Niall with his hands on her daughter, Nicolaus' precious wife, his brother's wife!

Constance tries to stay awake, however, she is just too exhausted as she worries about Deirdre and about Nicolaus. And now she has worry about Niall, as well. She had already decided that they must leave this house first thing in the morning. She is fearful that Niall will not abide by Ceil's command to leave the house and not return until Nicolaus is present. She knows they must leave at first light.

Francesca, Nicolaus' loving and supportive sister, enjoys the refreshing breeze over her skin from warm air off the sea in the Cayman Islands. She sits up from her sleep, feeling that something is terribly wrong. She cannot shake that feeling after briefly speaking with her brother, feeling he may be stepping into danger. Something just doesn't feel right. Francesca is greatly concerned about Nicolaus as she looks at her sleeping, handsome beau, in her luxurious hut inspired hotel room. She is not ready to leave him, though she knows she must get back home.

Francesca is very worried about this curse business that she found in the family book. She does not understand what it means, exactly. She is not able to decipher the paragraph, as Nicolaus easily would do. Using her phone, Francesca purchases her airline tickets for returning home.

Niall aimlessly drives through the city, incensed that his mother threw him out of the house. He understands if she is upset that he'd touched Deirdre, his American hero brother's wife, though he feels his mother has never been so rude to him, nor treated him so poorly. This compounds Niall's confused mind. He is furious that he did not get to fully take Deirdre, while feeling unworthy of Elsa, her pregnancy setting off all kinds of negative emotions for him.

Niall knows that he is nothing like "father material". He knows he has no business raising children. He is no one's role model, and doesn't want to be. Niall is riled up as he slams on his brakes for a red light. He revs the engine of his sports car, feeling impatient, angry, and rather incompetent.

Nicolaus briefly thinks of Deirdre as he leads his small unit of men up the side of the mountain, in Glavischtein, just outside of Spain. He left his post as the leading Vice President of his father's company, Villamae Medical Corporation, VMC, as the only option to rescue his former father-in-law, Jonathan Baird, Elsa's father. Nicolaus is trying to rescue Baird from the tangled mess he's gotten himself into with a deadly drug cartel. Nicolaus thinks of Deirdre, then brings his mind back to the matter at hand. After all, he is responsible for the three young men, James, Manny, and Sergey, provided to him through the U.S. State Department. They agreed to help him rescue Jonathan.

Nicolaus and his men each must watch the trail for snakes, and scorpions, and any other type of creature that could harm them. As they make it to the top of the mountain, the cartel's compound can be seen in the distance. Nicolaus spots the red house where Jonathan is being held.

Behind a cluster of rocks for protection, he rests his guys, as the sun has risen and is heating them up. They are sweating and panting. They rest, and refresh with water. Their upcoming task of rescuing Jonathan will be extremely difficult, with the unfortunate risk of death. Dealing with a cartel is no one's picnic. As Nicolaus peers over the rocks at the compound, he sees several men with military styled weapons. He has to develop a plan that will be the least risk to his men.

And Abigail Deirdre Omari, Deirdre's long lost twin sister, who currently lives in Johannesburg, South Africa, is having unusual symptoms and very unusual anxiety. Dominique, her beautiful best friend since childhood, looks upon Abigail with fright. She'd never seen Abigail behave in such a manner. Dominique observes that Abigail's eyes are wide, looking kind of bugged out. She watches as Abigail pulls at her long, curly hair, as if she may tear it from her head. Abigail is bunched up in the bed, under the covers, as if hiding from an approaching Armageddon.

Dominique grabs Abigail by the shoulders. "Abby, you have got to stop this," she tells her calmly.

"Dominique why aren't you listening to me?" she yells at her bestie of decades. "You aren't hearing me!"

"I do hear you! You keep saying we have to leave for Austin. We need to save Deirdre." Dominique looks at the clock. "Except it's two in the morning, Abby. What would we even be doing? Where would we be going? What are we even saving her from? If anything at all is wrong."

"If? If? I'm telling you something is wrong. I'm telling you directly. It's catastrophic! Why don't you believe me?"

Abigail begins to cry again. Her chest feels as though it may cave in. Her mind sees darkness, of which she has not seen before and cannot decipher. Abigail has never experienced anything like this before. She cannot seem to get ahold of herself, though normally she is the rock of the family, she is the one giving orders. However, now she knows it is imperative that she get to Deirdre.

In haste, Abigail stops herself crying, though looking and feeling disheveled, she picks up her phone. She gets the number for VMC in Austin, Texas, and calls the number.

"Oh my God, Abby! Who are you calling at this hour?"

"I must reach her. I have to talk to her." A recording is heard, as it is after hours for the office. "Oh God!" Abigail ends the call, and starts to cry again. "Please! Dominique, please get their number, please call her!"

"Abby! You think Deirdre's number is listed online?"

"Please! Try! I must reach her before it's too late. Please!"

Dominique sighs, "Okay, that's it. I'm getting your father." Dominique races from the room to awaken Cecil Omari, Abigail's father, suddenly feeling panicked for leaving Abigail alone. She bangs on the door. "Mr. Omari!" She calls loudly, loudly banging on the door. "Mr. Omari, please hurry! Abigail needs you! Please hurry!"

Feeling increased panic, Dominque races back to their room, only to find that Abigail is missing. She twirls the room checking for Abigail, and does not see her. She checks the bathroom ... no one. She checks the large closet ... no one. She had only been gone for a few seconds! Dominique twirls again and suddenly notices the window is open, which it wasn't before. The window is wide open, the curtains are blowing, ... and Abigail Deirdre Omari is gone.

After Niall's attack on Deirdre, and Ceil dramatically threw Niall out of the house, Ceil actually apologized to Deirdre for Niall's appalling behavior. She let the ladies know, which included Deirdre, Constance, and Deirdre's close friends, Ishani and Maggie, that she had made Niall leave the house, and that he would not be bothering them again.

This certainly put them all at ease, as Ishani and Maggie remained overnight. However, in reality, the ladies were lured into a false sense of security.

Unfortunately, as Nicolaus and his team had already trekked five miles up the side of a mountain to get Niall's father-in-law, and were now, literally making plans for the rescue, Niall comes back into the mansion, in the early morning hours. Ceil had not taken his keys, nor had she alerted security, nor the staff. She'd expected Niall to do what she told him; however, she is mistaken. The truth is, Niall has never done what Ceil has told him to do.

Niall's lust for Deirdre is excessively strong. By the time he re-enters the mansion, he has gotten himself angry about Deirdre's baby. He is angry about the way Deirdre ignores him at every turn. He has made up his mind and is determined to have Deirdre while Nicolaus is away.

Everyone is fast asleep in their respective bedrooms when Niall enters the mansion, shewing the staff away, after they let him in. Quietly, he makes his way to where he knows he should not be. Niall quashes the consciousness of his mind that tells him to turn back, or to at least go to his own wife. His feet, and maybe a streak of twisted darkness, leads him into transgression.

Deirdre stirs from unease and uncomfortableness. She is dressed in the special nightgown her mother bought her for her pregnancy. Constance sweetly bought Deirdre designer gowns for each night of her last month of pregnancy to accentuate the specialness of finally being married to Nicolaus, and them finally beginning their family.

Stirring, Deirdre sits right up into the arms of Niall. Immediately, Niall's hand goes around Deirdre's throat, in a tightened grip to keep her from screaming for help.

On the other side of the world, Nicolaus and his men begin the descent of the cliff to the cartel compound. They have brief exposure, which is extremely dangerous, if they were to be noticed by the cartel men. The plan is to land next to the rock wall, behind a building, which puts them inside the compound. Nicolaus knows they will most likely have to take out some men, as he is noticing an increase of the numbers of men with weapons patrolling and walking the compound. At present, those men seem relaxed, talking, joking, and snacking on morning bread and fruit.

Back in Austin, Deirdre becomes very frightened of what Niall might do. She is so shocked at his behavior towards her. She cannot believe he has entered her bedroom, the sacred space she shares with Nicolaus, only to attack her.

Niall violently shakes Deirdre. "You think you're better than me?" Niall harshly whispers to her, having already locked her bedroom door. "Women all over the city worship me and want my autograph. At every race show I go, all kinds of people want pictures with me. They want to touch me and stand next to me. But you … you don't even look at me anymore, Deirdre. You reject the love I have for you."

Feeling very uncontrolled, Niall violently shakes her again, tightly gripping her neck. "You completely ignore me, Deirdre! Why?" The question is not to be answered as he does not release her throat. "Well … you will not ignore me anymore, Deirdre." He shakes her. "You hear me? You're going to see me today! You're going to feel me today!"

To ensure her quietness, without love or mercy, Niall harshly backhands Deirdre across her delicate face, one, two, three times. She is sure she felt the snap of her jawbone on the right side of her face, as his grip tightens even more on her throat. She cannot breathe.

Niall slams Deirdre onto the pillow in the bed she shares with Nicolaus. Then playing out the fantasy he'd carried for years, Niall rips Deirdre's nightgown away from her body. This act is the international symbolism of stripping away a woman's dignity. The beautiful gown is now in tatters. Niall smiles, with a tinge of maliciousness, as finally, he sees Deirdre's full nakedness, which arouses him even more, if that were possible.

"Please, Niall, the baby," Deirdre pleads with him as best she can, hardly able to whisper, trying to release his stranglehold on her neck.

Her plead is rewarded with more cruelty of another backhand across the face.

Then, as if to purposefully bring harm to the baby, Niall yanks Deirdre from the bed to the floor onto her belly, never letting go of her neck. Harshly, he whispers to her, "That baby should have been mine!"

Meanwhile, in Johannesburg, Abigail is in a heap at the bottom of a small hill, on the lawn of their home. She is struggling to breathe. She fights immensely hard to get a breath, grasping her throat, not understanding what is happening, though sure Deirdre is going through something similar. Abigail fights with all her might and all her strength to scream, as she knows she needs help. She gets a scream out, and she screams again.

Dominique looks out that open window. "Abigail!" She calls out, hearing a faint scream. "Abigail! Where are you?" Dominique looks around outside in the darkness of three in the morning. She cannot understand what is happening. Suddenly, Cecil is by her side, looking out over the lawn. Dominique calls to her again, "Abigail!"

Abigail uses all her might and screams again. This time, she hears her scream echoing in the dark.

Cecil points to the bottom of the ridge below the window. "Oh my God, there she is! I see her!" Cecil bolts out the room to get his daughter. Dominique begins to cry. She grabs her phone to call for an ambulance, and walks following Cecil.

Back in Austin, cruelly, Niall drags Deirdre's dainty weight across the floor until he is done demonstrating the power he has over her. Then he lifts her and throws her onto the bed, jealous that Nicolaus can have her whenever he wants her.

The brutal assaulting begins.

The grip around Deirdre's neck is tightened. Niall proceeds to move forward with his filthy vile deed against Deirdre, his brother's cherished wife. He commits his unspeakable act against her. The feel of her body is beyond his imagination. However he is unable to reach gratification. He repeatedly violates her, yet in his rush to claim her, he is unable to draw any satisfaction or pleasure.

Deirdre suffers, hardly able to breathe, very worried about her unborn baby. She feels something wrong with the insides of her dainty body, most likely from Niall's whim to demonstrate his small power over her.

Deirdre cannot look at Niall as he repeatedly violates her. He is at his very lowest trying to prove to her that he is better than Nicolaus. That he matters more. When in fact, the only thing he proved to her is that he is a despicable low life, who doesn't deserve anything he has been given, not even his station in life, nor his birthright. Deirdre feels sorry for Nigel, knowing this will fall hard on Nicolaus' father.

Deirdre puts her mind on Nicolaus, her love, the only man on earth for her. She begins to say his name with the small breaths she could take. She utters the name of the man she loves, "Nicolaus. Nicolaus. Nicolaus." Niall's attack eases. The chokehold loosens, providing her more breath. She coughs out Nicolaus' name, "Nicolaus. Nicolaus."

Niall pauses, seeing that even while he commits his filthy vile deed against the dainty and elegant Deirdre, she still calls for his brother. Her cut and bleeding lips call for Nicolaus.

On the other side of the world in Johannesburg, Abigail lays in her father's arms and begins to scream excessively, holding her stomach, experiencing massive pains. The ambulance arrives to rush Abigail to the hospital.

Back in Austin, Niall looks upon the mess he's made of Deirdre, as she holds her belly in pain. Only the attempt of Constance trying to open Deirdre's bedroom door and calling for her, as she'd awakened and wanted to check on Deirdre, finding the door locked, is what makes Niall want to flee. Constance again tries to open the locked door, knocking and banging, knowing something is very wrong. Like the thief he is, after stealing his brother's sanctity of wifely love, Niall grabs his clothes, then climbs out the window onto the terrace, and runs away, without getting dressed. Constance calls to her daughter again. Ishani rushes to get help, and Maggie assists with the door.

It is Nigel who finally burst the bedroom door open. He, Constance, and Ceil enter to find Deirdre nude, bloodied, and bruised. Deirdre tries to cover herself as she struggles to breathe, and mumbles in hysterical panic as her amniotic fluid sac is now broken and oozing out of her, along with a sizable volume of blood.

"Oh God! Oh no!" Constance races to her daughter, and covers her nakedness. Constance holds Deirdre. No comfort is found, as Constance begins to wail with Deirdre's cries, holding onto her, helplessly.

Abigail faints in the ambulance on the way to the hospital. The emergency workers have placed oxygen on her. She wakes up, and grabs at her stomach, wailing a blood curdling scream. Cecil turns pail, scared for his daughter. He fears he will lose her.

Deirdre shakes in distress from having been powerless to fight off the repeated ravishing of Niall, while trying to remain as still as possible, afraid for the baby's life. She tries to speak, but no intelligible words fall from her mouth, only whimpers. Deirdre is suddenly gripped by labor pain. It rips through her as if there is a tearing in her inner body. She grabs her belly and screams out in agony.

Immediately, Ceil knew that Niall had been there. She knows Niall has done this. They all know what has occurred, as Deirdre screams in pain, they can see the bruising around her neck and on her face becoming prominent.

At this same time, Abigail is wheeled from the ambulance into the emergency room at the hospital. Dominique holds tightly to Abigail's hand, and Cecil does not know what to do. It seems that Abigail is having some kind of fit, having trouble breathing again, while flailing about. Only now she is again grabbing her stomach and crying a blood curdling scream. "Make it stop!" She yells before screaming out again.

Nigel hurries to ring for an ambulance for Deirdre. The mansion begins to stir with staff rushing around. Ishani and Maggie frantically hasten to Deirdre as well.

"Dear God, my Lord, protect my child!" Constance prays between tears. Constance holds tight to Deirdre, as she screams out again, the pain unbearable.

The noise alerts Elsa, as she notices Niall is still absent from her bed, indeed he is not in their bedroom. Elsa emerges from her room, and sees happenings in the direction of Nicolaus' wing of the mansion. Elsa rushes over, thinking Deirdre has gone into early labor. As Elsa enters the scene, suddenly she is shocked to discover what has happened to Deirdre. She shakes her head, numb, in unbelief. In her heart, and without asking, Elsa knows Niall is the perpetrator. She is saddened, and does not know what to do.

Chapter Three (TW)

Deirdre is rushed into the birthing room of the hospital, and several physicians and nurses attend to her. The ladies of the family insist they be in the room with Deirdre. Constance is at her head, holding her, crying with her, wiping her brow, as Deirdre screams out in pain. Ceil and Elsa are present. Elsa holds Deirdre's hand, surprised that Deirdre let her. She kisses her hand with humbled sorrow for her.

Immediately, the physicians know Deirdre is in trouble. They work quickly.

Nicolaus and his team are also working quickly, as they quietly enter the compound. They each jump the four foot brick wall that surrounds the land. As soon as they each are over the wall behind a building, they take machine gun fire, from a previously unseen machine gun station that has been lifted up out of the ground.

They dive for cover and roll around to the side of the building. However, before they are completely under cover, Nicolaus takes a hit to his lower left leg, and James is hit across his throat.

"James!" Nicolaus grabs young James, and holds him in his arms as he struggles. The open wounds pour magenta blood down his throat. The hot bullets have severed the arteries in James' neck. Nicolaus looks upon James and holds him as he shakes with death, and is swiftly gone.

"No, James! No!" Nicolaus holds the teen, who has now died, in his arms. Blood seems to be everywhere. "Oh God, no!" Nicolaus believes James is too young to die in such a manner. Sorrow immediately fills him, as he knows there is nothing he can do to save this brave young man who believed in their mission.

Joshua pulls James from a frantic Nicolaus, and gently places him on the ground. "Sir," he yells at Nicolaus to get his attention, "you cannot fall apart right now."

The machine gun has not stopped, and bullets are still whizzing by them. They are pinned down on the side of the building. Quickly, Joshua takes off his shirt and makes a tourniquet for Nicolaus' leg, as the wound is bleeding quite a bit. Nicolaus was so concerned about James, he hadn't felt his leg until Joshua tended to it.

The men stay against the side of the building, the bricks covering them. They hope and pray those men do not come upon them, as there is no escape. The machine gun continues to spray bullets at them as if the intent is to eventually kill them all.

Back in Austin, in the birthing room, the baby, little Nicolai, is removed from Deirdre by Cesarean Section. Ceil is next to the doctor, and she can see that the baby is folded, blue, and unmoving. The physician cuts the umbilical cord, and attempts to get him to breathe. He tries several techniques, none of which are successful. After fifteen minutes, the time of death for the baby is called.

"Oh no!" Constance is heard, already crying for her grandchild. She knows this is all very bad, and she is very much afraid of losing Deirdre, who is shaking with shock. She holds her daughter tight.

The baby is cleaned and washed before he is wrapped and handed to Ceil.

The physicians are still working on Deirdre, as she is now in medical distress.

Deirdre wants to ask about Nicolai, however she can't seem to talk. Deirdre holds onto her mother. Constance kisses Deirdre's forehead, and wipes her brow. Deirdre uses all her might, which is the last of her strength to call out. "Nicolaus! Nicolaus." Suddenly, Deirdre sees darkness covering over her.

Ceil holds her grandson who is lifeless and blue. His eyes had never opened. She looks at him, and hugs him to her. She begins to weep for her lost grandson, who looks exactly like Nicolaus. There is no denying this should have never happened.

"She is hemorrhaging," the physician announces of Deirdre's condition. "There is so much blood! Too much blood! Suction!" he urgently calls for the nurse specialist to use the medical device to clear away some of the blood so he could try to find from where it was all flowing from. "Again!" He sounds panicked. "Again!"

Deirdre tries to call for Nicolaus once more, then she feels herself slip away. She feels herself going, and there is nothing she can do to stop going. The machine monitoring her vitals flat lines. Promptly, the staff go into action.

Dr. Carrie Cox, Deirdre's obstetrician yells, "Crash cart! Stat!"

The team moves Constance out of the way and give Deirdre intensive CPR and electric shocks to her heart to try to restart it beating. They couldn't believe they were losing the one and only Deirdre Ravenell, an emblem of Austin society. The medical team notice that Deirdre's body is covered in bruises. They could clearly see that something terrible happened, something that no one would talk about.

Ceil holds the baby to her chest as she watches the medical team lose Deirdre. Ceil begins to wail with grief. How could this be happening? She feels distraught about Niall, as she holds Nicolai to her. How is this going to be explained to Nicolaus? Ceil begins to panic. Loudly, she says, "No, this cannot be happening!"

Constance can no longer hold back either, knowing her daughter is dying. "Please Deirdre, stay with us. Don't leave ... please," Constance implores her daughter.

Elsa runs from the room. She can't take it. She knows Niall is the cause of this tragedy. And this all happened while Nicolaus left Deirdre's side to rescue her father. Her stomach drops with emotion. She touches her pregnant belly, and it is too much for her.

"Elsa, what's happening?" Maggie is right on her, just barely catching Elsa as she faints.

Chapter Four

Deirdre senses herself be lifted up and out of her body. She could see herself in the birthing room, and sees much blood on the floor. As a white flowy robe covers her new body, she can see the physicians and nurses doing their best to work on her. In her arms, Nicolai is with her. He is warm and happy. He touches her face and smiles at her, with joyful laughter.

Straightway, Deirdre is matured into full knowledge. She looks up and sees three beings of what she knows are heavenly angels floating to her. She feels the pure love about them, and she is not afraid. Deirdre understands they've arrived to escort her and Nicolai. She understands that her time on earth is done. She understands that Nicolai is not to spend any time on earth, that there are other plans for him, as he is special.

Looking down into the birthing room one last time, Deirdre sees her mother grieving for her, and understands that Nicolaus will be her mother's anchor. She is very surprised to see Ceil genuinely crying for Nicolai as she holds his lifeless body in her arms. Suddenly an awesome peace overcomes Deirdre, as she is surrounded by soft, bright light. Deirdre can see a different kind of brightness from the sun shining through tree leaves. She can hear birds singing on earth; however, their chirping is in unison as if they were an invisible bird choir singing praises to the heavens.

Deirdre looks to her left, and in a vision, she can see her twin sister. Deirdre immediately recognizes that Abigail has the essence of DeeDee, their ancestor. She sees that Abigail will take care of her one and only love, her Nicolaus. She understands it is Abigail who is meant to be with Nicolaus for the second half of his life, and it is she who will give birth to his earthly children. Deirdre receives the understanding that Abigail's strength matches that of Nicolaus, and their combined intelligence and extraordinary efforts will bring even more positive change to children on earth. She understands that Abigail will finish her work, and go beyond her own imagination.

In real time, Deirdre can see Abigail sitting up from sleep. Abigail gasps for breath. She breathes deeply and looks around. Abigail can feel that something is not right. Her chest feels heavy with emotion, and she doesn't know why. She bursts out crying, and her friend, Dominique, is right by her side to console her.

Deirdre looks to her right, and she notices she can see through the space of time, as she looks upon her beloved. She sees that Nicolaus is in immense danger, and that he is injured. Suddenly, she wills herself to him, with Nicolai in her arms. Deirdre can see Nicolaus below her as he and his team are pinned from the gunfire.

Deirdre recognizes James, who is laying on the ground close to Nicolaus. She can see that young James is in his heavenly body and is being tended to by an angel group of his own, with several other newly formed and uplifted beings dressed in white. She realizes they are his peers of newly slain military and infantry men as well, from anywhere in the world.

Deirdre frowns, the angels understanding her resolve to help her Nicolaus. Provided with the angel's help and permission, with a wave of her dainty arm, Deirdre jams the machine gun and makes everyone in a two mile radius fall asleep, all except Nicolaus and his men and Jonathan and his militia men, who she can see locked up below.

Deirdre is able to see Jonathan, in the house shackled to a chair in a room with a barred door. With the help of the angels, Deirdre is allowed to release the shackles off Jonathan, making them fall to the floor.

Johnathan is shocked and amazed at the same time. He goes to the barred window and looks out, trying to see what is happening, as everything has become unusually quiet.

"Shh!" Joshua tells the team. "Do you hear that?"

They listen. They hear absolutely nothing.

Joshua takes off his shoe, and he waives it up in the air to see if it would be shot at. Nothing happens.

Nicolaus frowns at him, and pulls him back down, under cover. Nicolaus looks up into the sky, to listen. He looks right at Deirdre, though of course, his earthly human eyes cannot see her.

Deirdre grows sad for a moment, knowing this is the tearing away of her love. The unwanted and lifetime separation between she and Nicolaus, the only man she truly loved.

Deirdre understands she will not be with him again until his time arrives to make his afterlife journey. She feels sad at the thought of not being able to hug him, kiss him, or touch him, perhaps until the afterlife. She worries for knowing that Nicolaus will be devastated by her loss.

Deirdre feels sad until Nicolai touches her face with a smile and that joyful laugh. The angel beings provide Deirdre immediate comfort with a touch to her shoulder.

Nicolai looks into the eyes of his mother, and this makes her heart beam with joy. Deirdre knows it is time for she and Nicolai to go, as the angels bid her forward.

Then suddenly, Deirdre gasps. She looks to the left again, seeing through a different dimension of time, she hears the cries of children. Then she sees them appearing in spirit form, one by one, with radiant white coverings, same as herself and Nicolai. She and the angels go to them with no effort of movement. She looks below and sees a great earthquake has just occurred in Asia Minor, causing many deaths. Many children rise up in spirit body next to her, some with their mothers. With her thoughts, Deirdre joins the angels and comforts them, and they understand. Several of the children happily gravitate towards the angel beings, hugging onto them, none being afraid. They seem to understand what is happening.

Suddenly Deirdre hears more crying, from another dimension. She and several of the newly formed spirit children follow the sound of tsunami flooding covering several small islands in the Indian Ocean. Several children do not survive the tsunami wave. They too are drawn up and appear before Deirdre and the angels. When Deirdre looks around, she sees there are at least one hundred spirit children surrounding them. None are afraid.

Then moaning and crying is heard from another dimension. The sound is unmistakably of suffering children. The angels, Deirdre, and the spirit children go to the sound. They look upon the earth to see a village burning in an ancient town, also in Asia. One by one, the spirit bodies of children who did not survive the fire appear before them. The angels act quickly to restore these children, as they appear before them all. In thankfulness, with bowed heads, the children approach the angels, unafraid, in understanding their life on earth has ended. They are drawn to Deirdre. Nicolai reaches for the spirit children, and they react gleefully to him.

Once more, Deirdre hears crying of children. She, the new spirit children, and the angels follow the sound of suffered crying. They are drawn to a drought ridden African country. Children and babies are crying from starvation. Several children do not survive, despite their mother's doing everything they can for them. One by one another three dozen children appear in spirit form, with white radiant coverings, just as the other children. With quick movement, the angels place beams of love light on these children and they are restored, hungry no more. The children float to the angel beings with love and thankfulness, none have fear. These children acknowledge and greet Deirdre and Nicolai by name, as if they know them.

The three angels lead all the spirit children, the mothers who are there, and Deirdre.

Together, they all zoom past the stars and the planets, on their way through the unseen dimension of the universe. Together, they ascend through space toward the all-encompassing, golden swirling, intensely illuminating light of overpowering heavenly love. Each of them proceeding on their journey to the next phase of life.

Back on the ground on earth, Nicolaus edges himself out to see what may be happening. The silence remains. They can suddenly hear loud snoring of some of the men. Nicolaus edges out a little more, and he can see several men on the ground. They look lifeless, however, he can see them breathing, and some of them are snoring.

"How can this be?" Nicolaus frowns, then he hears Jonathan call for help.

"Help! Help! Over here!" Jonathan cannot exactly see what is happening. He found a white cloth and he waives it around, hoping someone can see it. "Please, help!" he yells again, very afraid that a guard will show up to shoot him. However, he decided to take his chances, seeing that all the guards near his cage had fallen down into sound sleep.

Nicolaus stands, ordering his men to remain in place for their safety. Suddenly, he can see all the men of the compound were on the ground where they once stood. He beckons the rest of the team to quietly get into the house, where Jonathan is being held. When they enter the house, they see that all the guards are on the floor, sleeping. Understanding this has to be divine intervention, Nicolaus hurries the team. They take away the weapons and place them away from the men. They open a door, and find Jonathan in a locked cage.

"Oh my God!" Jonathan exclaims, quietly. "Pretty Boy Nicolaus Ravenell, you're here to save me!"

Chapter Five

Jonathan looks at Nicolaus stunned. Not in a million years had he thought Nicolaus would save him. He sees that Nicolaus is not happy to see him, nor is he moving. Jonathan does notice that Nicolaus is covered in blood, and he sees a tourniquet of a shirt banded around Nicolaus' left leg, and blood is quickly dripping.

"Nicolaus!" He tries again with a happy countenance, extremely excited to know he is about to be rescued.

Nicolaus nods to him, seeing that Jonathan has wounds on his hands and his right shoulder. Calmly he asks, "Are you injured much?"

Jonathan laughs nervously. "I'm hurt, but I'm all right. I can walk, and I'll be happy to try running," he laughs again.

Manny moves to cut the lock on the cage door that held Jonathan.

Nicolaus stops his actions. "Wait a minute," he tells his eager team member. "Baird, you owe me," Nicolaus tells him flatly.

"Yes! Of course! I owe you my life! Right?"

"Your rescue comes with a price!" Nicolaus stands straight with crossed arms. "Freedom is not free for anyone. We all must pay something. I lost a brave young man to get to you today."

"Oh, I'm so sorry. Of course, yes, I owe for that. Of course," Jonathan laughs sheepishly the way Jonathan does.

"I want an apology," Nicolaus demands, unmoving.

"Oh, ... right, sure, sure ... an apology," Jonathan knows he's at Nicolaus mercy, and it hurts his feelings a little. "I apologize for ... your ... comrade ... for ..."

Nicolaus cuts off his words. "I want an apology for you forcing me to marry Gwen."

"Oh! Well,... yes, okay. I apologize for ..."

"A public apology," Nicolaus demands.

"Sir! We don't have time for this!" Manny moves to cut the lock again, only to be stopped by Nicolaus.

"Oh …. A public apology?" Jonathan quickly considers what is being asked of him. "Well," he contemplates, "Pretty Boy, you didn't travel all this way to turn around and leave me," he tells him as if he can talk his way out of such a dictate. When he sees that Nicolaus is unmoving, not budging, and saying nothing, Jonathan quickly decides he must do whatever is asked of him to be rescued. "Okay, okay! I'll give you your public apology. I will. I promise."

"In Spain, upon our arrival there," Nicolaus wraps up his demands, leaving no room for Jonathan to avoid the promise.

Jonathan looks upon Nicolaus, appreciating his cunning mind, though hating the situation and the pressure he is putting on him. They both know a public apology for such a thing will make Jonathan lose favor with any dignitaries, especially the international dignitaries. Jonathan sighs. "Okay. All right. I agree."

Nicolaus nods, then urges Manny to cut the lock, which is done quickly.

Jonathan is overjoyed to be released from the cage. He pulls Nicolaus into a harsh man hug, "Thank you! Thank you!" He shakes Manny's hands.

"Where are your men? They still alive?" Nicolaus asks him.

Jonathan nods. "I believe so. They are in the basement, last I knew." Jonathan leads Nicolaus, Sergey, and Manny to a door that leads to stairs and the basement. Turning on the light, they find thirty men, shackled together.

The men are all astonished to see that it is Nicolaus Ravenell who has arrived to rescue them. They can hardly believe it. They each remember that this is the same man they roughed up and hurt, when they forced him to marry Gwen. Immediately, many of them feel the sting of remorse, as they see that Nicolaus is covered in blood, that he'd been shot in the leg, yet there he stands, trying to find a way to free them, obviously having risked his own life to get to them.

Nicolaus quickly assesses the shackles and finds the primary chain that if broken will quickly free all the men.

Sergey looks around and finds an axe. Nicolaus shows him where to strike. After several tries, he breaks the main tangle, and the shackles fall off the men's arms. They are freed. Some of them cheer, they all stand and make haste to leave out of the place.

Several men, go to Nicolaus and touch his shoulder and his arm, seeing that he is injured.

"Thank you, Nicolaus. You are a badass! Just like they say!"

"Thank you," several of Jonathan's men tell him.

"After what we did to you ... here you are to help us. To literally free us." He touches Nicolaus' shoulder, "I'm sorry that I hurt you."

"I'm sorry, man," another tells him.

Humbly, Nicolaus accepts their apologies, then he wants to inform them of the situation, knowing their time is limited. "Listen up, everyone. Right now, we have divine intervention, and all your captors are asleep. I have no idea how long that will last. Let's go now. Be vigilant! Take weapons and let's move out quickly. You help me carry out my fallen man. Follow Manny, he will lead out down the mountain side."

All heads nod in agreement.

"All right, let's go," Nicolaus tells them, still in command of the operation.

Quickly, the men run up the stairs out the dark basement. The cartel men are still asleep on the ground. Jonathan's men grab weapons, food, and water. Four men gently lift James off the ground, place him into the soft cot, respectfully covering him with a blanket, and they quickly begin the steep descent down the mountain.

Jonathan is lifted off his feet and onto the shoulders of two of his men. When other men notice that Nicolaus is having trouble on his leg, two men quickly go to his aid, and he is assisted down the mountain.

Chapter Six

Francesca arrives to the Ravenell mansion in the late afternoon. She notices the staff seem somber. She is led to the sitting room where everyone is gathered. She sees a crying Constance, of whom Nigel is trying to console while tears drip from his own eyes. Francesca observes Ceil, who is also crying, holding hands with a weeping Elsa. Seeing Ceil cry is absolutely unusual, Francesca never thought such a thing was possible. Maggie and Ishani are hugged up and sobbing as well. She immediately understands that everyone is distraught.

"What on earth? What's happened? You're all acting as if someone has died," she notes in her British accent. Francesca stops herself and notices that someone is missing, and no one is answering her. "Wait a minute! What's happened? Tell me!"

Nigel leaves Constance and goes to Francesca. He hugs her, glad she is home. Nigel looks his daughter over, and hugs her tightly to him again, "Francesca. Oh, Francesca."

Nigel eases Francesca out of the room to tell her the news. He gently takes her hands, looks down, then looks to Francesca, a tear rolling from his eye. He wipes the tear, unable to believe all that has happened. "We've lost Deirdre."

Shock immediately ceases Francesca. "What?" Frowning, she shakes her head, "No."

"She went into labor early, and ... and ... she just didn't make it."

The shock cut her legs from under her. She falls to the floor, Nigel's arms around her, bringing her into a hug. Francesca's body convulses with mourning, she cries, silent tears at first, "No!" she says loudly. "How can that be?" She realized there was nothing she could do. Her mind immediately went to Nicolaus. "Oh my God! The baby?"

Nigel shakes his head negatively without words.

Francesca cries more. "How can that be?" she says again. "Oh my God! And Nicky?"

Nigel shakes his head again. "We haven't told him; we can't reach him. He doesn't know."

Francesca shakes her head negatively, "This gonna ... this gonna kill him. Oh God, not Deirdre! Not Deirdre!"

Chapter Seven

Jonathan and his men are so grateful to be at the bottom of the mountain. It took longer than Nicolaus would have wanted, and now that they are at the bottom, the exhausted men sit down. Some lay on the ground.

Suddenly, the men are surrounded by villagers- men, women, and children. Despite their tattered and emaciated appearance of poverty, the villagers are very curious to see what is going on.

The villagers of Glavischtein seem to be living in a time warp, as if the time of their lives stopped hundreds of decades ago. The people live in hut structures, much like those found in African villages or archaic European villages. They have no modern conveniences.

These people utilize well water which is centrally located in the middle of their community, and have little else besides some livestock, including cows, sheep, and horses. Their village is outside of the Spaniard border, and not part of any other country. They are in a no man's land. The cartel literally take care of all their needs.

The villagers are surprised to know that these men survived the cartel. If you did not come down that mountain with the cartel, usually in their helicopter, then it is common knowledge that you did not walk down that mountain at all. The world would never hear from you again, no matter who you are.

The villagers sit with the men, touching them, talking to them, not sure what to think. Nicolaus sees this and does not like it. Too much is being made of their presence. He knows too much attention is being shined on them.

Even though Nicolaus is injured, he does not want them to stop. He knows it is imperative for them to keep going, as the sun is just now setting. "Look, I know everyone is tired. We have got to keep moving."

"Nicolaus, Nicolaus, we can't! We must rest! My men need water and food. We are not like you. We are not used to all this physical activity, eh! We all need to rest. Nicolaus, even you need to rest."

Nicolaus looks behind him at the mountainside. He cannot see anyone following them down, though he is extremely worried this is about to occur. He didn't imagine the cartel were going to just let them get away so easily. "I understand. Believe me, I do! Look everyone, I know you need to rest and to eat, but we've got to keep moving. If they get on our heels, it will be tough for us to get away."

"No, Nicolaus! We will stay here in the village overnight. We eat, we rest, we sleep," Jonathan overrides him. His men make affirming noises in agreement with him, the villagers watching with fascination. "Then in the morning, we keep going, after we have rested," Jonathan instructs.

Nicolaus sighs. "Look, you all have gotten your freedom back. Don't let it get taken again just because you want to rest. We can all rest later! We must keep moving!"

Jonathan loses his patience and yells at Nicolaus, "You are driving my men too hard, Nicolaus!" He looks around and notices all the villagers seem mesmerized by this scene. Jonathan sighs, not wanting to lose face, seeing the angry look about Nicolaus. He is ready to compromise. "Five hours. Give us five hours, then we move again."

Nicolaus looks at him in disbelief, his anger about to boil over. He wonders if he should just leave Jonathan and his men on their own, calling the rescue done, though he knows this is not really an option. It would make no sense to leave him only for them to be captured again. Then the death of James and his shot up leg, and that great divine intervention, would have all been for naught.

Jonathan feels the look Nicolaus is giving him. He spreads his arms through the air, "Come on, the sun is setting," he says with nervous laughter, not sure what Nicolaus will do. "It will be dark soon anyway. And Nicolaus, you don't look so good. I think you may have lost lots of blood. You need to put that leg up for a bit."

Both Manny and Sergey stand next to Jonathan. "Sir," Manny tells Nicolaus, "... he has a point. That was a difficult trek down the mountain. They need to rest, Sir. And frankly, so do you, Sir."

Nicolaus sighs, knowing this is not a good idea, feeling increased anger and miffed that his own team is against him. "Three hours," he relents. "Three hours, then we get moving again. We've got to make it across the border to Spain for protection."

All men agree on three hours. They disperse to the nearby guest villa of the village, the villagers leading them, following them, and hanging onto them.

Miranda, a local villager, and the wife of one of the cartel members, stands in defiance, with her hands on her hips, having just witnessed the whole scene. She looks up the mountain and sees no one pursuing these men. She wonders if they have killed her husband.

Standing some distance from the men, she uses her cell phone and continues to get no answer. Worry and anger sets upon her, believing her husband must be dead. She looks to her sister. "That one there... that tall brown skinned one ..." she points to Nicolaus, who is unaware of her. Nicolaus is talking to a small group of men. "He seems to be the leader of this group."

"Miranda," her sister puts her arm down, and grabs her shoulder. "Miranda, don't go doing anything stupid. We know nothing of what has happened."

"I know what my husband would want me to do. He'd want me to take out their leader." Miranda stands with resolve, her hands on her hips again. "We keep our eyes on him. And when the time is right, I strike!"

Chapter Eight

Francesca now finds herself in the gloom that is upon the prestigious Ravenell family. The attack upon Deirdre is unspoken, as they begin to discuss how to handle the situation.

Elsa is oddly trying to comfort Constance. However, Maggie moves herself in, removing Elsa's hands from Deirdre's sweet mother.

Elsa feels in shock. She touches her belly, feeling her baby girl jumping around, most likely from the stress. "My God," she says, as if she has just had a realization. Slowly she asks, "What are we going to tell Nicky? How are we going to explain to him what's happened?"

Ceil is quick to take the lead, not wanting to divulge any negative information to Francesca. "We will tell him the truth. Of course! The truth ..." she says as if trying to convince herself. "That ... Deirdre, ... well, ... that she went into labor early ... and ... and ... and that she ... hemorrhaged, and ... they couldn't save her." Ceil sniffs with contempt. "After all, that is what happened."

Constance looks around to everyone and sees that no one is disagreeing with Ceil. She stands. "You hypocrites! The whole lot of you! We each know what has happened!" She yells at them.

Ceil stands and yells right back at Constance, defending the defenseless actions of Niall. "You have not one shred of evidence of what you are thinking. None!"

"Evidence?" She yells to them all, looking at them. "My daughter is dead! Murdered ..."

Nigel is quick to grab onto Constance. "No Constance, you cannot say that. Please! That is not true!"

"My innocent daughter is dead! She died right in my arms, Nigel! What other evidence do you need?"

"Constance ..."

"No!" She jerks herself away from Nigel. "Don't touch me!" She steps away from Nigel. "You know the truth, Nigel! Each of you knows the truth! No matter how fancy you want to spin your words, the facts do not change. My daughter is dead because of your son. The least you can do is say the truth! I will never forgive you for this, Nigel! Never!" Constance runs out of the house. Maggie and Ishani follow after her.

Elsa cries out loudly. She drops onto the floor onto her knees. She knows Constance is right. The trouble is no one actually saw Niall attack Deirdre. No one saw him, so it is very easy to cover for him. And Ceil is correct, there is no evidence.

Francesca stands, tears streaming from her eyes. "Sounds like there is some explaining to be done here."

Nigel sighs, ignoring Francesca's words, not wanting to entertain her comment. "We need to move forward with Deirdre's burial."

"Uncle Nigel, you have got to be kidding!" Francesca wipes her face, as the shocks keep falling on her. She tells them the obvious. "We have to wait for Nicky."

Nigel shakes his head in disagreement. "Normally that would be the thing to do. However, we don't know where Nicolaus is or when he will return. We should not wait."

"Uncle Nigel, Nicky would want you to wait, and it is his decision to make regarding ..."

Nigel cuts off Francesca, "We can have the formal services for her when he returns. We'll keep what's happened to ourselves, no announcements, as I don't want him learning of her death in the press. That would compound this horrid tragedy. We keep it close, and then when he returns, if he wants to announce it, he can."

"Uncle Nigel, please don't do this to Nicky! It's already too much. He can't come home to find her buried. Please ..."

"I'm sorry Francesca, it's the only way."

Chapter Nine (TW)

Manny and Sergey gently place James next to Nicolaus on the long porch of the guest villa. The villa is a one story building, square shaped with windows of each room facing out, has lots of dirt all around, consists of twenty rooms, and a grill for making food. Manny and Sergey help Nicolaus into the lounge chair. They place his leg up, bringing pain to him. Nicolaus sees that is leg is still bleeding. He is sure he will be needing surgery, at least to remove the bullets.

Nicolaus reaches into his back pocket and pulls out his wallet, after removing his jacket and bulletproof vest. Even though the sun has set, the atmosphere is still hot, and all of them are sweating. Nicolaus was going to relax, then put everything back on for the forward push into Spain.

Nicolaus whips out his credit card and hands it to Manny. "Here! Make sure everyone gets food and water. Make sure the guys buy water for the journey to Spain. Make sure you get us water, and I'll have some soup if they have any, if not I'll just have whatever fruit they have, please. And see if there are some bandages for our first aid kits, will you?"

"Sure thing, Nicolaus! Thank you!" Manny is amazed at the generosity of Nicolaus. He had not really thought about how these men would not have any money on them. He steps inside the villa and makes the announcement. "Everyone, listen up! Nicolaus is buying your dinner." The men erupt in loud cheering and thanks. "Hurry and get your orders in, remember we only have three hours. And make sure you get some water for the journey to Spain."

Jonathan exits the villa, looking for Nicolaus. He finds him sitting on a lounger, facing the mountain. Jonathan gently touches his shoulder, amazed at this young man. "Very kind of you to take care of my men like that, Nicolaus. Something I will never forget," he tells him.

Nicolaus looks at Jonathan, and slightly chuckles. "Don't worry about it. You just make sure you keep your promise about that press conference," he tells him.

"Oh, of course! Sure, sure." Jonathan sits down in the chair next to Nicolaus. He looks where Nicolaus is looking, at the mountainside. He sees no movement. "Hey, you still worried about them coming down after us?"

Nicolaus nods. "Very worried."

Jonathan sighs, "Well ... I think if they haven't been down yet, they ain't coming."

"Why do you think that?"

Jonathan shrugs. "I don't know. Why did my chains miraculously fall off me earlier? Why were they all asleep like that? Maybe ... it all goes with the territory, you know, ... with what happened."

Nicolaus nods. "Perhaps." He sighs. "I think we still have to be vigilant though. And anyway, I want to make sure you get home to see your grandbaby, my niece, Elaine Marie. I'm sure she will love to meet you."

Jonathan chuckles. "Elaine Marie? Wow!! So, she is born?"

Nicolaus nods, "She's a beauty. Just like her mom."

Jonathan looks to Nicolaus, appreciating this family banter. He'd always admired Nicolaus' military career, has an attraction to him, and now he owes him his life, after being selflessly rescued by him.

Jonathan admires Nicolaus. "You know, I think you should know something. Now ... I'm not trying to get out of the apology ... the public apology I owe you. I mean, I would never do that, not after you risked your life to save mine, no sir ... but Nicolaus, you should know it was your mother who put me up to that."

"Baird, what are you talking about?"

"Ceil! It was all her idea. She called me! It was all her plan! I mean, why would I have you marry my daughter? I didn't know you before that day."

Nicolaus looks at Jonathan feeling a little shocked. He thought about that day, long ago, and remembers that in his mind he wondered if Ceil might have been behind it all. Nicolaus shook his head, not wanting to believe it. "Your men, they roughed her up ... she was screaming .... You threatened to fatally hurt my parents if I didn't go along."

"I know, and I'm sorry for all of it. Really, I am. It was all an act on Ceil's part. The whole thing was her idea!" Jonathan sat back and sighed. "And Nicolaus, I really am sorry." He sighs again, "And I will make that apology. You deserve it more than you know."

Saying nothing else, Nicolaus rubbed his hand to his lip. He felt sick with disgust, learning that Ceil had again interfered with his marriage to Deirdre. Knowing that Ceil had threatened her own family, caused hurt to his father and hurt Niall. Why? Why would she do such a despicable thing? Now he realized that she really was trying to kill him with drugs through Gwen. She really did want him out of the way for Niall.

Nicolaus thought about his life, and he thought about Deirdre. He became very aggrieved at the time Ceil purposefully made him lose with Deirdre, all for her vendettas against him. His disgust is only tampered down when he thinks of Deirdre.

Nicolaus feels even more love for Deirdre for standing by him through all the appalling trouble and manipulations Ceil concocted. Suddenly, Nicolaus realizes that Deirdre is right to fear Ceil for their children. Again, he thinks about leaving all his responsibilities behind. He is considering hiring a replacement for himself at the company, though his father would be disappointed.

Manny brings Nicolaus his bland soup, which he eats, glad for the extra fluids. He knows he needs fluids, as he's lost much blood. He keeps his eyes on the mountainside, not seeing any lights or movement. He hopes the divine intervention is still taking place, and that he can get Jonathan and his men safely to Spain.

However, Nicolaus feels his leg painfully aching. Any slight movement hurt him greatly. He knew it was a mistake to stop, as he was unsure he'd be able to put pressure on his leg again. And now, he feels his tiredness, the exhaustion. He sits still and watches the mountain, while thinking of his Deirdre. He can't wait to get home to see her. He wants to hold her. He swears to himself he is never going to leave her side again, no matter what is happening or who needs saving. He tells himself this is the last time he would be leaving ... leaving ... leaving .... His body falls into sleep. Nicolaus sits up and shakes his head, not wanting to sleep. However, sleep slowly claims him, and he begins to dream.

His mind is on Deirdre, and he sees her. She is so beautiful. Her beauty strikes him. He wants to hold her and kiss her; he misses her so much. Nicolaus' mind is transfixed on their ancestral home. Peace surrounds Deirdre as Nicolaus lovingly embraces her under the bedcovers at their Estonian castle. They are in the room that once belonged to their ancestors, Nicohls and DeeDee, which now belongs to them.

The fire is ablaze, as the moon shines into the window.

Nicolaus gently holds Deirdre close to his body in the darkness. Softly, Nicolaus kisses Deirdre's face, and looks upon her. He cherishes Deirdre with all his heart.

"I love you so much," he tells her softly, kissing her forehead, and stroking her back. "We are destined to be together. It should have always just been us from the beginning."

Deirdre sweetly smiles upon the man she loves so dearly. "Nicky," she half sits up on her arm, and gently touches the strong, handsome face of her husband, "I thank you so much for being so kind and gentle to me. Thank you for treating me like a person, ... as your wife. You have always thought of me this way."

Nicolaus caresses her sweet face. "Is how it should be."

Deirdre earnestly grabs Nicolaus' hand and kisses it, feeling slightly embarrassed about her thoughts, also knowing she could tell Nicolaus anything. She continues, "Even when we have relations, I must admit, at first I was very scared, not knowing what to expect. The first time was painful, yet wonderful. You have never been cruel or hurtful, or ..." Deirdre ran out of words.

Nicolaus gently kisses her lips.

"Thank you," she tells him again, really wanting him to know she appreciates him.

"I love you so much, Deirdre," he tells her again. He felt as though he could not express himself enough. "I do not think I could ever live without you Deirdre. You have always been there for me. I would just fall away without you. I love you so much," he says again with a warm smile for her.

"I know you do Nicky, darling, ... I know." Deirdre settles her back against Nicolaus' bare chest. His warm, muscular *arms encircle her. Their breathing becomes as one, and they drift to sleep.*

Miranda sees that Jonathan is asleep as well, and no one is paying attention to these two men. She moves in, her weapon ready. Quickly, she kneels beside Nicolaus. She grabs his shoulder and whispers in his ear. "Fine Sir, you need anything?"

Nicolaus stirs.

"Anything I can get you, Sir? You want anything?"

Being jogged back into reality. Nicolaus opens his eyes, sees the woman, and sits up to respond. He lowly cries out in pain, as he has plunged himself right into her dagger. It entered his torso, just below his rib cage.

Miranda laughs, as she runs off, feeling she has done her rightful duty.

Nicolaus looks down and sees that blood is pouring from the dagger wound. He touches the blood, and it is slick and hot.

"Jonathan," he calls to him. "Jonathan, wake up! Jonathan!"

"What? Huh?" Jonathan sits up in fright, thinking the cartel men have found them.

"Jonathan, get your men, we have to go," Nicolaus says weakly.

Jonathan sees that something is wrong, and he goes to Nicolaus. "Oh no! What did you do?" He sees the dagger, and lots of blood. "What happened?" He sighs with panic, "Okay. Okay." Jonathan grabs onto the dagger, as he knows he must pull it out. He holds Nicolaus at the wound site, and slowly, he pulls the dagger out, as Nicolaus screams in pain. That dagger has a short, serrated blade, and Jonathan sees there is a purple substance covering it. Immediately, he knows the substance is poison. "Oh God." He throws the knife away from them. He sees Nicolaus turn ghostly pale, grabbing his wound, and trembling with pain. Jonathan looks around, realizing there is no medical care in the village.

Jonathan lays Nicolaus back. He puts pressure on the wound to try to stop the profuse bleeding. As he puts pressure, more blood gushes from Nicolaus. "No, no." Nicolaus grimaces with pain, grows cold and he begins to shake. "No, no, no, pretty boy. No you don't! You stay with me!" Jonathan looks around. "Help!" He calls louder, "Help!"

"Oh God, I'm gonna die here, in this place," Nicolaus says weakly.

"No, no, no, ... no, no. Pretty boy, you stay with me! Nicolaus!" Jonathan's panic increases, as Nicolaus shakes with shock, the poison already entering his blood stream.

Sergey, Manny, and other men rush over, seeing that something is wrong.

Jonathan shouts orders at them. "Quick, get me something to stop this bleeding. Get me some water! Jesus, don't let him die!" Everyone works quickly. Manny gets a powder substance that helps stop bleeding from his first aid kit. Jonathan pours the water over the open wound, trying to flush out some of the poison, then he puts the powder, and the bandages. "Horses! We need horses!"

"I'll get 'em boss." Several men run off, and within minutes they return with a few horses.

"Nicolaus, you stay with us. You are not going to die. You've got to get back to your little tart at home. What's her name?" Jonathan pulls Nicolaus to his feet, his weight heavy on him.

"Deirdre," Nicolaus says, feeling very weak. He feels his life force leaving him.

Jonathan walks him to a horse. "Deirdre! Yes, Deirdre! Pretty name for a pretty woman. You have to get back to your Deirdre. Now, you think of her. Okay? Keep her in your mind. You have to make it back to Deirdre."

Jonathan and his men lift Nicolaus upon the horse, and he lets out a painful yell, as his leg pains him as well. Nicolaus slouches forward onto the horse's neck as he slips into unconsciousness.

"Oh God! God, please help us! Let's go guys. We've got to get him some help."

Chapter Ten (TW)

Later that day, for some reason, Nigel feels eerie as he walks up to the door of Elsa's townhome. Niall had finally answered his call and told him where he was, as no one had heard from him since the attack on Deirdre.

Niall nonchalantly opens the door and bids Nigel to enter. Niall literally felt that he had nowhere else to go, and he didn't want to spend money on a hotel. He had not even informed Elsa of his whereabouts.

Nigel enters and follows Niall inside, noticing his son looks dazed. Niall stands away from his father, then walks to the large window, staring out. Niall feels numb and confused about what he'd done to Deirdre. He couldn't get clear about it in his mind. He realized that he had not thought about his actions all the way through. Niall had not thought about the after affects.

How could he ever face Deirdre again? He knew she'd be frightened of him. How could he face Elsa again? What could he even say to Elsa? And only now does he think of his daughter, his baby girl, Elaine. His actions are sure to bring trouble to her door as she gets older. How could he hold his daughter now, after what his hands had done to Deirdre. He looks at his hands in thought.

Nigel sighs with extreme disappointment in his son. "I suppose you are quite proud of yourself for having raped your brother's pregnant wife," Nigel comments dryly, confronting Niall with what he knows to be true.

Niall looks to Nigel, and then looks away. "Father, I do not expect you to understand."

"I understand that you brutally raped Deirdre."

Niall looks at his father again to face the accusation. "Do you not see? I love her!" he shouts.

"Love?" Nigel shouts back.

"I could not go on living not having her."

"That is absolutely stupid, Niall! You beat Deirdre and you raped her! We all told you that Deirdre was not yours to have."

"Do you not see? It was the only way. The only way I could have her." Feeling shamed, Niall turns from his father.

"And what of Nicolaus? Did you think of him? And Elsa?"

Niall sighs, holding his head back. "I can only think of Deirdre now," he says not wanting to admit that it is only now that he is thinking of them.

Nigel feels so heartbroken over all this. And now, he not only has to inform Nicolaus of Deirdre's death, but also inform Niall, who played a role in causing her death. Nigel sighs. "You have brought harm, not only to Deirdre, but also to the baby."

Niall looks to his father, knowing what he is saying. "If the child dies ... then so be it. That baby should have been mine anyway!"

Nigel feels the strong urge to strike Niall. At first, Nigel turns away from Niall, shaking his head in disbelief of his son, ashamed of him. Then, unable to control that urge, he walks up to Niall and harshly slaps his face one time, something he'd never done before. Did the slap bring Niall to reality?

The slap is hard, causing Niall shock. He holds his face and eyes his father. Nigel has never hit him, nor punched him. Niall is not sure what to do. He begins to tear, feeling he might lose control of himself, feeling like an ugly ogre, a monster, an insane fool.

"Your words and your actions have power Niall," Nigel yells at him. "Your dishonoring of the love between Nicolaus and Deirdre is utterly despicable. The debauchery you put on Deirdre has killed her and the child. They are both now dead because of you."

"What?" Niall asks in disbelief. "What? No! No!"

"Yes!" Nigel yells at him, waving his arms about, finding it hard not to strike him again. "You wished death on the child! On my grandson! Your wish is granted. You wished lust and debauchery on Deirdre, you did your evil act, only God knows why, ... and have caused her death!" Nigel breaks, "She is dead."

"Father!" Niall gasps. Never did he want Deirdre to die.

"Their deaths are on your hands Niall," Nigel says more calm. He moves towards the door, unable to provide any comfort to his son. "Our Deirdre is now lost to us. God help you if Nicolaus ever finds out what you have done! If the police show up, I'll not stop them, and you should go with them peacefully."

"Father ... I never meant to hurt her like that. I never meant ..."

"And yet you did! I am ashamed that you are my son." Nigel shakes his head in disbelief. "How is it that *you* are my son?" Unable to take more, Nigel leaves.

Niall falls to his knees. He weeps for Deirdre. He looks at his hands and he weeps for what he has done.

Chapter Eleven

Jonathan and his men made it to the border of Spain, and they easily crossed over. They had to travel several miles to get to the closest modern day town of Benlloch Village. Benlloch is set with Spanish heritage, including colorful houses, local businesses, and even sheep herders. The best they could do was get Nicolaus to the community health care clinic, however Jonathan knows he needs a hospital.

The physician at the community clinic is panicked when he sees Nicolaus' condition as they bring him inside. Nicolaus is unconscious, however he is still trembling and shaking, the shock taking over his body due to the loss of blood, and the poison.

"He must be at hospital. We cannot treat him here," the physician tells Jonathan. "His wounds are critical, and I don't have equipment or the ability to treat this kind of injury."

"Yes, please, he needs a hospital. Help me get him there. I will pay you any amount needed. Please, we must not let him die."

The physician nods. "This Nicolaus Ravenell, yes?" He recognizes Nicolaus from news reports of his marriage to Deirdre.

Jonathan nods. "Yes. Please!"

The physician has his nurses tend to Nicolaus and he rushes off to get an airlift to the nearest hospital, which is in Castellano, several miles away.

He returns with bandages to tend to Nicolaus. "The air lift is on its way. They will take you to the hospital in Castellano. He will receive good care there." The physician sees that Nicolaus' shaking has stopped. He checks for Nicolaus' vitals, to find them very faint. "If he can make it. Looks like he's lost a lot of blood."

Chapter Twelve

Deirdre is called on by the angels to assist with Nicolaus. Nicolaus finds himself being transported to a dimension beyond his dreams inside his mind. Mentally, he is still unconscious, however, his body is giving out, vulnerable against the fight of the poison coursing throughout his veins and his organs.

Deirdre goes to him. "Nicky, you must go back. Darling, you cannot be here. It is not your time," she tells him sweetly.

"Deirdre!" He sounds very happy to see her. Though they are completely surrounded by darkness, only indescribable illuminating bright white light shines on them. The environment and beautifully picturesque scenes of heaven are cloaked from his sight.

"Deirdre!" Nicolaus goes to her, taking her hands. "My love! My sweet love! I've missed you so much!" He gives her his usual look of love as he observes her, seeing she is dressed in a glowing white robe. "Wait ..." he frowns, "what is this place? Where are we?" Nicolaus looks around again, though he can see nothing.

"Nicky, my love, you can't be here. It is not your time yet. You must will yourself back."

Nicolaus looks around, and although he cannot see anything, he completely feels peace in this place, as he grasps Deirdre's hands. They are in the dark, except the radiating light shining on them. Nicolaus looks up at the light, to see where it is beaming from. He looks up, his eyes stretching as far as he can see, and the light continues on. He cannot tell from where the light is shining.

Deirdre pulls on his hands to get his attention. "Love, will yourself back. It is not your time," she tells him again. "You still have work to do. The foster children need you. Your own children are still waiting to be born. Your bride awaits you."

"My bride? You!"

"Nicky, my love, I know you don't understand this right now. You will understand later. Please. You must go back."

"Go back?"

"Nicky ..."

Quickly, Nicolaus takes Deirdre into his arms. "Please, let me hold you. I've missed you so much." Gently, he places a loving kiss to her forehead.

"Nicky ..." Deirdre is grateful for his love. She touches his chest, wrapped in his loving arms. She touches his injury. "Nicky, close your eyes." He does as she tells him. "Now ... think of our castle in Estonia. See it in your mind." He nods. "Now, think of the last time we were there together on our wedding night." A smile is across Nicolaus' face. "Our friends and family were there. The staff were so sweet to us."

He nods in agreement.

"Now think about your father, and how he helped us with our wedding. You felt the love of your father then, and I want you to feel that love again, right now. Really feel it, Nicky. Feel his love for you in your chest, in your heart."

Nicolaus nods again, remembering how happy he felt this day.

"And know that I truly love you, my darling." Deirdre gasps as Nicolaus is pulled from her arms and he drifts away from her. She knows he is returning. "I love you my darling Nicky. Always! No matter what! Forever, my darling love, forever!" Deirdre's voice drifts with him through the dimensions of time.

Nicolaus crashes back into his body on the emergency room table at the hospital in Castellano. The doctors and nurses are frantically performing cardiopulmonary resuscitation on him, using the shock paddles and oxygen. The monitor, which was flatlined, begins to beep with his heart rhythm again. Nicolaus breathes deep, and opens his eyes, which slowly focus to what is happening.

"We've got him back! We've got him!" The lead physician says excitedly to his team. They keep working on him.

Jonathan breathes a sigh of relief, as he'd been standing by, knowing that Nicolaus was in a bad state. He panicked when he saw several doctors and nurses rush in. He'd watched through the small square windows of the emergency room doors, and had seen Nicolaus flatline. He breathes again, relieved that he can hear the machine mimicking the pulsating beat of Nicolaus' heart.

Chapter Thirteen (TW)

Nigel was surprised when Constance did not fight him about Deirdre's private funeral and burial, which took place the following day. Constance let Nigel make the decisions regarding Deirdre, since he is Nicolaus' father. She gave him that respect. She felt it didn't matter anyway, as Deirdre is already gone.

Bishop Leighton and his priest officiate over the private services, which are solemn. Niall does attend the funeral, to everyone's surprise, as he has not been heard from. He just cannot believe that Deirdre is gone, not unless he sees it for himself.

Niall walks up to the open coffin and sees Deirdre. Immediately, he is emotional. "Oh God, no! Deirdre ...," crying cuts off his words. "Deirdre ... I'm so sorry," he whispers to her, though everyone can hear him, "I'm so sorry."

Constance stands in defense of her daughter, and Ceil quickly stands to block Constance. She signals to the ushers to take Niall out, as it appears he is about to dramatically drop to his knees again, and she wants him taken out before he begins to say things or confess anything, for which there is no evidence of.

Quickly, two male ushers grab onto Niall and take him out of the sanctuary so that he can get ahold on himself. No one else moves or says anything at this scene, as Constance sits down, and then Ceil follows, reseating herself.

After several minutes, Niall barely composed himself, and enters the sanctuary. Elsa is surprised when her husband sits beside her. She is not sure what to do, or what to say. She does see that Niall is very distraught. Thinking of Deirdre, Elsa takes his hand, which makes him cry loudly, unable to contain his grief. Bishop Leighton does note that Niall is the one crying the loudest of all the Ravenells on this sad day.

Crying, Elsa hugs her husband to comfort him. Niall balks at Elsa's actions. He has a great understanding that he deserves no comfort from anyone, least of all Elsa. This makes him cry even more.

Deirdre's burial plot is next in line of Nicolaus' wives, next to Gwen. Francesca tried to get Nigel to bury Deirdre next to their grandmother, without success. She didn't think Nicolaus would want her grave in line with Marguerite and Gwen. Deirdre is his true wife and should have been treated like a princess.

Constance grabs her hand. "I know what you tried to do for my Deirdre, and I thank you for that Francesca."

Francesca hugs Constance. "I promise you, I will make sure her headstone is large and the most beautiful of everyone here."

Later that night, Nigel receives a call from Jonathan. "Jonathan! Nicolaus found you then! He's rescued you!" Nigel beckons to Elsa.

"Yes, Nigel. Your pretty boy is very courageous. He is very brave. He lost a man to get to me, and he's been shot and stabbed."

"What?"

"He's bad off Nigel. He's lost a lot of blood. You'd better get over here, quick. He already almost died on us. He's in a low level little hospital in Castellano. It's the best I could do. He needs to be in a better place where they have the equipment to treat him. You need to move mountains for him, Nigel."

"I understand. I'm on it." Nigel hands the phone to Elsa, and goes to the family, who are gathered around to tell them the news. "Nicolaus has been critically injured. He's in a hospital in Spain. I need to coordinate his care."

"Oh my God! No! Not Nicky too!" Francesca says near tears. "It's that damn curse!" She tells them all.

Knowing eyes of Nigel and Ceil look at her without words.

"Francesca, don't," Nigel tells her. "We can't do this right now. Our priority has to be getting Nicolaus the care he needs."

Niall looks at Nigel, shaking his head. He can't believe he is about to lose his brother as well. He feels like he is going to fall apart.

"Dad?" Elsa says into the phone. "Is that really you? You all right?"

"I'm hurt, but nothing some bandages and a tetanus shot can't cure."

"I knew Nicky could get to you! I knew it!"

"Yes, well, at great cost to him. He is very brave. And he's been hurt very badly. We may lose him, Elsa. Get Nigel on a plane over here as soon as possible. Nicolaus does not look good."

"Oh my God!" Elsa is shocked at his words. "Okay, dad."

"Oh, and Elsa, I'm about to do a press conference, something I promised Nicolaus. I'm going to do it now, while he's still holding on."

"Dad, don't say it like that. We have to believe Nicolaus will make it."

"Of course! Listen, this press conference is going to upset Ceil when she gets wind of it. So, I'm giving you the heads up. I promised Nicolaus I would tell the truth about Gwen, ... and I'm going to do it. But I promise I will not tarnish your reputation, Elsa. I promise you this, my princess."

"The truth? What do you mean?"

"I don't have time to go into it. Just please, give Nigel whatever support he needs."

"Okay dad, I'll do what you say."

Nigel is on the phone making preparations to take a medical crew to Spain, on his private jet. He plans to transport Nicolaus to the renown medical center on the military base in Germany.

Chapter Fourteen

Jonathan checked himself into a hotel that is near the hospital. He cleaned himself up, and had his staff call for a press conference within an hour, as he sits down to enjoy a meal. Being grateful for his freedom, his life, and his health, thanks to Nicolaus, he enjoys a hearty meal of steak and fixings, with dessert of chocolate mousse in the hotel restaurant. By the end of his meal, several press, including international media are present in the hotel lobby.

Jonathan had written out what he wanted to say. He stands in front of the gobs of microphones to make his announcement.

"First, I'd like to thank each of you for being here today, to take an interest in what I need to say." He sniffs and clears his throat, "Actually, I wouldn't even be here today, at all, if it weren't for Nicolaus Ravenell, ... and that is Nicolaus ... Ravenell ... the retired military man, who has received several awards. He saved my life, and the lives of my men, from a vicious cartel. He's very brave. He didn't have to save me ... but ..." he pauses as emotion grips him ... "he risked his life to save me. And I want to publicly thank Nicolaus and his small team, and publicly acknowledge their bravery.

"And ... well ... I'm not a praying kind of man ... but I want to ask the world to say prayers for Nicolaus, because saving me ... he now has life threatening injuries. He's struggling for his life, in the hospital, and ... well," Jonathan looks down, then looks into the numerous cameras, "he needs prayers so that he doesn't suffer too much. Please."

Jonathan stops for a moment, pausing to get his mind clear. He clears his throat to get rid of the emotion. "Also ... aside from that ... I owe Nicolaus an apology. And I want to give him a sincere, heartfelt, public apology ... for ... something I put him through. Something that was not fair, or now what I see was not wise.

"My name is Jonathan Baird. I am the father of Elsa Baird, and Gwen Baird. I'm sure you recognize our names. My sweet Elsa, my princess, is married to Nicolaus' brother, Niall. And she's just had my first grandchild, Elaine Marie Ravenell.

"Well, Niall was not being very nice to my princess when she discovered she was pregnant. So ... I plotted with his mother, Ceil Ravenell, to get them married. And she came up with a plan to force them together and I went along with that plan. And well, for the most part, it worked. Only that, part of Ceil's plan was also to force Nicolaus to marry my other daughter, Gwen.

"Now, I remember seeing lots of stories about this ... asking why Nicolaus abandoned Deirdre, and asking who is Gwen. Well, Gwen was my daughter. And ... without getting into details ... let's just say, I didn't give Nicolaus a choice. I forced him to marry my daughter, Gwen. And ... well ... it was wrong. I was wrong. And that is what I am apologizing for. I am giving Nicolaus and Deirdre this public apology for forcing him to marry Gwen. And well ... as many of you know ... Gwen died in a car wreck, not too long ago. And we miss her, ... I miss her." He looks down again, feeling emotional, not knowing all these feelings would be emitted from him during this time. Jonathan sighs to relieve some stress. "And so,... that should clear up any questions or confusion about all this. And well ... that is all I have to say. Thank you."

Members of the press shout out questions to him, all at the same time, talking over each other.

"What hospital is Nicolaus in?"

"What was Nicolaus saving you from?"

"Why did you force Nicolaus to marry your daughter?"

"Are you really sorry?"

"Why a public apology?"

"What kinds of injuries does Nicolaus have?"

"How did you exactly force Nicolaus to marry your daughter?"

"Why did Ceil Ravenell plot against Nicolaus?"

Jonathan leaves the microphones. One of his men step up to stop the questions. "Hey, hey! My boss ain't taking no questions! He says that is all he has to say, so that is all!"

The press stop with the questions, and loud murmuring among them is heard throughout the lobby. Several press members are recording this conference live, and continue to wrap up the story with their live feed.

On the other side of the world, in Austin, Elsa turns off the television, as she, Constance, Francesca, and Ceil saw it live.

Elsa sighs, "Well, that wasn't so bad, eh?" She mostly directs her comment to Ceil, who is sitting very quietly.

Ceil knows this has put a bad light on her to all the dignitaries and elites she knows. She is thinking about the repercussions of Jonathan's press conference, as Nigel has already gone to Spain to assist in Nicolaus' care. She sees Constance looking at her with disdain.

Francesca begins to cry. She is very upset over Deirdre, and extremely worried about Nicolaus. And now she cannot believe what her ears have just heard about Ceil being behind the forced marriage to Gwen. She is getting a clearer picture of Ceil actually trying to kill Nicolaus with drugs. She feels so helpless.

Chapter Fifteen

Nigel arrives at the hospital in Castellano, with his medical team, ready to transport Nicolaus. He is shocked to see Nicolaus hooked up to several machines, though he is thankful he sees nothing like a ventilator.

"I am sorry, Mr. Ravenell. Your son is in no condition to travel. He will not make such ... flight," the Spanish physician tells him. "He already almost died. We got him back. Travel may finish him. And anyway, ..." the physician pulls the bed sheet back to reveal Nicolaus shot up leg, "this leg must be amputated. I'm just waiting for him to be more stable before operating."

"Amputated?" Nigel is alarmed at this news.

"And he has poison in him ... and ..."

"Poison? How?" Nigel frowns, as Jonathan had not mentioned this. "Look, that leg must be saved. No amputations. My son has already lost too much."

"Well ... I am sorry for this, but amputation cannot be avoided."

"I said no!" Nigel adamantly yells at the physician. He sighs, "Look," he lightly holds the physician on the shoulder, "I truly appreciate all you've done for my son. You saved his life, and I thank you. Truly! We must transport him. The American military hospital in Germany is waiting for us. They will handle his care from this point. I have a physician with me, and we'll take care of my son during the transport." Nigel goes to Nicolaus, and touches him. "Nicolaus," he calls to him. However, Nicolaus has slipped into unconsciousness again. "Nicolaus." Nigel looks to the physician. "Is he in a coma?"

"No. He slips in and out of consciousness. Probably the poison."

Nigel frowns, "Probably?" He beckons for the physician he has brought with him to examine Nicolaus.

"I tell you, he cannot travel."

"I'll take full responsibility. I'll sign whatever you need me to sign. Just get it quickly, please."

The Spanish physician nods in agreement, sighing, "Okay. I discharge him to your physician for transport."

"Thank you," Nigel tells him, grateful no additional resistance is given.

Chapter Sixteen

Niall walks into the church he and his family attend. It is the day after Deirdre's burial. Niall stands inside the entrance and looks around the church. It is empty except for the bishop and the priest he sees at the front, at the altar.

Niall cannot believe everything that is happening to their family, and he just wants to vomit all over the place. He feels heartbroken over Deirdre and sick in his soul. He now understands that what he did to Deirdre is wrong, regardless of how much he loves her. He thinks about other girls he'd forced himself on when he was young, and also as a grown man. Nothing like this had ever happened. It never occurred to him that he could cause such harm, fatal harm, to a woman.

Niall also is aware that he must ask forgiveness for his vile deed before he loses his brother as well. He did not want this guilt upon him, were Nicolaus to die of his injuries.

Bishop Leighton is surprised to see Niall. "Niall, it is very unusual for me to see you here at this early hour," he states as a matter of fact.

Niall ends his walk up the long aisle to the altar. "Yes, Bishop, I know. I ... I ...," he sighs near tears, never having done anything like this before. "I need to talk ... to relieve myself of this ...." He stops and looks at the bishop and the priest. "Anything I tell you is ... confidential? Right?" He asks both men, thinking about protecting himself.

Bishop Leighton nods, "Yes. Talks, counseling, and confessions are all confidential," he assures Niall. "Son ... what is it?"

Niall sighs, "I ...," he stops. Then tries again, "I ... I ...," he thinks he should back out, but forces himself forward, knowing he needs cleansing. Niall feels stupid again, and very much like a child who has done wrong. "I ... I've done a very bad thing, Bishop Leighton." His tears are back. "A horrid thing."

Bishop Leighton nods. "And this ... horrid thing you have done ... did it harm someone?"

Niall nods, "Yes. I want to confess, please ... I have to ..." Niall wants to cry and vomit at the same time. He puts his hand to his chest. "I need to make right the wrong I did ... and ... and ... I ... need your help, Bishop. Please! I want to change! I will change!" Niall begs, his body crouched, knees bent, not exactly on the floor.

The bishop frowns at Niall, knowing this is all very uncharacteristic for him, remembering his behavior at Deirdre's funeral. Bishop Leighton touches Niall's shoulder to calm him. He beckons for his priest to take Niall to the private confession space, in a different part of the church. Confession is done face to face, as the priest can better examine the person before him.

"Father Francois will assist you."

The men sit down, a seventeenth century archaic table between them. Father Francois makes the Sign of the Cross between he and Niall, "Bless us this day, our Holy Father." He nods to Niall, "Now, you may speak."

Niall sighs. He looks away from the priest for a few minutes, surprised at his patience, as he says nothing, and just waits. Then Niall speaks. "I ... put my hands on Deirdre."

Father Francois frowns. "Is this Deirdre Omari Ravenell you speak of?"

"Yes." Niall answers flatly.

"Put your hands means what?"

"I touched her when I shouldn't have."

"Touch her means what?" He forces Niall to speak the whole truth.

"I had her. Okay? I had her."

He shook his head. "No. If you need to clear your conscious, you must speak this horrid thing you have done. Had her means what?"

Niall sighs again, feeling emotionally sick and frustrated. He didn't want to say it. Could he say it? "I ... I ..." He shakes his head, internally fighting against himself. "I ... I raped her! Okay? Rape!" he shouts at the priest.

Father Francois touches Niall's hand. "Calm yourself." He instructs Niall, frowning at him, and feeling very upset about this. He knew Deirdre to be an exceptional young lady, a wonderful help to children and an example to the young women in the church. Father Francois fights against his rising flesh of wanting to hurt Niall for what he'd done to Deirdre. He remembers his place, inside the church, and his role to the community. He thinks about Nigel's tears and Nigel's words during the funeral. Scripture returns upon his heart.

"I love her, you see. And it was the only way I could have her ... because of my brother. But ...," he tears up, "I never meant to hurt her. I love her! I never wanted her to die! The baby, I didn't care if it died, but not Deirdre. Oh God, not Deirdre!" He stops to wipe his eyes.

Father Francois stops Niall's ranting with a frown. "Niall, let's think about this for a moment. You say you loved Deirdre, yet, you had to have her and you didn't care about her baby. You are confusing love with lust and jealousy. If you had loved Deirdre, than you would have been happy for her joy in her marriage to your brother. You would have cared about her physical condition, and her feelings. Instead, you were jealous and you wanted her, for which obviously she was not willing, so you raped her. That is not love," he says sternly. "Love is not violent, or greedy, or wanton. Love is caring and kindness, love is empathy and helpfulness. Love glorifies and reverences God."

Niall looks at the priest, nodding with understanding. "I'm so sorry. I'm sorry about all of it. Deirdre," he calls to her, "I'm so sorry." He grabs the priest's arms with emotional pain, "I want to change. I don't want to be like this anymore! Please! You have to help me change. Please. I want to change for Deirdre! I have to change for my own daughter, Elaine. Don't you see? Please! You have to help me! Please!"

Father Francois sighs away his own tribulation of this matter, putting the care for Niall above his own disappointment and hurt for Niall's atrocious behavior. "Are you truly sorry for what you have done?"

"Yes, yes, I am sorry."

"And do you ask for forgiveness?"

"Yes! I ask Deirdre's forgiveness. Can I do that?" He looks away for a moment, then back to Father Francois, "I ask God's forgiveness."

Father Francois nods. "You must complete your penance to be forgiven. If you fail to complete your penance, Brother Niall, you shall not be forgiven."

Niall nods ready to receive his penance.

"Your penance is to make amends to those you have hurt the most, beyond Deirdre, who is no longer with us. You shall make amends with her mother, for doing what you should not have done against her daughter. You shall make amends with your father, for dishonoring him and for bringing a stain upon your family name. You shall make amends with your wife for committing adultery against her. And you shall make amends with your brother, for dishonoring his marriage and for soiling his wife."

"My brother?" He feels this would be impossible. This is not the kind of penance he had in mind. "Father Francois, I cannot talk to my brother about this and anyway, he may be dying in a foreign country right now. Father ... can't you give me a different penance, one that hurts or something?"

"So now you mock God and think you can pick a penance of your choosing?" He frowns at Niall and yells at him in a corrective manner. "I have pronounced your penance. You may choose to carry it out or not. You will not be forgiven until it is completed. It is up to the victims to forgive you, not up to you!" He sighs to bring calmness to this situation.

"Now ... let us pray, you may fall to your knees in submission to God, and repeat the Rite of Penance number forty-five after me." Father Francois waits until Niall is on his knees. "My God, I am sorry for my sins with all my heart. In choosing to do wrong and failing to do good, I have sinned against you whom I should love above all things. I firmly intend, with your help, to do penance, to sin no more, and to avoid whatever leads me to sin. Our Savior Jesus Christ suffered and died for us. In his name, my God, have mercy."

"Niall, because of your entitlement attitude, and because of your haughty behavior, I am denying you absolution until you have completed your penance. And I will know that you have done so, because I will check with your victims, or you may perform your penance before me here in the church with your victims. Do you understand?"

Niall nods, still on his knees, "Yes, Father Francois, I understand," he agrees, very much feeling like a troubled child, and feeling defeated as well.

Father Francois reads that Niall feels the misery of what he's done. He lays hands on Niall and prays for healing upon his wicked heart.

Chapter Seventeen

"Doc," Nigel asks on the plane ride to Germany, "will my son make it?"

The physician and the nurses are tending to Nicolaus. He's been given morphine to alleviate his pain and uncomfortableness. His vitals are checked every five minutes, and he is hooked up to monitoring machines and intravenous fluids, as he lays in an ambulance bed in the plane.

The physician nods, "Yes, he'll make it. Your son is strong. He's lost a lot of blood, though, Nigel. Once we get to the hospital in Germany, we'll transfuse him to bolster his blood supply, and to clean out some of that poison. Then his blood will create its own cells, and will continue the process of rejecting the poison. We'll also be able to give him an antidote to diminish the poison. It will take a while, but he will be okay, Nigel."

Nigel nods. "And his leg? Will it have to be amputated?"

The physician shakes his head, "No. It looks bad now because of the poor blood circulation. Once we replenish him, I'm sure his leg will get better. He may need surgery on it though, it could be infected. I'll know more once we get to the hospital. I'll be able to do some imaging and really be able to see what is going on. Right now, my guess is his leg will be fine. After he heals from surgery, he'll need physical therapy."

Nigel nods and sits back with relief. "That leg seems to always be injured, since he was a child."

"We'll take care of him, Nigel," the physician reassures him.

Nicolaus stirs, and moans. "Where am I?" he asks weakly.

Nigel is quickly by his side. He touches Nicolaus' shoulder. "Son, I'm right here, son. You've been badly injured, but you're going to be okay."

"Father?" Nicolaus asks with a frown, unable to open his eyes due to the heavy dose of morphine.

"Yes, it's me. I'm taking you to the army hospital in Germany. It's all right, son."

"Baird?"

"You rescued Jonathan! He is fine! He was going to do some press conference, said ... he owed you, ... or something."

Nicolaus sighs and coughs, pain ceasing him.

"Son, take it easy!"

"Deirdre?" he asks weakly. "Deirdre ..."

"Okay now! Okay. Just rest right now. You're bad off, and we're going to get you better. Just rest son."

Nigel is again relieved as the medication takes his son to sleep, to get him away from the questions of Deirdre. The questions he knows he'd have to answer one day, in the not too far off future.

Chapter Eighteen

Niall decides his first penance, and probably the easiest to do is going to be with Elsa. Quietly, he enters his home, the one his mother had thrown him out of after his first attack on Deirdre.

Niall feels odd as he walks the mansion. The atmosphere is uneasy, yet sad. He realizes he'd never see Deirdre again. He'd never see her smile. He would never smell her beautiful aroma through the halls. He'd never get to grab her up again, and feel her push against his chest in protest.

Niall looks to the door entrance to his brother's side of the mansion. At first, he hesitates, then he goes through the door. He walks to the sitting room on the first floor. He observes the photos that are everywhere of Deirdre and his brother. He balks at the life sized wedding picture that graces the wall towards the stairs. He'd never noticed it before. He studies it.

Deirdre and his brother look very happy in this photo. Nicolaus appears dashingly handsome as he proudly holds Deirdre, her beauty shining through as she basks in Nicolaus' arms, and looks up at him with love, while wearing her beautiful, beaded wedding dress. The Saint Nicholas church of Estonia is behind them.

Emotion chokes Niall, as he remembers this day. He remembers how Nicolaus watched Deirdre as she walked the long aisle to him, then joined him at the altar, as if they were getting married for the first time. He remembers being excruciatingly jealous of Nicolaus on this day ... his brother's wedding day.

Niall climbs the stairs. He touches the door handle to open the door to his brother's bedroom, the same room in which he attacked Deirdre. He stops, pausing in thought. He remembers the first time he opened this door; he watched Nicolaus intertwined with Deirdre. The memory of it floods his mind, making a tear fall from his eye. He realizes how horrid his behavior is, that he didn't even think about those he hurt.

As Niall opens the door, his mind remembers what he'd done to Deirdre. He remembers violating her, and how she looked at him, with such contempt. He knew she'd never forgive him, but he continued to violate her anyway. Tears fill his eyes.

Elsa looks back at the sound of crying. She is also crying, sitting on the couch, thinking of Deirdre. When she sees it is Niall, she turns away from him. "Oh it's you! What do you want?" She asks him meanly.

Niall is very surprised to see Elsa here. "Elsa."

"Why are you even here? Returning to the scene of your crime?"

Quickly, he closes the door and goes to her, only for her to turn away from him again. "Elsa, please," Niall drops to his knees before his wife, "we have to talk."

She shoots a glance at him. "What do you want, Niall? I'm sure it's not me!" She tells him, again, with mean intent, tired of his antics, now embarrassed that he is her husband. Ashamed that she thought she could make it work with him. She'd been mulling over what had happened. It really got to her. This time he really made her angry.

"Elsa, I want to apologize to you."

Elsa looks at him, her baby kicking, feeling her stress. "Apologize? How do you apologize for what you've done?" She stands. "You should be in jail, Niall." She sighs, "And anyway, I'm not the one you should be apologizing to. Oh yeah... wait ... she's dead!" She steps up to Niall. "Dead!" She yells in his face.

Niall stands and grabs his wife by the upper arms. "Okay, okay," he tries to stay calm. "I deserve that, but I ..."

Elsa jerks herself out of his grip. "You killed Deirdre! You raped Deirdre, and you killed her."

Niall shakes his head at his believed mischaracterization of the situation. "Elsa, please, just hear me out." He tries to touch Elsa.

Elsa is quick to move away from Niall. "Don't touch me!" She shouts at him. "Don't you ever touch me again. Not me or my children!" Elsa moves towards the door. "Jesus! If you supposedly had love for Deirdre, I can only imagine what you had planned for me." She slams the door as she leaves.

Niall plops himself on the sofa in disbelief. He'd thought asking Elsa's forgiveness was going to be easy. He rubs his hand over his face, his eyes fixated to Nicolaus' desk. He sees books and maps and papers strewn over it, just as Nicolaus had left them, which brings to Niall's mind why his brother was away in the first place.

Chapter Nineteen

Nicolaus is placed in a private room in the military hospital in Germany, despite being in critical condition. The press had source reports of where Nicolaus is admitted, and already, they began to gather outside the hospital to run live news reports throughout the world.

Nigel began getting calls from reporters, dignitaries, leaders that Nicolaus and Deirdre met with, as well as the board members of VMC. Nigel had not expected such a reaction from people, and certainly not from people from around the world.

Within hours, telegrams of well wishes from dignitaries, letters of condolences and well wishes, and flowers from all over the world began arriving at the hospital for Nicolaus.

"Deirdre ... Deirdre ..." Nicolaus calls out often in his semi-conscious state. He is stabilized very quickly, and multiple blood transfusions are implemented to clean out his blood and hopefully his organs. Between calls for Deirdre, Nicolaus emits sounds of pain and sometimes has painful mini-convulsions of spasms due to the poison going through his organs.

After the first transfusion, Nicolaus' leg is much improved, and he is scheduled for surgery tomorrow.

Nigel is very worried for Nicolaus. He remains in the large hospital room, using the room furniture of the loveseat, and an eating tray as a makeshift office, in order to receive the calls and take notes, without leaving Nicolaus' side.

"At first the physicians at the other hospital told me they were going to have to amputate his leg."

"Really? Which leg?" Ceil asks.

"Actually, Ceil, it's the leg that he has always had trouble with," Nigel explains, without mentioning her prior acts of abuse towards Nicolaus and of being the one who first permanently injured his leg when he was a child. "The physician I brought with me told me no, it would not need amputating, and sure enough the physicians here at this hospital say the same." Nigel sighs, "Thank God I didn't listen to that first doctor. You know, Nicolaus has just lost so much already, I don't want him to have to bear an amputation as well."

"Well, yes, I see your point." Ceil is supportive. "So Nigel, you said something about surgery? When is the surgery?"

"Tomorrow, on the same leg. He will be the first patient for surgery. They tell me it will be a difficult surgery, but they are optimistic for him. Though Ceil, I'm ... I'm very worried."

"Nigel, why? Anything I can do?"

"He hasn't actually been awake yet. He's not in a coma, but he's not awake either. I'm concerned about it. Scares me."

"Well, you've got Nicolaus in the hands of the best doctors at one of the best military hospitals in the world. I think you should stop stressing about it and put your faith in those doctors. Maybe say a little prayer if needed."

Nigel nods. "Thank you for that, Ceil."

"I don't want you to make your health suffer over all this Nigel. You been eating? You sleeping? Taking care of yourself? You've been over there for several days now."

"I'm fine. I think I'll feel better after the surgery."

"Well, dear, for me, you have a meal today, and sleep, so you will be better for tomorrow. Nigel, it's important you take care of yourself. After all, you are still my husband. And I want to keep you around," she tells him.

"Why, Ceil, are you flirting with me?" A smile is across his face. He had not had such light banter with Ceil for quite a while. He is enjoying this.

Ceil chuckles, "Maybe a little! I kind of miss you. When this is all over and done with, you and I are going to the Bahamas for a long vacation."

"I would like that, Ceil. I really would," he tells her sweetly, glad to hear this side of his wife he had not heard for a while. "And tell me, how are things at home? Niall show up?"

Ceil chuckles again, "Funny you should ask! Niall is right here with me. You want to talk to him?"

"No, no. I just want to stay focused on Nicolaus for now. You able to handle Niall okay?"

"Oh, yes, he is fine. I was just telling him, that people started showing up at our gate, and are leaving flowers and cards and stuffed animals and what not for Nicolaus. Silly people."

"Oh wow, showing their concern for him! That's nice! I'm getting telegrams from all over the world. We'll need to talk more about this later and compare notes."

"I suppose that press conference Jonathan held has started all this. I am going to have Niall take care of receiving the items at the gate. And then I have some other tasks for him to do."

Nigel nods. "Okay, ... well ... I'll let you handle Niall for now."

"Of course!"

"Ceil, thank you for this call, and for your support. I appreciate you. I love you, my wife."

"Oh Nigel, now don't you go getting sentimental on me! I'll talk to you again tomorrow, after the surgery. But call me if you need anything dear."

"Okay, good night." Nigel had not seen the press conference to know about Ceil's misdeeds regarding Gwen. He is oblivious about it, strictly focusing his energy on the wellbeing of Nicolaus.

Ceil ends the call and looks at Niall. She smiles mischievously. "Finally, our time has come!" She stands with excitement, clasping her hands in joy. "Now, this is what you are going to do. Get upstairs and get yourself cleaned up. You are going to go to the gate, waive at the cameras, and put those items in the vehicle."

Ceil paces the floor as she devises her plan. "Better yet, I'll have you take the limo to the gate, and you have the driver put the items in the vehicle. While he's doing that, you waive to the cameras, and slowly approach. The reporters are going to be asking a lot of questions. No matter what they ask you, the only thing you are going to say is, 'We are very worried about Nicolaus, and we ask for your prayers, thank you.' And you just keep repeating that. Stay for about one minute, then get back in the limo and return to the house."

"Mother," Niall is frowning at her, "why would I do that?"

Ceil turns and looks at her most beloved and messed up son. She scowls at him. "What do you mean why? You are now going to be stepping into the limelight, ahead of your brother. And then ..."

"No. I don't want to."

"Now look Niall, this is finally our chance. And you've got to shake off what ... what you've done. Now don't you? It will be fine. Nicolaus will be gone for a long time. I will have the lawyers train you, and you will step into Nicolaus' place. If he returns, you'll work next to him, not even under him, but next to him."

"No! I don't want to!"

Ceil walks right up to Niall, and as hard as she can, she slaps his face. The slap is loud and turns his head. Niall grabs his face in pain, looking at his mother with a frown.

"Who the hell do you think you are, telling me what you will and what you won't do?" Ceil yells at him. "You're my son, and you'll do exactly what I tell you."

She steps back to look at him. "We can all see where running your own life has gotten you, carrying on like some sex crazed lunatic! You are going to do exactly as I say, when I say. And you are going to do it with a smile and no complaining, or I swear to you, I'll disinherit you, have you castrated, and have you disappeared and locked up for the rest of your life, faster than you can wipe a tear. I will make it as if I never had a son at all."

To reiterate her words, Ceil walks up to Niall and slaps him again. "Do I make myself clear?" She stands with crossed arms and waits for his answer.

Niall is shocked, as his mother has never treated him as such. Nicolaus yes, himself no. He's not sure what to do. Each of her threats certainly put immense fear in him, because he knows his mother, and he knows she is truly capable of carrying out what she says she'll do. Niall slowly nods, "Yes, Mother."

Ceil takes a breath, straightens her hair and sits down. "Good. Now, you will do what I have told you. When you get back from the gate, we will begin your training. I need you up and ready very quickly, so that we can move in fast while your father is away."

Chapter Twenty

As Nicolaus recovers from a complicated, though successful surgery, Niall is spending sixty hours a week in executive level development training.

Ceil hired university professors for Niall's at home training, which she also joined. Niall is imparted learning and wisdom from three accounting professors, two law professors, and three business administration professors. After two weeks of non-stop training, Ceil felt that Niall is prepared to enter the workplace.

She bought him expensive suits, got him a new stylish haircut, and reminded him of her promise if he failed her. Niall found himself with a new attitude and wanting to intertwine this newness with his willingness to make a change in his life.

However, Niall's relationship with Elsa did not improve. She refused him at every turn. Ironically, he feels that Elsa is treating him as Deirdre did, his very complaint that fueled his anger against Deirdre. So even though Niall looks better on the outside, he is still having trouble with his insides. His soul is still perturbed, and he isn't sure what to do about it.

Niall thought maybe he could talk to Constance, and ask her forgiveness and he'd feel a little better. However, when he pulled his sports car into her driveway, Niall found that he was unable to exit. He couldn't find it within himself to go up to the door. He is not able to face Constance, let alone ask for her forgiveness, which he is sure she would not give.

Sighing, Niall backs out of the driveway, and goes to his hangout downtown.

The following day is Niall's first day at the VMC office. This time, Ceil had Niall placed inside of the office with one of the lawyers. Ceil thinks placing Niall with the lawyers will make him less intimidated by Nicolaus. Additionally, he'd have someone to ask questions. Ceil provided Niall with a nice desk in the large office. She also had the professors provide Niall certificates of training completion, which she had placed on the wall behind his desk.

For his first task, she had him do the vetting of investment applications that were on Nicolaus' desk. The stack is large.

"Now, this is your first task to help your brother. Nicolaus goes through these to see if the investor applications are worthy of approval before we accept their money."

Ceil places the large stack of folders before Niall. "I imagine these haven't been looked at since your brother has been gone. So this is a good thing for you to help him with. Here is the checklist he uses. You must check and sign off each item in each folder, if all items pass the criteria on the checklist, then that company can donate. Let's get these done this week, as this is money waiting for us to have. I'll talk to Daniel to see if there is any other work he wants you to do, since he is the Chief Operating Officer."

With great confidence, Ceil leaves Niall to get to work.

Chapter Twenty-One

Nicolaus stirs as he fully awakes for the first time in two weeks. He breathes deep, looking around, and determines that he is in a hospital. He sees a nurse appear before his vision, though he cannot sit up, nor really move.

The nurse touches his shoulder. "Hello Nicolaus. Don't try to move, just relax," she says as she notices he is beginning to struggle against the bed straps. "I'll get the doctor." Instead of leaving him, she calls the nurse station and asks them to send the physician in. She returns her attention to him. "Relax. It's okay, you are in a hospital. Do you remember your full name?"

Nicolaus stops struggling. He breathes again. "Yes, Nicolaus Ravenell."

The nurse smiles at him and nods. "Good. You've been through a lot. You are definitely a strong and determined young man."

"Nicolaus, you're awake!" The physician greets him with joy in his voice. "How are you feeling?"

Nicolaus slightly smiles. "I don't know. Weird."

"For sure. I'm Dr. Peoples. Your father, who is here with you, just ... umh, I believe he is at a hotel to rest right now," he looks at the nurse who shakes her head in agreement with him. "We are here from the U.S. to assist in your care. We are at the military hospital in Germany. I've been working with physicians here to care for you. Do you remember what happened, Nicolaus?"

The nurse works on taking Nicolaus' vitals while Dr. Peoples talks with him. Nicolaus thinks for a moment. Suddenly, he remembers Jonathan. "Ah ... yes ... I remember I was just outside of Spain, helping my former father-in-law, Jonathan Baird. And ... we were waiting to get to Spain. It was hot, and ... rest ... his men needed rest. That's what I remember."

"Do you remember being shot in the leg?"

Nicolaus frowns, then remembers, happenings flooding his mind. "Oh yeah. Yes, I remember. Jonathan ... we ... rescued him. We rescued him, and ... yes, I got shot." Dr. Peoples nods. "And ... oh ... I remember a woman."

"That's good. Well, yes, your leg was shot up, lots of damage there. We had to do surgery. We removed the bullets and the infection. We were able to save most of the nerves, but not all Nicolaus. We repaired what we could. You also had a massive stab wound in your abdomen. You lost a lot of blood through that wound. By the time we got to you, a few days had passed, and you'd lost much blood. And you'd been poisoned as well."

"Poisoned?"

"Yes. The doctors lost you before we got to you, but were able to bring you back. Do you remember anything of that?"

"Lost me? You mean ... I died?"

"Well ... you flatlined. Do you remember seeing a bright light or anything."

Nicolaus pauses in thought for a moment trying to remember all that happened. He looks to Dr. Peoples and the nurse. Memories continue to flood his mind. He suddenly is surprised. "Yes. I think so ... maybe."

Dr. Peoples touches his shoulder. "It's okay. You'll most likely continue to remember things. Well ... we've given you three blood transfusions, patched up your abdomen, and provided the surgery I've mentioned. Now Nicolaus, I don't want you moving around, so you are bed strapped and will remain so. I know how you military leadership types are. You want to jump up and get going. Well ... you are not out of the woods yet, you see. You still have poison in your system. It has not completely cleared out, and is still going through your organs. And of course this is critical. Your heart, kidneys, liver, and brain are the ones we are mostly concerned about."

"My brain?"

"Yes. And the others. The poison could still potentially kill you. And ..."

Nicolaus suddenly has a convulsion. He cries out in pain, as it lasts for a few seconds. Dr. Peoples and the nurse tend to him.

"Just breathe through that Nicolaus, just breathe." Dr. Peoples immediately listens to Nicolaus' heart through his stethoscope, as Nicolaus does what he says. He sees that Nicolaus calms down. "You okay?"

Nicolaus nods. "It stings!"

Dr. Peoples nods. "Yes, that's the poison. That sting is the burning of your nerve endings. You'll still be experiencing that until the poison has cleared out, and you may have some nerve damage, Nicolaus, or you may fully recover with no nerve damage. Only time will tell. These episodes have lessened though. You are not experiencing them as often as you were a few days ago, so you are getting better."

Nicolaus nods in understanding.

"I want you to continue to rest. Sleep and rest will help to repair your injuries."

"Dr. Peoples, how long have I been here? What day is it?"

"You've been here for two weeks. It is July fifteenth."

"My wife ... Deirdre ... "

"Ah, that's who Deirdre is! You've been calling her name a lot," the nurse teases him with a smile.

"She is pregnant and due to have our son. I need to call her. Please ... is there a phone?"

"Okay, hold on there now. Remember, I don't want you moving around, and I don't want you stressed out. Let's get that coordinated with your father. Nigel should return in about an hour. That's when he's due back."

Nicolaus nods in understanding. He felt that he could wait an hour until his father returned to talk to his sweet Deirdre. He is excited to know about Deirdre's pregnancy. Immediately, Nicolaus begins to silently pray, thanking God for his life, and asking blessings upon his wife and son.

When Nigel returns to the hospital, he seeks out Dr. Peoples to check on Nicolaus' condition, as he'd been gone for about eight hours.

"Nigel!" Dr. Peoples pulls Nigel into an office. "Nicolaus is awake!"

"He's awake?"

"Yes, fully. He can't remember everything, but the memories will return. He is strong, and his vitals are very good. He is doing very well."

Nigel grasps Dr. Peoples' hand, "Thank you so much for helping my son."

"Of course!"

"When can we transport him home? I really want him to recover at home. I've already had my staff prepare an area for him."

"Sure, Nigel. Now that he is stronger, we can transport him ... say ... in about two days. And Nigel, he is asking about Deirdre."

"What did you tell him?"

"He wants to call her. I told him he could coordinate that with you when you return today."

Nigel nods. "Can we sedate Nicolaus until we get him home?"

"Sedate him? Nigel, he's just woken up."

"Look, I can't tell him about Deirdre, not here. It's going to be really difficult for him. I want him settled down at home before I tell him." Nigel pauses, seeing the physician's reaction. "It's going to be a really bad blow for him. It's going to set him back."

"Nigel, you want him sedated?"

"He has to rest anyway, doesn't he? Look, I don't want to ask you to do anything that is unethical. If you can't do it, I understand, but I am thinking of the health of my son. He is not going to be able to handle the news about his wife here. Just sedate him until we get him settled at home."

Dr. Peoples nods, hands in the air, "All right, all right. Let's arrange to transport him tomorrow then. He does need to be sedated for the flight anyway. Let me get on the arrangements."

Chapter Twenty-Two

It is hard for Niall to walk the mansion without remembering where Deirdre had been, without seeing her smile which lit up any room, and certainly without smelling her beautiful aroma that used to drift through the air wherever she tread. Niall imagined how much more difficult it would be for Nicolaus.

Niall thought about Elsa. He feared she would never forgive him, and now that Deirdre had been taken from them all, he realizes how blessed he is to have such a good woman at his side, who wants to bear his children and make a family with him. He realizes how stupid he's been about Elsa this whole time. He feels very bad about this as he looks upon Nicolaus. He stands where Nicolaus lay, in a hospital bed, in the sitting room.

Niall weeps at the sight of Nicolaus, who looks weak and helpless, aged and thin, much unlike his usual self. Niall had only entered the room because he saw that Nicolaus seems unconscious, otherwise he would not have entered, unable to face him, unable to own up to what he's done.

Nicolaus struggles to open his eyes; however, the strong sedative will not allow his brain to awaken. He whispers Deirdre's name, scaring Niall, making him back away.

"Niall, you must let your brother rest," the physician appears into the room. Niall reaches his hand to Nicolaus, wanting to touch him, but withdraws it quickly, afraid of waking him. "Go on now, son!" Dr. Peoples tells him, as he attends to Nicolaus. Niall leaves the room, feeling as though he is going to fall apart again. He does not want to be around when Nicolaus is told about Deirdre.

Chapter Twenty-Three

When Nicolaus finally opens his eyes from his forced induced sleep, he recognizes the golden sitting room curtains in the mansion. His eyes look around, and he recognizes the windows, the lighting in the ceiling, and the smell of his home.

He blinks his eyes, thinking he is dreaming, only to see the same scenes when he reopens them. He sees a nurse tending to him. "Hello Sir," she says sweetly to him. Nicolaus tries to respond and is unable to. He notices he cannot move his body, feeling the bed straps holding him down. As he attempts to pull against the bed straps, weakness falls over him, and he is again taken over by sedation.

Nicolaus' mind drifts on the medication, though he thinks of his Deirdre. He knows if he is home, he is one step closer to seeing her. His heart is glad and skips a beat at the thought of holding her and seeing his son. His mind calculates that Nicolai should have been born three days ago. He listens to hear sounds of his son as his mind and his senses float out of his control. The only sounds he can hear is the nurse clanging instruments, the friction of her scrubs, and the beeping of the monitor he is attached to.

Nigel enters to check on Nicolaus and the nurse. "How is he today?"

"Nicolaus is doing well, Sir. He opened his eyes a little while ago. Dr. Peoples is about ready to pull back on the sedation. It will take Nicolaus several days to get oriented, and much time before he'll be able to walk on his leg. Dr. Peoples brought some crutches for Nicolaus."

The nurse points to the crutches in the corner by the fireplace. They are placed there as if a scene from the famous Christmas movie, of a child with a lame leg. Except the crutches are long, for Nicolaus' height. "We'll need to measure them out for him. And then we'll probably start him on physical therapy in a few weeks. We can begin it here, at home, and then transfer to facility physical therapy."

Nigel nods, feeling worried about the questions he knows Nicolaus will have about Deirdre. He dreads the thought of explaining Deirdre's passing. He goes to Nicolaus, and touches him. He checks his forehead for fever, glad he feels none, then soothes his hair. Nigel is very glad the physician was able to save Nicolaus' leg. Emotions surface as he thinks about what Nicolaus has been through, knowing they'd almost lost him.

Suddenly, Nigel feels arms go around him. Ceil hugs her husband, and lays her head on his strong back for a few seconds. Then she stands next to him, and also observes Nicolaus. Nigel puts his arm around Ceil, and enjoys their tender moment.

"He will be all right," Ceil says softly. "He'll pull through."

"Yes."

"And now he will have help at the office. I've finally got Niall doing what it is he is supposed to be doing."

Nigel frowns at her, the tender moment gone at the mention of Niall's name. "What do you mean?"

"I've had Niall trained by some of the best minds in Austin. One hundred twenty hours of training. So now he understands what to do. He is helping at the office. Even Daniel is impressed."

Nigel balks at this news. "Hummh, I'm impressed too! That's wonderful Ceil. I hope he is cooperating as you want him to."

"More than what I want. I'm proud of him."

"Well, that's great."

"I'm heading back to check on things now. I just wanted to stop in and see how everything is going here, and ... to see you, Nigel. I missed you while you were gone."

Nigel smiles at Ceil. He kisses her cheek, and watches her leave out of the house. As soon as she is gone Nigel calls Daniel.

"Mr. Ravenell! How is Nicolaus doing? We all wish him the best and hope to see him soon."

"Thank you for that Daniel. We are home now, Nicolaus' recovery is going well, however, he will need more time before he can return to the office."

"Oh I see."

"How are things going there? I just heard that Niall is working cooperatively. I hope this is true."

"Uhm, ... well ... yes sir, he is. Much better than before. Seems to have better knowledge. Ceil has set him up as Associate Vice President, with the salary to match."

"Really? Hmmm ... well, that is good to know ... I mean, this could work ... though Daniel, I think we should have someone covertly double check his work, before it gets finalized."

"Oh yes Sir, we certainly are doing that already."

"I should have known you'd have my back and be diligently taking care of the company. Thank you, Daniel. I truly, thank you."

"Oh of course, thank you, Sir."

"I feel that you need to be offered a promotion, Daniel. I'll get to work on that!"

"Oh wow! Why, thank you Sir!"

Chapter Twenty-Four

Nicolaus opens his eyes, finding himself feeling very different, fully awake. He notices his arms and legs are still strapped to the bed, however, his mind feels much clearer. Before him, he sees the nurse, and also Elsa. Elsa is touching his face and roaming her hands through his hair, with a smile for him.

"Nicky," she whispers his name. "It's me, Elsa."

Nicolaus nods to her. He notices again that he is in the sitting room, glad he was not dreaming about this earlier. His eyes dart around the room, looking for Deirdre. He frowns when he does not see her. "Elsa," he says her name in a weak whisper, surprising himself. He thought his voice would be louder. "Elsa," he says again.

"Yes, Nicky, it's me." She continues to gently stroke his face.

"Deirdre. Deirdre?" He takes a breath. "Baby. Nicolai," he says in a whisper. "Where's Deirdre?"

Immediately, emotion grips Elsa, and tears roll from her eyes. She opens her mouth to say something, and closes it, saying nothing. What could she say? Suddenly, Dr. Peoples moves Elsa out of the way to tend to Nicolaus, checking his eyes, and his vitals. Slowly, Elsa backs out of the room, almost grateful for the interruption.

"Nicolaus! You remember me? I'm Dr. Peoples, and this is Nurse Haddie. We've been caring for you for the last few weeks. We assisted in Castellano, and then flew you to Germany, and assisted there as well. Your father hired me to take care of you." He touches Nicolaus on the shoulder.

Nicolaus nods. "Thank you," he says in a whisper, as he is still very weak.

Dr. Peoples relieves him of the bed straps, and rollie rubs out his arms and legs to get rid of any numbness Nicolaus may be experiencing. He checks Nicolaus torso wound, which has been stitched together. The bleeding has stopped, and is only oozing healing gunk, which most wounds do. "Let's get this bandage changed," he tells the nurse. She assists him to do so.

After the bandage change, he sits the hospital bed up a little. "There. I'm sure you will get stronger very soon. I don't want you rushing anything, though. You've had lots of trauma. Do you remember what happened?" He questions him again, to see if his mind recalls additional details.

Nigel enters the room, delighted to see Nicolaus sitting up. He goes to his son, and hugs him, kissing his head. "Son!"

Nicolaus grabs onto Nigel's hand. They have a moment, Nicolaus grateful for his father.

"I just asked Nicolaus to tell me if he can remember what happened."

Nicolaus nods, his mind fully engaged now. "My father-in-law, was up on a mountaintop, outside of Spain. Me ... and my team ... we climbed the mountain," Nicolaus pauses and frowns, remembering James, sorry for this loss. "I lost one of my men. He was young. James. We were under heavy gun fire. And ... I don't know ... everything suddenly stopped, but not until after James was hit. He died right in my arms," his whispering voice sounds shaky. Nicolaus clears his dried throat and takes a breath to continue. "Everything fell silent, and we saw that all the cartel men were sleep on the ground. It was crazy. But then ... I knew it was God, or the angels who helped us, cuz we were pinned down. And we went in the house, got Jonathan and his men, and came back down the mountain." Nicolaus sighs, pausing. Dr. Peoples signaled for the nurse to give Nicolaus some water.

"Drink it slow," she tells him.

Nicolaus drank some water, the best he's had in a long time. "And ... when we got back into the village, they wanted to stop walking to rest, and I wanted to keep going, ... but I was overruled.

So we stopped, and ...," he shakes his head. "The last thing I remember," he frowns, "... I remember ... uhm ... some lady ... some lady asked me something, but then I felt the dagger, and ... and ...," he stops talking, looks down at his torso, touching the bandage, then looks at the men. "I don't know ... I don't know what happened after that."

Dr. Peoples nods and looks to Nigel. "Wow!" He is astonished at Nicolaus account of what's happened. "Nicolaus," he touches Nicolaus on the shoulder again, "you are very lucky to be here, son. That dagger, it had poison on it."

"Poison?"

"Yes. And it could have severed your main artery. Luckily, it didn't. Frankly, I don't know how you are alive."

"Well, and they thought they lost him in Castellano. Remember Jonathan told us, how they got him back," Nigel adds.

"Oh yes."

Nicolaus' mind recalls that he'd seen Deirdre in a dark room. "Deirdre," he says her name to them, his throat raw from medical tubes and dehydration. "Where's ... where's Deirdre?"

The nurse began to remove Nicolaus' sweaty hospital clothes, and replace them with light clothing. Dr. Peoples and Nigel seemed to be talking amongst themselves, ignoring his question of Deirdre.

"Please," he asks the nurse, "my wife. Where is she?"

"Oh Nicolaus, I am so sorry," is all she says, and continues to work.

Nicolaus sighs, "Deirdre, where is she?" The nurse shakes her head to him and keeps working.

"Father," Nicolaus weakly calls. "Deirdre?"

Nigel and Dr. Peoples return to him, however, his question is not answered.

Dr. Peoples goes to the crutches, which lean against the fireplace. "I have these crutches for you. You may not remember that you were shot as well, Nicolaus. In your leg. We did surgery and repaired it and took out the infection. The crutches will help you walk. This is how you use them." Dr. Peoples demonstrates how to use the crutches for Nicolaus. "It is important that you don't put pressure on that leg of yours for now. We can practice using them after you have eaten and gotten some strength. You'll need physical therapy later."

Nicolaus sighs again. "Okay, thank you," he says gently, very grateful for the physician and nurse care. They are obviously doing a good job for him. Nicolaus looks to both men who are standing together again. "Where is my wife? Where is Deirdre? Is she okay? Nicolai? The baby ..."

Dr. Peoples touches Nicolaus' shoulder. "We shall discuss Deirdre after you have eaten."

"Discuss her?"

"Please Nicolaus. It is best this way. Now I will be right back with some food for you." Dr. Peoples and the nurse leave the room.

Nicolaus seems weak again. Nigel takes his hand and sits next to him on the bed. "Son, you've been through a lot. Let's get you stronger."

Nicolaus lays back, feeling his little energy waning. "Deirdre," he says weakly. "What's happened?"

Nigel touches Nicolaus to calm him, and says nothing.

Chapter Twenty-Five

Nigel watches as the nurse spoon feeds Nicolaus some chicken soup, as if he were a child. Nigel sees that Nicolaus is still weak. "Nigel, you will not discuss Deirdre with him right now. He's not ready, he's still weak, as you can see."

"How am I supposed to do this? He's already asking."

"Just give it a few days. You'll have to stall him ... judiciously, Nigel. Change the subject. Leave the room. Talk about something else."

Nigel chuckles. "You don't know my son. He loves Deirdre, with all his heart."

"Nigel, I know it's going to be tough, but trust me, he needs to be stronger before getting news like that. You must do this for him. I'm going to give him some medication to help him sleep. I don't want him out of bed. The catheter will remain, and the nurse will stay overnight."

Nigel nods.

After another hour, as the sun has already set, Dr. Peoples checks over Nicolaus. He gives him an injection of the sleep medication. "Nicolaus, you are doing very well. I don't want you out of bed yet. You're not strong enough yet, and I certainly don't want you falling on your leg. Now you get some rest, and I'll see you in the morning."

"Thank you, Dr. Peoples. Thank you for all you've done to help me."

"You're a great patient! I'll see you in the morning."

Nigel walks the doctor out, and by the time he returns to Nicolaus, he can see that the sleep medication has already taken effect. Nigel jostles up the covers over his son, kissing his forehead, grateful that Nicolaus survived this ordeal.

Chapter Twenty-Six

Nurse Haddie set her alarm watch to chime at five in the morning. She figured this would be more than enough time to get up and get ready before Nicolaus awoke. She slept on the sitting room couch, as a makeshift bed, to be close to Nicolaus during the night. She turned off her alarm, sat up and stretched herself. She looked over to the other side of the room where Nicolaus would be in the hospital bed. Except ... he isn't there.

She stands and walks over, feeling a little panicked. The bed covers are turned back, the catheter is placed on the bed, and the intravenous fluid needle is hanging from the pole. Nicolaus is not there, nor anywhere in the room. She looks to the fireplace and notices that the crutches are missing as well.

Nurse Haddie robes herself and goes out the room. She notices all is still quiet, as the family has not risen as of yet. She does not know the house, so she is apprehensive to just go about looking for Nicolaus. She decides to get herself ready for the day, then will deal with it. Perhaps by then he will have returned to the room.

Once she had readied herself, after thirty minutes of time, Nicolaus has not returned to the room. Nurse Haddie begins to walk the house to look for the staff, and Nicolaus.

"Well, there he is," one of the maids points to the other side of the mansion, seeing Nicolaus emerging from the door that connects his wing to the rest of the house.

Nicolaus hobbles, using the crutches he was given. His robe is loose, he looks strained, tired, and upset. "Where is Deirdre? I have looked for her, and I cannot find her. Her things are here, but she is not. Is she in the hospital?" He asks the maid. She turns away from Nicolaus without answering, feeling as though she wants to cry. They are all upset over Deirdre's passing. The maid runs from him.

Nurse Haddie rushes over to Nicolaus to help him. He is sweating from all the walking and stair climbing. "Nicolaus, you are not supposed to be on that leg just yet." She grabs onto him, to help his weight hobble across the room. He stops, stopping her too. "No. I have to find my wife. Has my father told you where she is?" The nurse shakes her head. Nicolaus hobbles away from her. "Deirdre!" He resorts to calling her, knowing she would be up by now, especially with the baby. "Deirdre!" He calls loudly and frantically. "Deirdre!"

Nicolaus makes his way to the kitchen. He is sure the staff would know where she is. "Mr. Nicolaus, Sir, please sit down." The ladies can see that Nicolaus looks worn out and sickly. They are very worried, knowing about the ordeal he has just survived.

"Please. Please tell me where Deirdre is. I cannot find her. Is she in the hospital?"

"Mr. Nicolaus," one of the ladies goes to his side, holding him around his waist, trying to edge him toward the table and chair. "Please, Mr. Nicolaus, sit down before you fall down."

He recoils from her, almost falling. "No, I'm fine. I just need to find my wife. Won't you please tell me where she is? Ms. Mary, please tell me?"

"Mr. Nicolaus," Mary shakes her head, saying nothing.

Nurse Haddie appears again. "Nicolaus, listen to me!" She half yells at him. "Your father will tell you about Deirdre. Now, right now, I need you to get to a chair," she produces a needle filled with fluid, "or you are going to force me to sedate you," she threatens him. "Now which will it be?"

Nicolaus sighs. "I only want to know about my wife. Why is no one answering me?" He yells.

Nigel appears in the kitchen, dressed and ready for the day. "Nicolaus ..." he frowns, "why are you out of bed?"

"I'm trying to find Deirdre! And no one will tell me where she is! Where is she, father? Deirdre! Deirdre!" Frantically, he calls for his wife again. "Deirdre!" His frantic state makes him lose his balance. He is sweaty and feels very weak.

Nigel quickly goes to Nicolaus' side. He supports his weight, and eases him out of the kitchen. The nurse follows.

Outside of the kitchen, Nicolaus stops their movements. "No. I want to know where Deirdre is father, and I want to know now," he half yells at Nigel.

"Sir, Nicolaus can be sedated and put back to bed."

Nigel holds his hand up to the nurse, "No no, that is okay. He's right. He needs to know."

Ceil enters the room, seeing what is happening. She understands that now is the time they will be informing Nicolaus.

"Son, let's get you to a chair, please, and I'll tell you."

Pained, Nicolaus hobbles to a chair in the sitting room that Ceil has placed across from the couch. All the furniture had been moved to the side to make space for the hospital bed inside the room.

Nicolaus sighs, out of breath, as he plops into the chair.

"Please give us some privacy," Nigel directs the nurse to leave them.

Ceil and Nigel sit across from Nicolaus. Nigel wants Nicolaus to catch his breath before they begin. Nigel's heart goes out to his son, seeing that his son of strength looks pitiful, weak, and sickly again, from trying to find Deirdre. Nigel is very worried about how Nicolaus will take the news. He knows he must be patient, no matter his reaction. "Son, you need some water or anything?"

"Father, the only thing I need is to know where Deirdre is. Please tell me, and tell me the truth. Is she in the hospital with the baby? You've said nothing of this, and you won't answer my questions about it."

"Nicolaus, I know you are upset about this, and I'm sorry. We just felt that you needed to be stronger before ... before we discussed it."

Nicolaus frowns. "There's that word again. Discuss." He shakes his head. "Where is she?" He knows for certain she'd be right by his side, holding onto him, unless she were in the hospital, unable to be next to him.

Nigel takes a long sigh. He is very worried.

Elsa was about to walk into the room. Nicolaus sees her. "Elsa! Elsa, you must know where Deirdre is. Why has she not been brought to see me? Is she in the hospital? Is she all right?"

Elsa gasps and places her hands over her mouth. When she sees the scene, she quickly backs out the room, telling him nothing. Nicolaus is puzzled by her behavior.

Elsa slides down the wall, just outside the door, out of sight. Tears fall from her eyes for what she knows is about to occur.

Nicolaus looks to Ceil for a long moment. She is unusually quiet. Finally, Nicolaus looks to his father. "Father, why have you not brought Deirdre to me? Where is my wife?"

Nigel frowns, tightening his mouth, thinking of the words to say. "My son, I am so sorry. No matter how we tell you, this is just not going to be easy. I'm so sorry, but ..." he sighs heavy, "Deirdre is ... Deirdre ... she went into labor early ... and ...," he couldn't bring himself to tell him.

"She's in the hospital then? But I asked you that and you wouldn't answer me. No one answers me." He stands. "I must go to her ...."

Nigel stands, placing his hand to Nicolaus' shoulder. "Hold on son, please. She is ... not at the hospital." Nicolaus looks at Nigel strangely, then reseats himself. Slowly he asks, afraid of the answer, "Where is she?"

Nigel reseats himself as well, he sighs. "Nicolaus, she went into labor early, and she lost a lot of blood. I'm so sorry, the doctors tried, they really tried, but ... they just couldn't save her. She died." Nigel didn't recognize that look on Nicolaus' face.

"What?" Nicolaus asks, as if he could not possibly comprehend such a thing.

"She died during childbirth," he softly states. "They did their best to save Deirdre and the baby ... but I'm sorry son, neither of them survived."

Nicolaus' eyes grew wide. His face is covered in dread. "Are you telling me ... Deirdre ..." He couldn't say the unimaginable words.

"I am so sorry Nicolaus," Nigel replies softly.

Nicolaus looks away from his father, then looks at Ceil. Ceil is unusually quiet, with her head hung. He looks between the both of them. "No," he half shouts, rejecting the statement. "I don't believe you. You are lying!"

"Nicolaus," Ceil reaches to touch him, and he jerks away from her.

"No! Where is she? Where have you sent her? What have you done with her, Ceil?" He half yells. "What have you done?" Nicolaus' tone is accusatory towards Ceil, as he remembers the scheme she plotted against him with Gwen.

Ceil sighs. "I was there! In the delivery room! So was Constance and Elsa. I held my grandson, little Nicolai. He was blue. He never opened his eyes, he never moved. I held him!" Ceil gets emotional, though purposefully omitting what Niall had done. "We watched as Deirdre slipped away," she stands away from the men. "They tried to save her, but they couldn't." She reseats herself next to Nigel, tears in her eyes, holding her hand to Nicolaus. "They couldn't save her," she says in a whisper, her hand unreceived.

Nicolaus shakes his head in unbelief. "No!" He shouts at both of them. "No! I don't believe you," he is pained to his heart. "Where is she?" Nicolaus yells to them.

"She is there!" Nigel yells back to get Nicolaus' attention, pointing to the back door of the sitting room, which leads to the place, in the courtyard, at the back of the mansion, that is the Ravenell family cemetery.

Nicolaus looks at Nigel with wide, unmoving eyes, understanding to where he is pointing. Nicolaus is so shocked he can hardly move.

His wide eyes follow the trajectory of Nigel's finger pointing towards the cemetery, which could be seen from the door window of the sitting room. Unsteadily, Nicolaus quietly rises from the chair. Using the crutches, he hobbles out the sitting room back door, on his own. Nigel is now the unmoving one.

Elsa begins to whimper loudly. She wants to go to Nicolaus, but she cannot. Mentally, she couldn't say anything to him. What could she possibly say?

Chapter Twenty-Seven

After Nigel had sent Nicolaus to the space where they lay their family members to rest, with that back door which Nicolaus slowly left still open, Nigel is unmoving in his chair. He sits and waits, not sure what to expect. He is not exactly sure how Nicolaus will react to the death of Deirdre.

Even though the Ravenell family cemetery is about a quarter mile from the house, the sound of Nicolaus' shock and immediate laments over Deirdre, and his questioning of God, is heard by the whole household, and by Nigel's ears, after the long time period it took Nicolaus to hobble to the gravesite.

"No!" Nicolaus is heard yelling again, with the feeling of being unable to do anything about the situation in his voice. "Not Deirdre! Oh God, why?" Nicolaus shouts up to the heavens. "Why? What did I do? What did I do? Oh God! My God! My Heavenly God!" Nicolaus cries loud laments over Deirdre.

Nigel is unmoving as he listens to the sorrow that fills the air.

He feels very inadequate as Nicolaus' father, at this very moment of time. What could he possibly do for his son? His son, the courageous military hero with a pious heart and love for God; his son, whom the love of God has directly touched on more than one occasion; his son, the CEO of the successful company he co-founded that helps hundreds of people daily; his son, the man who carried the family forward and made them more financially sound than ever before; his son, who worked to bring collaborative efforts to rescue families from imminent danger of war; his son, who'd ever only loved one woman, the young woman lost to all of them. His son, Nicolaus Ravenell, who will carry on the family name and the family empire.

The sounds of soul ripping is heard from Nicolaus. Nigel cries in silence. He remains seated and unmoving, unable to fathom what Nicolaus must be feeling, especially since Nicolaus had almost lost his own life recently. He knows Nicolaus fought his way from the brink of death to rejoin his wife in life and to prepare for the birth of their son, only now to find that all is lost, she is no longer here among the living. Nigel cries mournful tears for his son. Ceil grabs onto Nigel, hugging him, trying to comfort him, crying as well.

Chapter Twenty-Eight

Drenched from the downpour of rain outside, Francesca wasn't in a panic looking for Nicolaus. That is ... until she couldn't find him. She knew he was too weak to go out on his own. His bed in the makeshift hospital room is empty. He is not upstairs, nor is he in his side of the mansion. So now, Francesca is extremely worried that Nicolaus has been transported back to the hospital. The staff seem to be avoiding her when she inquires of them.

"Sorry ma'am ..." they say and leave from her, following the directives Ceil gave them to tell no one anything.

Francesca finds Nigel and Ceil in the sitting room. Nigel looks very somber and statuesque as he sits unmoving. Ceil is sitting close by, quietly looking through a magazine.

As Francesca enters the sitting room, Nigel does not look at her, nor does he give her his usual fatherly greeting. And Ceil says nothing. She finds this very odd.

Francesca goes to Nigel, and stands before him, thinking maybe he hadn't seen her enter the room. She frowns when he does not move, does not look at her, nor says anything. He is just there. Her anxiousness increases because now she knows for certain something has happened.

"Uncle Nigel! What's happened? Where's Nicky? I can't find him."

Nigel remains unmoving. He breathes a slight breath. "He's at her grave. He won't come in. He's been out there for three days."

His words and demeanor shock Francesca. "What?"

"And Nigel has been sitting unmoved in that chair for the same three days," Ceil informs her. Francesca frowns at Ceil. She cannot understand what is happening here.

"Bishop Leighton couldn't get through to him," Nigel continues strangely.

"Nicky's been out there for three days? But ..." her British accent is front and center, "it's pouring! It's been pouring for hours!" She notes of the seasonal torrential storm across Texas. The rain cell has been stalled over Austin, and has been pouring rain nonstop since yesterday. Upset boils out of Francesca. Her voice is now elevated as she yells directly at Nigel, "You left Nicky outside? For three days? At the grave? By himself?" She feels incensed, not caring that tears stream from Nigel's eyes at her words, or that Ceil is staring at her.

Nigel's eyes finally look at his daughter. He shakes his head. "I can do nothing for him. I cannot help Nicolaus. I cannot help him."

Francesca backs away from Nigel and Ceil, feeling gross disappointment. Nigel's eyes watch as Francesca turns from him and dashes out the back door to the yard, the same path that Nicolaus had walked three days ago. Tears stream from Nigel, though he remains unmoving. He listens to the rain pouring down, hitting the ground and the walls of his mansion, through the opened door. The fresh smell of rainwater floats to his nostrils. The thought of nature makes Nigel cry even more. Ceil provides him no more comfort. She leaves the room.

By the time Francesca made it to Deirdre's grave through the pouring rain, she is winded, and covered in mud halfway up her legs. Her designer shoes are ruined, though she is not concerned about this right now. Her only concern is her brother. She walks upon the back of the large headstone she knows to be Deirdre's. The large headstone she had especially made with a beautiful carved picture of Deirdre. Francesca had the talented artist use a photo of Deirdre from the baby shower, which was her last day on earth.

Francesca looks around and she does not see Nicolaus. She doesn't understand. Slowly, she walks around the side of the grave, and her brother's body slowly appears in her view. First his muddied, uncovered feet, his injured leg ... covered in mud. And then ... she sees all of Nicolaus as he is laying on his side on Deirdre's grave, his full body completely covered in mud. He looks a shambles, with glassed over eyes, in a state of confusion.

"Nicky," she softly calls to him. "Nicky." Francesca observes that Nicolaus is muttering something, she cannot make it out. He looks in her direction, but does not look at her. She kneels next to him, "Nicky, it's me, Francesca. What are you doing, Love?"

"Huh? Death? She's not gone. Angel's wings, angel's wings," he mutters. "She's not gone. Not gone ... no, not gone. No."

"Nicky, Love, you cannot stay here. Come on," she reaches her hand to him.

"She's not gone."

"Nicky. Come on, Love."

Nicolaus takes Francesca's hand, but does not lift himself beyond his head. "Francesca?"

"Yes, Love, it's me. Nicky," she begins to break down with crying, "let's go, please. Come on, Love," she tries to coax him, as the rain continues to pour down on them. Her hair is a muddled mess. She is now soaked, and half covered in mud, herself.

"She's not gone," Nicolaus loudly whispers to Francesca, as if she had not understood his muttering words. Then he continues to mutter. "Angels love her. She's not gone."

"Oh Nicky, come on, you can't stay here like this, Love. Let's go in."

Gently, he releases her hand, laying his head deeper on Deirdre's grave. "No. I can't leave her again," he whispers to Francesca.

"I can't leave her again. I can't leave her," he tells her.

"Oh Nicky!" Emotion grips Francesca to see her bold, strong brother, who always takes care of everyone else, in such a state. He'd just rescued someone, and now he cannot get his mind clear to accept what has happened.

Giving up, Francesca sits next to Nicolaus in the mud. She blurts out her cries, crying with him, as he repeats the same words over and over again, in a daze, only now whispering to himself, under his own crying. Francesca grabs hold of Nicolaus' arm. She lays on him listening to his chant, as the rain continues to drench them, 'I can't leave her again. I can't leave her again. I can't leave her again. I can't leave her again'.

Chapter Twenty-Nine

When Francesca enters the house again, she is without Nicolaus, completely covered in mud, and an emotional mess. "Uncle Nigel, Nicky cannot stay out there. His leg ... he's covered in wet mud! Where is his phone?"

Nigel shrugs, more tears escaping him, hearing the condition of his son. Neither Dr. Peoples nor Bishop Leighton, and now even Francesca could not coax Nicolaus off the grave.

The staff bring Francesca a towel. She goes to Nicolaus' bedroom and looks for his cell phone. She could not find it. However, she does find Deirdre's purse. She looks inside the purse and finds two phones. The first one she tries has a pin lock, which she figures is Nicolaus'. The other does not. She goes to the contacts list, and knows it is Deirdre's phone by the names of the people on the list. Luckily, she sees Roddy's number. Quickly, she calls Roddy. She is grateful when he answers.

"Oh Roddy, this is Francesca. Listen Love, we need your help. I know you don't know about this, but Roddy ... we lost Deirdre." Francesca starts to cry again, and then pulls herself together.

"What? What happened?"

"She went into labor and she bled out. They couldn't save her or the baby."

"What, Francesca?" Roddy is shocked. "My God!"

"Roddy, this happened when Nicolaus was away. And he got badly injured. Just sort of recovering, ... and ... and I just found out that he's been at Deirdre's grave for three days. Roddy, no one can get him to come back into the house, and ..."

"Say no more, Francesca. I'll be right over!"

Roddy arrives within fifteen minutes. He brought several other comrades with him. Francesca directs him where to go, and he and the men go out to the cemetery. The rain still pouring, they lift

Nicolaus and carry him inside, though he struggles against them, not wanting to leave Deirdre. Nicolaus is not strong enough to wrangle himself from the men.

Nigel is grateful, and leads the men upstairs to the shower, and instructs them where to place Nicolaus into bed, in his old room, which is now a guest room.

"Don't worry, Sir, we'll take care of him," Roddy assures Nigel.

They put Nicolaus into the shower and wash him, careful of his injuries. Nicolaus no longer grapples with them; he goes quiet. They wash him, dry him, lotion him, dress him, and place him into bed. Roddy combs Nicolaus' hair.

Roddy thanks his guys for helping him, as they leave. They touch Nicolaus on the shoulder and encourage him, and let him know they will be checking back on him.

Roddy stays with Nicolaus, sitting on the bed. "I'm so sorry about Deirdre. I didn't know about it." He puts water up to Nicolaus' mouth. When Nicolaus turns away in silence, Roddy knows his friend is hurting; how could he not be? "Drink it," he orders Nicolaus. Nicolaus drinks some water.

Nurse Haddie arrives. Roddy stays in the room as she tends to Nicolaus. Nicolaus says nothing, he only lays still, and lets the nurse do whatever she needs to do. She puts him on intravenous fluids again, rebandages his injuries, and makes him drink more water.

"Dr. Peoples will be here shortly to see about you."

Nicolaus does not respond. Roddy stays with him.

Chapter Thirty

Francesca showers and changes out of her muddy clothes, borrowing some garments from Elsa. She is present with Nigel when Dr. Peoples gives his report of Nicolaus' condition.

"Well, Nicolaus is in a weakened state," Dr. Peoples explains downstairs, away from the room where Nicolaus lay.

In the bedroom, Nicolaus removes the intravenous needle from his arm, surprising Nurse Haddie. "Now Nicolaus ..."

"No, I don't want this."

"Nicolaus, you need fluids."

"No. I have the right to agree or disagree with my treatment. I don't want this anymore. I don't want anything," he tells her.

Dr. Peoples continues to explain to Roddy, Nigel, Francesca, and Ceil. "He is now refusing treatment, even the fluids. He keeps pulling the needles out of his arm. Nigel, he has the right to refuse treatment." Dr. Peoples shakes his head, feeling a little defeated. "He will probably go down hill quickly. It's probably what he wants. I've seen this before."

"What? You mean he wants to starve himself to death?" Francesca asks. "He wants to die?" She begins to weep again, all this getting to be too much for her. Roddy hugs her. "He wants to go to Deirdre?"

Dr. Peoples nods. "I cannot speak for him, ... but that is usually the pattern. Unless you can get him to hold on to something, ... something very important to him ... we will probably lose him."

"Oh God!" Francesca cries. "Oh God!" She wipes her eyes with resolve. "What about a shrink? Obviously, he needs help to accept what's happened."

Dr. Peoples nods again. "I've offered, and he's refused, as is his right to do so."

Francesca finds the nearest chair in the hallway, and sits herself in it, feeling devastated. She feels for her brother, and certainly does not want to lose him.

After several hours, Francesca goes to sit with Nicolaus, Roddy now gone. Nigel still does not know what to do for his son. He ponders downstairs, having no appetite himself.

Ceil is off making plans for Niall at the office. She feels that perhaps Nicolaus will not return at all. She wants to be ready to replace him with Niall.

Nicolaus just lays in bed, on his side, staring out the window. Seeing him out of sorts and his uncharacteristic, downed spirit brings more tears to Francesca's eyes. She is very much afraid of losing Nicolaus.

Finally, he notices her. Francesca sits on the bed, and she touches Nicolaus' face. "Oh Nicky," she says softly, wishing she could fix this. She has no anthropological magic or wicken philosophy to heal his grief or remove his sadness.

"I can't do this," Nicolaus whispers to Francesca. "I can't live without her. How am I supposed to live without her?" He asks her the unanswerable question. How does one live without the love of their life; without their angel whose been by their side literally everyday of their life; without the love that helped bring them through the dark days; without their soulmate?

Francesca almost has no words. "You pray, Nicky. You pray for that strength. God knows your heart."

"Why?" Nicolaus breathes heavily, as if he had trouble breathing. He still does not understand any of this. "Why would God take her? Why?" The mental anguish in his voice made tears fall from Francesca's eyes. "What did I do? Where did I go wrong? I only tried to do right every day. To love God, and to love Deirdre as my wife. Every day ... since we were young." He cried in his words and in his thoughts. "Why did God take her?" He yells the question to Francesca, sounding desperate for answers. Francesca is glad that Nicolaus sounds logical, however, she is very worried for him.

"I don't know, Love," she tells him, feeling damn well the real answer is that freakin' curse that is set upon the family. She knew she could not tell Nicolaus about that right now. How could she damage his broken heart even farther. She also wants to know why God is breaking Nicolaus' heart ... all their hearts, over Deirdre.

Nicolaus retreats back into himself ... into his thoughts. He stares out the window, and he waits, in utter silence.

Chapter Thirty-One

Nigel placed a call to Helena. He had not seen her since Deirdre's funeral. He is sure she is broken up about Deirdre's passing as is the rest of the family. He calls her, in a last ditch effort to help Nicolaus. It has been another three days that Nicolaus has refused food or drink, has not gotten out of bed, and has just been laying still, listless, seemingly waiting to be claimed away. Not even Francesca can reach him. Nigel has had Bishop Leighton say prayers over Nicolaus.

"Helena, how are you my dear, it's been some time since I've seen you."

"Nigel? Oh my goodness," she sighs, "well ... I'm okay. Just here working. I'm definitely having a hard time getting over Deirdre. I really miss her. I'm sorry I haven't been back to the house, it's just hard to think of being there without Deirdre."

Nigel nods, sniffs tears, and clears the emotion out of his throat. "I understand. We all miss Deirdre. Nicolaus has returned ..."

"Has he? Did he find Jonathan?"

"Yes. As expected, he did a great job at that. Only, ... Helena, he was badly injured."

"Oh my God!"

"Yes, well, he has pulled through that, though we almost lost him. Since then, he's had surgery."

"Nigel!"

"Well, he's still in recovery,... only ... I had to tell him about Deirdre. He's heartbroken ...," Nigel shakes his head, "no, that is not the right word. I can't even describe his distress. He was out on Deirdre's grave for some days, and no one could get him to come back into the house. Roddy and other friends came over. They carried him in, and cleaned him up."

"Nigel, my God!" Helena is shocked to hear this. "Poor Nicky!"

"Well," Nigel sighs, "that's why I'm calling you. He's now been in bed for three days. He refuses medication, and I'm sure he's in pain. He refuses to eat, or sit up, or get up. He just stares out the window."

"Nigel, that is not good."

"We think he is waiting for death."

"My God!" Helena nods in understanding. "He doesn't want to live without Deirdre. I imagine he cannot see a way forward without her."

"Helena please, will you try to talk to him? I have Bishop Leighton in with him now, but the bishop has not been able to get through to him. I'm asking you because you seem to have an effect on him. He responds to you, and already you understand his mind."

"Well, Nigel, I don't think I really understand his mind. I do know that he and Deirdre had a special love, a different kind of love, and I can only imagine the pain he has."

"Nevertheless, please Helena, will you talk to him?"

"Nigel, I will, ... if ... if I can do it my way, without interference from Ceil."

"Hmm, you have my word," Nigel promises her, thinking about how intelligent Helena is. Nigel is desperate to save Nicolaus and he feels Helena is his last chance. There is no one else to call.

Bishop Leighton sits on the bed, next to Nicolaus. He notices that Nicolaus does not look pale as a dying person might, though he does seem to be weak from little nourishment. "Nicolaus, this is not what God wants of you," Bishop Leighton tells Nicolaus sternly. "God would not have spared your life out of an impossible situation, only for you to lay here and willfully die. Son, God still has work for you, and you know this."

Nicolaus finally removes his eyes from the clear blue sky to look at the bishop. "Why has God taken Deirdre from me?"

Bishop Leighton sighs. He shakes his head wanting to provide some comfort to Nicolaus. "Nicolaus, it is not for us to question God. Us earthlings cannot know God's mind, or exactly God's will. We must walk in God's light, in God's path, obeying God's commandments. This is what Deirdre has done. She was good and right. God will honor her. Don't you believe that?"

Nicolaus slightly nods, but then returns his gaze to the sky, as if he is trying to peer into the heavens, trying to telepathically communicate with God to get his questions answered. "By the grace of God, I cannot be here without Deirdre. And God knows this," Nicolaus tells the bishop quietly. "I cannot walk, I cannot breathe, I cannot be ... without Deirdre. God knows this."

Bishop Leighton touches Nicolaus' hand. "Son, I know this is hard. Sometimes life is difficult and sometimes we do not understand." He sighs, "Nicolaus, at times like this is when you hold tight to God. Let God lead you." He sits with Nicolaus and prays again, as Nicolaus has gone quiet.

Chapter Thirty-Two

As Helena enters the house, she is greeted by hugs and kisses from Elsa, Francesca, and Nigel. Ceil is not home at this moment, for which Nigel is very glad. Helena is even greeted by some staff members, having heard word that she will try to talk to Nicolaus. Even the staff are concerned about losing Nicolaus. They stand at the ready for any assistance such as food, bathing, liquids, cleaning, whatever is needed.

"Please," Nigel ushers Helena to the stairs after she places her things down. "He's in the middle room, his old bedroom."

Helena nods. She goes up the stairs slowly. On the drive over, she had been thinking about how to tackle this situation. As she ascends the stairs, she believes the best way to handle this is head-on, without mercy.

Helena enters the room, and sees what everyone else who looks upon Nicolaus sees. He's staring out the window, unmoving, lying in bed looking listless. She is shocked by this, as he does not seem his former self of being a strong conqueror of the world. Helena quietly closes the door.

Immediately, she gets into the bed, under the covers, right next to Nicolaus. She is at his back, and she grabs him around the waist, her chin on him.

"No," he says lowly, glancing in her direction.

"Oh you're not going to scare me away so easily," she tells him with lightness in her tone. "I'm so glad you are home safe and that you survived your injuries. Though ... it does seem that you are not glad."

Nicolaus sighs, as Helena's grip on him tightens. She kisses his bare back several times, making him glance at her again. Her intention for kissing him is to remind him that he is a human man, who needs love.

"So many people love you and care about you," she says to him between kisses. "We're all going to have double heartbreak if you leave this earth, trying to chase after Deirdre in heaven." She kisses him again.

He sighs, and says nothing. She knows her words are getting to him because he keeps sighing.

"I guess I'll have to inform the kids that you decided to starve yourself to death instead of helping them. They will be so upset."

"Helena."

"Oh, and what's your message to the Darfurian refugee families and children."

This makes him look at her. She can see he is thinking about what she is saying. "Message?"

"Well, yeah, I mean, you and Deirdre are their sponsors, right? Deirdre is in heaven. And if you are no longer here, they won't have a sponsor, and they will have to go back to the war zone, now won't they. So, before you can no longer speak, tell me the message you want me to tell them before they are kicked out of the country for no longer having a sponsor." Her tone is matter of fact.

Nicolaus sighs, shaking his head negatively to her. She brought up things he had not thought about. He shakes his head to the unfairness; he is being deprived of his ability to choose to die to go after Deirdre. He has fated himself to live without Deirdre, through his philanthropic efforts to help children.

"And those foster children. If you aren't here, for sure that program is going away. Can you imagine Ceil administering that program? I'm pretty sure she will close that down immediately, and all the work and all the effort that Deirdre did to develop that program will be wasted. Those foster children who once had a future will now have their futures ruined, being pulled right away from them without your presence."

She knew she'd got him when she saw the pain flick across his face as if her words cut right through him. "And who is going to mentor and help my older kids that are aging out of the foster care system? You've been such a help to them. Such an example. They really look up to you, even naming you 'Papa Nicky'. Oh God, I hope they won't think suicide is the way out of tough situations! And the young men at church ..."

Nicolaus can't take any more recounting of his responsibilities. He yells at Helena, "All right! Please!"

Her smile hidden from him, she kisses his back again, "I'm just saying! Even the business community ... what a loss. And oh, gosh, your little niece, Elaine. She's already lost Deirdre; she'll have to live without you too? What kind of future will she have? And Constance ... my Lord ... it will crush Constance if she loses you too. Who's going to look after Constance if you are not here? I'm sure Deirdre thought you'd be here for her mom."

"All right! All right!" He yells at her again, giving up his plight of starving himself. The thought of Elaine and Constance brings tears to his eyes. Her words and Bishop Leighton's words double down on him. It is clear how many people depend on him. He knows he must continue the work he and Deirdre were doing in the community. He is certain she would want him to.

"How about some water?" Quickly, Helena gets up and gets the water on the nightstand which has been waiting for Nicolaus to drink. She helps him drink some. She sits next to him, smiles, touches his face, wipes away his tears, and demands he drink more.

Helena pops up and cracks the door open, she sees the family at the foot of the stairs. "Nigel, we need soup."

Nigel nods and directs the staff to warm the soup they had prepared for Nicolaus. Tears flow from Nigel's eyes in gratefulness of Helena. Nigel bends with emotion which hits him in his gut. Elsa and Francesca help him to a chair.

Chapter Thirty-Three

Nicolaus is strong and healthy; therefore, his recovery progresses smoothly. He regains his strength quickly, and Helena spends time with him daily, after taking care of things at her children's home.

Nicolaus participates in physical therapy the following week, and he works hard to get his muscle tone back into his chest and his arms, and he works to get strength in his leg, to get to walking. He didn't like being wheeled around in the lightweight wheelchair Dr. Peoples ordered for him, or being on his crutches. He mostly used his crutches, once he had strength back into his arms.

Helena is with him, as he goes to see Constance. Nicolaus didn't think a phone call would suffice. Constance tears up at the sight of Nicolaus. She hugs him tightly to her.

Nicolaus drops his crutches, "Mom!" He hugs her, and they both have minutes of crying together. Helena is very moved by this. She goes into the kitchen to get them some water, or lemonade, or whatever she can find.

When the crying stops, Constance gently holds Nicolaus' face in both of her hands. "Oh Nicolaus. I've been praying for you. For your healing, and ... that you can hopefully get through all this."

Nicolaus gives Constance a sweet kiss to her forehead, the forehead of the woman who birthed his wife. "Thank you, Mom," he tells her humbly.

Helena returns with lemonade she'd made for them. "Here we go." She brings it into the living room, on a tray. She pours the lemonade from the pitcher into glasses. They sit down. "What else can I get for you. Constance, you look as though you haven't been eating." She notices that Constance has dark circles under her eyes. She looks withdrawn.

"No, not much. It's hard to eat." Nicolaus takes her hand and nods.

"How about some soup? I can make some, quick," Helena offers.

Nicolaus nods to Constance. "Let's try some soup, Mom," he tells her, knowing she must eat something. Constance slightly nods.

Helena disappears to the kitchen to make the soup.

"I'm sorry I haven't been over to see about you," she sighs, wiping her face with the tissue Nicolaus hands her. "I just can't stand to be in that house anymore."

"Mom, it's okay. Don't worry about that. I'm fine. Helena has helped me a lot. I just wanted to die when I learned about what happened, but Helena ... she reminded me what Deirdre would want me to do. And that I have a lot of things that are not done, and many people to take care of. Bishop Leighton told me the same." Nicolaus wipes his face as well, then takes a sip of the lemonade.

"Yes, that's true. Nicky, I told Nigel I didn't want a reading of Deirdre's will and things. None of it is Ceil's business!"

Nicolaus chuckles lightly at the fire he could still see in Constance. He is glad for it. "I understand, Mom."

"Anyway, she only left her money to you and me. She has given me two point five million, which is all her money. And she has left you her share of the castle and the lands."

"As it should be," Nicolaus comments.

Constance opens the desk drawer of the end table and pulls out a manila envelope. She hands it to Nicolaus.

Nicolaus briefly looks over the one page document. He nods. "Mom, I'm sure there is more money ... her bank accounts, her work insurance and investments. There should be more money for you."

Constance put her hand to her chin in worry. "I can't believe all this has happened," she begins to cry again. "My Deirdre," she wipes her eyes again, Nicolaus handing her more tissues. He sits next to her to comfort her. "She died right in my arms. I knew when she was gone, Nicky, I just knew it. And there was nothing I could do to help her. None of us could. Not even the doctors. They tried their best. We were all so ... shocked."

Nicolaus frowns, trying to hold himself together. He takes Constance in his arms and hugs her. What could he say?

"And now this. I don't even know what to do with this small fortune my daughter has left for me. I thought about paying off this house, and ..."

Nicolaus sits back. "No, Mom, you let me pay off the house. You take half of that money and get an annuity. That way you have income to live on every month for the rest of your life. And then the other half, you do whatever you see fit."

"But Nicky ..."

"I'll pay off the house," he insists. "I'm sure that's what Deirdre would have wanted. Please, let me take care of it," he insists. "And I know some reputable investors, so I can get you in touch with someone you can trust to set up your annuity."

"Nicky, son, thank you."

"Of course, Mom."

Later that night, Nicolaus had a conversation with his father. "Father, I want to thank you for what you did for me in Spain."

"Nicolaus, you don't need to thank me, son. I'm so grateful that you survived. I know you have much to work out in your mind, and I want you to know that I support you to take your time. None of this is easy."

Nicolaus nods. "Thank you. And ... I want to thank you for taking care of Deirdre."

Nigel sits next to Nicolaus, and touches his shoulder, as they are both filled with emotion. "Of course, son. I didn't know when you would be back. I did what I thought you would have wanted. She was buried within three days after her passing."

"And tell me again, what exactly happened? When I left her, she was perfectly fine. My son was perfectly fine. We were just waiting for her to go into labor."

Nigel nods. He knew Nicolaus would be trying to dissect exactly what happened. "Well ... she went into early labor, and ..."

"How? Why? Why would she go into early labor? Did something happen to cause that?"

Nigel clears his throat, stalling to think of what to say. "Well ... I ... I don't know son. When I saw her she was laboring. We called the ambulance and Constance rode with her. When we got to the hospital, all our ladies went in with her, Constance, Ceil, and Elsa. Francesca was still in the Caymans at this time. I was in the waiting room with Ishani and Maggie when Elsa ran out of the labor room. She was crying, and then she fainted. Some nurses took care of her, and then after some more minutes, a nurse came out and told us what was happening. And then ... then they told us the awful news."

Nicolaus looked down, frowning, as if he still had more questions. He didn't want to over tax his father too much, as he could see that Nigel, too, was upset.

"The date she was buried?"

"The eighteenth."

Suddenly, Nicolaus remembers the date on the headstone. He looks at Nigel. "Father, she died on the fifteenth?" Nigel nods. Nicolaus sighs. "She ... she was my divine intervention. Oh my God!"

"Nicolaus, what are you talking about?"

"That day! The fifteenth! That's the day we made it to the Cartel compound to get Baird. That's when I lost my young comrade, James, and when I got shot in the leg. They were shooting at us like crazy, for sure they wanted to kill us. And then suddenly, everything stopped. Everything! My God! Those men fell asleep where they stood. We couldn't understand it."

"Nicolaus ..."

"It all makes sense now. Deirdre really was an angel. Oh my God!"

"Okay, now Nicolaus ... "

"No, it was divine intervention, because of Deirdre. How else could something like that happen?"

"Well ... ah ... ah ... I don't know, son. Wow."

Nicolaus sat forward and placed his hand over his face in disbelief. He understood that because of his Deirdre they are alive.

"Nicolaus, wait a minute ... speaking of James. The staff passed me a message from his parents. They called this morning, looking for you." Nigel stands to retrieve the message and hands it to Nicolaus.

Nicolaus reads the message, then puts it in his shirt pocket. "Father, what about a public service for Deirdre? Did you hold anything?"

"No son. I made no announcements. I wanted to be sure you made those decisions."

"Oh, okay, thank you father. Well ... we must do something. The public should know."

"Only if you're strong enough now, Nicolaus."

Nicolaus shakes his head, "Nothing will ever be the same without Deirdre, father. Nothing. I'll never have the strength I once had, nor the joy. She was my life."

Immediately, Nicolaus dials Constance on his cell phone. "Mom, will you help me plan Deirdre's memorial service?"

Chapter Thirty-Four

D r. Peoples determined that Nicolaus would need to use a cane for the next couple of years, perhaps permanently. Nicolaus did not argue this point. He was patient with everyone, appreciative of the help. However, Nicolaus knew in his mind, he would not permanently be on that cane.

When Nicolaus was a young boy, the first time his leg was badly injured was after Ceil beat him with a metal fireplace rod. He was told he'd be on a leg brace for the rest of his life. His determination proved different, as he is sure would be the case this time around.

Helena is with Nicolaus as he re-enters the bedroom he shared with Deirdre, on his side of the mansion. The last time he had entered this room was when he had briefly sought out Deirdre. At that time, Nicolaus was missing information of what had happened. It is very painful for him to enter this room now, knowing that his sweet love, his Deirdre would not be there.

The staff had of course cleaned up the room, to restore it. Nicolaus lay on the bed, thinking of his wife. He curled his body and emotions rushed out of him. He mourned Deirdre. Helena sat on the couch, away from him, though she cried with him. She wanted to give him space, and dared not be on that bed with him.

The large house seemed empty without Deirdre's energy, without her giggles, without her smiles, and without her trying to make things right. Nicolaus grieved Deirdre. He didn't know how he was going to get through the rest of his life without her.

Chapter Thirty-Five

The following day, Nicolaus decides to go to Denver, to see the Darfurian refugee families. It has been quite some weeks now, since he has been to the Denver hotel, which he and Deirdre bought for the purpose of sheltering the families who were rescued from the horrid war zone. He wants to ask Helena to accompany him, as he is not sure what his reaction would be.

Nicolaus takes Helena's hand. "Will you go with me to Denver? I want to visit the families we have sponsored from Darfur?"

Helena is surprised at his request. "Of course," she answers quickly, not caring about what she may already have scheduled. She is thrilled to be able to assist him. Also, Helena had not seen the operation, and she is curious. "Though, before we go, Nicky," she looks upon his hair and she brushes her fingers through his haphazard long curly locks, which has lots of loose strays and seems a little dry, "let's get you to a hair stylist. You know any?"

Nicolaus chuckles, running his hands through his unruly hair. He nods. "Lots of them. Needs work, huh?"

"Just a little."

"Okay, I got it. Thanks."

Nicolaus received the hook up for his hair, and he looks debonair. His longer than normal curly locks now shined with moisture, and were retained to the back of his head with a large hair band, which many men sported. He is also sporting somewhat of a short beard, not really caring about his looks since he's been back. Most days he does not feel like tending to his regular grooming habits. He looks different and yet looks like himself.

As soon as Nicolaus and Helena enter the hotel lobby, in the early evening hours, they are surrounded by happy men, women, and children. Of course they recognize Nicolaus. The ladies hug on his strong frame and kiss his handsome face. They see he is on crutches.

"Nicky, what has happened to you?" Many ask him.

They look around him, seeing Helena. "Where is Deirdre? We miss her."

Nicolaus touches Helena on the shoulder. "This is Helena, my close friend. She helps children in Texas."

"Helena!" She is greeted.

The men also reach in to hug Nicolaus to them. All this love is starting to get to Nicolaus, remembering Helena's words of why he needs to stay present in the world.

"Deirdre? Where is she?" The women do not let this question go unanswered.

"She is ... she is ..." Nicolaus has trouble saying it. These are the first people he has said this to outside of his family. "She ... has ... died. She's gone ...." Nicolaus breaks down.

"Oh no!" The women hug him as he breaks down in tears. The men escort Nicolaus to the couch. The Darfurian people mourn with him, hug on him, and kiss him, and comfort him.

Helena is in awe of what she is witnessing, as seemingly, the whole count of the patrons of this shelter tend to Nicolaus to comfort him. Some of the ladies take her by the hand, hug her as well, and provide her a place to be seated.

Chapter Thirty-Six

Nigel got worried when Nicolaus asked him several times to recount what had happened with Deirdre when she went into medical crisis. This worried Nigel, because he knew that answers could possibly lead to Niall and his horrid behavior. Niall had purposefully been making himself scarce from the mansion at Nigel's request. He did not want Nicolaus to get wind of he and Elsa arguing over what Niall had done.

Nigel waits to see Dr. Carrie Cox, Deirdre's obstetrician. She was present in the birthing room, and was one of the physicians who went to heroic lengths to try to save Deirdre.

"Mr. Ravenell?" She approaches him, and Nigel stands with his hand out to her.

"Dr. Cox."

"My staff say you need to speak to me about Deirdre?"

"Yes, please. May I speak with you privately?"

"Of course." Dr. Cox leads Nigel to her office.

"Please," she asks him to sit opposite of her. "What is it I can do for you today?"

"Well, Dr. Cox, thank you for seeing me. I'm a little concerned about my son, Nicolaus."

"Deirdre's husband." Nigel nods. "I've met Nicolaus before. In fact, I remember that he excitedly attended all of Deirdre's appointments with her. This must be very difficult for him."

"Exactly. And Nicolaus has been asking many questions. I do think he will be here to pose more questions. I'm humbly imploring that you please, just give him the facts. No innuendos, no theories, just facts."

Dr. Cox eyes Nigel. "You mean, you don't want me to mention all the bruising we saw on Deirdre. What exactly was that bruising from, Mr. Ravenell?"

"Dr. Cox, ... please. I'm not asking you to do anything that is unethical. I'm just asking that you only give him the facts."

"Mr. Ravenell, you have not answered my question about the bruising."

Nigel sighs. "I ... I ... honestly, I can't say. I only know that Deirdre was in labor when I was called in, and we acted quickly to get her here. I just don't know why she had bruising."

Dr. Cox nods, feeling satisfied with his explanation.

"Doctor, Nicolaus has been through a lot. He was away when this happened with Deirdre, and he's clawed back from the grips of death himself, having been very injured. Now please, ..."

"Mr. Ravenell, I understand what you are asking me to do. And that is what I would do anyway, only give my patients facts. Sometimes when patients experience what Deirdre went through, bruising occurs in several places over the body. I don't think you need to worry."

Chapter Thirty-Seven

As soon as Nicolaus returns from Denver, the following day, he is at the church. He knows he'll find solace there. He needs spiritual strength. He feels that the Darfurian people helped to center him, but he still needs to feel the presence of God. He is not sure he is going to find peace of mind, though he does want to try.

Nicolaus vows to himself, that although he is angry, he is not going to turn his life away from God. This he refuses to do. He's carried God with him his whole life, and he is not going to let his anger of having to live without Deirdre turn him away from God.

Bishop Leighton enters the church sanctuary from out of the back rooms. He sees Nicolaus on the front church pew, sitting and grieving. Their eyes meet, and the bishop goes to Nicolaus and sits next to him. He gently touches Nicolaus on the shoulder. "Nicolaus, are you here to pray?"

"I need understanding. I don't understand any of this!"

"Loss of our loved ones is always difficult. So many people had love for Deirdre, just as she had love for many. She is your special one and she always will be. So, though she is not physically with us, she will always be in your heart, Nicolaus. And ... I'm sure you know this, but perhaps you need to hear it, from me, here, in the church.

"She is and always will be in your heart, just as you will always be in her heart. When she left us, she took part of you with her, a part that she holds dear. And you feel that missing part, as you had both given of yourselves to each other completely.

"And Nicolaus ... of your love with Deirdre, you both also gave of yourselves to others, to children, to lift them up. And Nicolaus, that work must continue, as you are still here, my son, and the world has not stopped, though we feel it has, and children have not stopped suffering. The children of the world still need your love, and the world still needs your example. Deirdre would want you to continue that work without her, ... or maybe because of her, ... or perhaps even, in her name. She would want you to carry that work of helping children forward. You can make it her legacy, her spiritual gift to the world."

Bishop Leighton takes both of Nicolaus' hands. "Let us pray."

Nicolaus takes the lead and begins to pray in the Latin language, as usual. He asks for blessings upon Deirdre's soul, as he had been doing, he asks for blessings upon the children they had already helped and upon those who are in his path to help in the future. He asks God for strength to get through this difficult time in his life, for which his crying starts up again. Bishop Leighton takes over the praying from this point, lifting the life of Nicolaus up to the good Lord for strength and guidance.

Chapter Thirty-Eight

As Nicolaus leaves the church, his next stop is the hospital. He seeks out Dr. Cox, who hugs Nicolaus in sympathy, and she guides him to her office, closing the door.

"Dr. Cox, please ... help me to understand what happened with Deirdre. I left to go assist my ex-father-in-law, and when I returned, my wife only has a grave," he says solemnly, with controlled emotions.

"Nicolaus, I am so sorry. Let me first confirm for you that Deirdre was never alone. Your whole family was in the room with us. She was brought in by ambulance, having gone into early labor."

"Why did that happen? She was perfectly fine when I left her. We'd just had an appointment with you the week before, saw my son, and everything was fine. Deirdre didn't even have morning sickness."

Dr. Cox nods. "Yes, I remember. This is difficult. I also want you to know that this type of situation happens to many of our black women, Nicolaus. Deirdre is not the only of our patients this has happened to. My own sister ... well ... I lost my own sister under similar circumstances. The pregnancy goes along quite well, without complications, and then when time gets close to the due date, the woman goes into labor and different things happen to different women. Blood clots, bleed outs- such as in the case of Deirdre, strokes, heart attacks, even. We do have an epidemic of this happening to our black sisters in this country."

Nicolaus tears, his hands over his mouth. He looks at Dr. Cox. "I'm sorry that you lost your sister as well."

She nods. "Thank you, Nicolaus. Please know that we did everything we could to try to save Deirdre. We were unable to find the source of her bleed out, and she went into cardiac arrest. We couldn't bring her back, we tried. She was just gone."

A tear streams from his eye. "Did Deirdre suffer much?"

Dr. Cox shakes her head, "No. It was quick. Her mother was holding her. Your mom was holding your son. Your son never took a breath. He never opened his eyes. Your mother cradled him, lovingly, Nicolaus. She cried for him."

More tears fall from Nicolaus' eyes. He nods in understanding. Nicolaus has no more questions.

Chapter Thirty-Nine

O nce the announcement of Deirdre's passing was published, the family began receiving flowers, condolences, telegrams, letters from adults and dignitaries, and poems and pictures from children. Items and hundreds of roses and flowers are left at the Ravenell mansion gate. The news media picked up on the announcement and ran major stories about Deirdre, her life, her work for children, and her life with Nicolaus. Several of the interviews Nicolaus and Deirdre did together were now being aired on several stations, including in Europe.

Deirdre's memorial service is beautiful, and held in the church of Bishop Leighton, where both families are members. Constance has beautiful white roses and white lace intertwined throughout the church.

Nicolaus sits next to Constance in the front pew of the church. His mourning appearance has changed, his soft hair, now curly locks that land at his shoulders, still pulled back in the men's hair band. His face displays thin jawline whiskers, and a thin mustache and light beard, which matches perfectly with his light caramel skin tone. Despite these changes, Nicolaus still has a strikingly handsome aura. He is dressed in a nice suit, what he thought Deirdre would like.

Nigel is seated next to Nicolaus, then Ceil, then Elsa and Niall, then Francesca, Helena, Ishani, and Maggie. Additional family members fill the second church pew behind the Ravenells, including Ceil's sisters Zoe and Janelle, and their husbands. Also seated in the second pew is Xavier, Nigel's brother, and Zhara, his wife, and their adult children, Ned, Cato, Bobby, and their wives and oldest children. The next pew holds the Ravenell cousins, including Claude. Other of Nicolaus' cousins and Deirdre's cousins spill into the following pews, along with scores of other family members.

Press reporters from around the world are crowded inside the church, and sprawled outside, trying to get a glimpse of the family. The number of press in attendance at Deirdre's memorial service rivals the number that attended their wedding in their homeland of Estonia. Nicolaus is astonished by this.

A small group of the Tallin City Choir arrived from Estonia to sing a few songs at the memorial service. Ladies of the Darfurian families sent a video recording of them singing several prayerful songs for Deirdre, despite their own suffering. This is played over the church's media system.

People from all over the United States, and people from several countries arrive to attend Deirdre's funeral, including Bishop Moratey of the Saint Nicholas church in Tallin, who married Deirdre and Nicolaus. Bishop Moratey is greeted into the pulpit, after tightly hugging onto Nicolaus.

The church is filled with community members, community leaders, business leaders, colleagues, peers, and friends of Deirdre and Nicolaus. Celebrity friends of the couple, and VMC board members also are present, many of which move down the line of the Ravenells, to offer condolences, including Daniel Araceli, the company Chief Operating Officer, and Andrejs Drone, the merger company CEO and Nicolaus' former father-in-law. Nicolaus is surprised at seeing Andrejs. Nicolaus' comrades, Roddy, Sanchez, and Washington, and their wives, along with other local military comrades and their wives also attend the service.

"Deirdre did wonderful work while she was here on earth among us. Her work with children will last beyond her time here. Her kind spirit, her infectious laugh, her concern for others is what leaves an impression on us all. We know that God has welcomed

Deirdre into the heavenly family," Bishop Moratey tells them. Nicolaus could not stop his tears from flowing.

"Deirdre's beautiful spirit and kind soul has touched many people, and many abandoned children, whom she made to feel loved and supported. Deirdre will be missed by all of us. Her mother did a wonderful job raising her, and pouring into her the theories of right and wrong, love for God, and love for mankind. Deirdre has provided all of us an example to live by in our own lives. We must strive for innocent love, and caring for one another, especially children. So many children in this world need caring for."

Bishop Leighton continues the eulogy, then provides a sermon about living the principles of brotherly love.

At the end of the memorial service, the Ravenells are crushed with love when the hundreds of people inside that church move forward to provide their condolences, kisses, and hugs.

Nicolaus is surrounded ten deep of people when he looks up and thinks he sees Abigail at the back of the church. She is disguised in a hat over her curly dark hair, hoping the press wouldn't notice her presence. She wore large shades to help cover her face, since she is Deirdre's identical twin.

Briefly, Abigail takes off her sunglasses, tears flowing, she blows a kiss to Nicolaus. Nicolaus recognizes Abigail, as she looks exactly like Deirdre, however, there is just no way he can get through all the people to run after her, and in fact is being hugged up, at this very moment, by an elderly lady who is wiping the tears from his face.

Nicolaus gives Abigail the international hand sign to call him, hoping she is staying somewhere nearby, for Constance's sake.

Manfred, the faithful family security staff member, steps forward, taking Abigail by the hand. He whispers in her ear, "I work security for the Ravenells. Allow me to walk you to your vehicle." Manfred had spotted Abigail long ago, and understood by her looks that she is related to Deirdre, and that somehow, she did not want to be known to be at the church or to be part of the family seating.

Abigail smiles and nods to him, thankful for this assistance, as she has a very hard time keeping herself from running down the aisle to meet her mother for the first time. She had been watching Constance and all the family from the back of the church, with Dominique by her side. Abigail knows that drawing attention to herself would be a grave mistake in this type of environment, especially with Ceil so close, and all the reporters present. She prays that Ceil did not actually notice her.

Nicolaus watches as Manfred gently escorts Abigail and Dominique on each arm, out of the church. Nicolaus recognizes Dominique as the same lady he'd seen in the museum the first day he'd ever seen Abigail. Nicolaus hopes he can meet up with Abigail later.

Chapter Forty

"Okay, so where are they?" Nicolaus questions Manfred several hours after the memorial service, back at the mansion.

"Well, I don't know! Isn't that something you would know?"

"Manfred, I don't know where she is! Did she tell you where they are staying?"

"No. They just got into a waiting vehicle and they drove off. How was I supposed to know that you wanted me to interrogate her? I figured if she was at the service, you knew who she was. She looks like Deirdre's family."

"Manfred, I do know who she is. She's Abigail, Deirdre's sister. I don't know where she is. I have no contact information on her."

Manfred throws his hands in the air. "Nicolaus, how am I supposed to know any of this?" he yells at him.

"I didn't know she was going to be here."

"Well ... I do have one lead. That vehicle was a local company. I can try to call them to see where they went."

"Manfred! Great! Please! Yes, let's get ahold of them!"

"Nicky? You alright? What's all the hubbub?" Helena asks, as she and Francesca enter the sitting room.

"I saw Deirdre sister at the service."

"What? Deirdre has a sister?" Francesca asks, shocked.

Nicolaus pulls Francesca to sit down beside him. "Shh! No one else knows. I saw her at Deirdre's service. Manfred is trying to see where she is staying. He's got a lead to track her down. I've got to find her for Mom."

"Oh my God, Nicky!" Francesca takes Nicolaus' hands. He sounds troubled over this.

"Boss ..." Manfred quickly enters the room, and stops his words and almost stops outside the door, seeing the extra people among them.

Nicolaus beckons to him. "They're okay. Tell me. Where is she?"

"No go. They were taken directly to the airport in a rush to catch a flight that has already left."

Nicolaus sighs with disappointment.

"Sorry, Nicolaus."

"Not your fault, Manfred. Thank you for trying."

Chapter Forty-One

Nicolaus finds himself antsy as he attempts to give himself more grieving time before returning to work. However, Nicolaus notices that reminders of Deirdre are everywhere. The day after Deirdre's memorial service is the day he calls the staff to the bedroom he shared with Deirdre. Brice, the head butler, and Ms. Mary, the lead housemaid, respond to him.

"Mr. Brice, please have my desk and any work items removed from this room and taken to the green room down the hall. After that is done, leave my wife's things, and I want this door locked, and no one ... and I mean no one is to enter it. Do I make myself clear?"

Brice and Mary nod, taken aback by Nicolaus' brash behavior. "Yes, Sir," they say in unison.

"And Ms. Mary, I want fresh flowers on my wife's grave every Sunday morning. One dozen red roses. Nothing less. This task must not ever be forgotten. You will have your team do this for as long as I'm living here. Do you understand, Ms. Mary?"

Mary nods. "Yes, Sir."

"I will not tolerate anyone forgetting to provide fresh roses for my wife's grave. No mistakes."

"Yes, Sir, Mr. Nicolaus." In a whisper, she tells him, "We love her too."

Nicolaus looks to her, then nods to them. "That is all."

Feeling unsettled, they both leave his presence.

Nicolaus is more than annoyed at dragging himself back into the so called game of life, as he drives through the stagnated city traffic to the office, the following week.

As Nicolaus enters the doors, he finds that he does not want to speak to anyone, so he does not. He does not speak to anyone, he does not look at anyone, he does not greet anyone. He just doesn't have it in him to do any of those things.

As he rides the elevator up to the top floor, having no one else with him inside the small electric box since the fifth floor, he crosses his arms with a frown. Suddenly, Nicolaus has the bleak understanding that he is going to have a very hard time trying to live his life without Deirdre.

As the elevator doors open, staff are surprised with the presence of Nicolaus, and they are surprised to see him using a cane. Luckily, Daniel is present, and he runs interference for Nicolaus, seeing the look of difficulty on his face, chasing the staff away from him, before they can say anything.

Nicolaus fumbles with his office door key for a minute or two, before he finally gets the door open. He enters his office then abruptly shuts the door, with a slight slam, something he's never done before. Daniel knows Nicolaus will need a few minutes, so he waits before entering.

Behind that door, Nicolaus finds that his anger has boiled up. Slowly, he looks around his office. Pictures of him and Deirdre are everywhere: there is a photo in the park, in the café downstairs, and there are several photos of them at different fundraising events. Nicolaus sits at the conference table as memories flood his mind.

Nicolaus puts his hands to his face, and begins to cry. He thinks about the last time he saw his Deirdre, in that dark place, ... that place where he didn't know where he was. Quickly and easily, he feels his anger turn to rage.

Daniel knocks on the door, then enters, "Nicolaus! Welcome back, ... oh!" Daniel can clearly see that Nicolaus is out of sorts. "Nicolaus, maybe it's too soon for you to be back."

Nicolaus looks at Daniel. "I'm sorry, I can't do this right now." He stands to leave. "Please, have someone get rid of these pictures, ... in both offices," he says, still in his brashness. Nicolaus rushes off.

"I'll take care of it for you."

Nicolaus hears Daniel's voice trail behind him as he goes to the elevator. Impatiently, he pushes the buttons, wanting to get away. He looks up and sees that the elevator is on the lobby floor. "Damn it!" He yells uncharacteristically, feeling like he wants to destroy anything and anyone in his path.

In anger, Nicolaus goes to the fire escape stairs, thinking he will jog down. Though, after the first step, he remembers he needs his cane to help him walk. Soon it is evident to him that going down twelve flights of stairs is a bad idea. He hobbles down to the next floor and enters the door, going straight to the elevator. It arrives sooner than he expected.

Chapter Forty-Two

When Nicolaus arrives back at the mansion, he rushes past Nigel in a silent fury. Nigel knows that Nicolaus is in emotional pain. He feels for his son, and still feels inadequate to do anything to help him.

Nicolaus changes clothes, yet continues to be enraged. He calls for the house staff. Brice appears. Nicolaus turns his back to Bryce and stares out the window. He snaps at him, "Mr. Brice, get rid of all the photos in every room!"

Bryce sighs before answering, trying to be patient with Nicolaus. "Sir, when you say, 'get rid of', you don't mean destroy, surely, Sir?"

Nicolaus turns on his cane to look at Brice. "No. No, I don't mean that. Thank you."

"And Sir, that rather large picture of you and Mistress Deirdre, at the entrance? Your wedding photo?"

"No. You can leave that one," Nicolaus says more calm.

"Very well, Sir." Brice turns to leave.

"Mr. Brice," Nicolaus calls after him, making him stop to turn and give his attention. "Thank you, Mr. Brice."

Brice nods to Nicolaus with a smile, then leaves to get the task done.

Nicolaus leaves the mansion. He looks at the note from James' parents. They want to meet with him. He sighs. He knows he is too angry to respond to them, so he doesn't. He shoves that note into his shirt pocket, then drives to Deirdre's house to see Constance.

Nicolaus could use his keys to enter, though he rings the bell instead. When Constance opens the door, she pulls Nicolaus into a hug. This action brings up his tears.

"Mom." They hug for a long time.

Constance breaks the hug. She touches Nicolaus' face, noticing the change of his appearance. "Nicolaus, how are you doing, son?" Nicolaus shakes his head in silence. She touches his chin whiskers. They are bristly against her delicate fingers. She touches his chest. "Talk, Nicolaus. How are you feeling?"

Nicolaus steps back from her. "I'm pissed! I'm angry! I want to rip up everything, but I'm trying not to." His words and tone convey his anger. "I tried to go to work this morning, ... and I can't!" He turns from her, putting his hand to his head.

Constance nods. She has been having long crying spells, every day since she'd lost Deirdre. She is tired of crying. "You know what I think we need?" Nicolaus turns to face her, to listen. "I think you and I need a vacation. Somewhere we've never been. Just you and me. We need a break away from all this sadness so we can collect ourselves to deal with it." Constance steps up to Nicolaus and puts her hand to his chest, similar to a move Deirdre would do when she wanted to calm him. "Will you go somewhere with me, Nicolaus?"

Nicolaus nods. They hug each other.

Later that afternoon, Nicolaus and Constance are on a flight to Los Angeles. He has reservations on the top floor of the posh, upscale hotel for rich folks, in Westlake Village, outside of Los Angeles. They are in a huge grand suite, which has two beds, lots of windows, and a jacuzzi. Constance is very pleased with the accommodation.

The first thing they do after settling into the hotel is put on their beach clothes and walk down to the beach. They stop by the shop on their way to the beach and get supplies, such as towels, chairs with umbrellas, and hydration.

Constance sits down and watches as Nicolaus walks straight into the ocean water. The cool ocean waters calm Nicolaus' emotions. He swims, and cries, and swims, and cries. The waves rush over him, mixing his volley of tears with the Pacific Ocean.

It is as if Mother Nature herself is wiping his tears away. The sun shines on him. The coolness of the water, combined with the warmth of the sun, gives him the feeling that maybe one day he could actually be happy again. Nicolaus is in the water for a long time, conversing with nature. Feeding his soul.

There are scarcely any people on the beach. When Nicolaus returns to Constance, she seems at peace, asleep. Quietly, he sits next to her and wonders when the last time was that she had such peaceful sleep.

By the third day, Nicolaus found that he too was able to somewhat sleep better than previously. He was in the ocean water for long periods of time each day, while Constance happily chilled on the beach. Constance enjoys the cool breeze that constantly drifts off the ocean water. She even takes a quick dip in the ocean water from time to time, though she is not an avid swimmer like Nicolaus.

Nicolaus was not sure how long their stay would last. However, Constance insisted they be pampered while they were there. Afterall, why stay at an upscale posh hotel if you are not going to be pampered? Constance had the hotel staff wait on them hand and foot, they received daily massages, and she spent time at the luxurious spa.

During this down time, Nicolaus checks online for Jonathan Baird's press conference public apology to him. He finds it and listens to it a few times, from different sources. He feels satisfied about this, believing it restores he and Deirdre's reputation about this issue to the public. The apology gives him a small peace about the matter. He closes the websites, satisfied with Baird's action.

By the fifth day, Nicolaus begins receiving calls to his phone. The real estate executive is frantic about what to do for deciding which property to purchase for the children's home. "Nicolaus, sorry to bother you, but hey, we've got to wrap up this property purchase deal. We've been waiting over a month now. Have you even looked over the documents yet? We can't wait any longer. We have to make a move by tomorrow."

"Nicolaus," one of the board members leaves a frantic whispered message, "when are you coming back? Ceil thinks she's taking over, and she's making some really bad decisions. We can't stall her much longer, and your dad seems ... uhm ... defenseless, shall we say, against her. I know life is difficult for you right now, but ... hon, if you could just make an appearance ...."

"Hello Nicolaus, I understand you are out of the office for a while now. We need the rent checks signed, or I'll have to evict your staff from all the offices on all three floors. Your staff tell me no one else but you can sign these checks. Call me, Nicolaus, this is an urgent matter."

"Hello Nicolaus, this is Lana, in the accounting department. I'm really sorry to bother you, and to have to leave this message, but your mom is refusing to provide us with numbers we need to get the quarterly reports done for our stockholders. I'm not sure what is going on. The report is due next week, and you know how we rake over the numbers several times for accuracy. Can you please just talk to your mom? I hope things get better for you soon. We miss you, Nicolaus."

"Hey Nicolaus, this is Mick in HR. We are trying to put together a town hall meeting for the staff. Remember, we need to discuss the upcoming changes to our benefits. We need to know when you might be thinking about returning. When would be a good date to set this up? Thanks."

"Hello Nicolaus, this is Simon, in HR. Sorry to have to call you, but your mom ... she literally just fired all the janitorial staff. Something about she didn't like the way they cleaned Niall's office. Uhm, ... she literally cannot do that. Please call me back and let me know what I should do. Thanks."

Another board member, "Hey Nicolaus, sorry to bother you while you're on sabbatical. Ceil is here, making a mess of things. She thinks she's taking over ... oh ... please tell me that is not true. She fired all the janitorial staff yesterday, and now we have a complaint filed against us. We need to know how you want us to handle this. And please let us know how we get a reign in on Ceil. Call me, Nicolaus. Please."

Another board member, "Hello Nicolaus. We have an urgent matter here. Ceil thinks she's taking over. We're getting emails from the staff. She's firing people, she tried to close down the café, she's yelling at the staff and being rude, she's violating EEOC rules. Can you get Nigel to retrieve Ceil out of the office?"

"Nicolaus, this is Ceil. I don't know where you are, but if you are getting calls from the office, just ignore them. I have everything under control. I'll hold down the fort until you get back, ... if you decide to return."

"Jesus!" Nicolaus exclaims. "Mom, I have to get back. Why don't you stay here for another few days and enjoy yourself." Nicolaus immediately grabs his bag to pack a few things. "In fact, I'll return next weekend, and bring you home then."

"Nicky, are you sure?"

Nicolaus nods and kisses Constance. "Yeah." He hugs her and is off. Quickly he is at the airport, and schedules a charter flight to get him back home quickly. He knows he will have to force himself back into his role tomorrow.

Nicolaus arrives back in Austin at seven in the evening. He decides to say nothing to his parents about all the calls. He will deal with everything tomorrow.

Chapter Forty-Three

As Nicolaus enters the office building, he is greeted by staff, and others who work in the building. He responds with a slight smile and a head nod. He'd been thinking about all he needs to clean up after being away. More revelations are imparted upon him about his responsibilities and things not working properly when he is away.

Nicolaus sighs as the elevator doors open to the twelfth floor. This morning, when staff greet him, he responds, though with the same slight smile and head nod. As Nicolaus opens his office door, he catches a glimpse of what he thinks is Niall, in the office to his right. Nicolaus looks over to find Niall, dressed professionally, at a desk, at eight in the morning. He can hardly believe it.

Nicolaus walks over. "Niall? You're working? Here?"

Niall looks at Nicolaus sheepishly. He nods. "Mother has me working."

Nicolaus is taken aback. No one had even mentioned this to him. "Really? Wow!" Nicolaus thought for a moment. "What is it she has on you, to make this happen?"

Niall is surprised at Nicolaus' insight. "Uhh, ... I don't want to talk about it."

"Well, okay. Well ... come on. I'll teach you how to do this work properly."

"Mother had me trained."

"Trained?"

"Yeah. Some professors, and ... stuff like that."

"Oh, you mean you had some advanced training. Well, good. Come on, I'll show you how it's really done. Come on," he beckons to Niall, to let loose of his desk.

Reluctantly, Niall follows Nicolaus to his office.

"And … Daniel …," Nicolaus calls to him. Daniel joins them. Niall is shocked to see all the photos removed. Nicolaus' office seems bare. Daniels sits at the conference table and Niall joins him. Nicolaus removes his jacket, tossing it to the couch, he loosens his tie, and he sits on the edge of his desk. He sighs. "So, where is Ceil? Where's your mother?" Nicolaus addresses Niall.

Niall shrugs.

"Nicolaus, I don't believe she has arrived yet. She usually gets here around nine." Daniel offers.

Nicolaus gives one hand clap. "Great!" He goes to his phone and dials a few numbers. "Hey, this is Nicolaus Ravenell, twelfth floor. Yep, I'm back. Thanks. Listen, if Ceil Ravenell arrives, turn her away." He pauses to listen. "That's right, turn her away. I don't want her in this building today. She can return tomorrow, but not for the whole of the day." He pauses to listen again. "I don't care what you have to do, don't let her in. Take her access card, or restrict it, or something." He slams the phone down. Then he dials more numbers. "Vinatalie, please enter my office, and bring a note pad."

Niall looks at Daniel, who seems very amused by all this.

"So, what happened with the janitors?" Nicolaus asks both of them.

"Nicolaus, Ceil arbitrarily fired all those staff. I've been trying to work with them since they lodged a complaint," Daniel informs them.

Nicolaus nods and looks at Niall. "Niall, for your future reference, if one staff person makes a mistake, you cannot just fire the whole department. Not only is that against VMC policies, but it's against the law." Niall nods, suddenly feeling very nervous. "What about the café, what's that about?"

Both men shrug.

Nicolaus scoffs. "She's just walking around creating havoc everywhere she goes. Niall for your future reference, we do not own the café. We do not even own this building. We are renting the space here."

Vinatalie enters the office. "Welcome back Mr. Nicolaus."

Nicolaus grabs some peanuts that he has stashed in his desk. He offers some to Daniel, Niall, and Vinatalie, all refuse with a smile. Nicolaus puts a handful of peanuts in his mouth. "Thank you, Vinatalie. Please be seated. You ready to take notes?"

"Oh yes, Sir."

Nicolaus nods. "Send one dozen roses to Ceil at the house. Have the note say, 'thanks for helping, I'm back now' and then my name. Try to have them delivered within the hour. Oh, hold on." Nicolaus uses his desk phone and dials the driver at the house. "Yeah, Ed, this is Nicolaus. Listen, if Ceil wants you to bring her to the office, tell her that I have given you orders not to do so. Yep, that's right, do not bring her. If she makes other arrangements, that's her business, don't worry about that. Just for today, do not bring her, nor my father here. Got it? Okay, thanks." He slams the phone again.

"Nicolaus, that is really going to make her mad," Niall informs him.

Nicolaus sighs, "Well, no one is more mad or pissed off than I am right now! Having to clean up all her damn messes. I don't care if she gets mad. Anyway, that is what the flowers are for."

He returns his attention to his administrative assistant, "Okay, Vinatalie, get our landlord on the phone, tell him I'm back and I'll get him his check by noon. Call all the board members and let them know I'm back and that I'll take care of all the problems.

"Daniel, can you have your team reach out to all the janitorial staff and have them come in today at eleven thirty?" Daniel nods. "That should give me enough time to get them some apology cash, and have them reinstated. And Vinatalie, get ahold of our real estate partners, and set up a meeting for two this afternoon. Tell him I'll sign the papers. Okay? Thanks."

Vinatalie leaves the office to get those items done.

Nicolaus gets on his desk phone and dials a few numbers. "Hey there Lana, this is Nicolaus. Send Niall an email, telling him which reports you need, and which numbers you need for your report and he'll get those to you within the hour. Yeah, sure."

Nicolaus ends that call then calls HR. "Hey Mick, you can go ahead and schedule that town hall. Just check my schedule and use what you see. Okay? Hey, please transfer me to Simon." He pauses to wait. "Hey Simon, this is Nicolaus. Look, I'm sorry for the trouble Ceil caused regarding the janitor staff. Listen, Daniel is going to ask them to be here at eleven thirty for a meeting. Let's get them reinstated with back pay for any days missed, and let's give each of them a bonus payment of five hundred dollars cash to place in their hands today at that meeting to make that complaint go away."

Daniel nods at Nicolaus in agreement. Nicolaus eats more peanuts. "Yep, today, Simon. We have to make a good faith effort apology to them to make the complaint go away. Yep." Nicolaus slams down the phone.

He stretches his arms to the side. "All right gentlemen, I think I've covered everything."

Daniel stands with a chuckle, and grabs Nicolaus by the shoulder, patting him.

"Oh yeah, one more thing!" Nicolaus tells them, as Niall's eyes have not left his. Niall stands to listen. "Daniel, I want to thank you for all the hard work you've done for us, and for taking care of our company, standing in while I was absent."

"Of course, Nicolaus! Any time!"

"Well, my friend, ..." Now it is Nicolaus who grabs Daniel by the shoulder. "I would like to offer you the Vice President seat, if you are willing to take it." Daniel looks at Nicolaus surprised. "You've been doing the work for a while, so you may as well have the title and the pay that goes with it. What say you?"

"Wow, I'm ... I'm honored. Yes, I will step up in that role. Wow, thank you for trusting me with such an important seat, Nicolaus."

They give each other a quick man hug. "The thanks belongs to you, Daniel. The board only needs majority rule to confirm the seat, and I'm more than sure you will have it!"

Nicolaus looks to Niall and nods one time, the same as his father usually does.

Chapter Forty-Four

The twelve janitorial staff are cordial when they meet with Nicolaus, Daniel, Niall, and Simon from the HR department. Everyone is standing, dividing the room between the two groups.

Nicolaus begins the discussion. "I want to admit to you that Ceil Ravenell made a terrible mistake when she dismissed you. That should have never happened."

One of the staff steps forward to speak for the group. "Mr. Nicolaus, we all know that you are a nice boss. We knew something was wrong, that you would never do anything like that to us. Man ... your mother ... she's a real witch!"

Nicolaus was taken aback by this observation. He places his hand in the air, palm towards them to stop such talk. "Well ... uhm ..., as I've said it was a mistake. I apologize for that, to each of you. I'm sorry," he says, looking into the eyes of each of them, "And I'm willing to go the extra mile. If you still want your jobs, we will reinstate each of you, with back pay, so that you don't lose any money. And ..." Nicolaus takes one of the envelopes from Simon, "I will give each of you a five hundred dollar bonus in cash. You can think of it like a raise. Only, to receive the cash, you'll have to drop the complaint."

The spokesman of the group laughs. "Oh, so you want to buy us off. Buy our silence."

Nicolaus sighs with a frown. "No. I would never do that. That is not in keeping with our policies. If you don't want the money, that is fine. It's just that it is not good business sense for me to give you cash, and then still have to pay lawyers to handle your complaint. I cannot do both." Nicolaus crosses his arms, signifying a closing of his negotiation stance.

Niall is taking all this in. He is surprised seeing that Nicolaus does not defend Ceil, not understanding that her actions against this group are indefensible.

"So, it's one or the other. It's your choice," Nicolaus tells them, knowing that they'd probably go for the cash.

"Five hundred dollars?" Several in the group ask to Nicolaus' affirming nod. They form a circle to discuss this amongst themselves.

"Five hundred dollars, that is half of a thousand," one says.

"I need that kind of money," another voices.

"Just drop the complaint and take the money," another whispers.

"Five hundred dollars? I don't even have gas to get home. Take the money."

"We've made our point. Take the money," another demands.

The spokesman emerges with arms crossed. "Mr. Nicolaus, you are nice and all, but Sir, we cannot be bought off so easily."

"Ayi!" Is heard from others.

"We said take it!"

The spokesman's arms go up to shush the staff. "We want a raise, Mr. Nicolaus. I think you can afford it."

Nicolaus chuckles, and looks to Daniel. With pursed up lips, he nods. "Okay, what are you asking for?"

"We want our jobs reinstated, the five hundred dollars, and a dollar and a half more per hour, for each of us, Sir. And in return, we drop the complaint."

Nicolaus looks at them with an eyebrow lift. He nods. "Consider it done!" Nicolaus looks at Simon, "Simon, make sure you give them the dollar fifty raise effective immediately." Simon nods. Nicolaus puts his hands out for the spokesman to shake on the deal. The two men grasp hands, and shake with manly vigor.

The mood in the office has lightened as the staff are smiling, laughing, and stepping forward to shake Nicolaus' hand.

Nicolaus grabs the envelopes and passes them out to each staff member. "I've kept my end of the deal, so I trust you to keep your end of the deal."

"Yes, Sir, Mr. Nicolaus. I will cancel the complaint right away," the spokesman informs him.

The staff leave in a group, though a few straggle.

"Mr. Nicolaus, thank you, Sir. It's a real pleasure working for you."

Nicolaus shakes his hand again. "Thank you."

"Mr. Nicolaus, you are a fair man. We appreciate you," says the other staff member.

Nicolaus also shakes his hand again. "Thank you. We appreciate the hard work you do for us."

Nicolaus stands against the door to watch all of them leave out. Once they are all gone in the elevator, he closes his office door. "Jesus! I thought they were going to ask for a five dollar an hour increase." He chuckles. "Simon, make sure you place a note of my approval of the increases for them. We'll expect them back at work tomorrow if not tonight. Just give them the hours and pay them."

"Yes Sir."

"Remember, we are providing them with backpay. Let me know if you need me to sign anything."

"Yes Sir." Simon leaves to get right on this.

Niall and Daniel leave his office with Daniel praising his style of negotiation.

Immediately, Nicolaus phones Helena. "Hey, my friend. What are you doing? Can you get yourself detangled from your work for a late lunch with me?"

Helena had to close her mouth from the shock of Nicolaus asking her to lunch. It is a first. She laughs, feeling stupid, trying to get back into the friend frame of mind, instead of thinking about him sexually. "Where have you been?"

"Constance and I went out to California for a bit. She's still there! I would be too if I hadn't got called back to the office to handle Ceil's freakin' shenanigans. So how about it?"

"Sure, ... sure! What time?"

"I'll pick you up at three."

"Okay, great."

Helena replaces the phone receiver, and has to sit herself down. She has a realization that Nicolaus Ravenell, the man she has been dreaming of being with for over a year now, is thinking about her. It scares her and excites her at the same time. She is afraid she will blow it with him. She knows this is going to be a delicate time. She shakes her head. 'He's just a friend. Just a friend.', she repeats to herself.

Helena grabs her keys and drives over to the mansion. She must talk to Ceil.

Chapter Forty-Five

"**Y**ou do know I can have you fired," Ceil tells the driver coldly. "Your behavior this morning ... no ... your insubordination this morning, and now again, is unacceptable."

"Ma'am, I'm sorry. Mr. Nicolaus gave me orders."

"I don't give a damn what Nicolaus gave you," she shouts at him. "I'm the head of this family, not Nicolaus! You'll do exactly as I say!"

"Sorry ma'am, I cannot do that."

The staff take Helena to Ceil. "Ceil, I'm sorry to interrupt, but I need to speak with you," Helena tells her.

Ceil looks to Helena, then back at the driver. "Helena, this is not a good time."

Helena looks to the driver, then to Ceil. "Well, yes, I can see that, but Ceil, I need to speak with you. It's important. Please," she steps closer to Ceil.

Ceil looks to Helena and wonders what she wants. Ceil is riled up and mad that Nicolaus has put the staff against her to keep her from getting into the office. Helena looks behind Ceil and sees there is a vase of fresh flowers on the floor. It looks as if the vase has been smashed. She looks to Ceil who is looking at her with angry eyes. Helena does not back down. "Now, Ceil."

Helena walks to the adjacent room, expecting Ceil to follow her, which she does.

"Ceil, I'm sorry if you are having a difficult day. I just need you to know that I want to break off our ... girlfriend ... relationship. I don't want to do that anymore; really is why I haven't been over here lately. And I don't want you to be mad about it Ceil, because I respect you. I admire you.

"And I want you to know, Ceil ... that I plan to pursue Nicolaus. I want you to hear it from me. And ... I want to be fair to you, Ceil,

148

... you know, so that if someone else might be interested in you ... so you can make yourself available. And Ceil, I don't want there to be hard feelings between us. You are a lovely woman, Ceil, really ..."

"Get out!" Ceil tells her coldly.

"Ceil, I don't want us to be at odds with each other."

"Get out!" Ceil yells louder, taking a step towards Helena, as if she might attack her. "Get out!" Now she is screaming at the top of her lungs. Each step she takes closer to Helena, makes Helena back away. "Get out, ... get out.... Get out!"

Helena looks at Ceil with sadness, then she turns and leaves.

Chapter Forty-Six

Helena is surprised when she gets into Nicolaus' SUV for their lunch date when he updates their situation.

"Francesca and Maggie are going to meet us for lunch, too."

"What? Oh! I thought it was just going to be us." She feels disappointed, however, she does not show this in her voice. 'He's just a friend', she tries to remind herself in her mind, though her heart sure feels differently when she looks at him as they drive through town.

"I was surprised to see both of them at the office on my way out. Hope you don't mind."

"Oh, of course not!" Helena put her head against the headrest. She sighs, removing her eyes from the handsome profile of Nicolaus Ravenell, and placing them on the road, her heart sinking a little. She was so excited earlier. She wonders why she feels disappointed. She shoves her feelings away, and turns to talk to him. "So how was the California trip? You going back?"

Nicolaus glances at her momentarily. He shrugs. "I needed the getaway. I didn't realize it, but I sure needed it." He smiles slightly, "I could use more time."

As he pulls into the low key Mexican restaurant, he sees Francesca and Maggie waiting for them outside. As a gentleman, as he normally would, and despite being on his cane, Nicolaus opens the door for Helena and helps her out the vehicle, a pleasure she'd forgotten about, as this never occurred with her husband.

"Helena!" Francesca is quick to greet the woman who pulled her brother from the brink of nothingness a few weeks ago. "Love!" She greets Nicolaus with a big hug and kiss.

Nicolaus reaches for Maggie and gives her a sweet kiss to her cheek.

"I hear this place has the best tacos in town!" Maggie tells them.

They order their food and get seated, the same as other patrons in the restaurant. Nicolaus hears low chatter behind him, a few gasps, a few shutters of a phone camera, and only one elevated voice followed by some hushing sounds. He hopes he is not fully recognized or their time is not interrupted. He is not completely ready to deal with the public yet.

"So, what is it that dragged you back from California, Love?" Francesca asks.

"Ceil ... what else?" The ladies chuckle. "I was getting calls from everyone. She fired a whole department of people. Everyone, rightly so, was freaking out. You can't just do that."

"My Auntie Ceil. She's always been such a mess."

"She made a mess." Nicolaus corrects her.

Their food was brought to them, and they got to eating. During their lunch, Francesca notices how Helena seems to be overly tending to Nicolaus. She noticed Helena sitting a little too close to her brother; awkwardly wiping Nicolaus' mouth of dripping taco sauce; and eyeing Nicolaus with a not so subtle look of love .... Or was it lust?

Francesca finishes her taco plate, and had more than enough of Helena's behaviors. She stands. "I've got to go to the restroom. Ladies!" She calls them expecting them to follow. When only Maggie stands, because Helena seems to be mesmerized by Nicolaus, who actually hadn't noticed her odd behavior towards him, his eyes on Francesca, Francesca grabs Helena by the arm, forcing her up, "Come on ... you've got to go too!" She tells her. "To the loo!" She pulls Helena along, the ladies giggling.

The restroom is on the other side of the restaurant. Once inside, Francesca begins pacing, much like her father does when he is nervous. "What the hell ... Helena!"

"What?"

"What? Now you gonna act all innocent?" Francesca badgers her, the British accent front and center.

"What did I do?" Helena asks, frowning.

"Jesus!" Francesca pulls out a cigarette from her purse and she lights it, and takes a long drag, then blows the smoke from her nose and mouth.

"Francesca! When did you start smoking?" Maggie asks her.

Francesca sighs, holding the cigarette between two fingers. "Since Deirdre. I'm so pissed about all this; I don't know what to do with myself. And if I'm pissed, imagine what my brother must be feeling."

Francesca takes another long drag of the cigarette, happy for the warmth it puts in her chest. "But don't tell Nicolaus I'm smoking. Can't get much by him. He ain't gonna let me. I can hear him now." Suddenly Francesca stands very straight to imitate Nicolaus, and makes her voice and tone sound close to his, but in her British accent, 'Francesca, what the hell you doing that for? You not gonna be smoking. Give it to me.'" She rolls out her hand in a demanding stance. The ladies burst out laughing at her impersonation of Nicolaus.

"Wait ... did you say Nicky is your brother?" Helena caught this morsel of interesting information.

"Shh! Don't tell no one. It's a family secret. If Ceil finds out we have the same father, she'll do Nigel in."

"Oh! That explains ... quite a bit."

Francesca nods. "Shh!"

Helena crosses her arms. "So why am I here? I thought you had to go!" She points at the stall.

Maggie puts Helena's arm down. "Girl! This is your intervention!"

"Intervention? I don't need an intervention."

Francesca laughs. "You were hanging all over Nicky out there, and looking at him like you are ready to jump his bones or something. Helena, we are not stupid!"

Helena sighs. "Obvious, huh?"

"Yes, girl! Nicky is not ready for that!" Maggie scolds her.

Francesca nods in agreement. "No, he's not. Look Helena, I appreciate that you love Nicolaus. Really, I do. And ... I'm sure he needs you in his life. I mean you are the only one who brought him back to us. And ... I don't know exactly how close the two of you are, though he sure does seem to let you into his personal space, which ... I've never seen him do that for anyone except Deirdre. And I know you've been with us for a long time Helena, and I know Nicky appreciates you."

"Yes, but it has only been a few months that Deirdre has been gone. And you have to remember, they waited a really long time before being together," Maggie adds.

Helena's head went back and forth between these two ladies as she listened attentively to what they were telling her.

"And Nicky is nothing like Benjamin Niall. Nicky does not just jump from one woman to the next. He's never done that."

"Nicolaus has always had Deirdre," Helena reminds them. "And Nicolaus strikes me as needing to be cared for. This has been a lot for him."

"What? He's the one that takes care of everybody else."

"Well, that's what I mean. It's too much. He needs someone to take care of him. And ladies, like it or not, I'm that one, whose going to take care of him."

"Helena, I get it. But honey, it's too soon. If you make a move now, Nicky's going to be pissed. I know my brother. He's not going to know what to do with you. It's going to piss him off."

"And it's not like you're exactly available, Helena," Maggie tells her.

"Damn, Maggie!" Helena is surprised at her comment, referring to her marriage to Joel, for which Joel refuses to grant her a divorce. "Look, I'm not trying to hurt Nicolaus or make him pissed. I just love him ... that's all," Helena surprised herself, saying such thoughts out loud. Well now she said it. "I love him," she repeats softly.

Francesca looks at Helena, while taking the last drag of her cigarette. She blows the smoke, and begins to chuckle. "You and about one thousand other women around the world." She puts the cigarette out in the sink, reaches into her purse and gets a small perfume bottle and sprays herself and her hair, to get rid of the cigarette smoke smell.

"I'm serious. I'm the one here with him. I love Nicolaus, and I know I have to wait. I hear you. But just know that I love him. And I'm hoping ... no ... I intend to have a relationship with him after he has time to grieve Deirdre. I'm still grieving her too."

"We all are," Maggie closes the conversation.

The ladies leave the restroom and return to the table. Nicolaus looks at each of them. "Everything okay?" He frowns, "You were gone a long time."

Francesca puts mint gum in her mouth and offers it around the table, only Nicolaus taking one. "Women talk. You know how we are," she tells him. Everyone giggles.

Nicolaus pays the bill with a hefty tip, and they leave the restaurant.

Chapter Forty-Seven

Nicolaus arrives home for dinner; except he has no intention of sitting down to dine with his family. The staff attempts to provide him with a plate. Nicolaus raises his hand, rebuffing the plate. "It's okay. I'm sure there is about to be some animosity going on here," he tells the staff. The staff nods and takes the plate away.

Nicolaus is standing, while Nigel, Ceil, and Elsa are sitting. He waits for what he knows is about to happen. He is ready. No one to stop him. No one to make him hold his tongue.

Ceil jumps right in, standing. She walks up to Nicolaus, making Nigel follow her. "Who the hell do you think you are, ordering my staff about? What the ... hell do you think you are doing?"

Nicolaus does not flinch. "What's the matter, Ceil? Didn't you get the roses I sent you?"

"Roses?" She asks as if it were a dirty thing to say. "Answer my question!" She demands of him.

Nicolaus crosses his arms. "Let me tell you something, lady. I know who you are. I know what you are capable of. And I know what you've done. I'm very certain you have done other things that I have yet to discover. And if you think that for one minute, I'm going to let you taint the name of my ancestors, or destroy everything that the Ravenells have worked so hard to build up, well ... you can just think again, lady," he says feeling very heated, emphasizing the word 'lady', separating her from his side of the Ravenell family.

"Uh! Don't you dare talk to me like that."

Nicolaus points in her face, yelling at her. "I know what you did, Ceil. Baird told me! I know it was you."

"Nicolaus, son, what are you talking about?"

"Don't tell me that you don't know what she did, father; how she made plans with Baird to destroy me?"

"Destroy you? Son ..., what are you talking about?"

"Remember when Baird and his men attacked us in our home to make Niall marry Elsa, and to make me marry Gwen? It was all her idea. She was behind it all," he yells towards Ceil, who stares at him and says nothing. "Yeah! He told me everything."

"Ceil, is this true?"

"Father, you don't need to ask her. In case you haven't noticed, your wife is a liar. I'm telling you! And just as we suspected, she used Gwen to try to kill me with drugs." Nicolaus waits for Ceil's response. When she only stares at him, he keeps going.

"Ceil," Nigel touches her and she jerks herself away, as she is now being exposed.

"And I can imagine that you are thrilled to the bone that I've lost Deirdre. You're probably happy about her death! I won't be surprised if I later find out that you had something to do with it." Ceil shakes her head negatively without words.

Nicolaus looks up to see that Elsa is trying to slip away from the scene. "Elsa, where are you going?" Elsa stops in her tracks and turns to face Nicolaus. She shrugs. "Where is Niall? He sure hasn't been around here since I've been back," he yells at her.

"Nicky, Niall and I are separated."

"Why? What do you know about Deirdre's death, Elsa? Tell me what you know," he roars at her.

Elsa is suddenly frightened of Nicolaus. She's never seen him like this. "Nicky," she shakes her head negatively, like Ceil, but says nothing further. Tears stream from her eyes. Elsa shrieks out cries and runs up the stairs.

Nicolaus' eyes follow her path, and his eyes land on Ceil, who is still staring at him. "Ah! There, you see? She does know something."

"Nicolaus," Nigel touches his shoulder to get him to stop.

"No!" Nicolaus jerks himself away from his father. "At the office today, I had to undo all the damn mess you caused," he says to Ceil. "And why? Because you are on some kind of power trip? You think you are going to run things?"

"Nicolaus, ..." Nigel fails in his attempt to get Nicolaus to stop. Nicolaus jerks away from him again.

"Father, did you know your wife fired a whole department of people?"

"What? Ceil ... why would you do something like that?"

"Yeah, Ceil, why? You do realize it is against the law to do something like that."

"Ceil," Nigel looks to her frowning.

"Well, I've got news for you, lady. You're not going to run anything. I've fixed it so that you will not get your grubby little power trippy hands on our company. The Ravenell company. I will not let you take it down with your irrational behavior. You hear me?"

Nicolaus feels his father pull him back, away from Ceil, because he keeps stepping closer to her to yell in her face. "No!" He jerks himself from his father, and steps up to Ceil. "You may have my father running scared, and you may have my brother running scared. Well ... I'm not scared of you, Ceil. I'm not afraid of you, and I never will be. You hear me, lady?" Nicolaus jerks himself from his father one last time before leaving their presence to go to his side of the mansion.

Ceil looks at Nigel, who is looking at her in astonishment. "Ceil, did you do those things Nicolaus is saying? You wouldn't do those things, Ceil, would you?" Nigel is at a loss. He doesn't want to believe that Ceil would fire a whole department of people, nor put Jonathan and his men up to what happened to them on that terrible day.

"I told you to send him away," she harshly tells Nigel. Ceil's mind has the keen realization that Nicolaus has dethroned her today. He took away her power with the staff, he took away her power with VMC, he took away her love of Helena, and now he's taken away her stance with her husband and the family. Ceil breathes deep and hard with anger. She seethes with hatred for Nicolaus.

"Ceil?" Nigel looks at his wife who is not answering him.

"I told you to get rid of him!" She yells at Nigel. "You never listen! And now look what has happened to our family. Our family is ripped to pieces because of Nicolaus, when I told you years ago to get rid of him." She breathes hard, her anger boiling over.

Nigel makes the mistake to try to touch Ceil, to take her in his arms to calm her. He receives a harsh backhanded slap across his face from her. In shock, he stands away from Ceil.

"I'm done with you, Nigel! You are useless as a husband!" Ceil yells at him. Then, in a more calm tone, "As usual, I'll take care of it," she tells him coldly, walking away from him.

Nigel watches Ceil leave the room.

Chapter Forty-Eight

The following day, Nigel went to see Nicolaus at the office, during a time he did not have any appointments scheduled.

"Nicolaus," Nigel gives his son a light hug, which is returned. He was glad to see that Nicolaus is calmed. Nigel looks around the office. "Why did you remove all the photos?"

Nicolaus shakes his head with a frown. "No way I could concentrate if I'm looking at Deirdre's beautiful face."

Nigel nods in understanding as he sits himself opposite of his son.

"Father, I'm glad you are here. I did some thinking last night, and I've decided I'm going to move out. Get my own place. I think it's time for me to do so."

"Nicolaus, you can't move out, son. Look, you definitely put Ceil in her place last night, I don't like the method you used, but ... overall, I think you did the right thing in confronting her. Though son ... you do know that means she is going to plot some kind of revenge against you."

Nicolaus nods. "I know. I'll have to pay for what I said," he sighs, sitting on the edge of his desk. "But father, what do you mean I can't move out? I don't think I can live under the same roof as Ceil any longer. I don't trust being around her, especially now. How do I know she won't poison my food or something? Do you feel comfortable around her? How can you even sleep next to her? I'm worried about your safety as well, father."

"Look, son, Ceil is not like that. As we've seen, she never directly does things. She always wants to keep her hands clean."

"Why do you stay with her? You love her so much you would risk your life, knowing what you know now? What's to stop her from getting one of the staff to do something against us? No, I want to get my own place."

"Nicolaus, you cannot move out. Son ..., marriage is not always about love. I stay with Ceil because if we divorce, she will take half of your inheritance. She'll take half of everything. Half of the Ravenell empire. So ... I stay with her, because I made a vow to do so, and for you, to protect what is rightfully yours. We have never had love the way you had love with Deirdre. What Ceil and I have is a partnership, from the time we agreed to marry. So, I'm asking you not to move out, Nicolaus. You can't move out."

Nicolaus looks at his father, frowning, "Can't?" He crosses his arms and waits for further explanation.

"Nicolaus, if you move out, you will forfeit your portion of your inheritance."

"Forfeit?"

"Yes. When my time with Rachel was discovered, Ceil insisted I put a stipulation on your inheritance."

"Stipulation? So, there is some kind of secret rule I don't know about?"

Nigel nods, "So to speak. If you move out, change your residential address, then you forfeit your inheritance. And the other part of the stipulation, is you are not to be told."

Nicolaus scoffs, "Deirdre and I were discussing whether to move out of the house. We only stayed because she wanted to."

"I would have asked you to stay."

"Father, do you know how unfair this is?"

"Unfair? Hmm, well, ... I don't think you are doing so badly, you've got your education, a wonderful place to live and lots of friends, you can travel anywhere anytime, you've got lots of money ... and ... I gave you a whole wing of the mansion, so you would have your own space."

"Okay, okay," Nicolaus chuckles, understanding his father's point of view.

"Anyway, now you know about it, but you must not let on that you know. You cannot use it to taunt her. She cannot know that you know, Nicolaus."

Nicolaus sighs. "So, I must remain in place, and continue to live with your wicked wife ..."

"Ceil is not wicked. She is vindictive, but not wicked. She is not all bad. She does have some good characteristics. Ceil is the one who picked the building locations for our first set of clinics. In fact, she had hundreds of people show up for the ribbon cutting ceremony, then people trickled through all day. After that, tons of donations flooded in.

"And Ceil is great at fundraising, she knows lots of powerful people. Ceil has raised millions for our operations, she easily raised one million dollars for Helena to help those children. She cried over the loss of Nicolai. The nurses told me they practically had to pry him from her. And Nicolaus, she does have love for her family."

"Love for some in her family," Nicolaus corrects his father.

Nigel chuckles. "Well, you get my point."

Nicolaus nods.

"So, will you stay the course? I'm not going to be here forever, and neither will Ceil. I'm sure you are at least halfway to the finish line. Will you stay on the Ravenell train?"

Nicolaus chuckles. "The Ravenell train? Yes, father, I'll remain on the Ravenell train."

"Thank you, Nicolaus. I cannot imagine turning everything over to Niall. You are the next generation of brains in our tribe. And your children as well."

"My children? Well ... I don't think that is going to happen now. It will have to go to Elaine, and the next little one born."

"Now, Nicolaus, you are still young. One day your heart will let you marry again, and bring your own sons into this world." Nigel stands, "Though it is much too soon for us to be discussing such matters." He goes around the desk, as Nicolaus stands, and he pulls Nicolaus into another hug. "I love you, my son. I'm very proud of you."

"I love you too, father."

Nigel continues, "You have really taken our family and business finances to the next level, so I really want to see you stay and manage the operations. By the way, I received a call for an interview from an international business trade magazine. They want to interview me for being the father of one of the most successful CEOs under the age of forty. Everyone is noticing you."

Humbly, Nicolaus smiles, "Really? Wow!"

Nigel grips Nicolaus shoulder with a father's pride. "You are really making a positive and global mark for our name, son."

Chapter Forty-Nine

Nicolaus disappeared from Austin, without telling anyone where he was going again. He only told Daniel that he could be reached on his cell phone, and that he'd be back before the board meeting in two weeks. This would be the board meeting to vote Daniel in as the new Vice President, something Nicolaus had not even told his father about. He didn't want Ceil getting wind of his plans to try to sabotage him.

Nicolaus went back to California to swim in the Pacific Ocean and to gather up Constance. On the way home, he stopped in Colorado, to visit the Darfurian refugees. They were very delighted to meet Constance. They gave her much love and heavily praised Deirdre. They gave Nicolaus additional love and hugs as well. The children, in anticipation of his next visit, made him drawings, and even created a new dance for him.

Constance is impressed with the operations, and she has a clear understanding that Nicolaus must continue this wonderful work.

As Nicolaus returns home, he is greeted by Francesca. Francesca looks over Nicolaus, and she hugs her brother and kisses his face. Though he seems weaker than he was before his horrid tragedy, he still seems to be strong in physical strength. She knows his spirit is still down, as she can see it. Losing Deirdre has broken him. "Nicky, where have you been? Dad said you went away for a while."

Nicolaus returns the face kiss and nods to her. "I was in Denver, visiting ..."

"Awh! The lovely Darfurian children?"

Nicolaus slightly chuckles, "Yes."

"Uh! I wish you had taken me with you! I would have loved to meet them!"

"Francesca, I didn't know you had an interest in them. I'm sure they'd love to see you and your colorfulness. Next time I go, you'll need to accompany me then."

She hung onto his arm. "How was the visit?"

Nicolaus nods, then sighs heavily. "I needed it. Those children and women help remind me of the work Deirdre and I did for them. They are so loving about her."

"And that helps you?"

"Yes."

"Good!" She hugs him again.

"Ah, Nicolaus, son! Welcome home." Nigel walks over to greet Nicolaus with a man pat to his back.

"Francesca," Nigel calls to his secret daughter.

Francesca quickly answers Nigel. "What is it, Dad?"

"Francesca!" Nigel looks around for lurking ears or lurking eyes. "We talked about this. You continue to address me as your uncle."

"I know, I know. I just wanted to see what calling you ... the other ... felt like. It would really take some getting used to."

"Well, and just trying it out can get us caught. Remember 'loose lips sink ships', darling." Nigel enjoyed getting a chuckle out of Francesca. Nigel watches as Nicolaus leaves them to go to his side of the mansion. He speaks again when he sees that Nicolaus is completely gone from them. "Look, Francesca, I don't want you to mention the curse issue with Nicolaus right now. I know you feel strongly that you need to say something to him about it."

"Well, yeah, we have to tell him. What if another woman gets involved with him? And anyway ... maybe it kind of explains what happened with Deirdre."

"Francesca, I understand where you are going with that. Look, I think I've come up with a better way of telling him. He's going to need support when we tell him. Imagine, ... it's going to be hard for him to take."

"Okay, Uncle Nigel. What have you come up with?"

"I want to get him to California. He needs to be around my brother and Zhara when we tell him."

Francesca nods in understanding while looking at Nigel suspiciously at the same time. "Uncle Nigel, you mean to tell me they know about this?"

He nods one time, his signature move of affirmation, "Yes."

"Oh my God!"

"Look, we didn't think it was really true. However, ... as you've said, now that we've lost Deirdre .... Let me talk him into going with me."

"Okay, Uncle Nigel, whatever you think best."

Chapter Fifty

"Nicolaus," Nigel is abruptly upon his son in the sitting room, once he sees that Nicolaus has returned to the main side of the house. He enters the back door, coming in from the family cemetery. Nigel grabs Nicolaus by the shoulder. "Son, I want you to go with me to California."

Nicolaus frowns at Nigel. "I've just come back from California."

"Oh. Well, ... there are some things we need to discuss with Xavier and Zhara."

"Business related?"

Nigel sighs, not wanting to lie, knowing this is going to be difficult enough. "No, family business."

Nicolaus looks outside the large plated windows. He looks in the direction of the family cemetery. He shakes his head. "I just got back. I don't think I want to leave her again, right now," he sounds solemn.

Nigel gives him a loving shoulder squeeze. "Son, Deirdre is not there. She's in heaven now. She's with Rachel, and Thaddeus, and little Nicolai, and my mother, and your grandparents, and our ancestors. She is an ancestor now. Right? She is living with the angels now. Right? We have to believe our religious teachings and beliefs. We know her body may be in the ground, but her spirit and her soul is in heaven."

A tear of understanding trickles from Nicolaus' eye. He nods. "Yes," he says lowly, agreeing.

Nigel feels that he wants to cry as well. "As you and I have discussed, none of us will live forever. We each have a given time on earth, and when that time is up, that's it. The separation from our loved ones is what hurts the most."

Nicolaus nods again, appreciating the wisdom his father put about his thoughts.

"Dealing with Deirdre's passing was the hardest thing for me. Harder than saying goodbye to Rachel, or my mother," Nigel confesses to him. "We all loved her very much. I think because she was so young and healthy ... is why." Nigel's voice cracks with emotion. "That suddenness just feels so devastating." He sighs, sitting down. "So, we have to understand that she is living her heavenly life now. I'm very sure that you of all people know this, son. You have to come up out of your feelings, and wrap your religious mind around it." Nigel pulls Nicolaus to sit next to him, then grabs him in a strong man's hug to him. "She did so much for so many. Her heart was so beautiful. And yes, we will miss her greatly." Nigel is relieved, and hopes that he is finally able to help Nicolaus, as he had not previously been able to really find the words to support his son through this ordeal.

"Thank you, father. Thank you," Nicolaus tells him softly.

Nigel looks upon Nicolaus, and sees that he is much more about himself, through his tears and his grief. He gently grabs Nicolaus by both shoulders. "We leave tomorrow."

Chapter Fifty-One

Nicolaus still seems solemn on the private plane ride to California. Nicolaus sits next to the window, the opposite plane side of his father and Francesca. He stares out, thinking of children, thinking about his future without Deirdre.

He understands what the bishop and his father have told him, however, he is not exactly sure how to go about everything without Deirdre. Nicolaus decided he had to keep living, now he has to figure out how to live and how to move forward. The thought of it strikes his heart, and feels like a gut punch, as sometimes happens to him every now and then. He tries not to cry, knowing that meeting up with his family members is going to be challenging for him.

Francesca and Nigel are very quiet as they sip their drinks. Francesca had given her brother lots of hugs and kisses earlier, and knows he most likely wants to be left alone to think his thoughts. She has brought the family record book, tucked away in her carryon luggage bag. She feels nervous about revealing the sad information to Nicolaus. She worries that it might send him over the edge again.

Nigel hired a limousine service to take them to Xavier's home. When they arrive, they are greeted by Cato, Ned, and Bobby, Xavier's sons.

Bobby chuckles, "Look at Uncle Nigel! Riding out here in style!" Nigel is the first to step out of the limo. He hugs his nephews, and Cato takes him right inside, followed by Francesca who receives loving kisses from her cousins. She greets their wives inside. Nicolaus is grabbed up by Bobby. Bobby hugs his cousin to him, also feeling the pain from the loss of Deirdre.

Zhara is quick to give Nicolaus some love. "Look at you! You are always so handsome!" She hugs him to her. "I'm so sorry about

Deirdre." She sees pain flicker across his face, and immediately takes him into another full on loving hug. Zhara gives the kinds of hugs that have meaning and you know they are filled with love.

Nicolaus met his cousin's wives, though their children are not present. Zhara had already prepared a meal for them, for which Nicolaus tried, and could not really eat much, as grieving sometimes does to a person. He listens as Nigel and Xavier chat about business and life. Nigel brags on Nicolaus and the record profits he'd brought into the company, while Xavier brags about being a grandfather.

Soon, they are in the living room of the high-end home in the upper middle class Santa Monica neighborhood. "So Nicolaus," Xavier begins, "we need to get to the family business of why you, your dad, and Francesca are here with us."

Nicolaus nods. "Before we begin that discussion, I'd like to say that I apologize to you Auntie Zhara for anything Ceil may have done in the past, that made you uncomfortable, or if she was rude in any way, or if she actually did anything to you. I apologize."

"Oh my goodness! Thank you for that, Nicolaus. You don't need to apologize. Ceil is Ceil. Nigel knew who she was when he married her." She threw a snarky look at Nigel.

"Hmm," is Nigel's response to Zhara.

"Well, I know that she makes you feel some kind of way because of her behaviors. And believe me, I fully understand, and just feel the need to apologize for it."

"Thank you for clearing the air, Nicolaus," Xavier tells him. "So, the thing we need to talk about is the family book."

"The family book?" Nicolaus looks to Francesca with a slight frown.

Xavier nods to Francesca, giving her the floor. "Love, there is something here that you have to know about. It's here on this page,

I found it as I was doing more research. And, well, Love, there is … a curse."

"A curse?"

"The curse that was placed on Nicohls," Zhara points out.

Nicolaus leans forward, "What exactly are we talking about here?"

"Nicky …" Zhara hushes Francesca, then continues.

"Nicolaus, that curse was placed on the firstborn son of each generation. Nichols was a firstborn. Did you know that?"

Nicolaus looks to Nigel, who is nodding in agreement with Zhara. "No, I didn't know that. He has siblings?"

"One younger brother in the Kiviste family line," Nigel tells him.

Nicolaus does not want to hear what he knows they might be trying to tell him. He didn't want to know, … though he does ask, while shaking his head negatively. "Like me. So, what are you saying?"

"Nicolaus, you are the next firstborn son in the Kiviste family line," Nigel heartbreakingly tells him.

Nicolaus sits back into the chair. Bobby touches both of Nicolaus' shoulders as he sees his cousin getting stressed. Nicolaus puts his hand to his forehead. He sighs, feeling this cannot be good news. He wonders why his father brought him all the way to California to tell him this. He looks at Francesca. "Francesca, what does that book actually say?"

Francesca feels nervous and sad at the same time, for having to tell this to Nicolaus at such a difficult time in his life. "Nicky, … Love, …" she sighs, "I'm not exactly sure of the translation, Love. Nicky, … everyone, maybe we shouldn't take all this so literally! I'm mean really! All these happenings could be a coincidence! Couldn't it?" Francesca is not so sure of herself about this as she previously was. She didn't want to be right about this.

"Well, at first, we didn't think anything of this. To us it seems like mumbo jumbo, ... like nonsense," Xavier explains. "But now ..."

"So, what's changed your thinking?" Nicolaus asks directly.

"Nicolaus, to be honest, Deirdre's death. We are very worried."

Nicolaus looks down in thought. "What does it say?"

"Needus (curse), Nicky, it says it here." Francesca points it out, then provides the book to Nicolaus. Nicolaus looks at the book in silence. All eyes are on him as he reads through it.

Nicolaus goes to the previous page and reads, then reads through a couple pages forward, then back to the page she pointed the word out to him. He is fluent in the Estonian language, as the pages are written in Estonian. He remembers the passage writing about the third wife is obliterated, as if it were purposely scratched out.

Nicolaus translates the passage in English for the family, "... because of infidelity with daughter of Fortis clan, a curse is placed upon the firstborn son of every generation, until this curse be broken. Curse placed by hand of Nicohls' first wife's mother, ... blame Nichols for her death, so no more happy. Külge siduv ... binding to ... any woman, motions curse. May each first born son be without joy ..." his words trail off as he pauses with the sting of it all, then continues, "of loved one, may joy be snuffed out, whisked away like a wind upon sand." He looks over the passage. "... truudusetus ...infidelity ..." He looks up to Zhara, who is nodding.

"I don't think the whole truth is revealed in the book," Zhara comments.

Nicolaus attempts to back track and does not find the whole story. "What ..."

Zhara moves forward and touches his hand. "Nicolaus, that is not important. Honey, the important part is the generational curse."

Nicolaus frowns. "This is like someone is paying for the sins of the father, except from a long time ago."

"Yes," Xavier agrees, "and is happening now."

"So, wait ... you think this is what happened to Deirdre? You're saying this curse is now on me? And because I married Deirdre ..."

"And the others ..." Zhara corrects him.

"Marguerite, Gwen ..." Francesca accounts.

"Hold on here!" Nicolaus stands, placing the book on the table. "That cannot be. We are really reaching here. I was absolutely not happy ... or joyful to marry Marguerite. That was forced on me ... as was Gwen. Hell, Gwen was an attack against me, so how can that factor in?"

"But Thaddeus, Nicolaus, our first grandchild," Nigel reminds him.

"And Alexander, Nicky. You were happy to give Gwen to him," Francesca notes.

Nicolaus steps back from everyone. He feels that his world is closing in on him. Are they saying he caused Alexander's death? "No! That's a stretch! It has to be! No!" He didn't want to believe it.

"Nicky, ..." Francesca tries to go to him.

Nicolaus backs away from her, not letting her touch him. "No!" He twirls in a circle at the confusion and unbelief in his mind. "You're all trying to tell me that I caused Deirdre's death? Because I married her?" He stops to think about it for a moment. "Oh my God! Then, she was fine before I married her? Twelve years ... and then .... No! Oh my God."

"Nicky, that is not exactly how curses work," Francesca tries to explain.

Nicolaus isn't hearing her, "No!" He moves away as Francesca tries to touch him again.

Zhara stands and goes to him. "Nicolaus, ..."

Nicolaus looks up at Nigel. "You knew about this, and you didn't say anything? You didn't tell me?" He half yells at Nigel, "At least warn me?"

"Nicolaus, none of us were sure about any of this. You've got to believe that," Zhara tells him. "And really, we are still not sure ... but it does make sense now."

Nicolaus looks at Zhara, then looks at no one. "If you are not sure, then why tell me?" He throws his hands in the air, questioning them. "Why all this?"

"Nicolaus, please," Nigel tries to calm him.

Nicolaus closes his eyes and he puts his hands to his head in disbelief. "My God! I don't understand. I'm so confused. It's her number of days on earth. She died in childbirth. I killed her with the curse," he recounts the scenarios. "I'm so lost! I'm so lost!" It appears as though he may fall down. Nicolaus stumbles for the door. Opening it, he hobble runs on his bad leg, out into the darkness, as the sun has set over the Santa Monica cityscape.

"Nicky!" Francesca cries, she starts to go after him. Nigel stops her.

"No, let him go," Nigel tells Francesca, holding her to him. "He needs time. He needs to let it sink in. He needs time to think. He'll be back."

Francesca struggles against Nigel, unable to get loose. "We can't let Nicky be alone right now. It's not right!"

Bobby touches Francesca. "Let me go. I'll look after him." Bobby proceeds to follow the direction of which Nicolaus ran out of their house, away from everyone.

Chapter Fifty-Two

Bobby found Nicolaus at the end of their long block of upscale homes. He is sitting on the curb, under a streetlamp. The street is long, however, Nicolaus got to the end quickly. When Nicolaus realized he didn't know where he would be going, and his leg was not going to take him much farther, he stopped, and dropped himself on the curb at the corner.

It didn't take long for Bobby to catch up to him, as he jogged at a slow pace, since Nicolaus was sitting and not in any danger. When he reached Nicolaus, he plopped down beside him on the curb, bumping him slightly, so he would know he was present.

Nicolaus used the sleeve of his casual shirt to wipe his face. His emotions were a blizzard these days, just popping up and everywhere.

"You okay, Nicolaus?" Bobby asks gingerly, not knowing what else to say.

"You know, for all my time in military service, over ten years, for all the missions I went on, and all the combat I've seen, not one time did I ever lose a team member. Not once! And to think that now I'm the cause of my own wife's death! It's too much, man. It's too much!"

"I hear you, Nicolaus. I hear you."

"I'm halfway around the world, chasing after my former father-in-law, to save him out of some heavy mess he's gotten himself into. I should have never left my wife's side in the first place! But no one else could go. It's so ... unfair! And in rescuing him, this time I did lose a team member, and I almost get killed, myself. I barely hang on, just to be with Deirdre again. That's the only thing that keeps me going." Nicolaus now sounds incensed, "Only to come home to her grave!"

"Awh man, that is tough to take. That'd be tough for anyone, Nicolaus."

Nicolaus sighs, emotions very intense within him. "If I had known she was already gone ... I would've just let go. And ... maybe we'd be together in the afterlife now."

Bobby gets emotional as well. "Nicolaus, man, I'm not exactly sure that's how that works. Is it? I mean, each of us have to go to the afterlife journey ourselves. Don't we? Walk our own path, and answer for whatever we've done while on earth. Don't we? I mean, there is no guarantee that you'd actually be with Deirdre. And what about the time and space continuum? One second could make a difference. Wouldn't it?"

Nicolaus looks to Bobby, wide eyed, wondering if this is what he needed to hear. He nods, "What you say does have merit. It does make sense. Though I do think I would eventually meet up with Deirdre. I think God would have to honor our love."

"Maybe. But that's for God to decide. Right? Nicolaus, you are a very important man. It's not your time to go, or like you said, you would have died already." He touched Nicolaus on his shoulder to make him hear his words. "And did you get your father-in-law? Did you save him?" Nicolaus nods in silence. "You see! It wasn't his time to go yet either. Obviously, you are a very important person, with very important things left to accomplish."

Nicolaus shrugs. "I don't know about all that."

"Are you kidding me? Look, this is the second time I've met up with you in our adulthoods that you were doing something very important to save people. Something that other folks are not capable of doing. Not to mention all your days in the military."

Nicolaus looks to his cousin in silence, thinking about what he is saying.

Bobby continues. "And you've got this mass of wealth that you must steer. Like a gigantic cruise ship. You'll be head of the family, your very wealthy family, when it's Uncle Nigel's time to go."

Nicolaus shakes his head. "I don't think so," he sounds defeated.

"What? You mean to tell me you're going to let your bonehead brother run things? My Lord, that is going to crash and burn quickly."

Nicolaus almost chuckles at Bobby's insight of Niall. "Ceil wants to run things."

"Auntie Ceil?" Bobby laughs heartily, "All your staff gonna quit within one week of her taking over. Nothing will ever get done."

His words make Nicolaus chuckle a little, because he knows Bobby is correct in his assessment.

"Look man, I know it's hard without Deirdre. She's always been with you. She was your purpose, that's why you feel lost. And now, you've got to find a new purpose. Look, us men, we are very linear. We see point A and point B," he puts his arm in a straight line and points forward. "And Nicolaus, you have lost your point B. Deirdre was your point B. So now, you've got to find a new point B to get yourself back on track."

"A new point B," Nicolaus slowly repeats after his cousin. "You sure are full of intricate wisdom today. So, ... how am I supposed to find a new point B? How am I supposed to do that?"

"Well, that I don't know. Really, I don't know. And Nicolaus, I never said it would be easy, ... finding that new point B. It may be the hardest thing you ever do."

Nicolaus sighs, with closed eyes, holding his head back. Slowly, he opens his eyes to the stars above, the ones he could see through the Santa Monica streetlights that lit up the whole of the city. He feels overcome with raw emotions.

Bobby sighs as well. He sees that look about Nicolaus and wants to jump into action for him. He wishes there was actually something he could do to make everything better for Nicolaus, to take some of his pain away. "Tell me what I can do for you. What can any of us do to help you through this?"

Nicolaus shakes his head. "What can anybody do?" He sighs, feeling as though he is going to break down again. "Bobby, I need to get to a church. Your family go to church?"

"We sure do! And I happen to know the church is open. United Methodist. You want to go?"

Nicolaus nods. "Please! I need to be in a church right now."

"You got it!"

They walk back to the house to get Bobby's vehicle, without going inside. Bobby drives Nicolaus to the church, then texts his father to let them know where they are.

"Bobby just texted me that they are at the church," Xavier informs the family.

"Oh, thank God!" Francesca says relieved.

"That is really good if my son is at a church. That's my Nicolaus. He always keeps God at the front of his mind."

Xavier touches his brother's shoulder. "Then all will be well. We'll get Nicolaus through this."

"Yes, he is seeking out God. You know, sometimes I don't know how to help Nicolaus. I don't know what to say. I'm too weak to do anything for him. It's been that way most of his life, and I know he feels it sometimes."

"And what about Niall?"

Nigel shakes his head. "I don't know what to do with him at all. Though he may have had a scare to make him do better in his life."

Chapter Fifty-Three

Nicolaus found solace inside the church. He sought understanding and answers for what to do. His tears of grief were touched by God, and Bobby stood back and watched as Nicolaus is wrapped in the love of God.

When Nicolaus returned to his uncle's home, it was late, though Nigel had waited up for him. Bobby left the two men alone.

Nigel touches Nicolaus on the shoulder, nervous that Nicolaus may reject him. "Son?"

To the contrary, Nicolaus hugs onto Nigel very tightly. Both men shed tears in each other's arms in a touching father son moment. Then in silence, they turned in for the night.

Nigel understood that Nicolaus accepted what was before him. He hopes his son has found a way to move forward.

Indeed, Nicolaus did move forward. When he returned home, the first thing he did was get a clean shaved face and a haircut, getting back to himself. He endured Ceil's cold stares across the dinner table when he decided to be home for dinner, and with each bite of food, he worried that it may be his last.

Nicolaus completed his physical therapy, trading it in for walking the mansion grounds in the mornings, finishing with a visit to the family cemetery. At the cemetery each morning, he said prayers for all his ancestors, and asked Deirdre for forgiveness and prayed for her soul, and the soul of his sons.

Little Nicolai giggles with heavenly delight each time his father thinks of him. Then he spreads his delightful joy to other little heavenly babies.

Nicolaus geared up all the new children's homes across the country, opening twenty-five houses within a two week period. He went to each home for the ribbon cutting ceremony, involving the mayor of each city, leadership of foster care service agencies, and the community. Helena was very happy to accompany him, at his request. Children were moved into the homes the same day of the ribbon cutting. Helena cried with happiness for these children, knowing that now they have a real shot of having a real future.

The energy between Nicolaus and Helena is good, palpable, and happy. They spent each day of these two weeks together. They slept in different hotel room suites, though enjoyed their meals together. Helena felt that she was really part of Nicolaus' life now, and when she gazed upon him at dinner, she could see her future with this man.

When Nicolaus returned home, he had additional duties to maintain these children's homes, so he often worked late. His morning routine remained the same, stopping by his wife's grave each morning. He very much appreciated that the staff continued to place fresh flowers for her.

Without Constance knowing, Nicolaus hired a private detective agency to look for Abigail and her father. He is determined to find her, and to try to correct the bad act Ceil did against the Omari sister's father. Furthermore, he had a great desire to reunite Constance with her family.

Surprisingly, at the office, Nicolaus is ready to give Niall additional duties, satisfied with the results of putting the investor vetting process on him, he wanted to give him some financial responsibilities. Nicolaus wants Niall to learn more about the company to groom him for a larger role.

Niall had been summoned and now sits in Nicolaus' office, across from his brother. He notices that Nicolaus has what appears to be dozens of accounting sheets with a huge mass of figures strewn all across his desk.

Niall looks around his brother's rather large office. Even though Nicolaus seems to be drowning in figures, his office is still pristine. Nothing on the floor, nothing in the trash can, nothing atop the filing cabinets. Nicolaus' office is much unlike Niall's office, which is a mess and littered with papers everywhere. Niall is messy and kept his office much like his living environment.

"Hey, Niall, how are you doing?" Nicolaus asks him with his eyes still milling over the accounting sheets.

"I'm good."

Nicolaus makes a mark on the data sheet, then looks up at his brother with a slight smile. He sits back into his chair, nodding. "So, you've been here for some months now. How are you feeling about working here?"

Niall sneers a little, not willing to tell Nicolaus how he really feels, bitter about Ceil's demands on him. "I'm good. It's all good."

"Hmm. And the work you've been doing?"

Niall nods. "The work is good. I like it well enough."

Nicolaus gives his younger brother another slight smile and head nod. "So, even though you were forced in by Ceil, the suit is fitting you okay," he comments.

Niall gives a slight smirk, wondering what Nicolaus is up to, and wonders why he is questioning him.

Being in Nicolaus' presence, and even just looking at him, makes Niall nervous because of what he did to Deirdre. He knows that Nicolaus is unaware of what really happened. However, Niall is very aware that Nicolaus could easily tear him apart when he does find out. The thought of this brings anxiousness over Niall, as he watches every move Nicolaus makes. When Nicolaus sits forward, it makes him feel jumpy, that flight or fright reaction vigilant in his brain. Sweat is now beading from the back of Niall's neck, he can feel it dripping down his shirt.

"Niall, you feel like you can handle all the financial receivable accounts?"

Niall balks at Nicolaus. He knows this is huge. "All of them?" He slowly nods. "Yeah ... sure."

Nicolaus nods, knowing he was correct a few years ago, that his brother could be part of the accounting team. "Since you are doing a good job vetting our donations and investments, you understand how the money is coming in, so I believe you will excel in this role as well, these tasks kind of go together. Only the insurance payments and self-pay arrangements will be included."

Niall nods. "Yes, I understand."

"This is sort of like a promotion for you, Niall. So please ... don't screw it up."

Niall nods. "Wow."

"You'll be reporting to Simon now, he's a great guy. You'll need to make sure all the money that we should be receiving is received, and you must account for everything. For anything missing, you'll work with Simon's team to retrieve it. It will be a great help to me if you could take this task off my hands."

Niall is shocked that Nicolaus would trust him with this. "Nicolaus ... I, I ... I won't let you down."

Nicolaus' eyes pop wide at Niall's nervous behavior. "You better not," he responds sternly. Nicolaus sighs and sits back in his chair again, eyeing his brother. "Do yourself a favor, Niall, and finally prove to your mother that you're worthy of her love. She wants to see you succeed so badly, she was willing to kill me to move me out of the way for you. Show her that you are worthy of that kind of love."

Niall is shocked again at Nicolaus' candor. He nods.

"When are you moving back into the house?" he asks Niall, with curiousness.

"Move back? Uhm ..." he shrugs, "I ... I, I ...," that nervousness is showing again.

"I mean aren't you going to try to make amends with Elsa?"

"Elsa ... uhm, I, ... I ... don't think she wants me back."

"Hmm. What happened between you two? Was it that bad? I mean ... gosh, you've just walked away from my nieces."

Niall laughs nervously. He looks around, wanting to bolt out of this office, and far away from his brother. "Uhm," is all he can manage.

"Did your breakup with Elsa have anything to do with Deirdre's death?" Nicolaus watches Niall as he seems to squirm in that chair at his direct question.

Niall avoids eye contact with Nicolaus. "I don't know. Look, are we done here? I mean with business."

Nicolaus sees he is not going to get any answers about Deirdre from his brother. He sighs, "Why don't you go see Simon and see when he wants you to start."

"Okay. Will do." Bolt out of the office Niall did. He couldn't leave fast enough. In the elevator, Niall wipes the sweat that is on his brow. He thinks he may be having an anxiety attack. After exiting the elevator, Niall goes into the men's room to breathe, before reporting to Simon.

Chapter Fifty-Four

The following day, Nicolaus grabs Niall as the board meeting is about to begin. He purposefully waited until the last minute to deplete Ceil of any subversions she could use against him. Nicolaus escorts Niall inside the conference room.

"Daniel, would you mind sitting on the other side of the table, next to Ceil? I'd like Niall sitting next to me."

Daniel nods gleefully, "No problem."

For this to happen, everyone along both sides of the tables shift down, and an additional chair is provided. Nicolaus nods to Nigel to begin the meeting, as he can feel Ceil's cold stare upon him. However, now, her behavior does not get next to him, as it did previously. Nicolaus has full control of the company.

"Thanks to everyone for being here. I'm sure many of you remember my younger son, Benjamin Niall, who goes by his middle name of Niall. Niall, welcome to the meeting."

"Father, if I could interject here, Niall should be attending all our board meetings, as Ceil has named him ..." Nicolaus purposefully looks at Niall pretending he forgot his title. He nods to Niall with a frown.

"Uhm? Oh, um, Associate Vice President."

Nicolaus nods. "Ah! Associate Vice President. Sounds important. Important enough for you to be here and know everything that is going on. We'll want your ... carefully thought out and logical opinions," Nicolaus tells him, knowing how his brother acts reckless and illogical most of the time.

Nicolaus looks at Ceil, and sees that she seems to be seething with anger. He smirks at her. "And ... Niall," Nicolaus touches his shoulder, "will now have oversight of our AR accounts. I have given him charge of this duty." He drops his hand from his brother. "Niall, any words for the board members?"

Niall looks at Ceil. She slightly smiles at him and shakes her head for him not to speak. "Ah, no, ah ... well ... except that I promise I will do my best in my new position." He offers his hand to Nicolaus, "Nicolaus, thank you for trusting me."

Nicolaus smiles and shakes his hand. "Of course! I'm sure you'll do well." Nicolaus looks to his father, "thank you father," handing the meeting back to him. He looks at Ceil to see she has a surprised look on her face on the trust connection with Niall. Ceil is not sure exactly what just happened. She is not exactly sure how she should feel.

Nigel calls on Vinatalie to read the minutes from the last meeting, and then he calls for any new updates or occurrences.

"Actually father, I have a major update, one that we need to vote on. I apologize it is not on the agenda."

"Oh sure, son, no problem. I give you the floor."

Nicolaus had not even told Nigel about Daniel's promotion. He didn't want Ceil to have any way of stopping him.

"Thank you, father. As you all know, Daniel Araceli is a valued treasure to our company. Daniel is currently our Chief Operating Officer, and he fills in for me when I'm away. Well ... Daniel has filled in for me quite a bit lately, and he has made sure that all operations have run smoothly. Thank you, Daniel."

Daniel nods and the board members clap for him, all except Ceil because she wonders what Nicolaus is up to, and Niall, because he doesn't know what is going on.

"Well ... previously, we operated under two Vice Presidents, and since the loss of Alexander, we have been operating with one leader, myself. The workload is quite a bit and I sincerely feel that I need an assistant. So today, I am asking that we take a vote to elevate Daniel from the role of Chief Operating Officer to Vice President. That would mean that I operate in the role of CEO, and Daniel will be the VP. Daniel has the qualifications, the experience, and the character to be second in command of our company. So I would like to ask for a motion to put this to a vote."

Nigel is as surprised as Ceil, however he says, "Well ... I believe this is a wise move. I place the motion for a vote to elevate Daniel Araceli to the role of Vice President of VMC. All in favor say aye and raise a hand for a count."

As Nicolaus expected, all members agreed in voice and by hand raise, except Ceil.

Nigel continues, "All opposed, say nay and raise a hand."

All eyes in the room are on Ceil. She sits unmoving, coldly staring at Nicolaus.

"Hmm," Nigel is surprised at her actions. "All sustained, raise a hand," he offers for Ceil. She is still unmoving. "Well ... the ayes have it," he closes the vote. "Congratulations Daniel, you are now the new Vice President of VMC. Would you like to have any words?"

The board members clap for him again, and he addresses them. "I just want to say thank you for this honor. I will continue to place this company and our values at the forefront of everything I do. Thank you."

"Thank you, Daniel, we appreciate your dedication," Nigel tells him.

"And," Nicolaus continues, "as the CEO, I shall appoint a new Chief Operating Officer, most likely from amongst the law team members, as we should always have someone with a legal background in that position."

"Agreed!" Both Nigel and Dwight say in unison. "This has been a boisterous meeting this morning. The next item is discussion on profits. Nicolaus, this is yours."

"Thank you father. Our profits are holding steady, as you can all see by the reports in front of you." Nicolaus reaches over Niall and opens the page for him. "I do want to make a suggestion, and ask for a vote this morning. I have had our investment team look at that Drone Pharma merger.

"They have analyzed that the merger is a drag on our stock price, mostly because investors are uncertain. This could cause our stock to drop."

A board member asks, "Uncertain, Mr. Nicolaus, what do you mean?"

"Well, because there has been no movement. It has been years since we've had this merger, and we have yet to receive one drug, one pill from them. For some reason, they cannot seem to clear the hurdle of red governmental tape. So there has been no movement.

"I do think that the idea of the merger was a ... good intended ... idea, aside from the marriage terms, which negatively affected me personally, I must say," he briefly eyes Ceil, "however, in reality it just has not worked out. There could be some benefit from the biomedicine portion of the agreement, yet there has been no movement on that front either.

"Therefore, I make a motion that we end the merger, effective immediately, as technically, they are in breach of the agreement anyway. And now that the marriage arrangement is over, there is no risk to our company if we end the merger. I can call them if you'd like, or we can send a letter, whatever you think is best.

"If we still want to pursue biomedicine, I propose that we provide a partnership agreement with them. What say you?"

Dwight nods and jumps right in with his support, "Nicolaus, I'm inclined to agree with you, especially if you have had experts analyze this. I feel we should trust your judgement, as you have brought us record profits."

Nicolaus nods, and briefly touches Niall's forearm, to get his attention, as a teaching moment. "Yes, of course, I would never insert my own opinion. In fact, our investment team believes that if we drop the merger, our stock price will increase. And of course this will make us even more money."

"Okay! Well, I second the motion to end the merger!" Dwight adds, gleefully.

"Great! Any more discussion?" Nigel asks. No one has anything. "Let's have a vote. All in favor, say aye and raise a hand." All agree with raised hands, except Ceil. Nigel notices the insufferable behavior of his wife. "All opposed?" Nigel sighs as Ceil remains unmoving. "The ayes have it!"

Nigel grabs Nicolaus' shoulder. "Nicolaus, I would ask that you let Dwight and I speak with Andrejs Drone regarding ending the merger. You have done more than enough for us, son." Nicolaus nods. "Next item. Ceil, you wanted to discuss the holiday party. I give you the floor."

Ceil has not taken her eyes off Nicolaus since the start of the meeting. Only she sees that this action that used to rattle him, no longer bothers him, and she doesn't know what else to do. She most certainly feels dethroned, and cut in size. She is not sure what to do about it. She'd never expected this to happen. She sighs heavily, "Table it," she demands.

"Hmm," Nigel is surprised by her actions today. He believes that Nicolaus may have finally cracked her. "Okay, then, item is tabled. This concludes our meeting. Thanks to everyone for your attendance. This meeting is adjourned." Nigel closes the meeting.

Niall is the first out of the room. Nicolaus and Daniel chat with the board members as they leave the room. After some minutes, Dwight and Nigel follow Nicolaus and Daniel out. Ceil remains sitting and thinking. She is thinking about her next move against Nicolaus.

Later that night, Nicolaus finally goes to visit with James' family. It is painful for any commanding officer to face up to the family of a lost comrade. Nicolaus felt that he finally had the strength, and the mental ability to face them.

As soon as the door opens, James' mother knows who Nicolaus is. She pulls him inside without words. Nicolaus assures James' parents that James was heroic, and that he did not die alone. Nicolaus described how he held James while he died, and that it was quick, so his suffering was minimal. "Your son made a great sacrifice for me, and for his country. I promise you, I will never forget that he was willing to give his life to help me in saving another."

The young man's parents appreciated Nicolaus.

Nicolaus left their home. He drove to a park, pulled over, and wept warrior tears.

Chapter Fifty-Five

E mily Brooke Ravenell is born into the world with loud crying drama, weighing six pounds and ten ounces.

Elsa is supported by Ceil's coldness, and only perks up when Nigel, Nicolaus, Helena, Maggie, and Ishani appear in the room. Nicolaus brings Elsa a beautiful bouquet of flowers, the only ones she received. He kisses her gently on the head.

"Awh! These are beautiful, Nicky, thank you."

"Another beautiful granddaughter," Nigel lovingly kisses Elsa's forehead, again standing in for her absent father.

"Wow, my niece is beautiful! Elsa, you are really good at this mothering thing."

Elsa chuckles at his comment. "Nicky," she answers him humbly with a smile. "You see Niall anywhere out there?"

"Sorry, he's not out there. And what a shame, he's missing the birth of beautiful Emily."

"Yeah, well, he's missing out on a lot."

Nicolaus touches her shoulder. "Sorry, Elsa."

Elsa sighs. "You know, I promised myself that if he didn't show up today, I'm filing for divorce. And there is no promise that I have made to myself that I haven't kept."

"Elsa, I understand. You do whatever you need to do, but stay at the house," Ceil tells her. "You need help with the babies, and I want my grandchildren with me."

Everyone looks at Ceil, amused at her sweet tone.

"Thank you, Mother Ceil. I appreciate that."

"Of course you'll stay with us," Nigel says factually. "I'd have it no other way, young lady."

"Ceil is right," Nicolaus agrees. "It takes a village to raise children, as the old African proverb says, and we are your village, Elsa."

Ceil and Nicolaus look at each other in a soft moment. They both look upon Emily together, then Elsa hands her to Ceil.

As Ceil rocks little Emily in her arms with a grandmotherly smile on her beautiful face, she thinks about the aspects of her plan for being rid of Nicolaus.

Chapter Fifty-Six

E mily is now three months of age.
  Nicolaus decided to step in as the male role model for both Elaine and Emily. He secretly used his lunch hour to be with the children before their nap, every day, unless his schedule got in the way.

Nicolaus would get on the floor and play with the little darlings, using their baby blocks and toys. He let them climb on him, walked with them on his shoulders and on his feet, he tickled them, and read to them, said the alphabet and primary numbers with them, and sometimes just sat with them. Many times, Emily fell asleep in his arms, being tuckered out from trying to keep up with her toddler sister. They adored their Uncle Nicky, and anticipated his arrival to be with them every day.

Additionally, Nicolaus kept his Saturdays reserved for foster children. He blocked off time to personally see the children at Helena's children's home. And he used at least three hours to video chat with the foster children in the homes across the country. He wanted to be sure he was helping them in any way possible to ensure their successful future.

In the foster homes he created, these children have the support services of a house mother, a case worker and a counselor to address any issues, and also to work on their future career plans. However, Nicolaus wanted to make himself available, and he still assisted them with testing preparations, and paid for any tests or certifications to assist them in their career choices.

On Sundays, Nicolaus resumed his mentorship of the young men in the church. Bishop Leighton insisted he return to this work, feeling it is part of Nicolaus' life mission. After church, he spent the afternoon with Constance, keeping his lifeline with her open.

Nicolaus maintained this busy schedule. His mornings started early, as he was not yet able to do his usual runs with his comrades, he replaced running with morning walking, ending with that visit to Deirdre's grave with prayers, before starting his day. His days were long, as he usually arrived in the office around eight-thirty in the morning, and ended his workday twelve hours later. He sincerely appreciated having the noon break to enjoy his time with Elaine and Emily.

Nicolaus is only able to sleep from a mix of exhaustion and a little whiskey. Night loneliness disturbed him, and he would find himself tearing for want and need of his wife, his Deirdre. He'd began receiving calls from single women interested in dating him, as now he is one of the most renown widowers in the country. He's also been receiving calls from mothers in high society circles, wanting to set him up with their daughters. Though he'd given slight thought to this, those calls remained unanswered.

The loneliness is heavy and pushes him to see Helena more often. He is aware that Helena had moved out of the mansion, and now similarly, lives alone in an apartment across town. Nicolaus notices how cold Ceil is towards Helena when he invites her over, or to dine with them and he doesn't know why.

Sometimes Helena stays overnight with Nicolaus on his side of the mansion, in mundane, drab, and innocent ways. Such as when they fall asleep in the living room watching a movie. Or when she lays against him, while they read together, also in the living room. Helena loves to curl up on Nicolaus and lay her head on his chest, and is surprised each time he lets her do this. His sleep breathing is even and unlabored. If they are awakened by the house staff, or for being in an awkward position, or from something else, they retire to separate bedrooms, Helena taking the guest room.

Though Helena finds that sometimes, even if Nicolaus is asleep, she cannot sleep for staring at him while laying against him, or fantasizing about him in the guest room, though there is no hint of romanticism about him towards her. She knows he is not thinking of her in this way, and it hurts. After several months of these mundane and unexcitable activities, Helena has become keenly aware that if anything were to happen between them, she must make the first move.

Though they sleep in separate rooms, Nicolaus actually let Helena into his private space. She is usually dressed and ready for the day before he is, as she moved herself into the guest room about a month ago now. She hears Nicolaus when he arises at five in the morning to go walking, and while he is gone, she readies herself for the day. Casually, she drifts into his bedroom when he returns, and he has never objected to this. Helena notices that usually, as soon as Nicolaus returns from his morning walk, he jumps into the shower. She normally enters his room when she hears the shower water.

"Hey Nicky, it's me, Helena. Good morning!"

"Good morning. I'll be out shortly." Is how their conversation usually begins.

Helena lounges around his bed, the covers are always jumbled and turned out in the mornings. She fantasizes about being next to Nicolaus in this very bed.

The elderly man servant, Mr. Adams, knocks and enters, placing Nicolaus' suit for the day on the valet stand. The man servant arrives at the exact time every morning, with a newly pressed suit for Nicolaus. He nods to Helena, as usual, "Madame."

Helena observes that this man has whisps of gray hair sticking out of his mostly bald head, a beak shaped nose, and has an involuntary permanent forward bend. She thinks it is kind of the Ravenells to have employed such a person. She wonders what his story is.

After Mr. Adams places the suit, he takes undergarment necessities out of the dresser drawers for Nicolaus and puts them on a shelf behind the dressing screen. Going into Nicolaus' closet, he retrieves shoes that match the suit, putting them on the floor close to the valet stand. He takes a small feather duster out of his pocket, slowly bends, and dusts off Nicolaus' shoes. Then he nods to Helena again, "Madame", he says lowly, then leaves the room.

Within five minutes of this action, Helena hears the water turn off, and she can hear bustling in the bathroom. Then, the door opens, and out pops a half dried Nicolaus, with a towel wrapped around his waist, and his soft curly hair dripping wet. Very rarely does Nicolaus ever completely dry himself. His soft curly hair reflects his Moorish heritage combined with his Estonian and African American mixed race, which perfectly matches his light caramel skin that covers his body.

"Sleep well?" His usual question to her.

"Yep." Helena must always control the terrible urge she has to rip that towel from Nicolaus' waist and get busy.

She follows him back into the bathroom as he looks over his face and chin, then goes into his shaving routine. She has finally discovered why Nicolaus smells of sugar cookies. It is the crème broulee scented body wash and aftershave he has been using for years.

Helena stands right next to Nicolaus, observing him shave, she watches how he is careful not to scratch his light caramel skin shaded face. She eyeballs his bicep muscle as it flexes each time he lifts his hand to his face, and she observes how his back muscle flexes.

Sometimes she flirts with him, grabbing onto his shoulders and kissing his tricep muscle, making him flinch with a slight chuckle.

"Your day full again?" She asks him.

"Yeah. I've been sneaking away to play with Elaine and Emily, though." He briefly looks at Helena in the bathroom mirror, not noticing her yearning for him. "Those little ones are so cute. Emily usually conks out."

"My goodness! Very sweet of you. Elsa know?"

He shakes his head. "I haven't told her. I'm just doing it. I can't believe Niall has just walked away from them. You know, he's never understood how lucky he is to have Elsa. He's never understood what a treasure she is. And now he has kids with her, and he's just walked away. Really, I don't get it."

"Right? How is he doing at the office, anyway?"

Nicolaus stops what he's doing and turns to look at Helena. He gives her a slight frown, considering her question as he wipes the shaving cream from his face, turns to face the mirror again, and quickly applies aftershave moisture. "He's getting along well enough. Not sure it's a great idea to force him in, but ... overall, he's performing well so far." He quickly applies a moisturizing facial cream as well.

Helena nods in agreement. "I'm where you are about Elsa though. He's been stupid about his relationship with her from the beginning, if you ask me."

Nicolaus grabs Helena playfully, and hugs her briefly. Her brain goes frantic at the feel of his bare muscular chest against her. She stays calm as he returns to his grooming routine, now doing his hair, only putting hair lotion and using his fingers, as the soft curls have already air dried.

Nicolaus gets dressed quickly using the dressing screen next to the valet stand. He doesn't bother about whether he likes the suit that was brought to him, as after all, he is the one who bought all his suits. He puts on all the clothes laid out for him. Helena always thought it was very interesting to see this side of the rich life.

Later that night, they are having a late night dinner at a local Italian restaurant, as a few of the last patrons.

Nicolaus chuckles as they finish their meal, "I'll need to eat out more often to avoid getting poisoned again," he mutters.

Helena frowns at him, "Poisoned? What do you mean?"

Nicolaus shakes his head. "Never mind, it's just an inside joke. Helena, I value your opinion, and I would like to know what you think of this idea. I want to start a foundation to help people, but especially people of color, like us, who own farms and small businesses, like yours. You know, help them with capital injection and probably mentoring. I'm still working out the details. I'm going to sell a lot or two of the castle grounds, which should provide at least seven million, maybe ten, to secure the funds."

"Nicky, you can get that much for the land? Millions?"

Nicolaus nods, "I'm pretty sure. It is lucrative. I'll be selling the plots at the far end, opposite the creek. I need to go measure and verify the boundaries. You should go with me!" He offers her.

"You're inviting me to the castle?" Helena feels excited about what he is describing. More so that he has just invited her to the famous Kiviste Castle in Tallin, Estonia, which he and Deirdre inherited from their Great Aunt Clara, an Estonian socialite. Helena looks at him amused.

"Of course," he says, thinking nothing of this, certainly not along the lines of where Helena's mind is thinking. "And I figure we can give out about three million of the ten million each year, and the rest goes in investments and financial growth instruments."

"Three ... million? A year? Nicky, that's a lot of money."

"Yeah, well, I figure we can provide ... I don't know, ... maybe between fifty to a hundred thousand, each, depending on the size of the business. And we mentor them to spread this out over several years."

Helena is astonished. "Nicky, that's a lot of businesses you'd be helping. That's like thirty to fifty businesses a year!"

Nicolaus nods, "Yeah," frowning, "hmm ... I've got to figure out the mentoring part. I can't mentor that many people by myself. Hmm, I'll have to get some partners. And ..." he stops talking when he sees how Helena is looking at him. "What? Why are you looking at me like that?"

"Nicky, ... that is such a wonderful idea. How did you come up with this?"

Nicolaus shrugs slightly, "It's not me." He points up. "It's our Heavenly Father. The ideas are from heaven, and I have the resources to make things happen. And this will be Deirdre's legacy. I need to honor her, you know, something with her name on it. I'm not sure about that yet either. I'm thinking something like Deirdre's Door ... or Deirdre's Box ... or Deirdre's Heart."

Helena bursts out crying at his words, with large tears streaming from her eyes.

Nicolaus quickly hands napkins to Helena. "What happened? What did I do? What did I say?"

Helena shakes her head and dabs her face. "Nicky, that is so beautiful, what you want to do. I think Deirdre's legacy is the children's homes, but this is really a beautiful gesture. I think you should go with Deirdre's Heart Foundation."

He nods. "I think it is what she would want me to do. Help people of color get a leg up. And this also pays homage to my ancestors as well ... sponsored by The Ravenells."

"The Ravenell Dynasty," she tells him.

"Oh, I like that! Sponsored by The Ravenell Dynasty."

"Nicolaus, you do so much for so many people. And you manage brilliantly. Never doubt your father, Nicky. Your father knew exactly what he was doing when he put the empire in your hands." Helena feels this moment. It is epic for her. "No wonder I feel the way I do about you." Helena decides now is the time she must be entirely truthful with Nicolaus, and put forth everything in her heart for him on the table.

"Nicky, I cannot go another day ... not another minute, without telling you how I feel about you." She looks into her empty soup bowl to solidify her courage.

Helena had been counting the days and the months since Deirdre's death. It has been nine months now. She looks at him, right in his eyes, as he is sitting right next to her. Nicolaus gives her his full attention, having heard her words. He looks like his handsome and fine self, only with a somewhat sad countenance, absent of the joy he once had.

"Nicky, I love you. I truly love you. And ... I want you. I want to be with you." She grabs his hand, and holds onto it.

Nicolaus rubs his forehead with the fingers of his other hand. He doesn't know what to say, or what to do. This was unexpected. He stays quiet, and lets her speak.

"I can be what you need. You know I can. I'm the one who can give you whatever you need."

Nicolaus sighs.

"I love you, Nicky," she confidently says again.

Nicolaus looks at her hand, as he gently rubs it with his fingers. He slightly shakes his head. "Helena, I ... I ..." he frowns, "I don't know what to say, ... I'm flattered." He shakes his head, "I don't understand how we would even begin to do something like what you're suggesting."

"Just let me be what you need."

"You are what I need. You're my good friend, Helena."

"Nicky, I'm talking about us being more than friends. I love your friendship, and I love you beyond that. I want to take care of you. Nicky, you need someone to take care of you."

He breathes out, momentarily looking away from her, frowning, considering her words.

"Don't you want me the way I want you? Can't you feel it, Nicky?"

"Helena ..."

"Don't you want me to hold you, and touch you, and love you?" She whispers to him, "I want to make love to you, Nicky."

Nicolaus' stress level goes up, and he closes his eyes to her words, and rubs his forehead again. He really doesn't know what to say.

"Helena, you're married," Nicolaus whispers back to her.

"Joel doesn't love me. He hasn't loved me for quite some time. Not even after the second chance you gave us, Nicky."

"Joel isn't going to divorce you. He's never going to let you go, Helena," he tells her, shaking his head.

"I don't care about Joel! I don't care about any of that. I only care about you, Nicolaus. I just want to be with you. For us to be together."

Nicolaus looks at her in thought, knowing such actions would go against his religious beliefs. Would he be able to live with such a decision? He sighs again, as her hold on to his hand tightens. He slightly shakes his head again, "Helena ... I can't ... I'm ... not ready for something like that, ... and anyway, there's a curse on me, ... or something. Every woman I've ever been with is ... passed on. First Marguerite, then Gwen, and now Deirdre. If I hadn't married Deirdre ... she might still be here."

"Curse?" She frowns, "Nicky, what are you talking about?"

"It's true. My family believes there is an ancestral curse on me. If I had known about it, I would have never married Deirdre. She was fine until I touched her, ... until I married her."

Helena could feel his hurt. "Nicky, Deirdre died in childbirth, you cannot blame that on yourself. Gwen was in an accident. You weren't there. Marguerite took her own life; she was ashamed of what she'd done. That's not on you either."

"No, don't you see? I'm the common thread. It's me that's the problem. Marguerite took her life because she was angry with me. Gwen died fleeing from me. Deirdre died in childbirth with my child. The curse is in motion once I am with the woman ... or something of that nature." He shakes his head negatively, "No ... I can't let anything happen to you, Helena," he adamantly says.

Helena sniffs her tears back, feeling rejected, refusing to cry. "I'm not ever going back to Joel. I'm staying right here for you, Nicky, whether or not you will have me. I love you that much."

Helena touches Nicolaus' face. Nicolaus gently kisses her hand for the kindness. Helena cherishes this gentle moment between them.

Nicolaus calls for the check, he pays, leaving a hefty tip, and they exit the restaurant.

Chapter Fifty-Seven

A bigail stares at the photo of Nicolaus on the VMC website on the 'About Us' page, as she did often these days. She is stricken by his handsomeness and the charismatic smile that plays on his lips. She understands why Deirdre was taken with him. She is sure she would be taken by him as well if she were ever in his presence and close to him.

Abigail wonders if she will ever see Nicolaus again, ever see him in her lifetime. She reads the memorial page they placed for Deirdre. The first thing mentioned is that Deirdre was Nicolaus' wife. Several of her accomplishments are listed, including the foster children's homes project.

Reading through the website leads Abigail to conduct online research about Nicolaus. Suddenly, she becomes fascinated with him and wants to know more. She thinks about going out to personally meet him, and then she figures this is a moot point. What good would it do? And she doesn't want to risk being so close to Ceil Ravenell again. She does not want to put her father in danger.

Abigail clicks back to the website and studies Nicolaus' picture, feeling a familiarity about his looks, something she just cannot put her finger on. She sits back in her office chair and she ponders what to do.

Chapter Fifty-Eight

Nicolaus chartered their private jet for the trip to Estonia. He wanted to avoid the possibility of the press and others swarming them and questioning him about Deirdre in the airport. Nigel was more than happy to provide the plane.

Nicolaus decided to make this trip a family affair, having Constance by his side, bringing along Francesca, and Elsa with her little ones, Helena, and he even invited Roddy and his wife.

On the plane, Constance holds onto Nicolaus' hand, as she sits next to him, and across from Roddy and his wife.

Nicolaus chuckles to Roddy, "Finally! We get to have some down time. I told you one day I was going to take you on vacation. Maybe we can fish while we are there."

Roddy laughs and nods, "Right!"

Helena sits next to Francesca, across from Elsa and the girls. They assist Elsa when needed, to keep the babies entertained. However, Helena has a difficult time keeping her eyes off Nicolaus, watching him on the other side of the plane.

"Oh, oh!" Francesca observes. "You got it bad for my brother, don't you?"

Helena chuckles. "It's weird to hear you call Nicky your brother."

"Oh, I love to say it. He's my brother. My brother. My brother," she slightly sings, making Elsa giggle. "And ... I noticed you didn't answer my question. Did you go all in for him already?" She whispers with that thick British accent of hers.

Helena nods. "I did."

"Well?" Francesca asks, annoyed that she has to pull the information out of Helena.

"He said 'no,'" she whispers, disappointedly. "That he's not ready and something about a curse."

"Yeah! I'm relieved he told you 'no', cuz yes, there is a curse. And we don't want you to be next, Helena. You got all them kids to take care of."

"Oh, I don't believe in curses, or stuff like that. I believe all the instances Nicky recounted to me is just coincidence. Nicky needs to be loved. He needs someone to take care of him."

Francesca lets out a shriek laugh. "Oh God! Girl! I told ya, Nicky is the one who is always taking care of everybody. Really Helena, he doesn't need looking after."

Helena disagrees. "Just look at him! He needs love."

Francesca gawks at Nicolaus making a playful face at him, drawing his attention to them. "Are we looking at the same person?" She asks Helena.

"What are you two doing over there?" Nicolaus asks them.

The ladies laugh and tell him nothing. Helena mischievously bumps Francesca, laughing, "You gonna get us in trouble!"

When the jet lands at the Estonian airport, the castle limousine is waiting for them. Once they get to the castle, they are greeted by the staff, as usual. Painfully, Nicolaus tells them about Deirdre.

"I just want to let all of you know ... well ... you may have already heard ... we lost Deirdre. She passed over nine months ago now, ... during childbirth." Francesca quickly hugs onto Nicolaus to support him, as the staff gasp, some nod, and some touch their face at the news. "She loved being here, and she really appreciated each of you." The staff gather around Nicolaus to give their condolences.

Helena is the only one among them who had never been to this famous Kiviste family castle. And she had never been to Estonia. She was in awe from the moment she stepped out of the airport. Upon turning to the road that leads to the castle, she felt as though she was in a fairy tale, she almost couldn't believe it. She felt as though she was dreaming. The rounded walls of the castle, and the multiple storied height looks like something out of a romantic novel or a fiction movie.

Walking into the stoned brick arched breezeway took her breath away in astonished delight. And now that she is inside, she felt mesmerized at the beauty of the place. The double grand staircase is similar to the staircase at the Ravenell mansion. She started to twirl in the enormous space, getting lost in the moment, when Constance stops her, grabbing her arm.

"It's okay, dear," Constance tells her, escorting her to Nicolaus. "This place can be overwhelming," she says with light laughter at Helena's behavior.

Constance gives her to Nicolaus, and Nicolaus quickly hugs her. "You all right?" He asks her.

Helena is amused. "This place! It's amazing!" Her eyes are big. She can't believe she is standing in a grand castle.

Nicolaus nods, and beckons for Butler Brown. "Mr. Brown, this is Helena, our close family friend. Will you show her around the castle and give her a brief history, please?"

Butler Brown nods to Nicolaus. "Most certainly, Sir."

Nicolaus promptly kisses Helena's forehead, her hand automatically going to his chest as he does so. "You'll be in good hands with Mr. Brown." Then he leaves Helena with him. Helena's eyes follow Nicolaus as he gracefully walks across the room, with a masculine strut, to attend to other things, and talk to other staff.

Butler Brown waves his hand before Helena's face to get her attention, seeing that her mind is preoccupied with Nicolaus. "Madame, right this way." He ushers her out of the room to begin the tour.

The real estate agent arrives, and Nicolaus, Roddy, and the stable manager, who knows the land like the back of his hand, ride out on horses to the lot site Nicolaus wants to sell. Nicolaus wants to get measurements and set boundary lines for the legal description.

Constance and Roddy's wife assist Elsa with the babies. Francesca talks with the staff about Nicohls and DeeDee while Nicolaus is away. "Who was the third wife? Why was her name obliterated from the family book? What happened to her?" Francesca is full of questions.

"Mistress Francesca, Butler Brown is your best source. I only know that Mr. Nicohls was indeed married four times. DeeDee or as we call her, Mari, is the fourth wife, and they had several children."

"Children?" Francesca says loudly. "This is the first time I'm hearing about children!"

"Yes ma'am, they had several little ones running all over this castle and the grounds. Nicohls was sickly as he aged, but he lived a long life, died when he was in his eighties."

"How did he meet DeeDee?"

"Hmm! That I don't know. Perhaps Butler Brown will know, ma'am. From my understanding, she was a harsh task master. She kept the house staff and her children very busy. I'm sorry ma'am, that is really all I know."

"Okay, thank you. That is good information. Thank you." The house staff nods and leaves her.

Francesca looks up to see Butler Brown standing with Helena by the family portraits wall. She sees that Helena has a look of surprise on her face as she is taking all this in, much like all of them did when they first arrived years ago.

Helena is amazed at how each family member in each portrait resemble each other. And when Helena gets to the portrait of Nicohls and DeeDee, her mind cannot comprehend what she is seeing. She cannot understand how what she is looking at is even possible.

Francesca snatches Butler Brown, encircling her arm through his, not caring if he is done speaking with Helena. "Mr. Brown, remember when I called you and every time I asked you about Nicohls, the phone went weird?"

Brown frowns. "Hmm, not exactly, Mistress Francesca. I remember we got disconnected, and when I tried calling you back, I couldn't get through."

"No, I remember that on my end, I was getting like high pitch noises and feedback. And you couldn't even hear me."

"Really?"

"Yeah, so I need to get some information from you. What do you know about that family curse?"

"Family curse?" He thought for a moment. "You mean the curse that was placed on Nicohls' ancestors because of an infidelity?"

"Yes, yes, that one!"

Brown clears his throat, and they continue to walk. "Well, Mistress Francesca, that curse brings misfortune to first born sons, that is ... until the curse is broken."

Francesca stops the butler. "Brown," she whispers, "is that what happened with Deirdre? The third wife. Deirdre was Nicky's third wife. The family book has the third wife obliterated. What happened?"

"Well," he turns and continues their walking, now up the castle stairs. "The third wife was not considered the true wife. I don't know why it was ... obliterated ... as you say ... why that was. The story goes that Nicohls fell in love with a woman that he had not seen since his childhood after the death of the second wife. He married her, and then somehow she disappeared."

Francesca pauses their walk at the top of the stairs. "Disappeared? How do you mean?"

"Well Mistress Francesca, the circumstances of the disappearance are not known."

"Wait a minute! Was he in love with her? I mean, was there foul play or something?"

Butler Brown shakes his head. "I do not think there were suspicions. From my understanding he was in love with her. However, DeeDee, the fourth wife, after years of marriage and bearing children, she did die suspiciously."

Francesca stopped their walking again. "What?" She sounds surprised. "That is not in the family book! And it says nothing about children."

"Well, yes, from my understanding, all the children were girls." Brown continues their walking, "I don't know why those events were not recorded. Perhaps the death wasn't recorded because it was a sad time. Though we are not sure what happened, Mistress Francesca." Brown pauses their steps. "And I do believe it is now Mr. Nicolaus who is the next in line."

"So Nicky is the next male in the Kiviste family line?"

"Yes," Butler Brown confirms.

"Oh my. And the third wife, who is she? What was her name? There is no name in the book."

"Her name was ..."

"There you are!" Helena interrupts them. "Francesca, you left me all alone in this big castle!" She grabs onto Francesca's arm and tugs her to go down the stairs with her. "Come on, lunch is being served."

"Oh, but ..."

"Come on!"

Helena and Francesca fly down the stairs as if they are schoolgirls.

"Brown, we're not done talking," Francesca shouts to him, as she is dragged along by Helena, "and those girls ... I need their names!"

Chapter Fifty-Nine

A s everyone settles into rooms to call it a night, Nicolaus walks the castle. Each room he enters, he remembers he and Deirdre taking inventory of each room together. He remembers her walking down the stairs in her blue coat to hide her beautiful wedding dress the day she gave him their surprise wedding. He remembers carrying her up those steps to the room that was once shared by Nicohls and DeeDee.

Slowly, Nicolaus climbs the dramatic staircase. He had not been upstairs the whole time he'd been here today. He wasn't sure his heart would be able to handle it. He sighs, and slowly climbs the stairs. He walks the hall to that wonderful room that was his and Deirdre's. He opens the door, steps in and closes it. The fireplace has a warm fire roaring. The bed and furnishings are just like they were the last time he and Deirdre were here.

Nicolaus undresses himself, washes his face in the cold water of the shelf basin, and climbs into bed. He is exhausted from the day. His mind is completely on Deirdre. He says prayers in the Latin language, then turns to observe the empty side of the bed. Tears seep from his eyes. His heart pines for Deirdre. His body aches for her. Loneliness closes over Nicolaus as he sadly drifts to sleep.

Chapter Sixty

The following day is Sunday, and Nicolaus leads the family into the Saint Nicholas Church for morning services.

At the door, Bishop Moratey greets everyone as they enter. He is happy to see Nicolaus and the Ravenell family members.

Bishop Moratey gives Nicolaus a tight hug. "You are looking well, my friend. Looking blessed. How are you, Nicolaus?"

Nicolaus nods slightly. "Holding it together." Nicolaus introduces Helena. "This is Helena Gaulkven, our family friend. This is the lady who inspired Deirdre ... and me," Nicolaus says smiling at her.

Helena feels tingly at his words. Even at a time like this, she has a strong urge to kiss Nicolaus, though she does not act on this urge as he greets the bishop. Additionally, Helena is again in awe for being at this historic church, the church where Nicolaus and Deirdre wed. Nicolaus leads her in, holding the small of her back, and the family follows them.

After services, Nicolaus speaks with Bishop Moratey alone, in the back private room. "Please." Bishop Moratey has an opened hand towards a chair opposite a large oak grained desk.

"Thank you for taking the time to see me, Bishop Moratey."

"Well of course! I always have time for one of the most important families in Tallin. Always! Tea?"

"Sure."

The bishop quickly pours tea for both of them, from a silver tea pot.

Nicolaus sips the cold, bitter tea. He looks at the bishop, remembering the last time he had such tea was at his home church. He sips the bitter tea, as it is a reminder to all who sip it, of the blessings they have in life. Nicolaus smiles slightly. "It was difficult walking through those doors this morning. My mind is flooded with memories of my Deirdre … in her beautiful wedding dress. She was so happy that day."

Bishop Moratey nods. "As were you. Such a wonderful day should never be forgotten."

"I need your counsel … on something that is a little … strange."

"I'm sure I've heard it all. What is it?"

"My father tells me there is a curse on me, placed on all first born sons of our ancestral line. Is that possible?"

Bishop Moratey sits forward with interest. "Well … anything is possible, Nicolaus. Curses are something that has to be believed in to be real. Do you feel that something is upon you?"

Nicolaus shakes his head. "No. Supposedly, it affects those who I … I'm intimate with. All of my wives, including Deirdre have died."

"Whether a curse or not, we must fight against that which is wrong with good, by the hand of God. A curse is ungodly, so it can only be broken with the help of God."

"If I had known about this, I would have never wed Deirdre, I would have never touched her. No one warned me. Only now, that it's too late." Nicolaus still had a hard time accepting any of this. He could not reconcile in his mind how a powerful, almighty God could let him live through an almost impossible tragic injury, yet take the very being who pulled him to survival and helped him be who he was. "I feel so lost without Deirdre."

"Nicolaus, sometimes what we think is a horrid problem, or a terrible act, is God opening a door to something else that may be more spectacular. We cannot read God, but we must trust in God. Yes, Deirdre's death is horribly sad, but it may lead to something greater."

Nicolaus absently nods. "How do I get rid of this curse? What do I do?"

Bishop looks to the ceiling in thought. His mind is searching for an answer. After about a minute he says, "I don't have an answer for that, Nicolaus. I don't know. What I do know is that you must remain close to God. Keep God in your heart."

"I do have God in my heart."

"Remain prayerful."

"I am! I am not letting go of God."

"God will lead you to what needs to be done. I don't have a direct answer for this sort of thing, I doubt anyone would. I say to you, put the thought of it out of your head."

Nicolaus feels as though he wants to cry. "I'm so lost without Deirdre," he repeats.

"Son, you are not lost. You are right here. God still has a hand on you. I have seen the work you have done recently for children. I'm quite sure you are doing good works that I don't even know about. You must stay on the righteous path."

"Yes, Bishop." Nicolaus is not sure this conversation is helpful. He finishes his bitter tea, and bids goodbye to the bishop.

Chapter Sixty-One

O
n the jet ride home, Helena was sure to sit next to Nicolaus. She wanted to remain close to him. Everyone pretended not to notice her blatant want for him.

Once home, Helena waited for Nicolaus to return from doing some errands. She is more determined than ever to have him, and she has decided to make it known again that she wants him.

Helena finds Nicolaus sitting at the office section of his large bedroom, studying some papers. Immediately, she goes to him. She hugs him about his broad shoulders, and puts her face against his.

"You enjoy the trip?"

She kisses his face and puts hers against his again. "It was fascinating. Thank you for inviting me along."

He nods, returning his attention to his papers.

Helena rubs his shoulders, his back, then his shoulders again. She hugs him again. "Why don't you come to my bed?"

Nicolaus chuckles slightly. "Helena ... no. I'll see you in the morning."

"Nicky, come on."

"Helena, I said no! That's not a good idea."

"We don't have to do anything. I just want you to hold me."

"Helena ..."

"We are two lonely people, in this big ole house. Why should we both be alone? We don't have to be alone. Just hold me."

"Helena, I can't. You know this! Respect me. Listen to me say no. Stop pushing!"

"Nicky, I do respect you. You know I love you. And I know you love me in some kind of way. I know you do, or you wouldn't do the things you do for me. So please, I'm just asking you to hold me. I want to be next to you."

Nicolaus sighs. "We know what will happen. We know what that will lead to. It's too risky, Helena."

"Nicky, I promise, nothing is going to happen!"

"Is that a promise you can keep, Helena? A romp with me is not worth your life, Helena. You're so much more important."

"Nicky, I don't care about that darn curse!"

Nicolaus looks at her with a frown. "This is your life I'm talking about here! Doesn't what I'm saying mean anything to you?"

"I just want to be close to you. Be next to you."

Nicolaus sighs, "Helena, I said no. Please, let's not talk about this anymore."

Helena hugs on him again. She kisses his face. "Just let me hold you."

Nicolaus sighs again, unable to get her off the subject. "I'll tell you what, I'll think about it."

Helena gives up. "All right." She kisses his face again, "Well, at least you'll think about it." She leaves him, knowing he will not be joining her later.

However, in the morning, Helena is present in his bathroom, as usual. Nicolaus tries to catch the towel that falls loose from his waist as he has finished shaving. He turns, trying to catch the towel, only to realize it has not fallen. Helena swiped it from him and threw it to the other side of the room. In an instant, she is upon him in a sexual manner.

Simultaneously, Nicolaus is in shock and aroused at the feel of her on him. In anger, he lifts Helena, shaking her by the shoulders, his face close to hers. "What are you doing? What ... are ... you ... doing?"

Helena feels herself being lifted off her feet, and she is on the bed before she knows what has happened.

Nicolaus is next to her, partially on top of her. "Is this what you want?" He asks her in an angry tone with a deep frown, "Is this what you want?"

"Yes!" She begs him, hopeful of getting what she wants, "Yes, please!"

Nicolaus lays his face on her shoulder, and takes hard breaths to calm himself. He turns away from Helena, throws on his robe, and leaves the room.

Helena reaches after him; he is gone. "Uh!" She hits the bed, slamming the mattress with her open palm in frustration.

Chapter Sixty-Two

L ater that evening, "Nicky," Helena calls softly, feeling very timid, afraid Nicolaus will never want to see her again. She finds him sitting at his desk, in his bedroom. She finds him in a very solemn mood. Helena kneels to the side of him, taking his left arm. "Nicky, you hate me, don't you?"

Nicolaus looks at Helena. He shakes his head, briefly closing his eyes to her words. "I could never hate you, Helena."

Immediately his words give her hope. She tampers down her excitement. "You're mad at me?"

Nicolaus shakes his head again. "I can't be mad at you."

Helena couldn't suppress the smirky smile that played across her lips. She grabs tighter to his arm, and now to his hand, noticing the marriage band to Deirdre still upon his finger. Helena places her head to the side of his. "Oh Nicky."

"I'm upset about what you did, ... but ... I can't be mad at you. You're just trying to show me love," he says softly.

"Yes, that's right. I just love you so much, Nicky. I want you to know how much I love you. I want to take care of you."

"I don't deserve that kind of love from you, Helena."

"What? Nicky, you have done so much for me ... and ... and you have done so much for the children. You're endeared to me. I don't know if you realize this, but ... I've loved you for a while now."

She presses her face against his again. She is elated with joy when he doesn't resist her. She makes up her mind to go for it. "Please," she whispers to him, moving close to his lips, "don't tell me 'no.'" Gently, she kisses the side of his mouth. "Please, don't tell me 'no.'" She moves for a lip kiss. She kisses his lips. "Don't tell me 'no,'" she whispers to him. "Let me hold you. Let me love you. You need someone to love you, Nicky," she says tenderly, "let me be the one to love you." She kisses him again, and this time he responds.

They kiss deeply, Nicolaus giving in to her. Quickly, Helena sits herself on his lap facing him, continuing the kiss. She is again thrilled when he doesn't resist her. The action of sitting on his lap reawakens Nicolaus' sexual desire. She feels his hands on both sides of her waist. Helena parts the kiss, looks at him, as he is looking at her. She looks in his eyes, then dives for his lips again.

Helena feels passion move through Nicolaus. He stands with her in his arms, her feet off the ground, legs wrapped around his waist, their lips sealed in kissing.

Helena concentrates all her might on Nicolaus, her heart is pounding a hundred beats a minute, as she gets extremely hot for this man, wanting him. She finds a way to think silent prayers for the action she has wished for so long to happen, as her mind is a frenzy with desire for Nicolaus.

She feels him maneuvering them around the room. She hears the door being shut. Helena is overexcited, realizing her fantasy of being with Nicolaus Ravenell is about to happen. She is bumped against a wall, and she hears things fall to the floor, glass breaking.

Helena feels their circling, and she hears other things being knocked to the floor and breaking, as she is now laying on a hard surface.

Helena concentrates on Nicolaus, not caring where they are, her lips not leaving his. She pulls at his clothes, opening his shirt. He takes it off, their lips keeping each other entertained. She rubs his strong, muscular chest, and his back. She feels him undressing her, and she helps him. Soon they are both fully undressed. She is lifted and feels the cold wall against her back. She takes to kissing his neck and chest, then he does the same for her. They are both moaning loudly at each other's actions.

Nicolaus continues to go with the flow with Helena. He doesn't know what else to do for her, except give her what she wants ... himself! His mind is torn between the sin he knows he is committing, and racing thoughts about what she wants and how all this is going to work. However, his body is harshly aroused from her actions on him this morning.

Helena's soft chest against Nicolaus makes him moan. He can see that she is more than ready for him, and immediately, he enters her with another moan and rapid movement. Helena is also moaning and shrieking, taking him fully, as they are still standing. Passionate sounds escape them, as their hot entanglement is deep, and intense.

Nicolaus finally places Helena onto the bed. Their fiery episode lasts for quite some time, and the song of their loud and scorching sex is emitted under the bedroom door, loud enough to concern the house staff.

Brice and Mary are listening outside the door, to make sure the couple is not fighting or needing assistance.

"I'm going to call Ms. Francesca! She'll know what to do," Mary says, hand over mouth in fright and shock, as she'd never heard such commotion from Nicolaus before. She runs from the area to the downstairs phone.

"Wait! Don't!" Brice tries to stop her, though it's too late, she is way gone. He scurries down the stairs to find Manfred and returns with him shortly.

They both listen outside the door, and it seems quiet, except for deep breathing. Manfred cracks the door open, and does indeed see that things are smashed on the floor, and he also sees Nicolaus in bed with Helena. He gently closes the door.

Manfred looks at Brice with a chuckle, "Um, yeah, I think I'd call what you were hearing, passion." He waives his hand, "They are just fine." He takes Brice around the shoulders to escort him away, "Let's go. Let's leave them to their privacy." The men scurry down the stairs.

Helena is overjoyed and thrilled that her fantasy is happening. She had never had such good sex before. She did not let up on Nicolaus. She got about working on him as no one ever had before. Nicolaus moans loudly, making Helena smile, getting what she wanted from him.

She frowns, "Nicky, no one has ever done this for you?"

He chuckles slightly, "Well, I've never had any one quite like you, honey." He moans as she continues to work him.

She gasps lightly at his comment, "Nicky, I hope you mean that in a good way."

"I do, of course," moaning.

"Nicky, you are too handsome of a man, too important of a man for no one to have ever done this for you."

"Huhm?" His mind cannot comprehend what she is telling him while her passion is crushing him.

Helena sits on him, facing him, making him moan uncontrollably. Their love making is quite intense. His size fills her deeply and completely. Helena groans with pleasure, as she quite enjoys herself on him, happily living out her fantasy of him.

After their many sessions of hot lovemaking, Helena couldn't sleep. She is too busy observing Nicolaus, as he breathes evenly, being knocked out by Helena's passion. She lays on his chest and listens to his heartbeat. She wants to memorize his rhythm. She runs her hands over his muscles and touches him anywhere she wants, as she happily realizes she could touch him anywhere now.

Her touching on him and her movements, stirs Nicolaus from sleep.

"I'm so lucky to have you," Helena tells him. "Nicky, I lo .... His kiss of her delectable lips, stops her words. The strength of his kiss is returned to him in the same measure.

"I don't know about lucky," he says softly. "Not as we have seen. No one who's been with me has been lucky. I'm really worried about that for you, Helena."

"Nicky, we had a wonderful time! I'll be fine."

"We can pretend that you'll be fine, but we know we can't take that literally. I appreciate you, Helena. I thank you for standing by me."

"Appreciate? Is that all I get?"

"I'm not going down that road." He repositions her, as she is still atop his chest.

"Nicky, how am I to know how you really feel about me?"

"I'm here with you! I gave in to you, and have given you what you wanted, didn't I?"

"Well ...yes."

"Then that will have to be enough, Helena. I'm terrified to go any farther, ... for your sake."

Helena nods. She scoots herself to kiss his lips again, grateful to finally have Nicolas Ravenell. After all, she does finally have him and he is all hers, as he is alluding to. She thinks of this situation as taking care of Nicolaus for Deirdre. Helena smiles at Nicolaus. She kisses him again, and he responds, encircling her in his arms.

Helena has never been happier with any man. "You're such a handsome ... beautiful man, Nicky. I can't get enough of you!"

"You're my naughty woman," he tells her in a teasing whisper.

"I am your naughty woman," she proclaims to him proudly in a sexy voice. "I'll be whatever you want me to be."

Without hesitating, she takes him again. They make rambunctious and passionate love. Nicolaus finds his experience with Helena very different than his previous encounters. Helena is a strong, tough woman. She does not give him one ounce of mercy in their sexual engagement. She is proficient at everything she does, including love making, especially with Nicolaus Ravenell.

Chapter Sixty-Three

The next Sunday after church, Francesca hands out cards to the family. "Meet me here in about thirty minutes. I have a reveal for everyone," she tells them. They look at her puzzled, not knowing what she is speaking of.

"When are you coming home?" Elsa has cornered Niall. He has been attending Sunday services sparingly.

Niall looks past her and sees Nicolaus. He notices that Nicolaus is carrying a baby girl, who is sleeping on his shoulder. And he sees that Ceil has Elaine. He sighs.

Elsa looks to the scene he is observing. She nods as she returns her attention to him. "Nicky has stepped in for you. In case you had not noticed, that is Emily who Nicky is holding, your second daughter, who you've never even met or held," she chides him, knowing it will do no good.

"Let him do it. He seems comfortable."

Elsa is shocked at his words. She scoffs, "That is not Nicky's responsibility. It's your responsibility, Niall."

Not wanting to hear any more of this, "Look, I have to go," he tells her. "I'll see you later." Niall departs the opposite way of his family to avoid any contact with his daughters.

Nicolaus notices that Niall is walking away from Elsa, and Elsa has her hands on her hips. Supporting little Emily, he goes to Elsa, and briefly hugs her to him with his other arm. "Elsa, ... come on," he coaxes her to join the rest of the family.

The Ravenells arrive to the address Francesca provided. They did not know what was about to happen. As they gathered on the front porch, Ceil rings the doorbell. Francesca appears in the open door, "Welcome! Welcome to my new home. Come on in!" She is excited to show off her newly built, sprawling two story townhouse. "I got BBQ grilling in the back, and drinks and goodies for everyone," she tells them with her thick British accent.

Nigel is the first to react. "This is beautiful!" The twelve foot walls have three foot windows up to the ceiling height all around on the first floor to let in sunbeams everywhere. The sun made the gold dust wall paint light up with golden sparkles. The home is fully furnished.

"Francesca, when did you do all this?" Nicolaus asks in surprise.

Francesca giggles. "I did it on a whim. I sold my other house and bought this one, got some new furnishings, and wha-la! I needed a good, positive change, you know."

"I agree with father, this is beautiful," Nicolaus tells her, being relieved of Emily by Helena.

"Well done, Francesca!" Ceil compliments her, a rarity. Ceil notices how Helena is looking at Nicolaus and knows that something has changed in their relationship, though they are trying to hide it. Coldly, she turns her back on Helena.

Francesca pulls the two away from everyone. "I got a call last Monday night from the staff. They were ... frantic, I guess you can say. Heard lots of noises and screaming from your room Nicky, and things being broken."

"What? Oh my God!" Helena is embarrassed.

Nicolaus chuckles, "Geez! What did you tell them?"

"Well ... at first, I didn't understand what the hell Mary was talking about. But then when she told me she heard a woman ...," Francesca claps her hands two times with a laugh, "I was like, ... oh! I told Mary not to do anything unless one of you came out of that room calling for help!" She bursts out in laughter.

Nicolaus chuckles more and nods, "We did leave a little bit of a mess," he confirms.

"I haven't heard anything else about it, so I have to assume all is well. And here you two are ... looking like two naughty canaries," she jokes with them.

Helena touches her chest, blushing with embarrassment. Helena is glad that she and Nicolaus have a better grip on their lovemaking. However, she doesn't make any comments one way or the other.

Elaine enjoys the grassy backyard, and runs over to Nicolaus, arms in the air for him to lift her. He swoops Elaine into his arms, and she cackles with the delight of being lifted so fast and so high off the ground. All the adults laugh with her. Elsa drifts over to them.

They walk over to the grill, and Francesca turns the meat. "Lunch is almost ready!" Francesca yells out to everyone. In a moment of slipped memory, Francesca takes out a cigarette, lights it, and takes a drag, holding it between her two fingers. Immediately, that cigarette leaves her hand.

Nicolaus is frowning at her, having taken the cigarette from her, he puts it out in a nearby ashtray. "Francesca, what the hell? Are you smoking?"

Francesca looks at the ladies with a big grin. "Oh Lordy, here comes my daddy," she tells them.

"Francesca, you're not going to be smoking," he tells her in a bossy tone.

The ladies look at each other and loudly crack up with laughter, remembering Francesca's imitation of Nicolaus over this subject. He is doing exactly as Francesca told them he would do. His words and his stance making Helena have to hold her stomach, she is laughing so hard.

"What's so funny?" He asks them. "I'm serious."

His words make the ladies laugh even harder.

Nicolaus frowns. "Francesca, where are the rest of these? You're not smoking."

Elaine throws herself to her mommy.

Helena touches Nicolaus on his chest, she frowns at him. "Nicky, this is Francesca's house. She's a grown woman. You can't just come in here and tell her what to do."

"Watch me. She's my sister. And she's not smoking. Our mother died of cancer. We both have a fifty-fifty chance of having the same fate. We don't need to rush it or usher it in," he lectures Helena and Francesca.

Francesca puts her arms around her brother's neck, and gets on her tippy toes to kiss his face. "He's right. He's usually right," she tells the ladies.

"Okay," he removes her arms from around him. "So bring me the rest and I'll get rid of them for you."

"Nicky," Helena is surprised at his forthright demeanor.

Francesca laughs at Helena's surprise. "Uh oh! You are learning something new about our Nicky today, now aren't ya?" She tells her. "After lunch Nicky darling, we'll destroy them together!"

Ceil watches from across the yard as Helena clings to Nicolaus. She feels her anger tick up.

Francesca serves lunch picnic style on the long table outside. The family enjoys the meal and is appreciative of Francesca. After about an hour, everyone leaves, however Nicolaus and Helena stick around to help with the cleanup.

Helena is in the kitchen doing the dishes, while Nicolaus assists Francesca outside to clean the grill and the picnic table.

Francesca enters to bring additional dishes. She bumps Helena. "So ... how are things going between you and Nicky? Is it everything you wanted?"

Helena sighs. "Actually, Francesca, it's not exactly as I thought it would be. Initially, I thought it would be the same as what I saw with Deirdre." Helena feels silly for thinking her relationship with Nicolaus would look and feel the same as what he had with Deirdre. She now realizes this would be impossible. Their relationship is difficult at best and strained at worst.

Francesca touches her, seeing she is frowning, not wanting her to cry. "Helena, I'm sure Nicky is not easy to be with in the first place. He's a type A personality, a military commander. And ... you have to remember that Deirdre was with us since she was a child, and they'd been together all that time. So, Deirdre knew everything about Nicolaus, and she supported him while he was on missions, just as he supported her while she was in law school. And here, you are just learning him." She side hugs Helena. "Anyways, I warned you that Nicky doesn't need looking after. He's the one taking care of everyone else."

Helena nods, "Yeah, I know. It's just that he's ... really distant most of the time we're together. His mind is still on Deirdre. He calls for her in his sleep."

"Wow, he hasn't gotten over her. Helena, he may never get over the loss of Deirdre. I mean, technically, they were together for fourteen years. He proposed to her when she was fifteen, and he waited for her. To finally have her, and then ... to so tragically have her taken away." Francesca sighs, "And I notice he's doing a lot right now, so his mind may be on other things as well."

Helena nods. "I know," she says humbly.

"Look, I will say that Nicky has always supported you, Helena. You've got to give him a little bit of a break. I mean, he's taking a significant risk being with you. He could lose a lot. And it means something big if my brother is taking such a risk for someone." She side hugs her again before going outside to help finish the cleaning.

Nicolaus looks to his sister. "So, while we were in Estonia, I asked Bishop Moratey about what to do to get rid of this curse," Nicolaus tells her while dismantling and cleaning the grill.

"Now that was a good idea. What wisdom did he drop on you?"

"None. He said he didn't have any answers. That I should just continue to walk with God."

"Nicky, really? Well, that's surprising."

"Yeah. What am I supposed to do? I'm really worried about Helena now. You know, now that we've, uhm ... you know."

Francesca chuckles. "Now that you two are lovers?" She says it for him.

"Right."

"Well, Nicky, from what I know about curses, in my Wicken studies, and for this type of curse particularly, you would have to be there to stop it from occurring at the time it is occurring."

Nicolaus looks at her with a huge frown. He didn't get what she said. "What? That sounds like a complicated riddle! Say it again. I have to do what?"

"Nicky," she stops what she is doing, and stops him as well so he can listen to her. "The way you break this type of curse is that you must stop the tragedy from happening at the time it is happening. In other words, you have to be there at the instant the tragedy occurs and then you must stop it from happening."

Nicolaus looks at her shaking his head. "How am I supposed to do that?" He sounds despondent.

"I don't know, Nicky."

He scoffs. "So ... I'm supposed to be with Helena twenty-four seven? Every moment of her life, from now on?"

"Nicky, I don't know. I only know you must be there, wherever there is, at the time the thing begins to happen."

Nicolaus looks at his sister, feeling devastated. He sits down to think about what she is saying. This sounds like an impossible thing to accomplish.

"Francesca, if I can do this, break this curse, is it broken forever?"

"From my understanding, once it's broken, it's broken forever. Like a seal. When it's broken, it's broken."

Nicolaus nods in understanding, and is almost certain the curse is going to be impossible to break. He stands and gives Francesca a kiss. "I appreciate your wisdom, Francesca. You're more knowledgeable than the bishop," he tells her.

"Nicky, while we're on the subject, I also spoke to Butler Brown about Nicohls' third wife, and ..."

"What did you find out?"

Francesca sighs, "Well ... the third wife was his childhood sweetheart. Only that ... oddly, she disappeared, and no one understands what happened."

Nicolaus frowns, "Disappeared?"

"Yes. And ... also ..."

"Francesca, what is it?"

"Her name. Her name ... was ... Abigail."

"Abigail? That's Deirdre's middle name."

"I know. I remember seeing several mentions of that name in the family book, though. I asked him if it was the same person. Mr. Brown says there were several ancestors with that name. So really, it doesn't prove anything."

Nicolaus looks at Francesca in thought. "Hmm. It probably does mean something. In time, the meaning will be revealed to us."

"And also I just learned that Nicohls and DeeDee had children. Gobs of them, apparently. Because of the curse though, DeeDee died suspiciously as well."

"What?" Nicolaus shakes his head, "that's not good. I've got to break this curse," he says determined, though feeling quite overwhelmed about it.

Nicolaus finished up what he was doing. "So now that we are done out here, let's go get those cigarettes."

Chapter Sixty-Four

The next morning, Ceil watches the awkward exchange between Nicolaus and Helena, from the window of the mansion, as Helena demands a kiss from Nicolaus as they leave for work. Nicolaus is reluctant to display public affections with Helena, due to the circumstances of her still being married, and his stance in the community. Frowning, he gives in to her demand with a quick peck kiss, helps her into her vehicle, and watches her drive away from him.

Nicolaus doesn't remember Helena ever being a needy person. He'd always thought of her as a pillar of strength. He worries that he is the cause of this change about her.

Ceil watches as he thoughtfully worries before getting into his newly acquired vehicle. Nicolaus turns off his phone, as he has several important back to back meetings today and he doesn't want to be disturbed.

Ceil had all the evidence she needed to confirm her suspicions about their relationship. Her anger and frustration grows with this new knowledge. Immediately, Ceil dials the mayor's wife. After a few minutes of small talk, Ceil gets right to her plan. "Well, you know, there is a rumor going around about Helena Gaulkven, and her children's home."

"Helena? Isn't she that lady we had that fundraiser for?"

"Yes, we raised a million dollars for that children's home. So, you can imagine how perturbed I am to hear swirling stories of cocaine and wild sex parties at that home ... with the children present."

"What? Ceil ... are you sure?"

"Imagine what that kind of exposure does to an innocent child's mind."

"What ...," the mayor's wife is infuriated, just as Ceil knew she would be.

She continues, "And I understand that home for abandoned children is right next door to a brothel type business. I don't understand how the city government ... your husband's office, could allow such an organization for children next to a place of ill repute. I don't understand it!"

"Ceil! Someone should look into all this! I mean really!"

"Well ... it's just a rumor ... I guess. But imagine if it weren't a rumor. What if it is true?"

"Ah!" The mayor's wife sounds exasperated. "Ceil, I'm going to make some calls so that we can be certain this is all just a rumor. And anyway, like you say, if it is next to a brothel, that is highly inappropriate. The least we can do is rescue those children out of there!"

"You think?"

"Oh, I'm certain of it! Let me make some calls!"

Ceil knew it wouldn't take much to get this going. Before the hour was up, Ceil called seven high level officials, half of them owed her favors. She told them about the "rumors" of cocaine and wild sex parties at Helena's children's home. All seven vowed to take some kind of action.

Before the end of the day, by four that afternoon, Helena is served a search warrant, and is overwhelmed with inspectors, child welfare workers, social workers, police, sheriff, and county officials. She doesn't understand what is happening. They all seemed to be searching for something, looking at her judgmentally, while talking on their phones and writing notes in their computers, tablets, and on their clipboards.

A lead police officer holds up a small package to her face, his hands covered with gloves. "And what is this?" He asks Helena aggressively.

Helena frowns at him. "It's an individually wrapped condom. There are seven of them in that drawer."

"Ah-ha! And why do you have condoms in this place?"

"What? Condoms? Because I teach my boys to be responsible if they choose to have sex."

"So, you encourage them to have sex?" His tone is accusatory.

"What? No! I said I teach them to be responsible."

He nods. "I've heard more than enough." He looks to everyone who is everywhere looking for something. "Shut her down!" He yells loudly for all to hear, "Shut her down!"

"What?" Helena is stunned.

He returns his attention to her, quickly writing on a clipboard. "We are closing you down, and taking the children."

"What? No! You can't do this!"

"An investigation must occur into allegations of sex and drugs at this facility. A judge will determine if you can reopen." He rips off a carbon copy of what he's written and hands it to her.

"Sex and drugs? That's not true!"

The officer holds the condom to her face again smirking at her in silence, as if she is lying.

"You're twisting things!"

He yells in her face, "No ma'am! We have it on good authority that sexual activities are happening in this place. And if we find it to be true, you can expect to be arrested in due time!"

"Arrested?" Helena is dismayed, she cannot believe what she is hearing. The police corral the staff to stand next to Helena. Her attention is brought to the children who are being dragged out of the house.

One of the young boys yells to her, "Ms. Helena! Make them stop!"

A young girl yells as she resists going, "I don't want to leave!" She tries to dig her feet into the floor, and grabs onto door frames, until her fingers are pried off and she is carted out.

"Get your hands off me!" Another young man yells, as he is being ushered out.

The children are all reaching for her and the staff, and resisting going, however, police officers block Helena and her staff from moving, placing their police sticks before them. The small children are crying as they are carried out. The babies and toddlers have no idea what is happening; however, they cry from all the tension in the air, knowing something is wrong.

"I'm so sorry, I'm so sorry," is all Helena can muster.

The police manhandle the older boys who resist leaving.

A young boy resists going, trying to grab onto anything solid, not to be dragged out. "Ms. Helena! Ms. Helena why you just letting them take us like this?"

"I won't go, I won't go!" Another young lady resists, and is carried out.

Within fifteen minutes all the children are gone. She has no idea where they are even taking her children. In another two minutes, all the inspectors, social workers, child welfare workers, police, and sheriff are gone, abruptly leaving the scene. The door slams shut to an empty house. The trauma is still there, and is very real.

Helena and her staff sit down in shock. Helena is shaking uncontrollably. Her babies are all gone. Her children are all gone. Who will feed them? Who will care for them? Who will keep the night monsters away from them? Who will make them feel safe? Who will read to them and kiss them goodnight? Who will make the boys properly shower and comb their hair? Who will teach the older boys how to shave? Who will make sure they study for their tests and do their homework? What about their schooling? Will she ever see these children again? Might she go to jail?

Despondent, Helena sends her staff home. She dials Nicolaus and only gets his voice mail. She calls him several times with the same result. It is then that she cries hysterically. She feels broken and all alone.

Chapter Sixty-Five

N icolaus rushes over to Helena's children's home. She sounded hysterical and asked him to meet her there.

"I've been trying to call you for hours," she yells at him. She could hardly look at him.

"I'm sorry. I've been in important meetings all day. What's happened?" Suddenly, Nicolaus thinks about the curse, which he'd forgotten about, business at the front of his mind. He panics. "What's happened?" He holds her, and observes her to see that she is physically all right.

"The City came in and closed me down. They took the children," she sounds defeated.

"What?" Nicolaus looks around and suddenly realizes the eerie silence.

"They took them!"

He frowns, "How could they do that?"

"Everyone was here, from all departments, the police, the sheriff, even inspectors. Something about sex and drugs. They took my babies, Nicky, they took them." She cried against him. "I don't even know where they are," she yells at him, not knowing what to do.

Nicolaus feels her pain, and he worries for the children as she does. "My God!" He leads her to a chair for her to sit down, taking her hands. "Okay, ... first we need to find out exactly what is happening. And where they have taken the children." He looks at his watch, it is already seven at night. He sighs, "It's probably too late to get ahold of anyone."

"And we have to go to my mother's. I promised her we'd be there. She's probably already waiting for us."

"Helena, I think we need to postpone that meeting with your mother. I can meet her at another time."

"No!" She shakes her head. "I promised her, and she forgets things, so I don't want to confuse her. We can just go sit with her for a few minutes." She sighs and begins to cry against Nicolaus again. She feels very stressed, and is still shaken by what happened.

"Helena ...," Nicolaus holds her. He sighs and reluctantly follows her lead, though it seems she is falling apart.

Nicolaus lovingly holds onto Helena, as he notices that she seems very nervous and is still shaking from the earlier events, before using her key to enter her mother's home. "Honey, you all right?" he asks, gently.

Helena sighs, wondering why she let the affect he had on her make her insist he meet her mother. "I don't know how she's going to react to you, Nicky, I've got to be honest about that. And please, don't mention anything about what happened today. She just really won't understand." She looks up at Nicolaus with concern, as he nods in understanding. She touches his chest and prays in her heart that her mother doesn't emotionally hurt him. She feels it wouldn't be fair, as Nicolaus has been through enough emotional turmoil.

He smiles at Helena. "You know you can trust me. And don't worry about your mother's reaction to me. It won't be the first time someone has been rude to me. I can handle it."

Helena smiles at him, unlocks the door and they enter the modest middle class home. Helena's mother is elderly, with gray hair. Helena kisses her mother, who is glad to see her.

"Mom, this is Nicky Ravenell, who I told you about."

Her mother smiles at Nicolaus, giving her hand for him to shake. "Oh! I've seen you before. On TV!" she tells him with a smile, as Nicolaus graciously and gently grasps her hand in both of his.

Nicolaus smiles at this little old lady. "It's very nice to meet you, ma'am."

"Am I right? I've seen you on TV?"

Nicolaus smiles, and nods, "It's possible! News reports ..."

"Yes, yes! Well ... come on in," she waives them into the interior of her home.

Helena grabs her melancholy man by the hand, and they follow her mother. She leads them to the large family room, and they each take a seat, Helena and Nicolaus next to each other, across from her mother.

Helena pops up. "I'll get us some lemonade. Mom always has some."

"So ... you are an item with my daughter?" Her mother directly asks.

Nicolaus is surprised at her directness. "Well ... I don't know if I'd call us an item. We're together."

Her mother frowns at him. "Together how ... then, exactly?"

Nicolaus suddenly feels uncomfortable. He shifts his body, and rubs his top lip, thinking. He never thought he would need to explain his relationship to anyone. "Well ...," he is relieved as Helena has quickly returned with small glasses of lemonade for each of them.

"Here we go." She sits next to Nicolaus, close on him, hating to be apart from him, even for a minute, even with all her current disorienting upheaval, or maybe because of it.

"Well ... what, dear?" Helena's mom looks directly to Nicolaus, not letting him avoid answering her question.

Nicolaus chuckles. "We're just together."

"So then, what are your intentions? Just sex? I mean ... you can't really ..."

"Mom!"

"Well ... where is this all going ... your relationship?"

Nicolaus looks at Helena and breathes. He realizes he actually doesn't have an answer to this question. He'd never really thought about this relationship with Helena "going" anywhere.

"Mom, can we just have a nice little visit? I just wanted you to meet Nicky. He means a lot to me!"

"Yes, yes, you get very excited when you talk about Nicky. You light up," her mother tells what maybe shouldn't be said.

"Okay, Mom!"

"No, it's okay. That's sweet," Nicolaus looks upon Helena with a smile. He clears his throat. "Well, to answer your question," he sighs to pause, pulling the words together, as now both ladies are looking at him. "Helena helped me through a very difficult time, and ..."

"I'm just not understanding. What about your wife? What is her name? Dearder? Dee ..."

"Deirdre, Mom. Deirdre."

"Yes, Deirdre. I thought the two of you were the love of the century. You know, like a Romeo and Juliet type of love, to conquer the world, or something."

Nicolaus bit his lip, feeling that stinging emotion about his lost Deirdre. He nods. "Thank you for that. We were ... ah ... yes ... I was married to Deirdre .. uhm, but ... uhm, I lost her. She died during childbirth, and uhm ..."

"Oh! I'm so sorry! I don't remember Helena telling me that."

"It's okay Mom, I did tell you. A while back, I told you. She was my best helper, ever, at the children's home."

"Oh!"

"Sorry Nicky, sometimes my mother doesn't remember things."

Nicolaus nods with a frown and a smile. He nods to her mother. "Thank you." He sighs. "That's what Helena helped me through. It was very difficult for me."

"I can imagine. I'm so sorry."

"And we just became very close. Your daughter is a wonderful woman," he says smiling at Helena. "She has an incredible heart."

"Oh I see, ... I see." She frowns, "But then ... how is this going to work, exactly? I mean ... Joel is never going to divorce you, Helena.

You know this. He said he'd never divorce you. Told both of us on more than one occasion."

"Mom!"

Nicolaus touches Helena on the leg to calm her. "It's okay, hon. Your mom is right to ask these questions. Ma'am, it is ... complicated."

"Uhf! I'll say! Complicated is probably an understatement, don't you think? And Joel can get very ... mean. He's mean! I told Helena so many years ago not to marry that man. I knew he was no good. No good! I tell ya'! No good! Any man that sets his hands against a woman is not worth the dirt he walks on, no matter how rich he is!" Her Mom had her say.

Helena feels more upset and quite embarrassed. Nicolaus sees this and hugs her to him. Nicolaus nods to her mother in agreement. "I agree, and I want you to know I would never do that to any woman. I respect women too much to ever bring harm to them. And we know that our situation is ... not ... proper or ideal, ma'am, we know it. We just want to be together. We sort of need each other."

"Hmm. I guess that is something I'll never understand."

Helena rushes Nicolaus to drink his lemonade, then she rushes them to the end of this little meeting. It did not go exactly as she had hoped, and she did not want to hear anymore of her mother's judgements against her.

Chapter Sixty-Six

Nicolaus is surprised at how fast Helena exited them out of her mother's house, having washed up the glasses, and giving her a kiss and all.

"I think you passed the world record for fleeing a mother!" He tells her in his vehicle on the drive back to the mansion.

Helena looks at him with a frown for the comment. She turns her back to him in the passenger seat. She looks out the window. It is dark out. She puts her hand to her face, resting her arm on the car door. "It's late. I'm really tired, and frankly, I don't want to discuss it, Nicky. Okay?"

"Helena, we need to talk about this."

The streets have light traffic and he lets the fifteen minutes of driving time pass silently. However, once home, as he opens the door for Helena to step out the vehicle, he begins again. "You know, you're mother is not wrong, Helena."

Nicolaus opens the house door for her as well, then assists Helena out of her jacket, to hand it to the waiting house staff.

Helena touches Nicolaus' face, pecks his lips, then says, "Please, I don't want to discuss this anymore. I have enough to worry about."

"Helena...,"

"Ugh!" she says in frustration, walking away from her man.

"Now you're fleeing from me?" He follows right behind her.

They both blow past Ceil, not having noticed that she was stealthily watching them from the staircase balcony. She observes them as they go towards Nicolaus' side of the mansion.

Ceil goes into the sitting room and pulls out her phone. She searches for Helena's landline number at her home and dials it, hoping that Joel will answer.

"Hello. Who is this?" Joel thought it odd he'd be receiving a call on his landline instead of his cell phone, and at this hour.

"This is Ceil Ravenell. I'm sure you remember me, Joel."

"Oh, yes ma'am. Sure I do. Um," he frowns, "what can I do for you?"

"I'm calling about your wife, Helena."

"Is she all right, ma'am?"

"You tell me! I'm sitting here wondering why you let your wife run around doing whatever she wants with my son, Nicolaus. It seems that she's with him twenty four seven, including in his bed. I'm wondering why you are so ... spineless ... shall we say, that you let that woman corrupt my family! Are you such a small man Joel, that you cannot even stand up for your own wife?" She could hear his anger over the receiver. "I mean she is still your wife ... isn't she?"

"Did ... did you say ..." he was sitting and is now standing, fuming with anger for receiving such a call, "she is with Nicolaus?"

Ceil smiles, knowing the type of insanely jealous, abusive man Joel is. She knew her words would get to him. "She is still yours, isn't she?"

"With Nicolaus?" He yells into the phone. Nicolaus has been his enemy, the thorn in his side when it comes to Helena. Even though he is separated from Helena, he would never agree to her being with Nicolaus Ravenell. No matter what he'd done for them in the past. "In his bed?"

"And just what the hell are you going to do about it, Joel?" Ceil yells back at him. "What?" She rudely ends the call with him before he can answer. With a smile, Ceil straightens her hair in the mirror, and leaves the sitting room to wait for the trouble to begin.

Chapter Sixty-Seven

Later that night, the unresolved disagreement brought palpable tension between Nicolaus and Helena.

Helena snuggles against Nicolaus, and he doesn't respond, he only stares at the ceiling, thinking. Helena sighs, "You're pulling away from me, Nicky."

He looks at her, telling her some of his thoughts. "Your mom is right. Where can this relationship go?"

"Oh my God! Nicky, please!"

He sits up, legs to the side of the bed, his back to her. He puts his head in his hands. "What are we even doing?"

Helena puts her arms around his shoulders, very afraid she is about to lose him.

"You are married, and unable to divorce," he reminds her.

"It's not true! I've filed the papers in court, and I am waiting on a date. I am going to get that divorce, Nicky. I promise you; I will divorce Joel."

"Then we should wait," he says discontentedly, not really believing her.

"Wait for what? I love you now. We don't need to wait!" Her annoyance is bubbling up. "Anyway, we've already had sex, so what would we be waiting for?" Helena sighs. This day has been overwhelmingly stressful for her. "We have too much to worry about right now, than to be thinking about this issue!" She sighs, feeling exasperated. "I don't remember you ever being like this Nicolaus. You seem easily swayed. It's like your gusto ... your ambition is missing."

He looks at her with a frown and a squinted eye, "Maybe it is."

"You're not the same since we lost Deirdre. Her loss has changed you," she complains. "We're together but we're not really happy."

Nicolaus nods to acknowledge her words. "Yes, Deirdre was my joy and now it's gone. I don't think I'll ever get it back," he says candidly. "This feeling," the emotions are present in his voice, "never goes away, I don't think it ever will. Helena, if we are going to be together, you'll have to come to terms with it. I don't know what else to tell you."

"You even call for Deirdre in your sleep, like you are talking to her, or something. I know you miss her greatly. Do you dream about her?"

"Sometimes." He turns and pulls Helena into his arms, wanting their spat to end. "Look, we will work on the children first thing in the morning. I'm with you on this. Okay? You don't even need to question my commitment to you. You should know this, Helena." Suddenly he wonders if what happened with the children today is the curse in action. After all, this did severely hurt Helena emotionally. "I'm very worried about you, Helena," he voices his thoughts.

They have a soft moment, as he hugs Helena to him, and he does not resist her kiss.

Chapter Sixty-Eight (TW)

The nightingale sings the sweetest song the best she can in the predawn hours. Several nightingales live in the beautiful tree groves at the Ravenell mansion. Only now, their beautiful song is interrupted by a drunken fool, a drunken Joel, who has managed to get himself onto the Ravenell property through the hills and trees close to the house, having avoided the security gate.

Joel stumbles with drunkenness at the front steps of the mansion. "Helena!" He shouts to the top of his lungs, with ridiculous theater. "Helena! I know you're in there!" The screaming scares the birds, and they all take to flight away from the mansion, all at the same time. Angrily and disrespectfully, "Helena! Get your ass out here, right now! I know you're in there!"

At first, Nicolaus thinks he is dreaming, then soon realizes he is not dreaming at all. He sits up to see Helena looking fearful.

"Helena!" Joel calls loud and long. The faraway neighbors can hear. Lights in the distance begin popping on.

Nicolaus' bedroom is on the back of the mansion, so he cannot see Joel, but he can surely hear him. He gets out of bed and throws on a sweat suit.

Nigel and Ceil are also awakened by the commotion on the outside of the mansion.

"What on earth?" Nigel looks at the clock to see it is three in the morning. "Doesn't that man have any decorum?"

"Helena!" Joel continues long and loud. "Get your whoring ass out here! You are my wife and you will do what I say. Now get out here!"

Helena gets out of bed and throws on a night gown and robe. Nicolaus takes her by the arms. "What are you doing? You stay right here."

A knock is heard at the bedroom door. Nicolaus can still hear Joel's ridiculous antics out front. He opens the door to Nigel and Manfred. He nods and the men go down the stairs together.

Helena follows them.

She grabs onto Nicolaus' arm, "Nicky ..."

"Helena! I told you to stay upstairs."

"Nicky, Ceil has done this. I've been thinking about it. She's getting her revenge on me. Who else would do all this? First she had my operations closed down, just like she said she would, and now she must have talked to Joel and told him something to get him angry."

Nicolaus frowns at her, knowing Nigel and Manfred are waiting on him. "Why would she do that? She raised money for the children. You were getting along famously with her ... though I have noticed she's been giving you cold stares lately."

"Oh!" She realizes his knowledge gap.

He balks at her. "Oh? Oh, what? What does that mean?"

"You don't know."

"Helena, ... I don't know what?"

"Nicky ...," she pulls him forward to whisper in his ear, "Ceil and I were lovers, and ..."

He pulls back from her with great surprise. "What? I thought you just said ..."

She nods. "Yes. We were, and she's angry because I'm with you now."

Nicolaus turns from her, then back to her again, making a circle, his mind blown by this new information. "When did this happen? Where was I?"

"You were on your honeymoon."

"Why? Why would you do that? I don't understand!"

"She threatened to pull all the money. I was scared. I didn't want to lose the home. I was scared for the children."

"Helena," he breathes in disbelief, frowning, "you should have told me she was threatening you. You didn't need to put yourself on the line like that. She doesn't control the money. I do!" Nicolaus sighs, this is all too much for him. "You know what,..." his hands up towards Helena, "I don't want to know anymore. And I absolutely don't want that image in my head. Look ...," briefly he hugs Helena, "just go back upstairs and wait for me in my room. Lock the door. I'm very sure Joel is not going to get past me, but lock it anyway. Wait there."

Manfred notifies his partners at the gate of a security breech. "We have him contained at the front. I imagine we'll be needing the police. I know it will take them a while to get here. We're about to confront this joker." Manfred opens the door, and the men step out, closing the front door.

Joel is dressed in his pajamas and a robe. "Where is Helena? I told her to get out here."

"Joel, I'm not releasing Helena to you. And certainly not when you are out here screaming like a maniac. Why don't you go back home?" Nicolaus observes him. "You're drunk out of your mind. We can call you a taxi," he offers.

"You! You done whoring with my wife, Nicolaus? My wife!" Joel yells at him, "She's ... my ... wife!" He says slowly and loudly, emphasizing the words.

"Okay. Go ahead and get off our property before the police get here. Do yourself a favor and just go home, Joel," Nicolaus tells him calmly.

"I'm not leaving here without Helena." He looks around. "Helena!" He calls her again. "Helena!" He steps closer to Nicolaus, just before the steps to the entrance of the mansion.

The front door opens. "Joel, what the hell are you doing? Just go home, I'm not going anywhere with you. You already know this,"

Helena tells him, no longer being afraid with the wall of Ravenell men before her.

Joel looks dejectedly at Helena, then pulls a gun and points it right at Nicolaus.

"Whoa!" Nicolaus puts his hands up, his mind quickly thinking how he can get the revolver away from Joel. Nicolaus yells at Helena, "Helena, get back into the house! Now!" He hears the front door close, then he gets in front of Nigel to shield him. "You going to shoot me, Joel? Is that your plan? Is that what you came here to do? Shoot me?"

Joel has pain on his face, as if undecided what to do, he turns the gun on himself, putting it to the side of his head. Then he gets an angry look on his face, changes his mind and he points the gun at Nicolaus again, right at his chest.

With quick action, Nicolaus grabs the gun from Joel in a fraction of a second, knowing he could be shot. As he does so, Manfred slaps Joel's face to distract his attention. Nicolaus empties the magazine of bullets, then chucks the gun as far as he can to the side of the house. At this same time, Manfred punches Joel, knocking him to the ground. Manfred jumps on Joel, subduing him. Joel is unable to get up or get loose.

Nicolaus turns to Nigel, "Father, you all right?"

Nigel nods with a chuckle. "Great work, you two! As usual, great work!"

One of the security team arrives to assist. With the help of Manfred, duct tape is placed around Joel's hands and feet. Joel is placed in the security vehicle, to wait for the police.

Helena flies outside to stand with the Ravenell men, specifically her man, her Nicolaus.

Nicolaus shakes his head to her, "Helena! Don't you listen? I told you to stay inside."

Helena chuckles at her bossy Nicky. She holds onto him, grateful for having him in her life.

Helena's stubborn actions make Nicolaus fully aware of what he must do to protect her.

Chapter Sixty-Nine

"Nicolaus!" Helena shakes her head negatively at Nicolaus, as he replaces her luggage bag onto the bed from where she removed it.

"Look Helena, I'm not going to force you to pack. You can leave with nothing if that's what you want. That's fine with me."

"Be reasonable, Nicolaus. I cannot just leave. I have to get my home back open, and I'll probably have to go to court. I've got to get the children back! We haven't even made any calls! And I cannot leave my mother!"

Nicolaus sighs, realizing how complicated his relationship with Helena is going to be. "We haven't called anyone because it is five in the morning. We can call them from Colorado. You are not staying here another hour. While Joel is tied up at the police station, I'm getting you out of here. That man came here with a gun and the intent to kill someone. Don't you understand that? You're not safe here, Helena!"

"Just put me in a hotel."

Nicolaus takes Helena by the arms. He looks her in the face, then he holds her to him. "It's not good enough. He can trace you anywhere in the city. I'm getting you out of here where he cannot find you. It's the least I can do to keep you safe. Okay?" He kisses her, then points open handed at the luggage, "You going to pack?"

Helena sits on the bed and begins to cry.

Nicolaus is right beside her. He hugs her, "Don't worry. We'll figure all this out. I promise. I've just got to get you safe first."

Helena followed what Nicolaus wanted. She packs some clothes and personal items, knowing she'd need to buy things when they got to where they were going, of which she had no idea where she was going.

On their way out the door, Ceil is standing next to Nigel. Several staff are present as well, getting things ready for the family, everyone up early now.

"If you wanted to hurt me, Ceil, you succeeded," Helena tells her, tears streaming from her eyes. "If you wanted to get Joel riled up against me, you succeeded." Nicolaus slowly pulls on Helena, making her walk backwards, as he carried her luggage. "If you wanted to close me down, you succeeded. And in the process of your little revenge against me, Ceil, you threw thirty children out on the street. Way to go in keeping with your VMC mission, Ceil. I hope you're happy. I hope you're happy, Ceil!"

Nicolaus finally gets Helena outside and into the limousine. He holds her close to him, as she cries in her upset.

Inside the mansion, Ceil watches the limousine leave the courtyard, then she watches as the staff close the front door. She turns to Nigel and in a moment of desperation, she cries against him. Nigel takes Ceil in his arms and comforts her. Ceil had actually loved Helena. She felt the loss, and was suddenly sorry for what she'd done.

Chapter Seventy

Nicolaus has them on their private jet, so that Joel could not trace them. Though it is early, he is already on the phone making calls, as it is midweek.

"Hey Dan, sorry, I know it's early. Listen, you did a great job finding the hotel for the Darfurian refugees. I need another property." Nicolaus chuckles, "No, not another hotel. This time I need a house. Yeah. I've previously looked at some properties, and I remember one on 6th Avenue. I believe it was a corner house, eight bedrooms."

Helena looks at Nicolaus, wondering what he's up to.

"Yeah, is it still available? Oh good! Yeah, I want that one. Right. Right. Oh good, no bids. See if they move for the asking price, if not just offer them a little over, and tell them I'll close on it today. Yeah, I'm on my way to Denver now. Okay. Just use the same title company, tell them I need it immediately, okay? Great, thanks!"

"Nicky, what are you doing?" Helena asks him, frowning.

Nicolaus doesn't answer her, though he does pull a furniture website up on his computer. "Helena, go through here and pick out some furniture for a large house with earth tone colors."

"What? Why?"

Nicolaus pulls her closer and puts her hands on the keyboard. "For real, pick out furniture. We need ..."

"Nicky, I don't want to do this right now. My life is falling apart."

Nicolaus sighs. "I'm not going to let your life fall apart. You saved me, now I'm saving you. Trust me, Helena."

"Of course I trust you!"

Nicolaus smirks, and nods towards the computer.

While Helena is busy picking out house furniture, Nicolaus phones Manfred. "Manfred, I'm going to need security detail for Helena. Can you hire a team for me?"

"Oh sure!"

"So, please do not tell Ceil that I'm moving Helena to Denver. I'm working on getting a corner house, which will be easier to secure, and I'll work on getting it fenced in."

"Makes perfect sense. Okay, you want a team of two?"

"I'm thinking I need four, two outside and two inside. I don't want to take any chances. One will need to be with Helena wherever she goes, and that will always leave three at all times on the property. And Manfred, I know they'll need to sleep, so maybe we need six instead of four. That way I can have them in shifts."

"You got it boss! I'll hire them local, and have them ready to start on Sunday."

"Okay, that works. I'll send you the property details once I secure the property. Thanks! Hey, can you pass me to Ms. Mary if she's around?"

"Oh sure, let me ring them Nicolaus, and I'll get back to you on this." Manfred transferred the call to the house staff.

Mr. Adams answers, "Hello, this is Adams."

"Mr. Adams! This is Nicolaus, how are you?"

"Oh fine sir. I understand you are out of town?"

"Yes, I had to leave abruptly, sorry I didn't tell you. Listen, is Ms. Mary around?"

Adams looks around for Mary, and sees her across the room. He beckons for her. "Oh yes, Sir, she is here. One moment."

"Hello Mr. Nicolaus, this is Mary."

"Hello Ms. Mary. Listen, I'm setting up house in a different state for Helena, and I'm wondering if you'd like to run the house for us?"

"Me? Mr. Nicolaus, me?"

"Yes! You get along okay with Helena?"

"Oh yes Sir, I think she is very sweet."

"Okay, if you are interested, I'll fly you out, and ... give you a raise of course for being the house manager. You can start on Monday. What do you think?"

Mary is so surprised, and grateful for the opportunity. "Well, yes ... Mr. Nicolaus, I'd love to!"

"Okay, great! Now listen, it's just a few states over, I want this all kept a secret. Don't worry about telling Ceil or my father, I'll take care of that. And I promise to take care of you, don't worry about a thing. Okay?"

"Yes, Mr. Nicolaus! Thank you Mr. Nicolaus!"

Helena looks at Nicolaus with a frown. "I don't understand what's happening," her upset is still present.

Nicolaus kisses her face. "Don't worry about anything. Just keep picking furniture."

Nicolaus then dials the number to his lawyer to see if they can get to the bottom of what happened with Helena that got the children's home closed down.

Chapter Seventy-One

Later that morning, Niall appeared at the house during breakfast time. He'd heard about the commotion, and he showed up to check on his daughters.

Elaine was happy to see her father. Niall almost cried when she hugged him tight with her little toddler arms. Children have the strongest power of forgiveness in the world. He kissed Elaine on her face, when Elaine stopped the hug to look at her father, then she hugged him again. Emily did not know Niall, and refused to leave her nanny's arms when he approached her. Children also have a way of being truth bearers.

Niall went to the breakfast room, where Nigel, Ceil, and Elsa were chatting over a light breakfast. Ceil wasn't much for talking, mostly sipping her coffee.

"Elsa, can I speak with you?"

"Niall! I didn't know you were here!"

He nods. "Our daughters seem happy and healthy."

Elsa nods. "You know what they say, ignorance is bliss. Though they won't be ignorant forever, Niall. Did I tell you Nicolaus has stepped into your role?" Elsa didn't flinch while announcing this to Ceil and Nigel. "Just as well, I'm sure you'll be completely gone soon, once the divorce is final."

"Elsa, please ... let's talk."

Elsa scoffs, she looks at her watch. "Anything you want to say, you can say it in the presence of your parents. And make it quick, Niall, we both need to be at the office."

Niall takes a breath. "Look, I just want to ask your forgiveness. I know I was wrong to have touched Deirdre." Ceil makes a loud coughing sound, and she looks to Niall with a deep frown of disapproval for his words. "I shouldn't be with anyone when you are my wife. It's disrespectful to you, and I'm sorry for it. I'm also sorry for ever hurting you, Elsa. You didn't deserve that."

Elsa looks to Niall with disbelief. "Hmm." Sarcastically, "Are you sorry for killing Deirdre?"

Niall drops to his knees with prayerful hands. "Elsa, I'm serious. Please. I'm asking your forgiveness. I never meant to hurt Deirdre, and ..."

"Niall, raping someone is hurting them."

Ceil looks to Elsa with a frown. "There is absolutely no evidence of what you are accusing my son of, Elsa," she tells her in a voice that sounds like a warning.

Niall ignores his mother and nods to Elsa. "I am sorry for what I did. I hurt Deirdre, and I hurt and disrespected you and my daughters. Please forgive me."

Elsa shakes her head in disbelief. "I know you, Niall. You do nothing without an ulterior motive. You probably just don't want the divorce."

"No, I'll give you the divorce, ... if that's what you want. I'm asking your forgiveness."

Ceil is rather shocked at Niall's actions. She is about to say something more, when Nigel touches her arm to quiet her. He wants to see this play out.

Elsa scoffs again. "Niall, I don't believe you. What's behind the ask, Niall? What do you really want?"

Niall feels exasperated, not sure how else to ask forgiveness. "I'm sincere, Elsa. It's my penance for God's forgiveness. I'm changed. I haven't been with any other women. I'm working. I'm praying. I'm working in the church. I'm changing, Elsa, I am. Please!"

Elsa looks to Nigel who is unmoving and listening. Elsa slightly nods. "Well, I'm glad to hear it Niall. I'll believe it when I see it with my own eyes. I'll be watchful, and prayerful for you, Niall.

And if I see that you've really changed, then I'll consider forgiving you," Elsa tells him, with a look of empty eyes, knowing in her heart she could never forgive him for the brutality he inflicted on sweet Deirdre. She looks at her watch for an easy exit. "Well, I've got to get to work." Elsa stands and touches Niall on the shoulder, as he is still on his knees. "I'll see you later, Niall." Elsa leaves out the house.

Chapter Seventy-Two

Two days later, Nicolaus checked them out of the luxury hotel in Colorado. It is time to enter the corner house he bought in the upscale neighborhood off sixth avenue, in Denver.

Without fanfare, they enter, as he carries in their luggage and things.

"Ms. Helena, Mr. Nicolaus," Mary greets them. She'd arrived yesterday, and prepared their bedroom, and bought groceries to prepare them a meal.

"Hello Ms. Mary! All go well?" Nicolaus asks her.

"Oh yes, Sir. This is a very beautiful house. I'm sure Ms. Helena will love it here."

Helena was taken aback. Approaching the door, one passes by beautifully manicured gardens. The exterior of the home shows there are several fireplaces throughout. There are plenty of windows, and the exterior paint is a golden brown color.

The interior of the house is immaculate. The design of the home is spectacular. A single half spiraling staircase, with a floral iron banister, in the sweeping foyer with a beautiful chandelier to greet everyone who enters. There are hardwood floors throughout the home with eighteen foot ceilings and extensive recessed lighting. Several arches and curvatures embrace cream colored walls.

As Helena enters the living room area, she sees the furniture she picked out, enhanced with a beautiful room rug, a large fireplace, built-in shelves, and beautiful large oval windows that peek into the back yard. The backyard holds a three tiered designer fountain, surrounded by lush green grass.

A hallway from the living room leads to the large kitchen, which holds a double Dutch oven and plenty of storage space, enchanted by large windows for the dining area. Helena sees the dining set she picked out. The outside patio is large, has a built-in grill, and the patio furniture Helena chose. The patio has ceramic bricks, and plays into the grassy area.

Nicolaus had been silently following Helena the whole time that she'd been in awe of the place. "Do you like it?" He finally asks her.

"Nicky ... this place is grand! How long are we renting it for?"

Nicolaus hugs Helena to his side. "I bought it."

She looks at him. "Are you serious?" She looks over the exterior of the home from the backyard. The Spanish tiled roof accentuates the golden brown color siding. "Nicky ..."

"Think you can live here okay?"

"Nicky ...," she puts her arms around him, tears spilling from her eyes.

He hugs her and wipes her tears. "Eight bedrooms, so enough for the staff, and for your office, my office, and a crafting room if you need one, a den, library, ... whatever you want."

"Nicky, truly, it's beautiful. I love it."

Nicolaus nods, a little relieved. "Ms. Mary will be here to help you."

"Oh, Nicky, I don't know what to do with staff. I've always done everything myself."

Nicolaus chuckles, "Well not anymore, you're with me now. Look, I hired Ms. Mary, so you let her do her work. She will clean, do laundry, and light cooking, mostly breakfast stuff. The chef will be here Monday."

"Chef? What am I going to do with a chef?"

He leads her to slowly walk back inside. "She'll cook for you,... for us. You can help if you want, but remember, I'm hiring her to do the job. You can just tell her what you want for the week, and she'll go to the store and get it and make it for you.

"And you'll have a security team. I've hired a team of six. They work twenty-four seven, and in shifts, so the back and the front of the house will be covered outside, and you'll have two inside. And Helena, they are to go with you any time you leave the house. You don't sneak out or sneak away. It's very important for your safety, Helena."

"Nicky, that's too much! You can't control every aspect of my life."

"We're not taking any chances. You'll have privacy when needed. They are professionals, they will know what to do. And oh yeah, I've got to work on getting the property fenced in."

Helena gazes at Nicolaus, realizing he is not only very serious about all this, but that now she is on a different level in life with him. She had no idea this was going to happen.

As they walk to the interior of the home a young woman is standing and waiting to greet them. "Ah, this is Leigh, your interior decorator." They all shake hands. "Leigh is going to help you design the inside of the home to your taste, you know the curtains, drapes, décor, all that stuff."

Helena looks at them both in awe.

Nicolaus peck kisses Helena on her lips. "Let's go see upstairs!"

Helena wants to cry at the perfect and pristine upstairs. The main bedroom suite is huge with skylights in every room, including the bathroom and the closet. The large window in the bathroom overlooks the large backyard. The bed she picked out is perfectly made and ready for them to enjoy. The furniture is decadent and lovely. The bathroom seems the size of the kitchen, with an elegant oval bathtub and large shower with rock tile. The closet is enormous.

Helena is shocked to learn there is a huge basement with a stocked wine cellar, a large movie room with luxury theater seats, enough for a dozen guests, another full kitchen with a huge refrigerator, and a fully loaded workout room with state of the art equipment, including a row machine. The home is completely beautiful.

Helena feels that she has never been so cared for. She finds herself to be absolutely speechless. Helena understands that Nicolaus is fulfilling his promise of not letting her life fall apart, and she is more in love with Nicolaus Ravenell than ever before.

Chapter Seventy-Three

Nicolaus takes everyone out for a light dinner at one of Denver's well known restaurants, as they had eaten what Ms. Mary had prepared for a lunch meal. The evening ended with he and Helena recounting the officials who were present to close down the children's home, so that Nicolaus could make contact with all of them in the morning.

Late into the night, as they got into bed, Nicolaus holds Helena in his arms.

Nicolaus chuckles, "Let's test out this bed." After a minute or two of silently laying still, he says, "Oh yes, my dear, you know how to pick a mattress!"

Nicolaus gathers Helena into his arms, and begins to drift to sleep.

Helena is not sure what to think, as they lay in their luxurious bed, in their luxurious bedroom suite, in their luxurious new home. She stares up at Nicolaus, as he drifts to sleep, not demanding or expecting anything of her, not even after doing so much for her.

She knows Nicolaus is already asleep as she observes his even breathing. She feels as though her fantasy of being with him has now turned into a life come true fairytale. She'd thought being at the castle was magical, however this real life magic seems very much more tangible to her.

The fairytale seems to be playing out as they all do; Nicolaus is the handsome prince, and she is the saved damsel in distress, now living in their little castle, tucked away safe from the dangers of life. Helena thinks about how easily Nicolaus did all of this within a three day time span. It not only impresses her, it scares her a little. How long would this fairytale last?

It is three in the morning when Helena pops straight up. She feels something about to explode from her insides. She runs to the bathroom and pukes unexpectedly. As soon as she is done, she washes her mouth and face, gargles with mouthwash, and heads back to bed. Only, ... no! She rushes back to the bathroom and pukes again.

By this time, Nicolaus is beside her. "Honey, you okay?"

Helena cannot answer because she pukes again, and again, and again. She feels Nicolaus holding her.

Oh how embarrassing! Puking before your handsome lover? She pushes at him to leave her, only to feel his strong arms go around her, holding onto her belly as she pukes uncontrollably yet again.

Finally, it stops. Helena feels weak, and stupid, and embarrassed. She cries as she does what Nicolaus wants as he pulls off her nightclothes and places her in the beautiful shower.

"It's okay, honey."

Helena lets the warm water pour over her, helping to relax her. She wonders how he knows what to do, as she sees him cleaning up the mess, and washing her clothes out. She watches the well-known, military hero, handsome stud of a man, Nicolaus Ravenell, clean up her vomit mess. She couldn't believe it.

After ten minutes of showering and washing her hair, she turns off the water, and there he is again. Nicolaus is right by her side, helping her out of the shower, and doing the drying of her body for her.

He kisses her, and ... she runs to the sink to brush her teeth and rinse with mouthwash. She cannot kiss Nicolaus in such a shabby state! Helena breathes, and grabs another towel and dries her hair, then applies moisture lotion to her waves, combs her hair out, then wraps herself with the towel, and ... there he is again, right by her side, to escort her back to bed.

Helena rests her hands on his shoulders. "How are you so wonderful? How ... are you ... how?"

Helena shakes her head, realizing the depths of this man. Pious. Courageous. Loving. Caring. Strong. Sexy. Handsome. The full package. The full deal for any woman.

"How are you such a wonderful man, after being raised by Ceil?" She shakes her head, feeling this cannot all be real.

Helena looks around wondering if she's in a coma and dreaming or something, until Nicolaus steps up to her, and hugs her close to him. The feel of his body makes her know she is not dreaming.

Nicolaus looks at Helena strangely, knowing being threatened by a spouse, and then uprooted, probably is shocking to her. "Hey, it's okay," he tells her.

"No really. How, Nicky ... how?"

Nicolaus chuckles, then lifts Helena into his arms and carries her to the bed, gently placing her down, as if they are filling the pages of a romantic novel. "Come on now, you need to rest. We can get a few more hours of sleep."

The scene is set again, as Nicolaus helps Helena into a clean nightgown, then holds her in his arms with even breathing and no demands.

However, in the morning, when Nicolaus returned to their bedroom with a breakfast tray for Helena, he knew something was wrong as he heard her puking in the bathroom again. Immediately he pulls up physicians on his laptop computer. When Helena exits the bathroom, looking pale and weak, he is right by her side. "You're going to see a doctor, right now. Which do you prefer a woman or a man physician?"

Dr. Phoebe Adelay looks at the couple before her, with a giant smile. "Congratulations! You're pregnant!"

"Pregnant?" Helena frowns. "Are you sure?"

Dr. Adelay chuckles at her reaction. She nods. "Oh yes! Helena, you are about seven weeks pregnant."

Both Helena and Nicolaus think back with a frown, then they both smile, realizing that was actually the first time they'd made hot love with each other, knocking things to the floor.

"Now is this something the two of you need to discuss?"

Helena looks to Nicolaus with a slight frown. "I ... I ...."

"Let me give you a few minutes." She leaves the couple to discuss the findings.

"I can't believe it!" Helena tells Nicolaus. "I've never been able to get pregnant." She looks at him in wonderment.

Nicolaus takes her into his arms. "Honey, whatever you want to do, I'm with you," he tells her supportively, though feeling very apprehensive because of the curse, and his past history. Would this child survive?

Helena touches her belly. "We keep the baby."

Nicolaus smiles at her with a frown of worry. "Wow. This is a surprise! A God given surprise, though Helena, I'm a little worried about it." He hugs her to him, moving past the obvious. "Hmm. Maybe you're supposed to be my fourth wife. Hmm. We'll have to get married. Well ... once you're divorced."

"Nicky ... did you just ask me to marry you?" Shock is in her voice.

Nicolaus hugs her tighter to him. "Well yeah. If you're going to have my baby, we need to be married," he states showing her respect, willing to do what is right by Helena.

"Nicky," her hands to his chest. She wants to cry again; she can hardly believe that her dream man just asked her to marry him. The curse is not even gracing her mind.

Dr. Adelay returns. "Okay, what's the word?" She sees that Helena is crying tears of joy and looking at her man with starry eyes. Dr. Phoebe Adelay already knows the answer.

Chapter Seventy-Four

Nicolaus and Helena got much accomplished on this Monday. Nicolaus has calls into several officials to see exactly why they closed down the children's home and to find out what evidence they had.

Helena now has a handle on her nausea and the puking episodes has lessened. However now, lying in bed with Nicolaus, she feels very vulnerable.

"Nicky, I don't want you to leave me."

He pulls her close and kisses her forehead. "I'm not leaving you. And you're not going to leave me," he orders her. "I just need to fly back and forth until I can unhook myself from the office, and then we'll just both work remotely. Or Helena, maybe you should just open a children's home here, and leave the other one closed. Ceil has no ties out here, so she cannot do anything against you."

"Hmm, I hadn't thought of that. But the house ... you put so much work into it."

Nicolaus shrugs. "We can sell it and put that money towards the new one for this city. It's your new beginning."

Helena is still in awe of Nicolaus.

As the week progressed, Nicolaus received scant information about the closure of the children's home. He realized he was going to have to get information in person. Tuesday, they paid a short visit to the Darfurian refugees. Nicolaus had plans to fly back to Austin on Thursday.

Wednesday night, Helena had a few revelations, and she started freaking out about it. Her first realization was that Nicolaus never initiated their love making. He was sweet, always a gentleman, and would always hold her, though he never initiated. She watched him as they made love, as she brought about the result she wanted from him, and he gave her what she wanted. Lovingly holding her while drifting to sleep.

The other revelation that occurred to Helena, is that now that she is pregnant with Nicolaus' child, she is in the same space Deirdre had been in when she met her deadly fate. As she looked at Nicolaus sleep, she remembered how he warned her about the curse. She started to worry and wonder what fate awaited her.

By morning light, Helena had a different take on things.

"Nicky, I ... I think ... no, I want us to take a break from each other for a while."

Nicolaus chuckles and looks at Helena with a frown, as he is getting ready to go to the airport. He thought he misunderstood what she said. "What?"

"I'm serious." She touches his torso, looking up into his eyes. "Nicky, we need a break."

He frowns at her, "Helena, what's going on?" He pulls her to sit down with him on the bed bench at the foot of the bed.

Helena stands away from him. "Just a little break."

Nicolaus shakes his head, "I don't understand." He's almost at a loss for words. "Uh, a few days ago, you just told me you didn't want me to leave. And now you're telling me you want a break. What's the matter? What happened?"

"Nothing has happened. I just think we need a break."

"Okay, ... I'm going to say no. We don't need a break. I'll be back Saturday morning."

She sits next to him again. "Nicky," she touches him, "please."

"What is this, Helena?" He stands, exasperated, "What's going on? Is it the pregnancy?"

Helena looks at her belly, then away from him with no words. She has worked herself into a terrified state about this curse business.

Nicolaus sighs, then sits next to Helena again. He gently takes her hands. "All right, what do you need? A week?"

She looks at him again. "Three months."

Nicolaus looks at her in shock, then half yells, "Three months? Three months. Why?"

"I just need time to adjust. And ... it will be past the first trimester."

Nicolaus is more calm. "Oh." He looks at her with searching eyes. "Oh, it's the curse. You're worried."

"Yes."

Nicolaus pulls Helena into a loving hug. "I get it. I'm worried too, but I'm not leaving you." He brings her face up to his and kisses her lips. "I'll see you Saturday, if not before."

Nicolaus leaves with security in place. He feels confident that Helena will be safe and secure until he returns.

Chapter Seventy-Five

Time went by quickly, and Helena's pregnancy progressed nicely. There were many times that she missed Deirdre. Nicolaus gave her the week, mostly flying back on Fridays.

They were able to find that the instigations of rumors about the children's home was brought about by the mayor's wife, prompting the mayor's office to launch investigations, which triggered several other agencies. However, now, six months had gone by, so Helena had little hope of getting the children or her reputation returned to her. She made peace with selling the home.

Ms. Fiona did not like that her friend, Helena, had her important work turned off. Ms. Fiona watched across the street, on the steps of her "love house", that afternoon, so many months ago now, when the social workers took the children away. It broke her heart to see those children crying, screaming, and resisting.

When Ms. Fiona saw the for sale sign placed on the property it got her blood boiling. She decided to get dressed in her best clothes, and march herself right up to the mayor's office and have a word with him.

Ms. Fiona is not about following rules, or listening to protocol.

"Ah, ma'am ... ma'am ... you cannot go in there. Ma'am!" The mayor's secretary is unable to stop Fiona once she blew past her desk with a confident walk, and a determined look on her face.

As Fiona threw open the door to the mayor's office, interrupting his video call with the governor, it is only a few seconds that she has his attention.

"Ah, Governor, please, let me call you back," the mayor says, as Fiona stands before him with her hands to her hips. Quickly, he ends the video call, and holds his hand up to the secretary, who is behind Fiona, to go out and close the door.

"Fiona," he is surprised at her show stopping behavior. "Now, Fiona."

"Don't you 'now Fiona' me, Chuck! I'm here on a complaint about my lovely neighbor, Ms. Helena. You had your people close down her children's home."

"Ms. Helena?" He frowns, trying to think of what she might be referring to.

"Chuck, don't you act like you don't know what I'm talking about! You had police, and social workers, and gobs of folks pulling the children kicking and screaming out of that home."

"Oh, oh, yes, yes, yes,... now I remember."

Fiona frowns at him. "Chuck, don't kid with me!"

"Of course not. Well, yes, I remember. What of it?"

Fiona looks at the mayor with a scringed up face, not liking his attitude. She steps much closer to him and he stands. "Chuck, that place is still closed down. What happened to those children?"

"Well, I don't know. Usually in cases like this they would be placed in foster care."

"Ms. Helena is an outstanding citizen, Chuck. She doesn't deserve what you did to her."

"Well ... there must be investigations, and ..."

"It's been six months now, Chuck! How long do them investigations take?"

"Well ... well ... I ..."

Fiona snatches the mayor up by his clothes, she is in his face. "Close it, Chuck! Clear her name of whatever happened, or I promise you,..." she releases his clothes and pulls out her phone to show him, "I've got all eight major network numbers right here ready to tell them all about the time you and I have spent together, the amounts of money you have paid me, how you paid me, what you like me to do to you, and I've got videos and photos to prove it." She stands with hands on hips, waiting for his response.

"Now, Fiona. You know something like that would ruin me."

"Yep! And I wonder what your missus will think."

"Okay, Fiona, okay, I'll make sure everything is cleared up. You have my word!"

"Yeah, and I'm not playing, Chuck. I better see news reports and newspaper articles that all is cleared up, with whatever excuse you give, and you better make Ms. Helena smell like fucking roses, Chuck, that she did nothing wrong, by the evening news tomorrow, or ... I launch 'operation tell all'."

"Fiona, you have my word! All will be cleared up! I promise you!"

"I'm counting on you, Chuck!" Fiona turns to leave. When she gets to the door, she stops and turns to face him with a smile, "And Chucky baby, get this done, and I'll have a special surprise for you on Friday." Like a storm blowing through his office, Fiona leaves, slamming the door.

The mayor sits down, wipes the sweat from his neck and brow, and gets to making calls to get the case closed, and to get his staff to make news reports.

Chapter Seventy-Six

Helena is ecstatic as Ms. Mary puts the national news on for her. She couldn't believe that the story of the closing of her children's home made national news. Together, they listen as she hears that all charges are dropped, and her name is completely cleared.

With joy, Helena hugs Ms. Mary to her. "We've got to go tell Nicky! Let's make a trip to Austin!"

Helena dials Joel after making airline reservations.

"Hello?"

"Hey Joel, this is Helena. I hope you are doing okay."

"Helena? Where the hell are you?"

"Oh Joel, I can't tell you that. Listen, I'm calling you because I need to get that chest that is up in the attic. You remember, it has photos of my parents and some of my high school stuff. Would you be okay if we came by to get it?"

"We?"

"Yes, Joel, Nicky and me. Look, Joel, I'm pregnant. Can you believe it? And I want our son to know his family. That's why I need the chest."

"You're having his baby? I thought you always said you couldn't get pregnant, Helena. So what ... you were lying to me all those years?"

"No Joel, I wasn't lying. I don't know why it didn't happen for us. Look, that's all in the past. Nicolaus wants to marry me, so that our son can be proper, you know. So, Joel, won't you please go ahead and sign those divorce papers? Me filing in court is going to make you look bad. You should just sign the papers so that we can all move forward. Our marriage has been over for years now."

"Helena ..."

"You just need to admit it to yourself, Joel. We're a thing of the past. We both need to move forward with our lives."

Helena listened to the silence, knowing that Joel is thinking about what she is saying.

He huffs a sigh. "Yeah, I'll think about the papers. You can pick up the chest tomorrow. I'll give you ten minutes around two. I'll leave, because I don't want to see that jerk you're screwing with."

"Joel, please don't do that. Nicolaus likes you. Remember? He helped us get rich. He believes in your work. I want you to be a part of all these good things too, but you've got to change your attitude, and stop drinking, Joel."

He huffs again. "Yeah, yeah. Tomorrow at two." Joel ends the call without niceties. He feels himself become furious that Helena is pregnant by Nicolaus. He sits down to think what to do about it.

Ceil is amused as she sees the national news reports of Helena being cleared of all wrongdoing. She doesn't understand how the story had gotten this far out. She wonders if Nicolaus had something to do with it.

Back in Denver, Helena's security is resisting her demands to prepare for the immediate trip. "Ah, Ms. Helena, Mr. Nicolaus would have to approve such a trip. Has he been notified?"

"Oh nonsense! He'll know I'm there when I arrive. Look, aren't you tasked with going anywhere I go?"

"Well, yes ma'am, but ..."

"Okay then, let's go! I'm going to Austin to see my honey!"

"Ah, ma'am ..."

Helena proceeds to quickly pack a bag, and intends to be at the airport on the next flight to Austin. Nicolaus had Helena's vehicle brought over several months ago; so she and Mary are ready to go. Two of the security detail men run to get into her vehicle, before being left behind.

Later that afternoon, Nicolaus returns to the mansion earlier than usual. He'd left the office early after hearing the news reports clearing Helena. He is sure she would be pleased and want to talk about it.

Nicolaus gets a shock as he walks into the mansion to find Helena there, in person, speaking happily to Nigel. He puts his briefcase down, and gently touches her about the waist. "Helena?"

She turns, "Oh Nicky! Have you heard? It's all over the news. I've been cleared of all accusations and all investigations are closed!" She hugs Nicolaus to her, feeling so elated.

Nicolaus returns her hugs, and her kisses. He looks astonished at his father, who shrugs with an eyebrow lift, then looks to Helena. "Helena ... honey ... what are you doing here?"

"To share the good news! And look at this, Nicky!" Helena unfolds a tri-folded paper and hands it to Nicolaus. "They sent it by email."

Nicolaus looks over the paper, and it says the same in writing, that she is cleared of all accusations, and all investigations are closed, and that she may reopen the children's home. Nicolaus nods with a painful grimace. He eyes the security detail.

"Sorry, Sir, I couldn't stop her."

Helena hugs Nicolaus to her again. "Isn't it great, honey?"

"Yes, great! Wonderful! Congratulations! I'm still not clear on why or how you are here."

"Nicky, don't be unreasonable. It's good news! And I spoke to Joel and he's going to let us go to the house to retrieve the chest I told you about. He says ..."

"Helena, you called Joel?"

Helena continues with childlike excitement. Nodding, "Yeah. He says we can go over around two. He will leave and give us ten minutes to get the chest that has the photos of my father, and my parents, and lots of high school mementos. I know exactly where it is."

"Helena, so now Joel has your number?" Nicolaus seems a little shocked at her actions, after all the steps he's taken to hide her from him.

"Oh Nicky, it's okay, Joel is harmless."

"Harmless? Helena, that man tried to kill you! And somehow I'm sure that wasn't the first time. How many times has he hurt you, Helena? You're trusting him too much!"

"Oh Nicky, he was drunk!"

"Helena, what if it's a trap?"

"Oh Nicky, Joel is not that smart. You're giving him too much credit. And anyway, we'll have security with us. I brought two. So, what's he going to do? Hmm? Oh Nicky, it will be fine. It's just for ten minutes." She kisses Nicolaus, completely dismissing his concerns, and happily bops herself off to tend to other matters on Nicolaus side of the mansion.

"Keep your eye on her. Don't let her leave alone," Nicolaus orders the security staff. They nod, popping into action, quickly following the path of Helena.

Nicolaus puts his back against a wall, leans his head back, and sighs.

Nigel chuckles. "Looks like she's quite a challenge."

Nicolaus shakes his head. "Good Lord! Challenge is probably an understatement. We argue all the time now, over everything I say or do."

Nigel holds onto Nicolaus shoulder. "Helena is a beautiful woman and a strong woman. Probably not what you are used to. Though I think when my grandson gets here, she will slow down a little."

"I don't think so. Helena doesn't slow down for anything."

Nigel chuckles hardily, making Nicolaus laugh as well.

Chapter Seventy-Seven (TW)

The following night, Helena is so happy to have been able to obtain her family chest. She felt this would be something she could pass down to her son. She was also very happy to have spent time with her mother as well. She and Nicolaus visited with her for a few hours.

Helena is excited and unable to sleep. She observes Nicolaus as he sleeps soundly, breathing even and steadily. She looks at his handsome, un-aged, and unweathered face. She observes his muscular chest and arms. His curly hair, his nose, and his smooth caramel colored skin.

Helena lays on her back and rubs her six month pregnant belly. She wonders what her son will really look like once he is born. She thinks about how she will need to start preparing for her son's arrival. Her fears about the curse has lifted, as she looks forward to the future.

Helena's phone chimes with a text message. Quickly, she turns it down, not to disturb Nicolaus. She sees that the message is from Joel. It is two in the morning.

'Helena, I thought about what you said,
and am willing to sign the divorce papers.'

Helena is happy that her words got through to Joel. She imagines this new beginning.

'Great Joel. Tomorrow?'
'No. Right now.'
'Right now? It's 2am!'
'Best do it now, before I change my mind.'
This panicked Helena a little. *'Okay, then.'*
'I'll meet you at the house for the kids.
Come alone Helena, or no deal. Hurry.'
Helena did not like this. She frowns.

'Joel'. No response. *'Joel??'* No response.

Helena sighs, nervous about what to do. She looks at Nicolaus and then she decides to trust the goodwill that Joel has shown her. After all, maybe he wants a hug or a kiss to end their marriage.

Helena eases out of the bed, and quickly dresses. She eases out of the room, not disturbing Nicolaus, or anyone else. She does not see either of her security detail men standing guard, so she makes her way to the vehicle keys, which are kept in a central location inside the mansion. With stealthy quietness, Helena retrieves Nicolaus' keys, and she is out the door.

Helena feels desperate to get the divorce papers signed, so that she and Nicolaus can marry. As she drives up to the children's home, she can see Joel's vehicle. The for sale sign on the property makes her feel sad, and then she feels her son move inside of her. This reminds Helena of the new life she has started with Nicolaus.

As soon as Helena exits the vehicle, Joel is behind her.

She turns and sees him. "Joel!"

Immediately, he ceases Helena with rage, then punches her away from him. Helena loses her footing and falls to the ground. Joel lifts her, only to punch her across the head again, this time knocking Helena unconscious.

"Get your hands off her!" Fiona yells from across the street. "What are you doing?" She yells loudly, her voice echoing throughout the neighborhood.

Joel sees house lights pop on, up and down the street. He moves hastily. He lights the grass of the children's home property on fire and it catches quickly, as he'd already poured several gallons of gasoline on everything before he called Helena.

Fiona runs inside to call the police and fire departments. Joel picks up Helena, and takes her inside the house, barricading the front door.

Immediately, Joel runs upstairs and sets it alite, then back downstairs, and sets every room ablaze. The next task, he pours the gasoline in a circle around himself and Helena, who is still unconscious, on the floor.

Without hesitation, Joel lights the circle of gasoline, and they are now trapped in a ring of fire. He stands and waits. It does not take long for the whole house to be ablaze with fire, from the roof to the front lawn, upstairs, downstairs, the whole of the house.

Hysterically, Fiona calls Niall. "Benjamin! Benjamin, wake up!"

Niall frowns. "Who the hell is this?"

"Benjamin, it's Fiona!"

"Fiona! You're calling me?" This was a blast from the past for Niall. He had not been to Ms. Fiona's for a girl since before Elaine was born, although mostly because he treated the girls so abusively, Ms. Fiona banned him.

"Benjamin, hurry! Get your brother down here, hurry, the house is on fire with Helena inside!"

"What? What are you talking about?"

"Benjamin wake up!" She yells at him. "And listen! The children's home is on fire. Helena is inside. Get your brother down here. Hurry!"

Niall looks at his phone, frowns, then calls Nicolaus.

"Yeah?" Nicolaus turns to see that Helena is not next to him.

"Nicolaus, this is Niall. Wake up!"

"I'm awake. What's going on?"

"Nicolaus, I just got a frantic call from Fiona. Something about the children's home is on fire, and Helena is inside."

"What?" Nicolaus jumps out of bed and looks for Helena in the room. He checks the bathroom; she is not there.

"Isn't she supposed to be in Denver?"

"Oh God! Yeah, she ... she ... she is here unexpectedly," Nicolaus' mind is racing. Dread suddenly covers him. "Thanks."

Nicolaus ends the call with Niall, and calls his father.

"Father, I think Helena snuck out, and she may be in trouble."

"Oh no! Okay, I'll meet you downstairs."

The Ravenell men and security take Nigel's SUV and rush down to the children's home. "Oh God!" Nicolaus can see the glow of the fire lighting up the sky, well before they get there. Once they arrive, the men jump out the vehicle and are confronted with a huge inferno.

The firemen of several firehouse ladders are working to put the fire out, as they already have it contained.

"Help me!" Nicolaus can hear Helena's voice from inside behind the raging flames. Through the front window, he can see Joel and Helena surrounded by fire, and Joel is holding Helena down. She screams, "Help!"

Nicolaus immediately runs to get in, however, the force of several men hold him back, stopping him.

"Sir, you cannot go in there."

"People are inside! Please! My fiancé, I can see her!"

"We are working to help them."

Nicolaus finds it difficult to get loose of the force of four men, holding him. He is suddenly being wrestled to the ground.

Nigel knew that Nicolaus would be determined to get inside to save Helena. He talks to the fire chief, and they release Nicolaus.

Nicolaus quickly jogs around the back, getting a sense of how bad the fire is. One of the firefighters follows him. On his way to the backside of the house, Fiona runs over to him. She touches Nicolaus' face, having never seen him in the flesh before. "Nicolaus. Be careful."

Nicolaus nods to her, touching her hand, then goes to the back with the fireman following him. The house is fully engulfed, except the back yard. "There is a trap door, here," Nicolaus points to the door. "It goes down into the basement, then up into the house. Let me try to get her."

"Okay, let's go!"

Nicolaus stops the eager fireman. "No, no, no. I don't expect you to go in there. We may not make it out."

"You're not going in alone, Sir. Let's go!"

Nicolaus nods, and lifts the trap door. The fireman uses his flashlight to flood light into the darkness. They go quickly. Nicolaus is able to get the basement door open, though it is very hot. He runs in, seeing the huge and hot flames everywhere. All he can think about is Helena. He sees Helena and Joel, both now lying unconscious, surrounded by large flames of fire.

The house begins to collapse, large interior beams and wooden planks begin falling all around them. Nicolaus jumps into the fire ring, and grabs Joel, handing him to the fireman, who places Joel over his shoulder and carries him down the basement stairs, then up and out. He calls on this radio to get help to the back.

Nicolaus jumps back into the fire ring. He begins having trouble breathing. He coughs, trying to get air. Nicolaus begins to pick up Helena when he feels the flames biting him on the arm.

Ignoring the pain and the danger, Nicolaus lifts Helena, jumps through the flames, and another beam falls, barely missing them. The sound of the roaring fire is loud. Helena remains unconscious; a rather large bruise covers the side of her forehead. Nicolaus carries Helena down the basement stairs, then puts her over his strong shoulder, and climbs up and out.

EMS technicians are nearby. Nicolaus lays Helena on the ground and checks her breathing, while wheezing and coughing himself, his clothes are smoking. The top portion of his hair is singed and smoking. "Please! Help her," he calls to them, "please save her!"

Immediately, they place oxygen on Helena, and check her vitals. She moves and coughs, and tries to speak but cannot. Nicolaus stays with her, his hand on her belly. Tears escape him. "Oh God!" He begins to pray over Helena. Quickly, they place Helena on a gurney and put her in an ambulance. Nicolaus is right beside her.

Suddenly, a huge crack is heard, then a large whining sound as the house implodes on itself. Everything buckles, folds, and drops, until it is just a burning pile of house.

"Sir," the firefighter finds Nigel. "Your son is very courageous. We did get those two people out of the house. The man is deceased, but the lady is still alive. She and your son are in the ambulance on the way to the hospital if you want to follow. I believe they will take them to Saints Hospital."

Nigel shakes the fireman's hand. "Thank you very much!"

Nigel finds the Fire Chief. "My son, Nicolaus, has been taken by ambulance to the hospital. The other two are Joel and Helena Gaulkven. Helena owned this property; it was a children's home before the city shut it down. This couple has been separated for some time now, Helena filed for divorce, though Joel was not in agreement. I fear their disputing is what may have led to all this." The Fire Chief makes notes. "My son's vehicle is there," Nigel points to it, "Helena drove it here. Do you need it to remain, or can we take it?"

"Mr. Ravenell, I appreciate this information. Feel free to take the vehicle. Better it is not left out here. The trouble occurred inside, and that is where our investigation will be." Nigel nods. "I hope you are open to further discussions, if we need additional information."

"Of course. You know how to reach me."

Nigel had the security staff drive Nicolaus' vehicle. They went directly to the hospital. They can see an ambulance with the doors flung open. Nigel parks and they go inside. Nothing they can do, but wait.

Nigel phones Ceil. "Ceil, Joel set the house on fire with Helena inside. Nicolaus helped get them out, but ... they say Joel is deceased. Helena and Nicolaus are in the ER now."

"Nigel ...," tears fall from Ceil.

Nigel hears her crying. "Ceil, ... I'll let you know when I hear something. Try not to worry." Nigel knows that Ceil is not crying for Nicolaus, but that she is crying for Helena. Nigel felt himself tear up for both of them. He has no idea if Nicolaus is seriously injured. Nigel is very concerned about the baby. And then all of a sudden, that dreaded curse weighs heavily on his mind.

Chapter Seventy-Eight

C eil dressed herself hours ago. She paces the mansion, her phone in her hands, waiting for news. She has just made up her mind to go to the hospital when the front door to the mansion opens. It is four in the morning.

Ceil freezes as she sees that Nicolaus' clothes are tattered and has burn marks. His face has black scorch marks and blistering. His hair is singed. His arm is bandaged. It is clear that he'd been directly in a fire. He smells of burning house. He looks devastated. Nigel looks depressed as he enters the house after his son.

Ceil steps up to them. "Well?" She impatiently wants information. "Tell me! How is Helena?"

Nicolaus looks up at Ceil, with tightly closed lips, he shakes his head negatively. "She didn't make it," he can barely manage. "She didn't make it," his voice breaks with tears.

Ceil steps back from them in shock. "No." Nigel abruptly goes to Ceil and takes her in his arms. "No! That cannot be."

Nicolaus sits himself on the first stair step. His head in his hands.

Ceil pulls herself from Nigel. Her cold hard shell returns for Nicolaus. She doubly hates him. "This is your fault!" She shouts at him, "It's all your fault Helena is dead!"

"Ceil, dear," Nigel tries to pull her back. Ceil won't let him. Ceil pushes at Nigel in his chest to get away from him.

She wants to attack Nicolaus, but she stops short of it. "You did this!" She harshly yells at Nicolaus, "You did this!"

Nicolaus looks up at Ceil, and sees that Nigel is trying to stop her. "No father, let her go. She's right. This is my fault. She's right," he sounds uncharacteristically defeated.

"Son ..."

"I failed Helena. I failed her, and now she too is gone." He shakes his head, crying emotional tears. "She's right." Nicolaus then wipes his eyes with a groan. He looks at Ceil, "You win, Ceil. You win. I give up. Winner takes all."

"Nicolaus, ... son ..." Nigel has never seen Nicolaus like this, though of course what's happened is demoralizing.

Nicolaus stands and goes to his side of the mansion with no more words spoken.

Ceil is speechless. She just watches Nicolaus walk away.

Chapter Seventy-Nine

N icolaus showered and cleaned up as much as he could. He found himself at Constance's home. It is early, but when she opens the door, Nicolaus falls into her arms. Constance manages to get Nicolaus to a nearby chair, for which she sits, and he somewhat collapses onto her lap, his legs on the floor.

"My God, Nicky, what happened to you?" She sees that he looks as though he's been through a fire. She sees burn marks on him. His hair is crunchy and singed when she touches it. He smells of fire. Emotion has gripped him so much so, that for now he cannot speak.

After about an hour, Constance goes with Nicolaus to inform Helena's mother. Constance is able to console her mother, whereas Nicolaus cannot. However, Nicolaus quickly arranges twenty four hour professional nursing care for Helena's mother, so that she would not be alone at her home.

Nicolaus informed Bishop Leighton of Helena's passing, and asked that he officiate her funeral within the next three days. The ceremony was private, only friends and family, including Ms. Fiona. Nicolaus insisted Helena be buried in the family cemetery since she was carrying his son at the time of her death. Nigel is adamant that Helena was part of their family.

Ms. Fiona is sweet on Nicolaus, feeling that he is treating Helena properly. She kisses his face and holds onto his hands in a gesture of gratitude, before leaving, and is glad that Helena's name was cleared of any wrongdoings before her death.

Nicolaus takes care of any property payments for Helena's mother to ensure she can live out her life in her home if she wanted. He also hires permanent nursing staff to care for her. Nicolaus managed Helena's finances and provided all monies to her mother as well. Fortunately, Helena had already placed her mother on all her accounts, and made her mother the beneficiary to all her life insurance policies.

Nicolaus works quickly for his professional transition. He has not returned to the office. "Daniel, I hope you are doing okay."

"Nicolaus, I'm so sorry to hear about Ms. Helena. Her home was our first foundation project."

"Yeah," Nicolaus acknowledges his words. "Look Daniel, I'm really sorry to do this to you, and without notice, but ... I'm not returning to the office. In fact, I've already resigned."

"Nicolaus!"

Nicolaus sighs. "I left my keys and computer for my father and for Ceil. Obviously, you should be in the lead role, though honestly, I'm not really sure what will happen from this point forward. I suspect Ceil will be there to take over, if she has not already."

"Oh! I was wondering why we've been getting emails from her."

"It would be so appreciated if you could have security box up my personal affects today, and have them send it to me by courier. Other than that, I'm out. I ... I just cannot do anymore. I just don't have the mental capacity to keep going."

"I understand, my friend. Nicolaus, it has been an honor to work under your leadership. We have always known where we stand with you. And we all, all the staff, we trust you."

"I really appreciate that Daniel. Thank you. I hope your awesome talents will continue to be recognized. I implore you to speak with my father. He may know what plans are coming about."

Nicolaus takes leave of his father's mansion, without moving out, as melancholy doubles down on him. He stays with Constance for now, with plans of shifting to Denver, remembering his promise to his father of not literally moving out of the mansion.

"Ms. Mary, are you still interested in managing my Denver property?" Nicolaus asks her over the phone.

"Of course, Mr. Nicolaus! Anything you need, Sir."

Nicolaus nods. "Okay, I'll fly you over, and will you please gather up all of Helena's things and donate them to a charity that works with families? It's what she would want. Think you can have that done by the end of the week?"

"Of course, Sir."

Nicolaus has decided to become recluse and stay away from everyone, especially women, and largely withdraw from society. Helena's death has broken him again. He feels there is too much against him, between the stress of work, Ceil, and the losses caused by the curse, to continue forward.

Nicolaus remains prayerful, keeping his faith in God, hoping solitude will protect others from him. He is now worried about Elaine and Emily. He thinks it best if he removes himself from them, mostly to protect them.

While Nicolaus is working on his transition, Ceil is working on her own transition plans.

"Hello Penelope! This is Ceil Ravenell."

"Ceil Ravenell? A surprise call. I thought you done with us since you dump our merger and try to ruin us," she says spitefully, in her Latvian accent and broken English. "I not forgotten that I still owe Nicolaus his punishment for Marguerite's death! So why the call?"

"My, my! Feisty, now, aren't we?"

"I think us very partnering with your company was the worst decision father ever made. The worst!"

"Well, I hope not Penelope. I thought you and I had a productive relationship."

"Productive for who, Ceil, who? You only?"

"Now Penelope, that is no way to address your in-law. Especially not when I'm calling with an offer that I'm very sure you will not want to refuse. An offer to help you with your ... punishment ... against Nicolaus."

"Hmm! Okay, I listening."

"I want Nicolaus out of my hair. For good! He has just resigned from the company, and I need to make sure he never returns."

"Hmm!" Penelope is intrigued. She has been thinking of revenge plots against the Ravenell family since she is now running Drone Pharma, brought about by a hostile takeover against her father, after his breakdown. With this call, Penelope fully sees an opening. "Well then, who runs your company?"

"Me, of course! Benjamin Niall is the figure head, the new CEO, which I will announce tomorrow."

"Hmm! I see! Okay, I still listening."

"I will pay you ten million dollars to take Nicolaus off my hands. He will be yours to do with whatever you want."

"Say again?" Penelope couldn't believe her ears.

"You are still in love with Nicolaus, yet you want your punishment, right?"

"Yes."

"Well, I will pay you ten million to take him. I don't care how. Get your team to abduct him, or whatever. Then he will be yours, to keep, forever."

Penelope laughs gleefully at first, then a little deviously. "Hmm. What Nicolaus has done to you? You must really hate him, Ceil Ravenell, to be selling him. You own son."

"For me, it's an even trade off. We both get what we want, and you get ten million on top of that. Now, what do you say?"

"I say sounds like kind of a trap! I not really trusting you, Ceil Ravenell."

"Penelope, I'm being straight with you. It's no trap. I promise. I want to be rid of him!"

Penelope thinks carefully, just as Ceil has taught her to do. She thinks about what she wants, and she smiles as an idea enters her mind. "I the only offer, Ceil?"

"Well, yes, for now. If you pass, I'll find someone else."

"Okay, no. I want Nicolaus. I agree, but only you bring him and you family celebrate my birthday with me here."

"What do you mean?"

She impatiently yells at Ceil, "My birthday! You celebrate with me, here to Latvia. And bring Nicolaus!"

"Oh, I see. When?"

"One month from now. All of you, even Elsa. I like Elsa. I send you details. We celebrate, I then to take Nicolaus."

"Okay," Ceil nods, feeling a month or six weeks is not such a long time to wait to be rid of Nicolaus for good. "Okay, it's a deal, Penelope. We will look forward to it."

Chapter Eighty

Niall is shocked to learn that Nicolaus has resigned. He steps into Nicolaus' office and sees that all his items are gone. This brings some panic about Niall.

"What are you looking for?" Ceil says from behind him, startling him, as she intended.

"Daniel says that Nicolaus resigned." He looks to his mother for confirmation.

Ceil nods. "That is correct! Finally! And we'll be completely rid of him soon."

Niall frowns, "What does that mean?"

"Never you mind. Your first task as the new CEO of VMC is to fire Daniel Araceli."

Niall looks at Ceil in disbelief. "I'm the new CEO?" He shakes his head. "No. I don't want it."

Ceil closes the door. "What have I told you before?" She eyes Niall. "You will not be arguing with me, whatsoever! Obviously, the company must pass to a Ravenell. This is finally your time, Niall. What I have been preparing you for! Now, this will be your office. After you fire Daniel, get your things moved in here. I expect this to be done within one hour Niall." Ceil opens the door and walks out.

Full panic is all about Niall now. He knows he is not ready for such a move. And how is he to fire Daniel, the most senior leader of the company behind Nicolaus?

"Niall, all okay?" The voice of Daniel Araceli is behind him.

Niall turns to see Daniel checking on him. Niall nods, then stands straight. He looks at Daniel. "Your fired," he says flatly, with a mean tone.

Daniel looks at him astonished. "What?"

"You heard me. Get your things and get the hell out of here. You're fired, dude!"

"On what grounds?"

"I don't need grounds!" He yells. Then thinks, "Do I need grounds?" He looks silly inadvertently asking the question to Daniel. Niall frowns for a moment, thinking up a lie or something. Niall shakes his head to get on with it. "We are no longer pleased with your work. Therefore, you are fired. Now get out of my office before I have security escort you out!"

As Daniel leaves, Niall sits his shaky self into the cushy chair behind the desk. He uses a tissue to wipe the sweat from him. He feels sick in his stomach. "Vinatalie!" He calls Nicolaus' administrative assistant loudly through the door. She enters the office. "I'm your new boss. Get my things from my other office and bring them in here," he orders her.

She looks at him with a squinted eye, "Sure Niall, right away."

Niall sits back into the chair, with a realization he does not have to be Nicolaus. If he is the boss, people will run and do whatever he says, ... so he thinks.

After ten minutes of staring out the window with his feet on the desk, Niall gets up, wondering why it is taking Vinatalie so long to get his things. He steps out of the office door, and sees several staff members exiting the building with their belongings boxed up. He sees that the whole of the law team is leaving with Daniel.

Niall frowns. "Where the hell do you all think you're going? No one gave you orders to leave."

Laughter ensues from the group as the elevator doors open. Several of them get into the elevator with Danniel.

"You can't just leave!" Niall tells the remaining people.

"Sure we can. We quit, Niall. We refuse to work for you. If Nicolaus is gone, we are gone as well. Good luck."

The other elevator door opens, and the rest of the law team gets into the elevator to exit the building.

Once the word was out inside the agency that all members of the law team quit, several other important staff immediately quit.

Niall is hoping this is a rumor that staff were quitting. Before noon, he walked the floor of all the departments and found most spaces empty, except one or two low level employees.

By days end they lost the whole human resource department, the investment and finance team, all department directors, and all section managers.

The dislike that people had for Niall is now unmasked. Niall does realize that losing so many staff in such a way is going to be a problem.

"This is going to be a problem, Mother!"

Ceil shrugs. "Stop panicking. We'll just hire replacements."

"The HR department is gone! Who's going to hire anyone?" He half yells.

Ceil looks at him sharply. "Watch your tone with me, Niall. We can outsource all those jobs anyway. We'll work on it next week.

"I have already closed down the foundation and all those children's home thingies. Any donated money will need to be returned. So get on that."

Niall felt exasperated, and extremely stressed. "The finance department has quit. I have no idea how to do that."

"Figure it out, Niall!" Ceil yells at him. "Weren't you over the accounts? You should be able to figure it out. Anyway, all those kids will be returned to ... wherever they came from. I want all those houses closed up by the end of the week. We will put all those properties up for sale, and bring that money back into our business."

"What properties?"

Ceil rolls her eyes without answering. "And tomorrow, I'm announcing you to the board, so I want you to be ready." Ceil looks around Niall's new office. "I told you to get moved in here hours ago. Why haven't you done so?"

Niall frowns, having forgotten about Vinatalie. He looks for her and sees she is not at her desk. He walks to her desk and finds that it is completely empty. She has also left.

Chapter Eighty-One

Nigel feels depressed at the events over the last week. Nigel looks at the mail and sees a letter from Penelope addressed to Nicolaus; he thinks this is odd. He calls for Mr. Adams.

"You rang, Sir," Adams addresses Nigel.

"Yes, can you place this for Nicolaus until we get it to him. Wherever we are keeping his mail." Nigel hands him the letter from Penelope.

"Very well, Sir. I shall place it on the huge stack of these we have for him, though your wife likes to hide these, Sir."

"Wait. There is a stack? You say hidden?"

"Why, yes, Sir."

"Adams, bring all those to me."

"Why yes, Sir."

Nigel wonders what Ceil is up to. He is shocked when Adams returns with a stack of over fifty letters, all from Penelope, addressed to Nicolaus, and unopened. Nigel looks at the dates of the letters and sees they begin around the time of Marguerite's death. Nigel begins to open them and briefly scan them. He sees that they are mostly letters of Penelope declaring her love for Nicolaus and offering him marriage in the place of her sister, and then in the place of Deirdre.

Nigel feels a bit perturbed by this, and now worried, knowing that Penelope has a volatile attitude when it comes to Nicolaus. He keeps the letters with the intent of giving them to Nicolaus.

Later, at dinner, for which Ceil and Elsa are present, and Francesca, who surprised them with her presence, Nigel asks, "So what happened at the office today, Ceil? I received a call from Daniel. He tells me Niall fired him without cause. And he informs me that he could sue us if he chooses to and he'd win, and I'm sure he is right. Why would Niall fire Daniel? He's our most knowledgeable ally, and should be the next CEO."

"Daniel will not be the next CEO, because that slot belongs to a Ravenell. Niall, to be exact."

Nigel sits back and sighs. He has a keen realization that things are already falling apart and Nicolaus has only been gone three days, counting today. "Ceil, Niall is not qualified to be CEO."

"He is! He's a Ravenell. I will have him voted in tomorrow."

"Ceil. I am nicely asking you not to destroy everything Dwight and I built up."

"Destroy?"

"Ceil! My email inbox is full of staff, former staff, asking for references. What happened today?"

"So some people left. That is expected."

"Some people? I have over fifty requests. Ceil, we have to ensure things are run properly."

"Pops, sounds like you may need to come out of retirement," Elsa suggests.

"Oh, by the way Elsa, your position of writing grants is no longer needed. I closed down the foundation. There are plenty of other jobs for you to choose from now, unless you want to go back to being an administrative assistant."

Elsa looks at her shocked, "Oh!"

"Ceil, you closed down the foundation? Why would you do that? Such actions need board approval, of which I'm sure you are aware, Ceil."

"I'm on the board, and I approve. Case closed."

"Ceil, that is not how this works, and you know it! How are the children's homes going to get funded if you close the foundation."

"Oh, I closed those too!"

"Ceil!"

Francesca looks at Ceil with disapproval. She can clearly see that Ceil intends to undo everything that Nicolaus did to help children. It makes her sad for the kids.

"Nigel, I'm tired of all these questions. If you want to be a part of the happenings, you really need to be at the office, dear. Otherwise, just leave everything to me!" Ceil stands from the table and orders the staff to bring her food to her room. She leaves the area.

Chapter Eighty-Two

There is much chatter amongst the board members as they enter the VMC conference room. All the chatter makes Niall very nervous. He wipes the sweat off him.

Soon, the questioning begins.

"Nigel, is it true that Nicolaus has resigned?"

"Why would Nicolaus resign? He's brought in record profits."

"Was Nicolaus run off?"

"And I hear that the staff has walked off the job. Are they on strike or something?"

"I heard that Daniel Araceli was fired. What happened?"

"What's happened with Nicolaus?"

Nigel calls the meeting to order. "Okay, okay, please everyone." Quiet falls over the room. "Thank you all for your questions and concerns. Let me fill everyone in with the facts. Yes, it is true that Nicolaus has unexpectedly resigned. He has some major personal issues and he feels he can no longer lead the organization. It is true that we have lost many staff members." Nigel looks at Ceil, "Whole departments to be exact." He turns his attention back to the board. "They are not on strike, they have quit. I think most left when they learned that Nicolaus had resigned. And ... as far as Daniel ... I will defer that question to Ceil. Ceil ..."

Ceil smiles at the board members. "Daniel is out, and Niall is in! I'd like us to take a vote to install my son, Niall Ravenell, as the new CEO."

The board members look at Ceil with frowns, no one speaking to affirm her request. They remember Niall and his previous irresponsible behavior at a previous board meeting. They remember some incident with the supply closet, though they were not exactly sure of the full details. And they know Ceil has placed Niall at the company, giving him an unearned title that sounds important. As the seconds go by, their frowns grow deeper.

"You remember Niall. He is the Associate Vice President, so now that ..."

"Ceil, this is highly inappropriate, don't you think?" Dwight, the co-founder, tells her. "I know nothing of this."

"And so, what happened with Daniel?" A board member asks.

"Well, he was fired," Ceil says without explanation.

"Nigel and Dwight, this is very troubling. Didn't we just have something like this happen with the janitorial staff?"

"Yeah, and Mr. Nicolaus fixed it. Restored them," a board member confirms.

"So, Niall, can you please tell the board what your credentials are? I think we missed that," another board member directly asks him.

"Credentials?" Niall frowns, not understanding.

"Where you went to school. What is your degree?"

"Oh college? Well ... I haven't gone to college."

"Nigel, isn't the requirement for our CEO to have a master's degree?"

"It doesn't matter if he went to college," Ceil snaps at them, "he's a Ravenell. The company must be in the hands of a Ravenell!"

"Oh, like Mr. Nicolaus," that board member throws back at Ceil.

"Okay, wait, I have a question. Mr. Niall, how are you going to do accounting and investments?"

"I've been doing accounting. Nicolaus put me in charge of the accounts. I don't need college to do that. Just give me a good calculator!"

The board members chatter amongst themselves at his response. Then another asks, "So then, what about investments? Do you know what instruments we are currently using?"

Niall looks to his father for help. Nigel remains silent with eyes closed, not wanting to watch the humiliation of his youngest son. Ceil has risen Niall to where he should not be, with no possibility of success. Nigel knew the board was not going to accept Niall. "Well, I ... I'm not sure. Instruments? Like multiplication and division?" Loud chatter abounds, until another question is asked.

"Mr. Niall, how many clinics do we currently have?"

"Clinics?" Niall frowns, he looks to Ceil. "I'm not sure. Twenty-five?"

"The correct answer is fifty-two, Mr. Niall. Do you know where our newest clinic is located?"

Niall shakes his head. "No, I don't know."

"Mr. Niall, what does VMC stand for?"

Niall sits back into his chair. He's starting to get heated as his ignorance is on full display. He sighs. "Gosh, I don't know."

"You don't know? It is the acronym of our business, Villamae Medical Corporation. How are you doing our accounts and do not know this basic information, Mr. Niall?"

"Oh, yeah, sure, I do know that. I thought you meant something else."

"Okay, well do you at least know our mission statement?"

In frustration, Niall throws his hands in the air, and sits back into the chair, next to his father, which was once Nicolaus' chair. "I don't know!"

One of the board members stands. "I've heard enough! Ceil and Nigel, it seems that you have lost control of the agency, and now you are trying to install an incompetent, unqualified successor to run things. This is dangerous! I'm very surprised by all this. This is very risky and for me ... the liability is too high. I resign my position effective immediately. Call me if Mr. Nicolaus returns, or if you figure out some viable option." The board member leaves the room.

Following his lead, all the board members, except Dwight, stand.

"Too risky. I resign."

"I resign. I cannot believe this is happening."

"Nigel, I'm really surprised at you. I resign!"

"Nigel, call me when Nicolaus returns. I resign."

"Look, I think you really need to talk to Nicolaus, and provide him whatever support he needs to bring him back. I think we're in real trouble here. I also immediately resign for now, unless Nicolaus can be brought back, or you figure out something else."

One by one, twenty-two of the twenty-five board members give a reason, and resign, walking out. The only ones remaining are Ceil, Dwight, and Nigel.

Dwight stands, feeling offended. "Ceil, this was a fiasco! I imagine that next we'll see the stock prices drop. What on earth are you thinking? You have no right to force any of this without discussing it with me first. And Nigel, I don't blame you my friend. I know how Ceil can spring these things on you, but we have got to get a handle on this. I'm sorry to know that Nicolaus resigned. That makes me very sad. I'm sorry to know he is having personal issues. Please let me know if I can do anything for him."

Nigel nods. "Thank you, Dwight, I appreciate that."

Dwight chuckles, "Looks like we may need to come out of retirement to get this all cleaned up. I'm really worried about the stocks. If we had staff walkouts, it is most likely that word has already gotten to market avenues. We've got to turn this around quickly. Let's talk and come up with a plan." Dwight heads for the door.

"Okay Dwight, thanks." Nigel sighs heavily, then looks to Ceil. He says nothing to either Ceil or Niall, as his emotional pain is too immense. He stands and walks out the conference room.

Chapter Eighty-Three

The following day, Nigel and Dwight return to work from their retirements. They invited all staff who left to come back into the company, as if they were never gone. For staff who did not want to return, they promised to provide them a nice reference letter.

Dwight had his eye on the VMC stocks. He'd noticed that since Nicolaus had voided the Drone Pharma merger, their stock prices had actually risen. He noticed that they held steady for now, most likely since he'd sent that press release to inform the world that he and Nigel were stepping back into leadership roles until Nicolaus decides to return. Dwight described Nicolaus' departure as a hiatus, with an expectation of his return after a period of rest and relaxation.

Nigel talks Daniel into returning to his role of Vice President, with a promise that neither Ceil nor Niall were going to be in charge of anything. As Daniel returned, so did the legal team, as well as the HR staff. By the end of the week, most high level staff return to VMC with a letter of gratitude signed by Nigel.

Nigel also reversed all the closures that Ceil made. Undoing the damage that Ceil caused helped to lift Nigel's depression. He felt power in being the bridge for Nicolaus, and in protecting Deirdre's legacy.

The children were all safe from being sent back into the foster care system. Nigel's top priority was to protect these vulnerable children. Nigel could clearly see what a fully prepared and complete job Nicolaus and Deirdre did to ensure the services for the children was more than adequate, and also providing a future for each of these children. He felt that this may be the thing he could use as leverage to get Nicolaus to return to his post.

Nicolaus decides to sell his home in Denver, and obtain another one. He knows he cannot officially move out of his father's house, as such an action will put his inheritance in jeopardy. So he leaves his belongings there, and does not change his mailing address.

"Nicolaus!" His real estate agent is surprised to learn that he wants to sell his home, and he doesn't know about Helena. "Are you sure you want to sell it?"

"Yes, ... I just ... I just need another place." He pauses at the pain of losing Helena. He knows he cannot stay in that house, no matter how lovely it is. He cannot even walk it. "Please, sell it with whatever furnishings are there. We hadn't furnished all rooms, but I think it is enough to lure a buyer. And ... I do have my eye on a different home."

"Really? Okay, same neighborhood?"

"How did you know? Yes, I really like the sixth avenue neighborhood. I was looking at the home on Bellaire street, I think it's listed for two point three mil."

"Nicolaus, I know exactly the house you're speaking of. Three fireplaces, seven bedrooms, and a huge basement."

"Yes, that's the one. Pool in the back, large front yard, outdoor grill with patio."

"Seven bedrooms, Nicolaus, just for you?"

Nicolaus pauses for a moment. "Yeah, I know. Um,... it seems like that's the one I should buy. Only I want the wall color changed. I like that cream color on the walls of my current home. So I want to get it painted before moving in."

"Sure, I can arrange that. You want a walk through?"

Nicolaus flew out with Ms. Mary. He abruptly went to the property for sale on Bellaire street. Something overwhelmingly drew him to this property, though he didn't know what it was.

"This house is eight thousand seven hundred square feet."

The backyard also made an impression on Nicolaus, and the pool out back is of medium size, with a beautiful garden on the side, and a sauna with a large square tub in the main bathroom. The interior is intimate, though large. There are several white rock arches throughout the home, with arched wooden doors, almost resembling the doors of a castle. The basement is huge with a full kitchen and wine cellar.

Nicolaus nods. "Yeah, this is it. Feels right."

"Hmm. I think you may be covertly planning your future, Nicolaus," the real estate agent jokes with him.

"I think I will have peace here. Just look at this backyard." Nicolaus spreads his arms out over the lush plants that fill up the yard. "Please put in the offer. If there is competition, just go ahead and outbid them."

Nicolaus and the real estate agent shake hands. "You got it, Nicolaus!"

Chapter Eighty-Four

Francesca waited a month before visiting Nicolaus. She notified Ms. Mary, then swore her to secrecy, wanting to surprise him. She takes Elsa with her. It is their first time in Colorado. The quick change in weather has caught them off guard. They shivered while waiting for the door to be opened.

"Oh my, this house is beautiful," Elsa tells Francesca, as she shivers in the light snowfall, wearing her light fashion sweater, with no overcoat.

Mary welcomes them inside the warmth of the home with hugs. "He has no idea! He'll be so surprised!"

"Ms. Mary, did I hear the door?"

The ladies giggle at hearing his voice from somewhere in the house. Absent mindedly, Nicolaus jogs down the stairs, then stops when he sees Francesca.

"Francesca! Elsa!"

"Surprise!" Francesca has wide open arms. Immediately, her brother grabs her up in a loving hug. Then he swoops Elsa in the hug as well.

"What are y'all doing? I didn't know you were arriving!" He dusts the snowflakes out their hair with a chuckle. "Here ..." he pulls both ladies by the hands to the fire to get warmed up.

The fireplace is large, warm, and inviting.

Francesca looks around. "Nicky, this place is beautiful."

"Yes, lovely!" Elsa agrees.

He nods. "I like it! I have peace here."

"It looks peaceful. Kind of like a little castle or something."

Nicolaus hugs Francesca tightly to him again. He has a look of loneliness about his eyes. "I've missed you." He seats the ladies.

"So tell me what's happening. Elsa, how are my nieces? Growing, I imagine. I miss them, too!"

Elsa nods with a smile. "Nicky, they sure miss you! The staff told me you used to visit them, and that they look for you every day."

"I'm so sorry about that. I just feel that it's better if I'm not around them, for their protection."

"I understand, Nicky, I do. And yes, they are growing." Elsa pulls out her phone. "I'll send you pictures."

"Thank you. Elsa, will you send me pictures every month or every couple of weeks, so I can see them growing?"

"Sure, Nicky."

"I had to see you, Nicky, for two things. Here is the first." Francesca pulls out the wrapped letters from her backpack. She holds them up, then hands them to Nicolaus.

He frowns. "What is that?"

"Letters! From Penelope! Years of them!"

"What? More letters?" He looks at them and sees years of dates on the postage marks. He chuckles.

"Apparently, my Auntie Ceil was hiding them. Father asked me to bring them to you."

"Hmm! Well, you can put these right on the fire."

"Curiosity got the best of us, and Elsa and I just had to open a few. That woman is really in love with you, Nicky. She offers to be your new wife, ... like in every letter."

"Oh God!" He says frowning. "And she's probably serious." Nicolaus stands to put the letters into the fire. They blaze quickly.

"Nicky! Aren't you even going to read them?" Francesca asks him half teasingly, with a chuckle. "She put a lot of effort in to proclaiming her love for you."

He reseats himself. "Lots of wasted effort! Isn't that thingy for her birthday in two weeks? Father told me something about it."

"Nicolaus, aren't you going?" Elsa asks. "Pops says Mother Ceil is insisting all of us go. He wants us to show up as the Ravenell clan," she chuckles. "Supposedly, lots of Latvian dignitaries will be there."

Nicolaus chuckles. "Ceil wants us to go. More reason for me to not attend." He brushes the subject aside. "So what else you got for me? How is my father?"

"Our father! Well, you know he's back to work at the company. He tells me he's filling in, waiting for your return."

"Yeah, I saw news reports that said I'm on hiatus. I keep telling him to hire someone else, but he won't listen."

"Nicky, are you seriously not going back?"

Nicolaus nods. "I can't deal with Ceil anymore. And this curse business ... it's best if I just stay away from everyone."

"Oh Nicky! That sounds lonely. You can't give up, Love. Someone will be in your life again."

"No. I'm done with that now. That season of my life is over. I've had to get to a place to accept it, and I have accepted it. That is not meant for me. After losing Helena ... and Deirdre, I know I'd be endangering any woman. I stay in contact with my military brothers, have forged new friendships, and have joined one of the active methodist churches here."

"Well Nicky, you left the foster children vulnerable to the whims of Ceil. She tried to close down everything you and Deirdre put in place. I felt so bad about it. Although now, father has restored all the programs."

Nicolaus shakes his head in disbelief. He sighs. "I was hoping father would ensure everything continued to run smoothly. I didn't want to leave them. I have already told you why I left. I'm glad father responded. As far as my work is concerned, I continue my support calls to all the children, I have kept the business grants going, and am looking to start some scholarships for young people. I also have the Darfurians to look after."

"So sounds like you really are trying to disconnect yourself from VMC. I'm very sure father is not going to accept that kind of change, Nicky. He fully expects your return."

"I can't deal with Ceil anymore."

Francesca frowns. "You know, once Helena told me that you needed love. I didn't believe her. But looking at you now and listening to you, I do think she was right. You need love in your life Nicolaus. That is the one thing that's always been elusive for you."

Nicolaus shakes his head. "I've had my big love. Deirdre!"

"You still wear your wedding ring," Elsa points out to him.

Nicolaus looks at the ring that binds him to Deirdre, he touches it. "Oh, I can't imagine ever taking this ring off. Deirdre has always loved me, and I have always and will always love her. I was blessed to have her for the time I did. And so blessed that we married. I miss her so much." Nicolaus felt himself getting sad. He sighs thinking of Deirdre.

"As far as my Auntie Ceil, I think the two of you have to work out her issues about you. You know, just bury the hatchet and get on with living."

"Maybe someday." He stands, "How about drinks?" Nicolaus disappears for a minute or two, then returns with drinks for each of them.

The alcohol warms Francesca and Elsa even more. "So, Nicky, the other thing I've flown all this way to see you about, is to tell you I'm also leaving. I've accepted a position at Cambridge, my alma mater. Can you believe it?"

"Are you serious?" Nicolaus was right on his sister to hug her again. "Congratulations! Tell me everything!"

"Anthropology! I'll be the lead chair of the department."

"Wow! That is fantastic, Francesca! When do you start?"

"Next week!"

"Awesome! My sis, department chair at Cambridge! I'll have to visit and see about you. Will you have housing?"

"Yes! Right on campus! I'm so excited!"

"What a great accomplishment! Our mother would be so proud of you!"

Chapter Eighty-Five

Nicolaus recognizes the call from Estonia. He immediately answers it.

"Mr. Nicolaus, this is Brown from your home in Estonia."

"Hello Mr. Brown. Is all okay?"

"Oh yes, Sir. I'm calling to let you know that we have a few special guests here, Sir. They arrived eight hours ago, which would have been late your time, so I am just now calling."

"Special guests?"

"Yes Sir. Miss Abigail Omari and her father Cecil."

"What? Abigail is there?"

"Yes Sir. Said she just had to see the castle, the grounds, the family gallery, and the church. When I saw her, Sir, when they first arrived, I immediately knew she is of Ms. Deirdre's family. She looks just like her. So I had no hesitation, Sir."

"You did good, Mr. Brown. Exactly as I would have wanted. Thank you for welcoming them. Abigail is Deirdre's sister, and Cecil is their father. Please make them feel at home, they are family. They deserve the same treatment you would give to me and my family."

"Oh yes, Sir. Just as I have instructed the staff."

"Mr. Brown, is Abigail there now, and available?"

"Oh yes, Sir, she is right here beside me. Would you like to speak with her?"

"Yes, please!"

Butler Brown nods to Abigail, then hands her the phone.

"Hello."

"Abigail, is that you? This is Nicolaus."

"Nicolaus!" Hearing his voice for the first time brought butterflies to Abigail's stomach. She imagines his face before her. She tries to remain calm and assured in her voice, although her insides are demonstrating a swirling feeling.

"I hope you don't mind that I took the liberty of stopping by. I just had to see this place. My dad has been talking about this castle for years. It truly is amazing!"

"Of course I don't mind. It is your home as well. Abigail, I think of you as family. In fact, I've been searching for you."

"You've been searching for me?" Dominique steps forward to put her ear to the back of the receiver to listen in.

"Yes, since the memorial service. You left without seeing me."

"Oh, well, there was so many people, which is wonderful to see such love for my sister. But Nicolaus, I didn't want to chance running into Ceil. She has wrangled legal issues over my father. I didn't want to chance causing further problems."

"I understand. Did you see your Mom?"

"Yes. She looks well, under the circumstances."

"Yes, she is well, and ... somehow I want to bring the two of you together. Is it okay for me to fly out to see you?" Nicolaus feels something here. The sound of Abigail's voice, which is unlike that of Deirdre, does something to him. He feels jumbled at the prospect of seeing her again, especially the possibility of seeing her in a personable way. He brushes his feelings aside, remembering the curse, not wanting to endanger her.

However, Abigail's giggle is exactly like Deirdre's. "Nicolaus...," the way she says his name moves him, "I wouldn't want you to trouble yourself. Anyway, this is just a stop for us. My dad is taking me to Greece to visit family. I believe our ship leaves in eight hours. We're just going to get some sleep and be off in the morning. A storm is blowing in, so my dad wants to get ahead of it."

"Your ship?"

"Cruise ship. My dad is terrified of flying. And I'm terrified of the water, and more so of the ocean. I don't want my dad traveling alone, so Dominique and I bear the ocean to support him."

"Abigail ... I'd really like to talk with you. In person."

"Oh, well ... okay, uhm ... I'll be here for the next eight hours! Though Nicolaus, we have to get to the ship early, so probably really only seven hours."

"Okay, let me see what I can do. I thank you for being open to meeting with me."

"Of course, Nicolaus. We are family!"

Upon ending the call, Abigail touches her hand over her heart as it is racing, and Dominique seems to be providing a few little jumps for joy, with great laughter for Abigail. Dominique can see that Nicolaus had an effect on Abigail, just from talking to him over the phone.

Chapter Eighty-Six

Nicolaus' private jet is delayed by the weather, as they have to wait out the storm, before making the flight over the ocean.

By the time Nicolaus makes it to Estonia, and intensely and dramatically enters the castle, knowing he is late, ... he has just missed Abigail.

"Oh Sir, I am so sorry," Butler Brown tells him. "They have just left, about fifteen minutes ago, now. They did try to wait for you, Sir."

Nicolaus sighs with his hand to his head. He begins to pace, as Nigel would, thinking about what to do. "Mr. Brown, did they tell you which cruise ship they will be on? Maybe I can meet them at the dock."

"Sorry Sir, they did not. They were anxiously awaiting you, though Sir."

"Well, did they leave a phone number or contact information?"

"Sorry, Sir, they did not."

Just then, they hear the door opening by another staff member. She'd opened the door, before the guests could knock. Nicolaus turns at the sound of the closing of the front door. There she stands ... Abigail. Dominique and Cecil are behind her.

Abigail reaches her hand out to Nicolaus, and he connects with her. Abigail looks at Nicolaus with heightened consideration, out of breath from running.

Immediately she knows in her heart there is something special about him. Now that she is meeting him in person, she feels the strong connection, even though she doesn't even know him. Abigail feels his charms, his striking good looks, and appealing physique are having an effect on her, though she knows this is something deeper. His eyes are warm and inviting towards her, the same as in his photos. She understands her sister's attraction for him, as she has a strong magnetism to Nicolaus herself, of this she is certain.

Abigail's mind recognizes Nicolaus' face from her dreams of her future children. At this realization, her hand grip on him automatically tightens.

"Nicolaus," Abigail says his name with a sweet smile. "It is very nice to formally meet you."

Nicolaus gently grasps her hand between both of his. He cannot believe that she is standing here before him. "Abigail."

Abigail continues to smile at him, his touch stirs her. Purposefully, she does not release his hand, as she half turns to introduce her party. "This is Dominique, my dear, dear friend. She's like a sister to me." Abigail continues to tighten her hold on his hand for him not to release hers. Nicolaus obliges and greets Dominique with his other hand. "And my father, Cecil Omari."

"Mr. Omari! Thank you so much for returning."

Cecil steps close to Nicolaus. "So, you are Nicolaus Ravenell," he states, more than asks. Nicolaus nods, and offers his free hand. Cecil grabs Nicolaus' hand as he keenly observes the man who held Deirdre's heart, whom he notices is having a real time effect on his other daughter.

Cecil knows all about the Kiviste family folklore. He knows all about Nicohls and DeeDee, and has often told Abigail of the destined love story of her ancestors, so she would know where she came from. DeeDee having traveled from Greece to Estonia to help put an end to a devastating war, only to fall madly in love with Nicohls.

Cecil is stunned to see the romance piece of this story playing out before his eyes, in modern times, with his own daughter. He's never seen Abigail look upon a man the way she is now looking upon Nicolaus Ravenell, Nicohls' direct descendent. It worries him, having already lost one daughter to that dreaded curse.

However, Cecil is also well aware that where love and matters of the heart are concerned, it does no good to fight against this.

Cecil strongly holds onto Nicolaus' shoulder. "You resemble Nigel, yet mostly look like Nichols, your ancestor. Nigel and I are old friends, you know."

"Yes Sir, I understand that you had some connection to our family, and that Ceil has ..."

"Your mother, Ceil," he suddenly sounds upset and takes a step back, "she pulled a dirty job on me all right."

"Sir, I am so sorry. That is partially what I'd like to speak to you about. Please," Nicolaus sweeps his hand to the furniture for them to sit and speak, "shall we?"

Cecil nods.

"See dad, I told you we should return to at least see what Nicolaus would like to speak with us about. It is important! Aren't you glad you listened to me and postponed our trip until tomorrow?" Abigail puts her full support towards Nicolaus.

Nicolaus notices that Abigail has not let go of his hand. He looks to her and is taken by her. She stands strong, though she is the same height of Deirdre. Her grip is strong on his hand, though her hands are small, similar to Deirdre. Her mannerisms and her hair is different from that of Deirdre. She has an aroma, as did Deirdre, only it is very different, more sexy, than innocent. Her eyes are strikingly daring.

Abigail giggles as he stares at her. "Stop staring, Nicolaus." She slowly releases his hand, though she does not really want to. She frowns, not sure what has come over her. "I'm not the ghost of Deirdre! I'm her twin sister!" She tells him, following her father to sit down by the fireplace, Dominique in tow behind her.

"Of course, please forgive me. It's just ... the resemblance."

"Her twin, honey," she tells him with a giggle. "I wish I could have met my sister. Tell us about her!"

Nicolaus sits across from Abigail and Cecil, next to Dominique. He shakes his head with endearment. "Deirdre was amazing and wonderful! A spark, for everyone. She loved children. Helping children was actually her idea, and I just supported anything she wanted to do. And then ... the ideas grew, I believe divinely inspired, and we began helping children globally, and getting kids out of foster care using my family's company and donated money. Deirdre had a happy laugh, just like yours, Abigail."

"And you were married," she pushed to know more.

Nicolaus nods. "Yes. Yes, we married at home, and then publicly, here in Estonia."

"We saw it all over the news!" Dominique informs him.

"Really?"

"My daughter seemed very happy to be married to you, Nicolaus."

"Yes Sir, we were happy." Frowning, "I love your daughter very much. We were engaged for ten years. I asked her to marry me when she was fifteen and I was sixteen. And then I left to serve in the military."

"You just left my sister?" Abigail sounds concerned, though her mind is all about Nicolaus. She watches his movements, his eyes, his lips, his hands. Though her own intrigue of Nicolaus is apparent, Abigail did not realize that Nicolaus was doing the same, as Nicolaus felt mesmerized by Abigail, and it scared him.

"Well ... no," his frown deepens, "I knew she had to finish school. And then she started college, and graduated with a law degree, took the bar exam and passed it, so she was a lawyer. She did law work at the state capital. Then, she finally gave me a wedding date. We were going to marry, and ... things got interrupted."

"Yes with Marguerite and then Gwen," Abigail tells him in a reporter's tone, showing him she knew about everything.

"Yes. And ... after all that, we married, here at the historic Saint Nicholas church across town. And the year was great."

"And she was pregnant?"

Nicolaus nods. "Yes. Our son ...." Suddenly he stops talking and shakes his head, as the mention of his son, Nicolai, grips him with emotion. Tears spill from Nicolaus' eyes. "Can you give me one moment, please?" He gets up and leaves the room. In privacy, Nicolaus sighs, and wipes his face. He wants to cry more, though he knows that instead he must pull himself together. It takes him a few minutes to enter back into the room.

While Nicolaus is out of the room, Dominique makes keen observations, quietly, while Cecil has also gotten up to look out the window. "Girl, that man is fine!" Dominique puts emphasis on the word 'fine' as she waves her hands as if there is an aura where Nicolaus was sitting. "Mmm! Fine!"

Abigail giggles, and shushes Dominique, fanning herself, trying to stay calm.

Butler Brown serves drinks, and leaves one for Nicolaus as well. Nicolaus enters and reseats himself, downs his drink, and decides to change the subject.

"So what I wanted to discuss with you is ..."

"My Constance," Cecil interrupts him, bouncing back into the chair.

Nicolaus looks at him with surprise. "Well yes, actually. I call her Mom, because she is like my mother. And so I want you to know that she is all right. She is healthy, and she very much wants to see both of you."

"My Constance," Cecil says again, this time with a hint of remembrance. "I couldn't find one photo of her online, though I did see her in that interview Deirdre did."

"Oh!" Nicolaus pulls out his phone and looks through his photos, "I'm sure I have a picture. Yes, here you go," he hands his phone to Cecil.

Cecil smiles. "She's just as beautiful as ever! You know, we wouldn't have been separated if it weren't for Ceil." His demeanor changes to that of a mad and upset person again. "That woman is rotten to her core. She's a vindictive ... witch!" He sighs to try to calm himself. "Sorry to speak of your mother like that, Nicolaus."

Nicolaus chuckles. "What you say is not a lie. And turns out, she is not actually my mother. Rachel was my mother. Did you know Rachel?"

"Rachel? Yes, yes I know Rachel. And Janelle and Zoe as well. Janelle and Zoe are nothing like Ceil."

Nicolaus nods. "So, I want to clear your name of whatever has transpired all those years ago that kept you away from Mom. Can you tell me what happened?"

"I doubt that you can help me."

"Please let me try. I want to right the wrong Ceil has done. It's the least I can do."

Both Cecil and Abigail look at Nicolaus with unbelief, as not even Nigel has offered to do such a thing. "Well," Cecil begins, "hard to know exactly what she did. All I know is that all was well between all of us. Then I'm being accused of embezzlement for millions of dollars at the financial firm I worked for. Millions. I was arrested, paid bail, and released. Then I'm suddenly accused of embezzlement of your father's company, VMC. Accused of stealing millions."

"What?"

"I learned these accusations were all coming from one source. Ceil. Ceil in cahoots with the mayor, at that time. So there is another warrant. How am I supposed to get from under accusations of the city mayor? So that's when I decided to run.

Unfortunately, my sweet Constance goes into labor, from all the stress. We didn't know why Ceil was doing this to us. I swear to you, I've never taken nothing from anyone. I would never ..."

"Mr. Omari, of course I believe you. I know how Ceil is. So you have no idea why she turned against you?"

Cecil shrugs and puts his hands mid-air, "I have no idea. For some reason she wanted me gone. I couldn't bear to leave my family and the double burden on Constance. So, I took one of the babies," he takes Abigail's hand, "and we go into hiding."

Nicolaus shakes his head. "I am so sorry, Mr. Omari. I'm so sorry that Ceil did this. I promise you, I'll get the best lawyers on this, and I promise to get you exonerated."

"How? I don't want DeeDee exposed to Ceil."

Nicolaus frowns at him. "I'm sorry, who?"

Cecil grabs up Abigail's hand again. "My DeeDee. Right here!"

Dominique and Abigail giggle. "DeeDee is Abby's nickname," Dominique explains to him.

Nicolaus crosses his arms looking at all of them. "Okay." He sits back and rubs his forehead, apprehensive of such a double meaning regarding the family line. "Okay, yes, I understand. I will have them be discrete. Knowing Ceil, it is most likely that if she got the mayor in on it, there is no evidence. And the charges were probably just never dropped. So let me work on this."

Cecil stands to shake Nicolaus' hands, and Nicolaus stands as well. "Nicolaus, anything you can do to clear me. I will be so appreciative!"

"Of course, Sir. And my home is your home. Please know you are welcome here any time at all. Just as you arrived, I do not need to be present. As you experienced, my staff know how to treat family."

Cecil nods, "Yes, they were very kind. And thank you. This castle is magnificent, just like all the stories say. Tomorrow we go visit my family in Greece. I really hate that my Deirdre never met this leg of my family."

Abigail is standing close to Nicolaus again. She gets his attention by grabbing onto his arm. She smiles at him. "That portrait gallery is incredible."

"Yes, and ... your full name, Abigail?"

"Abigail Deirdre Omari, the exact opposite of my sister. Wasn't my mother clever, doing that?"

Nicolaus nods, "I remember Mom telling me about it."

Dominique chimes in, "And we call her Abby for short, and DeeDee is her nickname. You know, DeeDee, like her ancestor."

Nicolaus slowly nods, getting that confirmation of his fear. "Yes," he says slowly. He removes himself from the ladies as his insides are getting all riled up. The feeling brings fear to him. Nicolaus pours himself another drink and downs it, trying to squash the pain, the fear, and the dread.

Later, as everyone is sleep, Nicolaus makes calls, since it is daytime in the United States. He phones the private detective and fires him, since he has not detected the whereabouts of Abigail, though she is right here with him. Then he dials the number to the lawyers, and hires them to assist in clearing Cecil's name. Nicolaus also decides not to say anything to Constance as of yet. He knows he must get Cecil's name cleared before he can take them to see Constance.

Abigail looks at the moonlight that drifts into the window of the bedroom inside the castle. The light drifts over her. Her mind cannot stop thinking about Nicolaus. That face. That handsome face! The face of her children. She thinks about his soft, strong hands, which gently held hers without hesitation. She thinks about his voice, and the way her insides flitter at his mere presence. She could see his curly hair, his soft warm brown eyes, and the way his lips curl when he smiles.

Abigail turns from the moonlight and closes her eyes. However, sleep eludes her, as all she can see when she closes her eyes is ... Nicolaus Ravenell.

Chapter Eighty-Seven

C eil is annoyed and a little worried that Nicolaus has been ignoring the phone calls and text messages of her demands for him to join them on this trip to see Penelope. She knows she will need a backup plan, as he has not shown up to meet the family as they are getting ready to leave for Latvia.

Nigel used his private jet to fly the family over to Latvia for Penelope's birthday celebration. They had received an official invitation. The celebration is to be held at a dilapidated medieval Latvian castle for which Penelope is remodeling, and she renamed this property 'Drone Castle', in honor of her family.

Both Ceil and Nigel notice on the drive to the property, it is isolated, far from the nearest town, and far from neighbors or people. When their hired ride from the airport pulls up to the large land mass and moat bridge, they see no other people. No other vehicles. No dignitaries, no other persons.

Nigel sighs, "Well, let us see what is happening!" He assists everyone out of the vehicle, lifting Emily into his arms, as Niall carries Elaine. Nigel leads the family over the sturdy bridge that crosses over the moat. Then they carefully walk the land mass that led to the large, drab castle walls.

The castle is a gray brick structure. Plain tall walls, looking out of place on the surrounding plentiful foliage grounds. Half of the castle has fallen in. Nigel hoped them to be gone before sunset.

As they enter, the castle itself is cold, drafty, and dark, lit by several lanterns. Entering the castle is like entering a different era of time and day. Going from daylight to darkness. There are several security type guardsmen present, outside the doors, and also inside. Nigel finds this intriguing.

Nigel takes Penelope's hand as they are greeted. "Penelope! We've been looking forward to celebrating your birthday!"

Elsa carries in a few gift packages. "Hello Penelope." She frowns, not seeing other people. "Looks like we are the first to arrive! Where would you like these?"

"Hmm, I thought we were a little late," Nigel comments.

"Well, you the only ones here. Over there Elsa," she points to a bare table. "I surprised you bring gifts, very kind of you." Penelope looks at the door, as if she is looking for someone else. "And Nicolaus? Where is Nicolaus?"

"Oh, Penelope, Nicolaus no longer lives with us. I told him about this event, though I don't think he is attending. He has other things to take care of today," Nigel informs her.

"Other things?" She asks with indignation, frowning. "How is this? Ceil, did you not tell me you to bring Nicolaus?"

Ceil chuckles, taking Penelope by the arm. She turns her from everyone. "Don't worry about him not being here. That will not change anything you and I have discussed. Shall we?" She stretches her hand forward for Penelope to walk with her. The family follows behind. "So tell me about the work you are doing here."

Penelope smiles at Ceil, with a frowned sigh. She was prepared for such a deception of Ceil going back on her word and not bringing Nicolaus. She makes a hand gesture to one of her men, who nods, then disappears.

For about fifteen minutes, Penelope walks the family through the castle, showing them renovations, and also tells them her future remodeling plans.

"And Andrejs? Shall we see him today?" Nigel asks, noticing that no other guests are arriving.

"No. My father is no longer in charge. You see, Mr. Ravenell, my father had a ... how you say ... breakdown."

"Breakdown?"

"Yes. The day you called to dismiss the merger. That day you try to kill our company."

"Now, Penelope, that is not true. We just merely, ..."

"You merely break my father. Our stocks drop like crashing rocket. Plumet. No more funds. No more investors."

"Oh no, Penelope."

"Do not say you sorry," she yells at Nigel. "You no sorry. My father devastated. Almost to file for bankruptcy."

"Almost? He pulled through?"

"No! I take over! Ceil help me!"

"Oh! Penelope, I had no idea. Ceil?"

"Well ... I only provided a little advice."

Penelope started them walking again. She eased them down some stairs through a passageway, lit only by torches. "Good advice. Advice that worked. And another offer." Ceil, Niall, Elsa, and Nigel followed Penelope down the steps thinking they are still touring the castle. Elsa carries Emily while Niall carries Elaine.

Penelope leads them into a room with several toys and goodies for the girls. "Please!" She tells them pointing at the toys. "I have these especially for your little ones."

"Oh how nice!" Elsa comments.

The whole family attends to the happiness of Elaine and Emily, except they had not realized that as they walked, they had been descending into the dungeon of the castle, and that now they are standing in a barred jail cell. Penelope steps out and slams the door shut, locking the Ravenell family inside.

The sound of the clank of the barred door immediately gets Nigel's attention. Straightaway, he attempts to open the door, seeing Penelope step back from the other side. Several of her men join her. "Penelope. The door."

"Yes, you locked in, and shall remain for Nicolaus arrives to free you," she tells them in her broken English.

Nigel looks to Ceil, then back to Penelope, understanding they have walked into a trap. "Penelope, I told you, Nicolaus is not with us. Please don't do this. Our grandbabies ... they cannot stay in here."

"They will! You will do what I say now!"

Penelope pulls out her cell phone, is surprised to get a signal, and dials Nicolaus' number. She hears an operator's voice, 'This number is blocked. If you feel this is an error contact the person you are trying to call'. Penelope's anger looms larger, learning that Nicolaus has blocked her number. "Ugh!" She shouts loudly in frustration.

Ceil places her hand on Nigel's arm to stop him from pulling out his phone. She smiles. "Penelope, perhaps this is not the best idea. Why don't we all go upstairs to talk about this? You can tell us what you want, and we will get it for you."

Penelope steps up to the bars. "No more talk, Mrs. Ravenell. You break you promise to me. You break it! You say you deliver Nicolaus and he not here. So no. No more talk."

Nigel looks to Ceil again. "Ceil, what is she talking about?" Ceil shakes her head and does not answer him. "Penelope, what about your other guests?"

"No. No other guests."

"Oh. Well ... please, I agree with Ceil. Our babies cannot stay here, it is cold and damp. Let's go back upstairs to talk."

"No! No more talk." Penelope points to Niall. "You!" She head gestures to one of her guardsmen. Quickly, the door is opened, the family is pushed back, Niall is dragged out, and the cell door is relocked on the family.

Harshly, he is pushed up the stairs, leaving the family.

Nigel looks to Ceil. "Ceil, what have you done?"

Upstairs, Penelope has the guardsman force Niall to sit at a desk table. Penelope places some papers before Niall. "Sign me your shares," she yells at him. She strikes him, then the guardsman negates any wishes he has of reacting. "Sign!" She harshly yells at

Niall. Each time he signs, she removes the top paper, for him to sign another. "All your properties." He signs it without arguing. "All your rights." He signs. Smiling, Penelope looks over each paper. Then in a fit, she slams her hand on the table before him.

"You have three days to bring Nicolaus. Your babies no eat until Nicolaus here. No three days, then I decide what next to do. And no police, no authorities, or I decide what next to do. Don't make me hurt those little babies. Got it?"

Frightened, Niall nods. He is manhandled out of the chair, all the way to the front door, then harshly shoved out the castle. The door is slammed on him.

Niall scrambles to his feet, and takes off running.

Chapter Eighty-Eight

After Niall finally returns to Austin, he directly goes to Bishop Leighton, not knowing what else to do. He doesn't even know where Nicolaus lives, and he does not want to call Nicolaus alone. He had no idea how to explain all this to Nicolaus.

"Calm yourself, Niall," Bishop Leighton touches Niall on the shoulders.

"I can't!" Niall paces the church office. "That witch might kill my daughters."

Bishop Leighton stands, "I demand you calm yourself, son! You will respect God's house."

"Sorry Bishop."

"This is what happens when you do not prepare yourself to be a man, Niall. You should know everything your father knows. How is it that I know where Nicolaus lives and you do not?"

Niall walks over to the Bishop, and grabs his shoulders. "Please! You have to help me! Nicolaus and I are not exactly on speaking terms."

Bishop Leighton frowns at Niall, realizing the situation in the family is worse than he had suspected. "And why is that Niall? Haven't you asked Nicolaus' forgiveness?"

Niall looks at the bishop with anger. "We don't have time for this, Bishop Leighton. My children are being held captive!"

Bishop Leighton nods. "Umhum, and I want to know what may happen when we arrive at your brother's home. What state is your relationship with him, Niall?"

Niall sighs. "I don't know ... strained, I guess you could say. And to answer your question, no I have not yet spoken to Nicolaus about Deirdre. I haven't asked his forgiveness."

Bishop Leighton nods. "Hence, your apprehension." He thinks for a moment. "Okay, best we just show up. Let's go."

A few hours later, Ms. Mary is surprised to open the door to Bishop Leighton and Niall, on this cold Saturday night in Denver. The bishop nods to her. "Is Nicolaus home? We have an emergency." He keeps the smile on his face as they are bid inside.

"I'll get him. He's outside in the garden. Please have a seat."

Both the bishop and Niall look around the beautiful home.

Nicolaus enters the room promptly, frowning. "Bishop Leighton? Niall? Ms. Mary tells me there's an emergency? Oh God, what's happened?"

Bishop Leighton takes Nicolaus' outstretched hand to shake it. Nicolaus touches Niall on the shoulder, then offers them to sit down.

"Nicolaus, son, please, sit with us," the bishop tells him.

Nicolaus looks at him as if to brace himself. He has a seat opposite of them. "Niall, what's happening?"

The bishop touches Niall's leg to stop him spewing out the situation, as he knows this needs to be handled with care. "Nicolaus, your family, they are in Latvia."

"Oh, okay, so they are safe. No plane crash or accident?"

"Correct. However, there is a problem. Of which Niall will explain."

"Niall, you didn't go with them?"

"I did ... I ... I did, I was there. Oh God! Nicolaus you have to help. You have to help! Penelope has everyone. Even my daughters."

Nicolaus frowns. "Penelope has them? What do you mean?"

Niall stands, furious. "That witch! She has them locked in a dungeon. My daughters ... in a dungeon!" Niall begins to pace.

Nicolaus stands. "What? Niall, slow down. Tell me what's happening."

"It's all your fault!" Niall shouts at Nicolaus. "It's always about you!"

Nicolaus shakes his head, wide eyed and frowning, not understanding. He looks to the bishop.

The bishop stands and pulls Niall to sit down again. "Niall, you are not making sense. From my understanding, they went to a party in some castle. And she has everyone locked in a dungeon."

Nicolaus cannot believe what he is hearing. He frowns. "Penelope?"

"That little witch is not the same person she was before. Something's happened to her. She's changed. She's mean. She says you have to go to release them, or she might hurt my daughters. We have three days, one and a half now, to get back."

Nicolaus sighs. "Let me call her." Nicolaus goes to get his phone, returns to the room, and calls Penelope.

Penelope answers. "Oh, so I bet I have your attention now, Nicolaus Ravenell!"

"Penelope, my brother is here telling me that you have my family locked up. And I told him that could not possibly be true, because the Penelope I know would never do such a thing."

"The Penelope you know is no more, Nicolaus Ravenell. I do have your family, and they will stay locked up with no food until you get here. Do you hear me?"

"Penelope, my nieces are babies, please, you have to .... Hello? Hello?" Nicolaus looks to the two men who are looking at him. "We got disconnected. Let me try again."

"She most likely hung up on you," Niall comments. "I told you ...."

"Penelope, this is Nicolaus ...." The phone is disconnected again. "Hello? Hello?"

Niall takes the phone from him. "Forget it, man! She's not playing! My girls' lives are at stake here! You have to go back with me, Nicolaus. Please!"

Nicolaus silently nods, knowing he will be walking right into whatever trap she has set for him. He sighs. "What is she so angry about?"

"Hell if I know. It's always all about you! Even the VMC board members wouldn't work with me. They walked out on us and quit because of you!" Niall is yelling at Nicolaus. "So what did you do to Penelope?" Niall throws his hands in the air, not waiting for an answer. "Awh forget it! You have to go back with me to get them out!"

Nicolaus nods in silence again. "Let me make some calls."

"And no police or authorities. She says she'll hurt my girls if we do that."

Nicolaus nods in understanding.

The bishop stands. "Let us pray." The bishop lays hands on Nicolaus. "This day, God returns your authority back to you, Nicolaus Ravenell. Men will follow you like lambs follow a shepherd. You will do mighty things. It will not be an easy road Nicolaus, and there may be a time that you might feel extremely overwhelmed, but you must not give up. The whole of your family and its empire will hinge on you, Nicolaus Ravenell. Our great God Almighty, we ask for strength of mind, heart, and spirit, the fighting spirit needed to accomplish this task," Bishop Leighton prophetically prays over him.

Nicolaus receives the prayer with added worry.

Chapter Eighty-Nine

Nicolaus charters a private jet plane to get them to Latvia as quickly as possible. Roddy is on board, and they are on their way to pick up his other trusted comrades, Sanchez and Washington.

Nicolaus observes his brother. He can see that Niall is nervous, and looks determined at the same time. He touches Niall's shoulder, as he is sitting next to him. "Niall, it's really good to see that you've risen to the occasion for your daughters."

"Well of course I did," he snaps at Nicolaus. "I don't want any harm happening to them." He looks at his watch. "We're going to make it really close on time."

"They need you to show up for them like this every day though, Niall. Not only in an emergency, or when their lives are at stake. They need you every day."

Niall looks at Nicolaus with a smirk. "Are you seriously about to lecture me about having kids? My kids?"

Roddy chuckles, noticing Niall's abrupt attitude. "Hey, you two, we need to stay focused. Niall, I'm wondering about the castle, can you tell me about it?" Niall tells him what he knows and what he saw.

It is not long before Sanchez and Washington are aboard, the jet refuels, and they are on the way to Latvia.

"So where is this castle, exactly?" They question Niall.

"I'm not sure. I just know we drove about twenty miles from Riga."

"Twenty miles. Okay, that's good. Do you know the name of it, I mean before she changed the name?"

Niall shrugs. "No. That is all I know."

"What is waiting for us though, Niall?" Nicolaus asks him. "Does she have an army, security, or what?"

"Well, I'm not sure what they are. I did see a lot of them though. It's like being in some medieval nightmare or something."

"What does that mean? Are they armed?"

Niall nods. "Yeah. I saw swords, and guns ... and rifles."

"Swords?" Nicolaus frowns with a sigh. "Okay, guys, look, when we land, that is as far as you go. I don't want you risking your life for this."

"Are you kidding, Nicolaus?" Roddy chimes in. "We did not travel this far only to drop you, then turn around and run. No. We need to see this place. The least we can do is get the coordinates to send for help."

"Look, I don't want any of you to risk your life for this. It's a Ravenell mess, and I'll have to clean it up. If I can."

"No, Nicolaus, no," Roddy is more adamant, "there's no question about whether we risk our lives or not. It's what we do. Guys, are we all in this together?"

"Hurrah!" They make a military sound. "We are all in this together," Sanchez and Washington say in unison.

Nicolaus is moved. "You guys are amazing."

Chapter Ninety (TW)

When the jet plane lands at the Riga, Latvian airport, Nicolaus and the guys are suddenly surrounded by people, asking Nicolaus for autographs, as though he is a celebrity star.

This, of course, only makes Niall more angry, as again, it is all about Nicolaus, and none are asking for his autograph. "What the hell?"

Roddy and Sanchez chuckle at the scene. Nicolaus attempts to oblige a few people, as the crowd seems to grow with onlookers who have curiosity of who the celebrity might be. As the crowd continues to grow, Roddy, Sanchez, and Washington step forward to try to protect Nicolaus and Niall, while attempting to push through the crowd. With great effort, they finally make it to the exit doors, and into a taxi to take them to the castle. Niall angrily eyes Nicolaus most of the twenty mile drive.

Once they arrive to the isolated castle, which is far from any other properties, they exit the taxi down the way from the castle grounds, not to be detected. They trek the short distance and hide behind some tall bushes for cover. Niall watches as the men seem to scout out the grounds.

Nicolaus retrieves his binoculars from his backpack and he looks towards the castle. He notices this is an unused historic property, with the whole right side fallen in on itself. He passes the binoculars to Washington.

"Okay," Nicolaus begins, "Niall is right. They do have swords and guns. Okay, guys, this is where your journey ends. Niall and I will take this line of bushes and try to sneak into the back of the castle, and ..."

"Nicolaus, what the hell are you talking about?" Niall says rather loudly.

"Shh!" They all tell him, Nicolaus quickly putting his hand over Niall's mouth. "Quiet Niall."

Niall whispers, "We can't sneak in, there is no way ..."

"Maybe we can. It's the best option to try to get in undetected. There are too many of these men out front."

"Those dudes are all over, including the back."

"I say we just charge them. Charge them and get it over with. Then they will all know we are here," Roddy suggests, feeling bold.

"No," Nicolaus disagrees. "That puts you guys in direct firing line. No. And this is where your journey ends," he repeats, knowing the guys are ignoring him.

"Nicolaus, we are not leaving. So, I say we charge. And since they won't shoot you, Nicolaus, you lead."

"Well, I ..."

"Okay, let's go!" Roddy doesn't wait. He waves everyone forward, and charges.

"Oh God!" Nicolaus jumps up, grabbing Niall by the arm, pulling him along. Nicolaus must run fast to get ahead of Roddy, forgetting his leg injury. The men make yelling sounds as if they are charging into battle. Niall is in the rear, not knowing what to do. Niall stops in his tracks when he sees his brother and the guys fearlessly take on hand to hand combat fist fighting with the large group of guardsmen who have swords, guns, and rifles.

Nicolaus looks for Niall as he flips a guy over his shoulders, then takes another out by punching him. "Niall!" He calls to him, shouting, "Get to the castle door!"

Niall seems very confused as he sees men's bodies flying through the air as they are thrown by Nicolaus, Roddy, Sanchez, and Washington. He sees Nicolaus use that throat punch he once received when he stupidly accosted Deirdre. Niall runs for the castle doors, out of harm's way and he watches.

Inside the castle cell, Elsa can hear the loud commotion and rumbling through the open air barred window. She climbs on the hard bench bed to look out. "It's Nicolaus! He's here!" She says excitedly. "Mother Ceil, Pops, it's Nicolaus and his buddies! They are fighting!" Elsa's voice has the belief and certainty that Nicolaus would save them.

Nigel chuckles, "That's my son! Dear Lord, help them."

"Bring her to me," Penelope tells one of her guardsmen, pointing to Elsa.

During the boisterous fighting outside, Nicolaus and his crew retrieve weapons. Niall watches his brother and the guys bravely sword fight trained men. He watches them fist fight them, barely taking blows themselves. He watches as they remain on their feet after taking on each man.

Nicolaus has already saved Niall several times, while battling other guardsmen himself, as men approach his brother with swords drawn.

The fighting noise grows louder and additional guardsmen rush onto the field. "There is too many of them," Nicolaus shouts. "Niall, go inside! There is too many!"

Suddenly, Niall gets dragged inside the castle and down the steps towards the dungeon. He fights against the man whose got a grip on him, feeling that he should do more. For the first time in his life, Niall wishes he was more like Nicolaus. He tries to throw a punch at the guardsman and misses. He is shoved down the stairs, being held on by his clothes, then pushed into the cell, while Elsa is pulled out. Ceil has her grandchildren in a loving hug, as if she could shelter them from the madness.

"Elsa, you stand here with me," Penelope tells her nicely.

Outside, the fighting noise grows even louder, as Nicolaus and his guys are starting to have trouble holding off all the men. "There are too many," Nicolaus says again, seeing that they are being overrun.

Suddenly a massive number of guardsmen rush Nicolaus, closing in on him. There seemed to be hundreds of hands bearing down on Nicolaus. He fights against the force holding him, however, he is unable to get loose. Nicolaus knew he was being carried inside the castle. He sees that his comrades are captured as well, and also being dragged inside, behind him.

Once they enter the castle, Nicolaus continues to fight against these men with all his strength, trying to break free. He is carried over the men's heads, down the stairs to the dungeon. Once they get there, Nicolaus is still being held in the air, over the men's heads. Bravely, Nicolaus is still struggling against them, trying to get free. Briefly, he can see his family members locked away. They are watching with eyes of terror.

With a nod of her head, Penelope gives her guardsmen permission to subdue the strong and mighty Nicolaus Ravenell.

Nicolaus is thrown to the floor, amongst the many guardsmen.

Nigel stands to oppose the treatment of his son, though he is locked behind the cell bars. "Don't hurt my son."

His comrades also make loud complaints of their treatment. "Make them stop, Penelope!" Roddy demands.

"Arrgh!" Washington struggles mightily against the four captors holding him.

"Get off me!" Sanchez gets in a good punch, and almost gets away, but is captured again. They all continue to struggle to break free.

Nicolaus anticipates what is about to happen and quickly he gets in a defensive position on the floor of the dungeon, covering his head, face and groin the best he can. Immediately, Nicolaus feels himself getting struck with objects, kicked from all sides at the same time, and stomped from various angles.

After about a minute, the guardsmen harshly pull Nicolaus to his feet, and hold him up in front of them to face their Penelope.

Ceil feels more terrible by the minute for what she's done. She remembers that she once told Nicolaus that she wished he would get beaten within one inch of his life. Her own words haunt her as she bears witness to this terror. She watches as Nicolaus is held forward, almost like a rag doll.

Again, Nicolaus uses his strength to wrench himself against the guardsmen, trying to get free, and again Penelope nods. Nicolaus is taken down.

"No! Please! You will kill him," Elsa shrieks, pleading with Penelope.

When Nicolaus is pulled forward again, blood runs from his mouth. He pants painful breaths, feeling defeated. His body is already beginning to bruise.

"Welcome, Nicolaus," Penelope tells him with a smirk and a strange smile, a smile that is not of Penelope. "You think you may be able to save your family," she steps forward, close to him, "well ... the joke is on you," she touches his bloodied lip, wiping the blood, "cause you here for me to collect you, at request of your mother, for ten million dollars. Ten million! But then I stop, and think, ..." she begins to pace before him while she speaks, "handsome Nicolaus not care about me, he no answer, not even one of my letters," she complains.

"And it very clear that if mother is so willing to sell him away, then why I should not take all from them? My company would be so much richer if I own VMC, and I get Nicolaus too!" She laughs a little. So ..." she sighs, "here we are." Penelope stops pacing to look at the man she loves, "so what you have to say to me?"

Through his slightly blurred vision, Nicolaus can see that his family, including the babies are locked up. He knows that he is the one she wants. "Let them go. You have me. This is between you and me, Penelope. Just let my family and my friends go. I will stay with you and do whatever you want."

Penelope gives another head nod and Nicolaus is dragged back into the gang of guardsmen. Roddy, Sanchez, and Washington try to break free from being held, and are briskly locked into a cell room, across from the family.

It is clear to all that Nicolaus is being savagely beaten. Elsa cries, fearing they will kill him. Nicolaus' moaning and painful groans can be heard amongst the punches, hits, kicks, and stomps. The guardsmen are delighted to get their chance to shred Nicolaus Ravenell.

"Your son is so courageous. That is one of things I love about him. Courageous."

Elsa shrieks again, crying, her hand to her mouth. "Please make them stop! They will kill him!" She says in excited concern, her tears flowing. "Please Penelope, if you love Nicolaus, why do you let them hurt him?"

"Why? Because I will break him. Make him obey."

"Oh no, Penelope, please," she begs for Nicolaus' sake.

Nicolaus is pulled before them again, looking weaken, more bruised, and more bloodied. Blood is now trickling from the side of his head. He could no longer stand on his own.

"Son," Nigel says in despair.

"Now Nicolaus Ravenell," Penelope says, teasing him, "if I let family go, how you to behave? Huh? How you obey what I say?" Penelope motions for Ceil to be brought forward. Niall takes the children.

Nigel attempts to leave out the cell instead of Ceil. "No! Take me!" His plea is discarded and he is harshly pushed back into the cell, making him fall.

Nicolaus is being held tightly, cannot stand on his own, and cannot do anything to help his father. He feels like he may be passing out soon.

Ceil is placed to stand next to Penelope. Penelope hands for a sword from one of her guardsmen, and is given one. She holds the sword to Ceil, the point at her heart.

"So Nicolaus, I wonder, what you do to save Mrs. Ravenell?"

Nicolaus frowns through his pain. "I'd do anything. Please don't hurt Ceil. Don't hurt anyone else." He finds strength to talk, to negotiate. "Penelope, what's happened to you? Why are you doing this?"

Penelope laughs, removing the sword, handing it back to her guardsman. "What happened? You happened! And ten million dollars to buy you happened. Mrs. Ravenell, tell Nicolaus what you tell me." She gives Ceil a little shove to make her talk.

"It's true," she says through tears, broken spirited, clearly seeing there is no way out of this situation. Ceil cannot imagine how this will end. "I ... I offered her ten million to take you." Her words shock Nigel, as well as Niall and Elsa, and the guys. Nigel is disturbed that Ceil would do such a thing.

"See?" Penelope says joyfully, seeing the hurt on Nicolaus' face, through his pain. "I tell you what, Nicolaus, ..."

"No! I'll stay. I'll do what you want. Just let them go. Please!"

Penelope frowns at him, "Are you tell me what to do, Nicolaus? Are you?"

"No, no ... I'm just asking to please, please, let them go, and I'll do whatever you want."

"Uh, you begging now," Penelope chuckles.

"I'll beg you, whatever you want. Please, please just let them go."

"So Nicolaus, you think you in position to ask, to beg, to bargain?" She grabs his face by the chin and looks him in his eyes.

"No! It's whatever I say! That's what to happen. What I say! So I say I let everybody go. Your dad, the babies, your friends, even you, ... everybody, if you say I keep Ceil chained down here in the dungeon to die, all alone. Your revenge, eh? You say it, and you can all go."

Nicolaus looks at Ceil and sees her crying, something he's never seen before. He shakes his head, "No. No harm to anyone else. I stay, and you let everyone else go."

Ceil and Penelope look at Nicolaus in surprise. Penelope laughs at Ceil. "Woman, you a outright fool!" Ceil looks to Nicolaus, tears flowing.

Niall feels shame wash over him. He realizes it is just as the bishop said, that only Nicolaus can save them all.

"Please Penelope, we can work this out, you and me, let everyone go and ...." With a nod of Penelope's head, Nicolaus is dragged down amongst the guardsmen and pummeled again. A loud crack is heard, followed by a painful cry, as Nicolaus' forever injured leg is broken.

Everything happens very quickly, as a broken Nicolaus, with a rebroken leg, is pulled before Penelope again.

"Do you surrender, Nicolaus Ravenell?"

Nicolaus gives a painful sigh. "Yes. Yes, I surrender," he says slowly.

Penelope smiles brightly. "So you stop fighting?"

"Yes, I will stop."

"Very good, then." Penelope smiles, "You say you do anything I want?"

"Yes," Nicolaus answers softly.

Penelope walks before Nicolaus. She observes the man she loves. He is beaten, bloodied, and bruised; broken, just as she wanted, and he is now her captive. She laughs loudly, remembering Ceil's words, "To do what I please with him, is that what you say, Ceil?"

Nicolaus briefly looks at the homely Penelope Drone, his former sister-in-law, then he looks to Ceil, who says nothing, only cries. Nicolaus body throbs with pain, and he fears this is only the beginning of such cruelty.

Penelope turns to the devastated family. "If you thought my sister horrid person, you will now deal with me, the new me. I no so nice!" She claps her hands to her guardsmen, and nods.

Suddenly, Nicolaus is knocked unconscious, and dragged to an adjacent cell, separated from everyone, to the pleads and complaints of his family and friends.

Elsa cries hysterically at Nicolaus' treatment, in the depths of the dungeon cell, as a stream of blood from Nicolaus' leg is left on the floor from the path he was dragged.

The dilapidated dungeon is cold, dark, and drab. The children are hungry. Elsa does not know what is to become of them, and she fears for Nicolaus.

Both Niall and Nigel are in utter shock of what is happening. As the guardsmen harshly usher Ceil and Elsa back into the cell, they both know there is absolutely nothing they could do to stop any of this. Niall grabs Elsa and his children to him. He looks at his mother who was silently crying, being comforted by his father.

Nigel comforts Ceil as a husband would, while inside of himself, he cries for Nicolaus and worries about his life. He worries that they will never be released. He worries about his grandchildren. This is all very traumatic.

Ceil realizes the magnitude of her selfish actions. She realizes they may lose everything, and the one person they have always relied on is now bound and stripped of his strength, defeated, and helpless to the least, if they do not kill him.

This nightmare that Ceil created is just beginning.

Chapter Ninety-One (TW)

Everyone knew that Nicolaus was being harshly handled by guardsmen, because they could hear him groan with pain every so often. Without mercy or medical training, the guardsmen tend to Nicolaus' broken leg, for which the bone had been snapped and is sticking up. They remove his clothing, except his underwear, cutting off his pants. From the moment they touch his leg, Nicolaus moans in pain.

Quickly they lift up Nicolaus' leg.

"No, wait," he begs them, to no avail.

Abruptly, they untwist his leg, and snap it straight, making Nicolaus yell out in great pain, writhing about on the floor.

Roddy and Sanchez complain loudly about the treatment of Nicolaus, though it does no good.

Nigel wants to cry at the echoes of his son's suffering, as Nicolaus continues to make sounds of pain. The guardsmen harshly wrap his leg with sticks placed on either side, a sort of crude middle ages medical treatment.

Not long after this suffering, Nicolaus finds himself being carried out of the cell, and tied and stretched in the hallway of the dungeon between the cell rooms of his family and his comrades.

"Take me instead! Let me stand in for Nicolaus," Roddy offers.

"Hey man, we'll all three stand in for Nicolaus. You have hurt him enough," Washington shouts. The offers are ignored.

Nicolaus is already having difficulty breathing as his hands are tied, spread apart, above his head, to a thick pipe that runs horizontal along the ceiling of the dungeon room. His legs are tightly bound at the ankles, also spread apart. Nicolaus gives manly groans of pain, especially when they touch his broken leg.

Nicolaus has no muscle strength left to struggle against the ropes that bind him. His wrists are tied so tight, he knows he cannot break free. He is stretched in extreme pain.

"Nicolaus," Roddy calls to him, "just hold on, Nicolaus."

Weakly, Nicolaus responds to his comrades, "I've got to get you out of here."

Though Nicolaus is weak, he begins to pray in the Latin language, to Nigel's dismay. Everyone goes silent as he prays. Elsa shields her babies' eyes from the sight of their uncle.

Suddenly, Penelope appears. She walks up to Nicolaus and touches his muscular, bare torso. She missed touching him. Then she puts her hand to his crotch, just to see what he will do. He frowns, without moving, controlling himself. Penelope giggles.

"What's happened to you?" He asks her weakly.

"Oh Nicolaus, you ask me again?" Penelope sighs, feeling the full power she has over Nicolaus Ravenell. She gently touches his torso again, momentarily. She stands back from him. "I am me. I am who you and Ceil made me to be."

He frowns at her. "I'm sorry," he says softly. "I should have read your letters. I should have responded. I'm sorry."

"Oh! So now you sorry!" Penelope laughs again. "Too late Nicolaus Ravenell. Too late."

"Have mercy," he tells her. "Please, an ounce of mercy."

"Mercy? Oh I give mercy." Penelope gestures for them to bring Ceil to her. Two guardsmen enter the cell. One guardsman harshly pulls Ceil from Nigel, who is pushed back by the other. Ceil is brought to stand next to Penelope, before Nicolaus. "Now is time for your punishment, Nicolaus. I told you I give you punishment for your part of Marguerite's death some time in you life. Time is now. You ask for mercy, here your mercy. You take twenty-five strikes with boards," there are two guardsmen holding two-by-four wood boards, "or you leave Ceil chained to die, and no strikes and you all go home."

"Let me take the strikes!" Roddy offers. "Please Ms., let me take the strikes for him."

"Wow! You got nice and caring friends." Penelope tells him to hush with her finger. "No. This Nicolaus punishment. Now you quiet or I have you gagged and chained. You hear?" She turns her attention back to Nicolaus. "Nicolaus, what you choose?"

Nicolaus sees Ceil tearing again. Ceil is absolutely expecting Nicolaus to get his revenge and leave her there to die. She gets a surprise at his answer.

"No, I'll take your punishment."

Penelope laughs at Ceil. "Mrs. Ravenell, you complete fool! You sell away Nicolaus and he willing to die for you. You complete fool!" She turns to her men, "Okay boys, you heard him."

Penelope steps back pulling Ceil with her, as the guardsmen step up, ready to do their grisly task.

"Wait!" Nigel yells. "Wait, please don't do this. I will pay you handsomely to walk away. I will give you land and millions more than ten million. Please, my son has suffered enough. Please don't!"

Briefly, the guardsmen consider Nigel's offer, then turn to provide their work for their employer.

One to the front, the other to the back of Nicolaus. They strike him, almost at the same time, in a continuous manner.

At first, Nicolaus does not cry out, and then as the men heartlessly use the boards, his already bruised flesh gets soften, then broken, causing bleeding. The pain becomes unbearable. Any man, any human, would yell in pain.

Niall cries, knowing he could not be as strong as Nicolaus. He could never measure up to his brother. The babies cry at the distress happening, though Elsa shields them the best she can.

Tears pour from Nigel as his son suffers. He listens as Nicolaus cries out, but never begs for it to stop, though Nigel does pray for it to stop. With each strike, he prays harder, falling on his knees.

After the fifteenth strike, suddenly, it stops.

"Nicolaus," Penelope calls to the barely conscious Nicolaus Ravenell, "Nicolaus, you have ten more to go. I make it stop, and I let everyone go, except you and Ceil, and if you agree that Ceil gets chained in dungeon. You agree I chain Ceil?" she toys with him, now knowing he would never agree.

Barely able to respond, Nicolaus says through his pain, "No. No harm to anyone else. I'll take the hits. I'll take your punishment."

Penelope laughs, tickled at Ceil's foolery. She gestures for them to continue.

With five strikes left, Nicolaus falls silent and unconscious due to the severe pain. The guardsmen finish the twenty-five strikes. Then they proceed to pull Niall and Nigel from the cells. Niall is fearful that he is next. The guards push them towards Nicolaus, giving Niall a small knife to cut his brother down. Penelope escorts Ceil back to the cell, as Niall and Nigel carry Nicolaus and gently place him on the hard stone bed.

The Ravenell family hear and see the cell door lock, and Penelope and the guardsmen leave.

"Oh God!" Nigel exclaims, "My son, save my son, do not let them take him this way. He has done good work. He is courageous, and he loves you so," he pleads to God, with humbleness. Nigel cries as he holds Nicolaus' unconscious body to him. These acts against Nicolaus are horrid.

"Mr. Ravenell, it will be all right," Roddy tells him. "Nicolaus is a strong warrior, Sir, he can take it. I know it looks bad now, but believe me, he'll be up in a few days. He's one of the strongest men I know."

"Thank you for that, Roddy."

"And Mrs. Ravenell," Sanchez calls to her, "I hope you understand what Nicolaus has just done for you."

"Yes," Ceil replies quietly.

"He stood up for you,... saving your life."

"Yes," Ceil answers softly, her tears freely flowing.

Chapter Ninety-Two

Ceil had not been able to look at Nicolaus since he was brought unconscious into the cell. However now, Nicolaus begins to stir and moan.

Ceil slowly turns to look at what she has caused. She can only put her hand to her head in silence, damning herself. Her grandchildren are crying and hungry; Elsa is sad while doing her best to tend to Nicolaus; Niall, her beloved son, is bewildered and frightened. She feels broken as tears spill from her eyes.

Ceil cries for Nicolaus, for what has been done to him. She wonders to herself if this is what she wanted to happen to him? No, it is not what she wants. He risked his very person to protect her, which bemuses her, since he understood what she intended for him. She looks at him, sorry for his intense pain.

Elsa tends to Nicolaus' wounds. With tears, she places two over the counter pain pills in his mouth. She has a bottle of them in her purse. Elsa also has diaper wipes for the babies. She uses them to gently clean any open wounds she sees, hoping she is not causing Nicolaus more pain, though he is still semi-conscious. Then she places petroleum jelly on the wounds.

"Where am I?" The pain cut off Nicolaus' words, as he tries to get up.

"Please son, do not move yourself," Nigel is by Nicolaus' side, holding his shoulders. Nigel can see how much pain Nicolaus is in. His son, the pillar of strength in mind and body, is laying in his arms, bloodied, bruised, and broken. Words escape Nigel. What does a father say to such an outstanding son, at a time like this? "What you did was very brave my son."

Chapter Ninety-Three

As night fell, food was finally brought to the Ravenell family, and to the guys. Nigel is not sure if Nicolaus is drifting in and out of sleep, or in and out of consciousness.

The children want to be next to Nicolaus, recognizing him as the uncle they'd been missing. They fuss until Elsa lets them crowd and curl next to him. Even the children seemed to realize the specialness of Nicolaus.

Elsa raises Nicolaus' head, and with the help of Nigel, they make him drink water, fearing he'd get dehydrated, which would bring additional pain. After eating their meal of chicken sandwich bites, with chips and water, the little ones drift to sleep.

Two days passed with no word from Penelope. By this time, Nicolaus seems to be getting stronger, as he painfully sits up, to the amazement of Nigel. Nicolaus observes the many bruises that cover his body. His head hurts, he is sure his ribs are cracked, most likely on both sides, as he feels immense pain when taking a deep breath, and his leg hurts horribly at any movement. Nigel assists him with his leg. "Thank you, father." Having no clothes, Nicolaus wraps himself in one of the blankets.

"Wow, Nicolaus, I don't understand how you do it," Niall comments. "You really are very tough."

Nicolaus acknowledges Niall's comment.

"Guys, you okay?" Nicolaus calls to his comrades.

"I knew you'd be up!" Roddy says excited to hear Nicolaus's voice. "I told your family so. We're okay, they haven't come after us as of yet."

"Nicolaus Ravenell leads the badass team of our nation," Sanchez jokingly tells him.

Nicolaus chuckles at his comrade's banter. Smiling with some relief, Elsa takes a baby wipe to his face and pats his bruises, then pats the cuts on his chest. Niall watches as Elsa runs her hands through Nicolaus' hair to make it look as neat as can be, under the circumstances. "Thank you, Elsa," he tells her softly. She touches the sides of his face with both of her hands, and kisses Nicolaus on the cheek, happy that he is alive and up, despite the pain.

Elaine and Emily make baby noises of elation to see Nicolaus awake and sitting up. Briefly, he holds the little darlings, as breakfast is brought to the captives. They munch on toast, fruit, and water.

Elsa had a hard time keeping the children from crying and being cranky throughout the day. The small cell the family had been put in is cold and damp; hardly a place for babies to play.

With both, physical and mental strenuous pain, Nicolaus looks to Ceil. He believes he is ready to confront her in this small space. She has said nothing to him, nor has she looked at him all day, and his heart will not let him stay quiet any longer. "Ceil, is it true, about the ten million?" His question is soft and respectful.

Nigel sits next to his son, across from Ceil. She has her back to Nicolaus, as she has not been able to face him since this morning. Ceil sighs, and turns to look at Nicolaus. Only now, instead of the cold stare she usually gives him, her face seems to be softened, the face of a sorrowful mother. She nods, "Yes," she says in a whisper. Immediately, she sees the hurt across Nicolaus' face.

Nicolaus shakes his head with a sigh, in disbelief. "Wow." He is not sure how to respond, so he just says what appears in his mind about this. His tone is even and respectful. "Ceil, if I have done something so horribly wrong, to make you hate me so much, that has made you commit such an act against me,... against all of us ... then I guess I owe you an apology. So ... I sincerely apologize for that thing I have done, which, frankly, I cannot imagine what it is. Nevertheless, I sincerely apologize to you. Although, Ceil, if your absolute hatred of me directly stems from my birth, then that is a conversation that you'll need to have with God, to resolve that issue within your soul. Because Ceil, if our family is able to survive this, we cannot go through something like this again. I ... cannot go through this again. This is the last of the strength of all of us, Ceil. We all must be prayerful that we survive this."

Ceil is surprised by Nicolaus' words. She had no answers for him one way or the other.

Suddenly the cell door flings open and there stands Penelope. She steps inside and the children cling to Elsa, terrified of her. Penelope has a crutch in her hands, and she offers it to Nicolaus. "I have this for you, to help you." He nods, and uses the crutch to stand. She touches his arm, "You walk with me."

Penelope motions to her men, who without words, step into the cell, and carefully lift Nicolaus. They carry him up the stairs, and carry him to a one story house that is on the castle grounds. When they enter the house, Nicolaus immediately notices it is warm inside and smells of food.

They take Nicolaus to the bedroom, gently sit him onto the bed, and they leave them, closing the door. Penelope uses a water basin and cloth to gently wash Nicolaus. Her actions shock him. He is not sure what to do, so he lets her wash him. She uses soap and water to gently wash the blood from his face and torso. He tries to read her, and is not sure what to make of all this.

"Would you like clothes?" She asks him, standing.

Nicolaus nods, "Yes, please, thank you."

As if having this moment preplanned, she hands him men's clothing of underwear and a sweat suit. With the predicament of his leg, she knows he will need help getting dressed. She attempts to remove the blanket, but Nicolaus holds onto it.

"Please, Penelope. I need my father to help me."

"Your father?"

"Yes, please."

She sighs, and thinks about the request. She nods. "Okay."

He is surprised at her response, so he asks for more, "And the babies, Penelope. They are just little babies freezing in that dungeon. Can't they please be brought in here?"

She chuckles at him. "So then Elsa too?"

Nicolaus nods, "Yes. At least for a little while to warm up. Please, I know you have kindness in your heart and you wouldn't want to make babies suffer."

Penelope chuckles at him again. She is very thrilled to have Nicolaus with her. She sits next to him on the bed. "You just keep push and push." She sighs and nods. "Okay. Okay." She calls for her guardsmen and gives them instructions. Within five minutes, Nigel and the rest of the family enter the bedroom.

"Oh thank God, it's so warm in here!" Elsa exclaims.

"Elsa, warm the babies by the fire," Nicolaus tells her, as the fireplace has a warm fire going. Elsa is helped by Ceil.

Nigel immediately understands he needs to help Nicolaus dress. "Thank you, Penelope. I'll help my son." Nigel takes the cloth, douses it in the water, and washes Nicolaus on his unhurt leg, carefully on his back, and elsewhere. Then covering him, he and Niall assist Nicolaus to get dressed.

Penelope stands back and watches the family. They seem grateful to be in the warmth. Once Nicolaus is dressed, Penelope motions for Nigel and Niall to move away, and they do so, standing by the fireplace with the ladies. Penelope motions for them to leave the room, and they file out, as she sits next to Nicolaus.

Understanding Penelope's mood, Nicolaus asks for more, hoping to push her to do what is right. He touches her hand and looks into her eyes. She acts bashful, so he grabs hold of her hand. "Thank you for the kindness, Penelope. My friends, ... they just came along as good men to help me. I'm begging you to please, please release them ... unharmed. Just let them go."

She looks down at his hand which is holding hers. "Hmm. And so then, Nicolaus, if I do that, what will you give me?"

Nicolaus notices that her tone is teasing again, which makes him hesitant, unsure if she is switching her mood. He decides to keep pushing for his friends. He realizes that if he can get her to release his comrades, there may be a chance that he can get her to release his family. "What do you want?" He set his tone in a teasing manner as well.

His words make Penelope giggle. She looks up at him. "A kiss. I want a kiss. You give me darn good kiss, I set them free."

Nicolaus raises his eyebrows in surprise, seeing where all this may be going. "Unharmed?"

"Yes, unharmed."

"Okay," he nonchalantly agrees with a nod. Nicolaus suppressed the dread of this. He never thought he'd be forced to kiss Penelope Drone. He takes his hand and lifts her chin, then kisses her, with involvement. Her response is almost nonexistent, making him realize she may have never been kissed before now. He breaks the kiss and kisses her again, which may have been overwhelming for her, as she pulls away, giggling like a schoolgirl.

Penelope touches her mouth, then her face, as if the kiss may have changed her appearance for the better. Penelope is in awe of having just been kissed by Nicolaus Ravenell. She's been dreaming of this moment for at least a decade now. She stands with resolve and a straightened spine; very sure she will be having more of this. She opens the door, startling the family who are in fear of her. She calls for her guardsman. "Release his friends, and do not harm them. Give them bread and meat, and their things, and send them on their way."

"Yes ma'am."

"No harm, do you hear? Do not hurt them!"

"Yes ma'am!"

As Roddy, Sanchez, and Washington are released, their phones are not working. They take off running, zig-zagging through the nearby forest, staying close to the road. They know Nicolaus expects them to send help.

Penelope brings Nicolaus out of the bedroom to join the family. "Now you all shall eat." She claps her hands and her staff get to work.

Chapter Ninety-Four (TW)

Penelope had the meal with the Ravenell family. After the meal, she places papers before Nicolaus, and gives him a pen.

"Here. You sign."

"What is this?"

"You signing to me your VMC shares. And property and claims. I taking it all, Nicolaus. Will be in my name, but you and me will take care of it all."

Nicolaus sighs, frowning. "What happened to you Penelope? This is not you."

"It is me. I exactly who you and Ceil made me into. Me."

"I can't sign this! It has to be checked by a lawyer. The information may be wrong."

"No, you sign. Everybody already sign. Now you sign."

"Penelope, I ..."

Penelope slams the table. "Do you really want to argue with me right now, Nicolaus? I've learned from the best," she nods her head to Ceil in acknowledgement, "and I get what I want."

Nicolaus looks at Penelope. "Where is Andrejs? He would not approve of all this. Kidnapping, extortion, and torture," his voice is elevated to match her mood.

With more extreme force, Penelope slams the table with her fist on the papers before Nicolaus. "I in charge of Papa now! He does what I say! So stop stall and get to signing," she yells at him in his face, her nice mood gone. She feels angry that Nicolaus has spoiled things. "Just try me, Nicolaus," she threatens him. Not taking her eyes off Nicolaus she orders her guardsmen, "Bring her to me. And that little one too."

Nicolaus is unmoving, keeping his eyes locked with Penelope as she has not moved out of his face. He understands that his tactic did not work. Penelope moves to grab up Ceil, placing her hands next to the papers, while Elsa and Niall struggle against letting them take Elaine from them. They are both struck, making them fall and the guard jerks Elaine away from them, placing her to stand next to Nicolaus. Penelope whips a large sharp knife from her belt holder and places it over Ceil's hand.

Penelope nods for the guard to hold Elaine's little hand next to Ceil's. Penelope holds the knife over both hands, with the intent of him not knowing which one she would slash.

"Try me, Nicolaus," she tells him with a mean tone of voice. "Try me!" She stares him down, ready to cut Ceil's hand. "Try me!" She yells at him, moving a little closer to his face.

Nicolaus slightly shakes his head, keeping his calm. He blinks. "You don't have to do that. I'll sign them." He looks at Ceil who seems terrified, and Elaine who is shaking, staring wide eyed at that large knife.

Quickly, Nicolaus uses his left hand to sign the papers. This is a security strategy taught to him when he first joined the company. A strategy that he thought he'd never be using. Since Nicolaus is right handed, the left handed signature would not be recognizable as his signature, making the documents void. Nigel had taken the same action earlier. In haste, he signs all the documents before him, without reading any of them. He just wants to get Penelope calmed again. He knows if they survive this ordeal, by the grace of God, everything he signs would be null anyway, because he is signing under duress.

Nicolaus hands the papers to Penelope, and she puts the sharp knife away, replacing it in the holder of her belt. She takes the papers, looking at them with a big smile. She nods. "Okay. Okay. Lock them up!"

Chapter Ninety-Five (TW)

It is hard having to leave the warmth of a nice home to be returned to a cold, dark, drab dungeon cell. Elsa sits with her children and cries in despair.

"You just had to go and piss her off, Nicolaus!" Niall yells at him. "You just couldn't keep your mouth shut and sign the damn papers! You're going to get us killed!"

"I'm sorry." Nicolaus sighs. "I'll fix it. I have to fix it, and I will," he says with determination.

"If I could take all this back, ..." Ceil begins, her words stopped by her tears.

Nigel is right beside her to hold her. "Now, now," he tells her, not wanting her to fall apart.

"How?" Niall yells at Nicolaus, riding him, still wanting to blame him again for everything. "How are you going to fix it? We're locked down here again!"

"I know what I have to do," Nicolaus says with something different in his voice. Perhaps sadness or disgust. "Guards," Nicolaus calls to whom he knows is outside the dungeon door.

"They are not going to respond to you," Niall yells at his brother, feeling his plan, whatever it may be, is not going to work.

Nicolaus yells louder, "Guards!"

The dungeon door opens, and two guardsmen appear before him. Nicolaus looks at Niall, "Never give up, Niall," he says softly. Then he addresses the guardsmen, "Please, take me to Penelope. I must speak with her."

The guardsmen look at each other, shrug, then open the cell door and assist Nicolaus. After they secure the rest of the family inside, they carry Nicolaus up the stairs.

Niall is shocked as the dungeon door closes again.

"What you think you doing, Nicolaus?" Penelope tells him with a frown, seeing her guardsmen bringing him to her.

"Please, I want to apologize for what I said earlier. I think I messed up." He touches her shoulder. "I've made you angry with me, and I don't want you to be angry. Please."

Penelope steps away from Nicolaus. "Yes, you mess up!"

Nicolaus knew he had to get her while she is impassioned. "I'm sorry," he says softly, stepping closer to her. "I don't want us to be adversaries." He steps even closer to her, in her space. He touches her shoulder again. "In fact, I know what you want, Penelope, and ... I want to give you what you want." With his fingers, he gently touches her face.

His gentle touch brings Penelope's eyes to his. "And what you think I want, Nicolaus," she says more calm.

Nicolaus steps closer, right upon her. "Me. You want me to be your husband," he says softly, then nods one time, "and that ... I will be,... your husband," he says almost in a whisper.

Penelope does not remove her eyes from him. His fingers are still gently touching her face, bringing chills about her now. She studies his lips.

"Right? I mean ..." he stops touching her and takes a step back, playing this teasing game with her. "that is what all this is about, anyway. The letters. Taking everything we have, including our persons. Punishing me. Bending me to your will. Making me obey. What you really want is for me to be your loving husband. Right?" He waits for her to answer.

"I ... I... I...," she breathes out, words escaping her. She suddenly feels herself flush as she looks at him and his sexy smile. She is not sure what to do.

Nicolaus steps up to her again. "I'll give you want you want. I'll be your loving husband."

Penelope cannot seem to stop from flinging herself to Nicolaus. She pulls him to kiss her, and he does. She grabs onto him, wanting him. She shews the guardsmen away with her hand. Nicolaus breaks the kiss, and slowly pulls her by the hand into her bedroom. "Let me bathe you," he says sweetly.

Because of his leg, it is a struggle for him to run a bath for Penelope. She watches him in silence as he adds whatever he sees handy, realizing that Penelope seemed to have made herself at home in this little cottage, away from her father. He wonders if Andrejs even knows what she is up to.

Once he got the bath ready, he turns his attention to Penelope, and slowly, helps her peel her odorous clothing off. Nicolaus is revolted at the thought of putting himself into this woman, but he knows he must do this to get his family out of that dungeon.

She is too shy to strip before him, so she doesn't let him take her undergarments. She gets into the water, which now has bubbles, and then Nicolaus manages to get her out of her undergarments. Gently, he bathes her, ignoring the pain that is searing through his leg, which reminds him that they are trapped because of Ceil.

With the soap, he cleans her with teasing motions, making her moan at times, especially as she lets him clean her vaginal area.

Penelope is in fantasy land, unable to believe that Nicolaus Ravenell wants to touch her. After several minutes, he takes her hand to lift her out of the bath, having a towel ready to cover her nakedness. Penelope touches Nicolaus' face, very satisfied at his actions, especially now that he kisses her neck, making her giggle and shiver. She turns to kiss him, and cannot believe it when he takes her into his arms.

Penelope pulls back and touches the chest of the man that is standing in front of her. She can hardly believe it. Finally, after decades of fantasizing about this, he will be hers. This handsome man, for which her sister wasted time and energy, will finally be hers. Penelope looks at Nicolaus, pats him on the chest, then goes to the door to call for her guardsmen.

"Yes ma'am?"

"Release the family from the dungeon. Bring them here. Settle them in the other bedroom, and give them food and drink."

"Yes ma'am."

Nicolaus looks at himself in the mirror and sees how awful he looks. He has bruises on his face, and most of his body. He tries to make himself as presentable as possible, running his hands through his curly hair. He looks into her drawers, and on the tables.

"Nicolaus, what you looking for?"

He turns and steps up to the towel wrapped Penelope, taking her into his arms, wanting to keep the momentum going.

"Thank you for freeing my family," he tells her and gives her a peck kiss, which she greedily accepts. "I'm looking for condoms, hon. I don't want to chance getting you pregnant. I know you are very busy, Penelope." He disguises his concern.

"Condoms?" She thinks for a moment. "Oh, those!" She shakes her head, "I don't have any."

He takes her in his arms, "That's okay. Well, I'm ready to make love to you, if that's what you want."

She steps away from him, next to the fireplace. "Yes, what I want. First, though, Nicolaus, I want make you mine."

"I am yours." He steps up to her.

"I want mark you, Nicolaus."

"Mark me? What do you mean?"

Penelope takes a fireplace poker, and puts it in the roaring fire.

Nicolaus takes several steps back from her, his hands out in a defensive posture. "Penelope, what are you doing?"

"I want mark you. You only be mine, Nicolaus."

He scoffs, "No. That is not necessary. I am yours. I'm telling you. I'm saying it to you ... I am yours."

Penelope shrugs. "You know, I really admire Ceil. She strong woman. I want to be like her. So I say, no, we do it my way. You say you do what I say, so," she turns with the hot fireplace poker in her hand, "I say ... pants ... now."

"Penelope, please, put that down."

She can hear her guardsmen entering the cottage with the family. She calls for them, and several of them enter her room. She nods towards Nicolaus, "Subdue him." Immediately, two men grab onto Nicolaus.

Nigel and Ceil can hear immense scuffling and things breaking behind the closed door of Penelope's bedroom, as she is giving her men orders about Nicolaus. 'Well ... don't let him do that! Stop him! Get him!' they hear through the hallway.

Nigel knows that for whatever reason, Nicolaus is fighting the forces against him.

They hear sounds of men yelling in pain, things crashing and being overturned.

"You mean to tell me you cannot get him? There are more of you than there is him?" Penelope yells.

Nigel laughs to himself, amazed at his son's tenacity. 'Nicolaus!' Penelope sounds exasperated through the castle hallways.

Suddenly, the door to Penelope's bedroom is open and a ruckus is heard as several men stumble out, as if running from what is inside. Some are bent over in pain. Others have blood streaming down their face from gashes in their heads, others have bloodied noses. Nicolaus' strength is too much for them. Several other men rush into the room after hearing the commotion.

"Subdue him!" Penelope orders the dozen men under her command who have entered the room.

She shouts orders at them. "Hold him down!" The men follow her command, as several of them have ceased Nicolaus. The searing heat and hot iron bring harsh burning pain to Nicolaus. He is unable to contain a loud, painful and anguished sounding yell, though she is only cruel to him for a few seconds.

Andrejs, Penelope's father, enters the cottage during the sound of the yell. He frowns deeply, especially seeing the Ravenells here. Nigel is quick to go to him.

"What going on here?" He asks perturbed, in his broken English. "Nigel? Nigel, what you doing here?" He looks to the bedroom door, from where the yell is emitting. "What happening?"

"Andrejs! Andrejs!" Nigel grabs Andrejs by the forearms in desperation. "Please you must help us. Penelope has us captive, and ... I do fear that she is harming Nicolaus worse than before."

"Captive?" Andrejs looks around Nigel's shoulder and sees Ceil, Niall, and Elsa and her babies, as well as guardsmen with weapons. He shakes his head, staying quiet about receiving a call from the embassy.

Penelope exits the room to the worried stares of the Ravenells. Slowly, she walks over to them, chuckling. "That Nicolaus! What I'm to do with him?"

Nigel releases Andrejs, and now clings to Penelope's forearms. "Penelope, please don't hurt him anymore," he begs her, "please Penelope, he's suffered enough."

"Hurt him? Did you see what he did to my men? I thought I weakened him, but ... hmmm ..., maybe guess not!" She laughs into the stare of her father. "Oh, Poppa! I did not know you here. What you doing here, anyway, Poppa?"

"Me? What you doing?" He frowns at her deeply. He yells at her, looking at her bedroom door. "What you doing?" Several of her guardsmen are now exiting the bedroom. Nicolaus does not appear. When Nigel attempts the direction of the bedroom, he is stopped, and pushed to stand next to Ceil.

"Please, my son."

Andrejs looks at the door, then to his daughter, who is in a night robe, with a towel underneath. "Your obsession with Nicolaus going too far! Embarrassing!"

"No, Poppa, I promise you. I take VMC, for us. I own all of it now. They sign it over to me. Nicolaus mine too, now. We richer and we have Nicolaus."

Andrejs looks at his daughter as if she might be crazy. "What they doing here?" His hand points to the family. "Here?" His hand grazes the air, as if revealing the cottage.

Penelope yells at her father, offended that he would ask about it, "This is mine, Poppa!"

Andrejs looks at them, then to his daughter. The Ravenells grow gravely disappointed when Andrejs does not demand their release or rescue them. Instead he grabs Penelope by the wrist to drag her out of the cottage. "Let's go, we have important meeting in Italy. You making me late!"

"Oh Poppa, I forgot all about that meeting."

They leave the cottage, closing the door. The guardsmen remain in place.

Chapter Ninety-Six (TW)

Nigel watches Penelope and Andrejs leave the grounds, out the window of the cottage bedroom. He knows they have little time to get a plan of escape going, as Penelope would be gone for at least two days, maybe five. The guardsmen would not let the family see about Nicolaus, keeping them separated. However, never leaving home without cash, Nigel bribed one of the younger guardsmen with two hundred dollars to let Elsa check on Nicolaus.

Although they were being closely watched, Nigel whispered brainstorming ideas with Niall. Considering the babies and the condition of Nicolaus, it would be almost impossible to escape through a window.

"I think we leave Nicolaus, and come back for him with the police," Niall says.

"No, we are not leaving Nicolaus. They could move him, or kill him. No."

"I'm just saying, father, he's dead weight to us right now."

Nigel looks at Niall feeling as if he wants to strike him. "Don't you talk about your brother like that. Nicolaus is a decorated military veteran. He's very courageous, risking his own life to save ours. Could you have withstood everything they have done to him?"

Niall sighs. "No. I'm sorry."

"Think about that next time you want to make a disparaging comment about your brother. Now, I said we are not leaving him. What about the back door?"

"There are guards everywhere. How is any of this supposed to work? We can't get away from the sight of any of the guards."

Nigel nods. "Quite right. We need Nicolaus to help us here. I'm very sure he'd know what to do."

"I don't think even Nicolaus can help us, father!"

Elsa returns and reports, "Nicky is okay. He is in pain, but he is up and moving around."

Nigel chuckles. "Wow. You see that Niall? Now that's my Nicolaus. That's ... my ... son," he says slowly, and proudly.

The family is provided food and drink, and allowed to sleep in the spare bedroom.

The following morning, there is a large commotion on the castle grounds, so much so, all the guardsmen inside the cottage run out to assist. Nicolaus hobbles out the open bedroom door and sees his family huddling together, in fear.

"It's okay," he tells them. "I think we are being rescued."

Just as Nicolaus says these words, the front door is thrown open, and the silhouette of Jonathan Baird appears before them. He stands in the doorway, tall, like a picturesque hero, with his hands to his hips, looking refreshed and rested.

"Dad!" Elsa jumps up with glee, and runs to her father to hug him. "Oh Dad, thank God!"

Jonathan laughs heartily. "Of course it's me! Who else?" He hugs Elsa and Emily to him. "My Elsa! You all right, my princess?"

Elsa nods, without words. Happy tears stream down her face.

Nigel then greets Jonathan with a hearty handshake, and a manly hug, tears of joy escaping him. He'd never been so happy to see Jonathan Baird.

Nicolaus also shakes Baird's hand though he is elated enough to hug him. Baird's grasp on Nicolaus lingers longer than need be, and he looks at him with happy eyes of mischief.

Baird made the rounds, hugging Ceil to him, then Niall, and holding up Elaine and kissing her.

The Ravenells could see that Jonathan brought his army of men who are disarming Penelope's guardsmen. They seem to be obeying, throwing down their weapons, and having a seat on the grassy castle lawn.

Nigel leads everyone to sit in an oval circle in the cottage main room. Baird and Nicolaus on the lead ends, with Elsa and Niall to Baird's right, and Nigel and Ceil to Baird's left.

"May I start by saying we are so wonderfully glad you have stepped up to our aid. I really was not sure how we were going to untangle ourselves from this nightmare," Nigel pats Baird's arm, as he speaks joyfully.

"Yes," Nicolaus agrees. "I assume my comrades made contact with you."

Baird nods, "Yes, through Manfred, whom I believe is heading here to assist as well. I hear your gratefulness for my aid to you, and sounds as if you are ready for your freedom." Baird clears his throat. He knows he has the upper hand over Nicolaus in their silent one-sided feud, and he intends to use it. Jonathan has a history of being jealous of Nicolaus' professional successes. He was upset when Nicolaus was called on years ago to save ambassadors, instead of him receiving that call. He's never forgotten about this. His jealousy is laced with his sexual attraction to Nicolaus.

Jonathan draws both of his granddaughters upon his lap. One on each knee as he eyes Nicolaus, who is directly across from him. "I am here to help and to take you home. In fact, I have made sure Penelope and her father will never bother you again."

Nicolaus meets Baird's gaze, as he is staring at him with mischievous eyes. "Wait ... you didn't hurt them?"

Jonathan frowns. "Hurt them? Of course not! What kind of man do you think I am?" He looks to the family. "The international police has arrested both of them on corruption and abduction charges, and anything else they can find in their Latvian books."

"Oh, thank you Baird," Nicolaus says. His pain is immense, and he can hardly wait to get out of this cottage.

"Of course. And so, now, we are down to my help. Yes, I will help you restore your sense of self, and get you home, only ... Nigel

... my help has a price. Someone once told me that freedom has a price." His eyes meet the gaze of Nicolaus, as Nicolaus is surprised to hear his own words of the past reverberate in the present.

"Well of course man, you can have anything you want. We understand," Nigel fumbles with words, surprised at this unexpected demand, but not concerned. "We are so grateful to you. Just name it! Money, property, ... anything you want!"

Baird looks at Nigel with an eye squint. "Nigel, I told you before, I don't want your money. I don't need your property. In fact, what I want cannot be bought with money." The look on Baird's face changes as Nigel is stunned by his words. "What I want, Nigel, is right in front of me. I want your son."

Nigel looks at him strangely, not understanding. He looks at Ceil, then at Nicolaus. Everyone is looking at everyone else, trying to understand this request.

Even Elsa is frowning upon her father. "You mean you want Niall to assist you?" She guesses at his meaning.

"No," Baird says quickly.

"Nicolaus! You want Nicolaus to assist you with a project or something," Nigel tries to clarify.

"No." During this whole exchange, Baird's eyes had not left Nicolaus. "I mean I want him. I want Nicolaus with me, to do what I please, for the next two days. That ... is my price."

Nicolaus laughs nervously in disbelief. "Surely, there is something else you want."

With seriousness, Baird answers steadily, "On the contrary, there is nothing I want more than to have you."

"Father!" Elsa shrieks. She pulls her children away from her father and covers their ears, knowing they should not hear such things.

"This is preposterous," Nigel protests.

"It is my price. There is that something between us, Nicolaus, isn't there? That unspoken thing." Jonathan elevates his sexual desire for Nicolaus above rescuing his family.

Nicolaus looks at Jonathan with unbelief in his eyes, knowing he is referring to the time Jonathan sexually touched him, when forcing him to marry and consummate with Gwen. Nicolaus slightly shakes his head. "That thing I let slide when I decided to risk my life to save your ass from the cartel? And you have the nerve to bring that up? Now? You going to hold that over me to save my family?"

"Dad, what are you talking about?" Elsa asks, confused. None of the other family members knew about this. Nicolaus never spoke of it, as many men would never do.

Jonathan smirks. "Just as easily as me and my men are here, we can pack up and leave again. I will let you decide, Nicolaus. As I say, well, Nicolaus, you are my price."

Nicolaus shakes his head in disgust.

"What the hell?" Niall yells at Jonathan. "What does any of that, whatever that is, have to do with rescuing your grandchildren and the family of your grandchildren? What the hell is wrong with you?"

Nicolaus touches Niall on his leg and briefly looks at him to calm him. He then returns his eyes to Jonathan, knowing in his mind that after sacrificing his actual body, he'd now have to sacrifice his morals, his sexuality, and his piousness in order to save his family. There is no other way. They have no other options.

Nicolaus' eyes are locked with Jonathan, as the smirk across Jonathan's face grows larger. "What are you going to do? Rape me? That is the only thing you can do to me that hasn't already been done."

"No," Jonathan says in a calm, even tone. "I am not going to rape you, Nicolaus. You will be with me of your own free will, or the deal is off." He nods at Nigel, then Nicolaus, "Now, the choice is yours. You say yes, then I give the signal and we move forward with the rescue. You say no, and we leave."

Niall yells at Jonathan, "You cannot do this! You cannot abandon us. These people will kill us!"

"You, of all people, should know by now Niall, that everything has a price. And your brother is my price."

"How does this make you more of a man?" Niall yells. He's in shock and unbelief how everything seems to evolve around his brother. "Putting a price to save your grandchildren?" He stops as Nicolaus grips his arm.

"I will do it then," Nicolaus says simply, with hushed anger, only looking to Baird. "You have to give me your word that you are going to get my family out of here as soon as possible."

Jonathan nods. "You have my word."

Ceil holds her head down in silence. Her tears flow with hurt for Nicolaus. She knew damn well Baird's intentions toward Nicolaus, and he has just agreed to it, so that they could all be out of this nightmare that she created.

"Please," Nigel tries to negotiate something else.

"I believe it is settled then," Baird cuts off Nigel. He smiles at Nicolaus, "I intend to have a good go with you," he half warns him. "Shall we?" He stands and reaches for Nicolaus. As quickly as Nicolaus can hobble out, they are gone.

Chapter Ninety-Seven (TW)

Approximately one hour after Nicolaus had left with Jonathan Baird, Manfred and Roddy arrive with the police, an ambulance, and a helicopter to rescue and assist the family.

Roddy and Manfred are quick to look around. "Where is Nicolaus?"

Nigel shakes his head. "Jonathan Baird took him."

"What do you mean, Mr. Ravenell? Where?" Roddy is perturbed.

"I don't know. As a tradeoff for rescuing us, he took him. They left about an hour ago, and Jonathan's men have been assisting us. Please, we need to find them."

Manfred grabs Roddy's shoulders. "No, you stay with the family. Let me go look for them." Roddy nods in agreement. Manfred goes to Baird's men to get information.

Baird brings Nicolaus to a private first floor condo, in a small condominium complex just off the straight highway, on the border of the city. Before entering, Nicolaus looks down the street, thinking of trying to bolt away from this predicament of madness, though he knows it will be difficult with his leg.

Baird sees Nicolaus' hesitation, and tightens his hold on him. "There is no turning back now," Baird says, "a deal is a deal."

Once inside, Baird happily showers Nicolaus. Despite the awkwardness of Baird's behavior, Nicolaus needed help to shower. He is grateful to have the hot water pour over his pained injuries, as this made him feel a little better. He is grateful for the opportunity to wash himself.

Baird also helps Nicolaus with his leg. The dirty wraps are undone and fallen off. Nicolaus is in much pain. Jonathan checks his bag, and finds some over the counter pain pills, giving two to Nicolaus. Jonathan decides to use extra bed linens for bandages, ripping it, and wrapping it around the two sticks that line each side of Nicolaus' leg. Nicolaus holds the sticks with great discomfort and pain, while Jonathan wraps them. He makes the wrap tight so it will not fall off.

Then he helps Nicolaus lay back on the bed. Jonathan grabs fruit and water for Nicolaus, certain that he needs to eat.

Nicolaus thankfully eats a little, and drinks some water, feeling very nervous about what is about to happen with Jonathan. He does not speak, and takes breaths, to try and calm himself. Nicolaus tells himself he is not going to beg or try to find a way out, as he believes this is the only way to free his family.

Nicolaus has no idea that Baird is exploiting him, since he did not know others were enroute to rescue them. Baird quickly manipulated Nicolaus and his family into thinking he is the liberator in this scenario.

Silently, Nicolaus prays, asking God to help him accept this fate, and to help him get through it all.

Jonathan watches Nicolaus closely. At first, he chuckles at how nervous Nicolaus is. Then suddenly, Jonathan has a realization that he should not be attempting to ravage Nicolaus Ravenell. However, he fights against his conscience.

Jonathan has a propensity to go either way sexually. He knows that in his mind he has always wanted the chance to get at Nicolaus. He knows what he wants at the time he wants it, and he made no qualms about forcing his way to get what he wants, Nicolaus Ravenell. He thrives and revels in the fact that again he has the famous and courageous Nicolas Ravenell in his grip. Jonathan is completely in control of the situation at hand. Nicolaus is at his complete mercy and he does not want to let go of the idea of taking him.

Jonathan knew by the mindset and the physical positioning of Nicolaus, that he is silently praying. Fighting against his thoughts,

Jonathan moves forward with tying Nicolaus to the bed. First he runs his hands over Nicolaus' bare chest, unable to keep himself from touching him. He sees that Nicolaus is not resisting him. Then he ties his right leg, leaving the hurt left leg free.

Nicolaus stops praying and breathes, trying to ready himself for the sexual attack.

However, Jonathan stands, not able to bring himself to do it. Jonathan hits his own hand with a closed fist, as he stands back and looks upon Nicolaus, in all his defenseless nakedness. He sees that Nicolaus' body is covered in bruises. He can clearly see that he has suffered in the hands of Penelope Drone.

Nicolaus looks at Baird. "Well, go ahead ... let's get this over with." His tone makes him sound defeated.

Jonathan sighs. "I could take you right now, this very moment. And I want to, believe me, that was the plan." He backs away a few more steps. "Somehow, I just can't do it. There's something about you, ... and I just ... can't do it. You're too important. I don't want to mess you up."

Jonathan sits on the bed, and gently, he runs his hands over Nicolaus' body, noticing the scar on his abdomen from when he was stabbed. "You survived being poisoned after saving my life. I know that you've done a lot for many people. I want you to keep doing what you've been doing." He touches Nicolaus once more on his chest. "You make a difference in the world. People need you." Jonathan rises from the bed.

"Wait ... my family, please, you have to save them."

Jonathan waves his hand at Nicolaus. "They are already rescued, probably on their way home by now. You have my word."

Jonathan takes a good look at Nicolaus once more, "I gave you that public apology you demanded, you saved my life, I saved your life, I think we can call it even now." Jonathan sighs, "I'll see you around, Nicolaus." Jonathan grabs his stuff, and leaves the room in a hurry, before he changes his mind.

However, Nicolaus is still tied to the bed. He cannot exactly move about. He struggles against the ropes, but remains bound, unable to get free.

Chapter Ninety-Eight

Manfred followed the only highway road from the castle. He found the described jeep vehicle that Baird was driving, parked outside of a residential complex. He happened to see the door from which Jonathan exited, across the property courtyard, as he was trying to figure out which condo Nicolaus' was being held.

He busted open the door with a kick of his foot. He sees Nicolaus naked, and tied to the bed. Immediately, he goes to Nicolaus to free him.

"Manfred! Oh my God! Thank you! How did you know where to find me?"

"I followed the street, and saw these buildings, then I spotted the jeep."

Nicolaus covers himself with bedding, then hugs Manfred. He wants to cry. "I didn't know how I was going to get loose."

"Did he hurt you? I'll get that ... jerk!"

"No, no he didn't. He wanted to, but he didn't, by the grace of God. Said he couldn't."

Manfred sighs relief. "Thank God! Well let's get you dressed. Your family will be waiting for you."

Nicolaus shakes his head. "Manfred ... I ... I ... I can't go back."

"What do you mean? We'll scoop you all right out of there. I brought an ambulance. There's even a helicopter."

Nicolaus shakes his head. "I can't face them. I can't. And anyway, Ceil has made it very clear how much she does not want me around."

"What do you mean? Nicolaus, your father wants to know you are all right." Manfred talks while he helps Nicolaus get clothes on.

Nicolaus shakes his head. "No, please, just tell him."

Manfred frowns. "Well, where are you going, then?"

"I don't know." He sounds despondent, then says the first thing that appears in his mind. "Switzerland, I suppose."

"Switzerland? Nicolaus, you don't even have any money on you. You need medical care, and ..."

"It's okay, I'll figure it out. Can you just drop me at the dock? I'll figure it out."

Manfred can see that Nicolaus is in physical and emotional pain. He thinks driving him around will give him time to talk Nicolaus out of this. "Okay, sure, I'll take you wherever you want to go, Nicolaus."

Chapter Ninety-Nine (TW)

Manfred informed Roddy of the situation, then took Nicolaus to the docks. There are several cruise ships, some ready to depart. Manfred was unable to talk Nicolaus out of this. He walked with Nicolaus. "Nicolaus, come on man, let me take you to your father."

"No." Nicolaus held his hand to Manfred for a handshake. "Thank you for all you've done for me and my family." He nods as Manfred shakes his hand, then pulls Nicolaus into a hug.

"Nicolaus, at least get some medical care and a decent crutch, for God's sake!"

"I'll see you later," Nicolaus dismisses Manfred.

Manfred begins to walk away, but then hesitates. He looks back at Nicolaus and sees him staring into the ocean water. He's just standing there, staring at it, as if he needs to make a decision. Immediately, Manfred is right next to Nicolaus, holding his shoulder. He eases him back from the end of the dock. "Nicolaus, come on, let's get on board."

Nicolaus looks up frowning, his thoughts interrupted. "What?"

"Let's get on board. I'm going with you."

"No, you need to get back to your own family."

"Sure, I'll catch up with them later. You need help right now, and I'm here for you. I'll go with you."

"I don't need a babysitter, Manfred. Just go. I'm fine."

"No, Nicolaus. You are not fine. Let me do this for you." Manfred eases Nicolaus to walk with him. Manfred uses his credit card to purchase departure tickets. Luckily, since they are only at half capacity, he received a large discount.

They board, and are immediately upgraded to a larger room, once a few staff members recognize Nicolaus. "Here you are, Sirs!"

The staff bring them to a medium sized suite with two beds. "And here," he pulls papers out of his jacket pocket, "meal tickets for you, on us. Oh, and, if you give me your measurements, I'll be happy to get you clothes. They can be charged to your room. We have a store deck, it's on the fifth floor."

"Wow, young man, thank you kindly for such help," Manfred tells him looking over the meal tickets. "I'll be sure to put in a good word about you to your boss!"

"Thank you, Sir." He nods to Nicolaus, "Mr. Ravenell."

Manfred uses a paper to write down their sizes for the clothing.

"And we do have a doctor on board if needed."

"Oh, perfect, thank you."

As the young staff person leaves, Nicolaus collapses his exhausted self into a chair.

"Hey, how about a drink?"

Manfred pours Nicolaus a drink of bourbon and ice.

Nicolaus finds himself exhausted, humiliated, and in much pain. He downs the bourbon, and within minutes, he is asleep.

Manfred phones Roddy, and speaks with Nigel to update him on the situation.

Chapter One Hundred

When they arrive in Switzerland, it is chilly cold, as the snow season has begun. Manfred girded himself with several layers of winter clothing, including a coat, hat, and gloves for the weather. However, Nicolaus refused such purchases, and would not let Manfred buy him anything. The most he dawned was a men's sweater and a blanket he wrapped himself in, while sitting on the park bench as the snow began to fall and stick on both of them.

Children see Nicolaus and Manfred from the other side of the park, where they live in a huge storm pipe. Little by little they begin to visit the men, curious about them. They visit as a game of hide and seek, as they hide their appearance, and seek out what the men are doing. Nicolaus notices them, and when he acknowledges them, they run away with giggling laughter. He sees that the children are of all different ages, races, and sizes, once he sees them across the park. This reminds him of the street children he and Deirdre assisted.

"Nicolaus, we cannot stay out here. It is too cold," Manfred complains. "And you are not well. It is freezing out here and you are sweating like you're on a beach! That cannot be good. Let's get you to a doctor."

"I'm fine, Manfred," he states the obvious opposite. Nicolaus sighs, "Look, you should go home to your family. They need you."

"I'm not leaving you. Okay? Stop telling me to go home!"

"Your wife keeps calling and ..." Manfred's phone rings.

Manfred chuckles, "Speaking of." He answers, "Yes my love, how are you?"

"Don't you give me that, my missing in action husband! When will you be home? I'm feeling like a single mother these days."

"Now Dottie, you know I'm working with Nicolaus."

"In Switzerland? If that is really where you are," she mutters with disbelief in her voice. "Sounds like a vacation without me. Why does Nicolaus have you in Switzerland, anyway? Are you even with him? Put him on the phone. I want to talk to him."

"You want to talk to my boss?"

"Manfred!"

"Okay, okay, hold on." Manfred hands his phone to Nicolaus. "My wife would like to speak to you. Why should I be the only one getting yelled at?"

Nicolaus takes the phone with a frown. "Hello?"

"Nicolaus? This is Dottie, Manfred's wife. I'm just wondering why you insist that I be a single mother here with my four children, while you and my husband are galivanting off somewhere in Switzerland? If that is truly even where you are. And what are you two doing there anyway? I'm wondering when my husband will be back home," she gripes at Nicolaus.

"Yes ma'am, I understand you need your husband. I think he should return to you as soon as possible ..."

Manfred takes the phone from Nicolaus, frowning deeply at him, "Don't tell her that!" Manfred gets on the phone, "Dottie, now you listen here, I'll call you back when I'm not working and we'll discuss this. Okay? I love you, honey. I promise I will not leave you stranded with the kids. I'll call you later." Manfred ends the call, feeling annoyed more than anything else.

Nicolaus looks at him, "You should go home to your wife and kids. You don't need to babysit me."

"I'm not leaving you," Manfred reiterates, as he shivers in the chilly artic air. "We need to get inside."

"Those children are not inside. If they can handle the cold, we can handle the cold."

"What? Those children were born in the cold."

"Manfred," Nicolaus frowns at his statement.

"Let me call your father and get some money. We need a place to be. We cannot stay out here, Nicolaus."

"No. Don't call my father."

Manfred sighs, "Stubborn," he murmurs of Nicolaus under his breath. "I can see a town square or something in the distance. Let me see if I can find us some food. You do plan on eating to survive, I hope, Nicolaus."

Nicolaus nods without words.

"Please, just stay here. I don't want you gone when I get back. Please do me that courtesy."

"I'll be right here. I can't get far on my leg anyway, and not in this icy snow."

Chapter One Hundred One

The following morning, the men awake to the sunrise, though they are covered in snow on the park bench. They are awakened by the sound of laughter of several children who paid them a visit while they were sleeping. The children are running away from them, across the park, with their food of left over crackers and soup.

Nicolaus chuckles at them and gets an idea. "Manfred, today when you go to get us soup, can you bring extra crackers and some peanut butter, and peanuts for the children. We can help them fill their tummies." Nicolaus bellows an unusual cough that does not sound good.

Manfred looks at Nicolaus with great concern as he has never heard him cough before, and he notices that Nicolaus is covered in sweat. He knows this is not good. Manfred looks around and notices something he had not before. A building, in front of them, at the edge of the park, with a large sign that says 'doctor'. He sighs with relief. "I will, only if you see a doctor today," he tries to bargain with Nicolaus.

Nicolaus looks at Manfred. He had seen the sign previously and was thinking he should have his leg looked at, as such an injury was scarcely able to be cared for aboard a cruise ship. He had said nothing of his burn injury. In silence, he nods.

Manfred assists Nicolaus to hobble the distance. Manfred is relieved to find the office is open for business. When they enter, Manfred is again relieved to feel the warmth of heat throughout the building. He asks to speak to the physician.

"I've noticed you two in the park since yesterday," the physician tells him. He looks through the glass of the hallway door at Nicolaus, then turns to Manfred with a look of shocked surprise on his face, having now seen his friend up-close. "Is that ... Nicolaus Ravenell?"

Manfred chuckles. Even as terrible as Nicolaus looks, he is still recognizable by strangers. "Yes. And please, don't let on that you know who he is, or he may turn around and leave. Doc, really, he needs help. He's sweating, even though it is freezing out there."

"Wasn't he missing? With his family? I saw news reports on this."

"Yes. I'm part of the security team that found them. And Nicolaus ... needs to ... take a break away from his family now. He was hurt and he has not seen a doctor and now he has a bad cough and he's sweating a lot, and ..."

"Sounds like an infection. I see he's hobbling. His leg is also hurt?"

"Yes. Please. Will you see him? I don't have money on me to pay you, but I can get it from his father, I promise. I will pay you more than you ask if you just care for him."

"Yes, I'll see him. Just wait there, and I'll treat him the same as all my patients."

Manfred shakes the physician's hand. "Thank you."

As Nicolaus is called back, the physician hears the awful cough, and sees the trouble he has walking.

"I'm Doctor Elias Pearson. Please undress so that I can fully examine you," he tells him.

Nicolaus does as he asks, with assistance from a medical assistant. He is still bruised over his body. The linen wrap on his leg is worn out.

The physician examines the burn injury. "Nicolaus, is this a burn?" Nicolaus nods with no explanation. "It is very infected. Your leg is broken, my goodness. And your ribs? Does it hurt if I touch ... okay," he says as Nicolaus reacts from tender ribs. "Hmm, I need x-rays. Luckily, we have a modern, easy use machine here. Let's get imaging, then I can diagnose you properly."

Nicolaus nods. The mobile x-ray machine is utilized by the medical assistant, and Dr. Pearson has results in minutes.

As Dr. Pearson examines the results, he scratches his head. "Hmm. We talk with your friend, okay?" Nicolaus nods, then Dr. Pearson asks Manfred inside the exam room.

"Please," Dr. Pearson bids Manfred to sit down. "Nicolaus, you do have some broken ribs, to both sides, a few cracked more than once. You are starting to get fluid in your lungs, hence that cough. Your leg is broken, needs resetting with screws, and must be casted properly, or it will not heal, could cause worse issues. You are lucky, even though I see no infection there, I want to give you an antibiotic shot anyway to stave off infection. Your burn is very infected. It must be cleaned out properly or will for sure cause other problems. We caught it in time.

"Nicolaus, let's get rid of these infections first, then I will have you transported to a hospital for surgery on your leg. You must be off your leg for at least two weeks, maybe three after the surgery. So for now, you will be on an antibiotic, I'll give you electrolytes for dehydration, and you must rest. Now, where are you staying?"

Manfred feels elated at the news of Nicolaus finally receiving proper medical care. "Doctor, we are ..." Manfred looks at the park, "we don't have a place."

Dr. Pearson frowns, "No, you cannot live outside, Nicolaus. Look, I have a private room upstairs. I don't use it. It is not big, but there is a bed and a bathroom. You can make it work for now, at least for the next few weeks." He takes Nicolaus by the shoulder. "You must be in bed to get better. My medical assistant can tend to you when needed."

Manfred takes Dr. Pearson's hand to shake it. "We will pay you, I promise you, Sir, thank you so very much!"

Chapter One Hundred Two

After two days in bed, Nicolaus' melancholy doubled down on him, until little footsteps were heard on the stairs outside, that led up to the upstairs room above the clinic. The children have been watching all that is happening from the park area. The peanut butter and crackers held their tummies for one day, though now they find themselves hungry again.

The outside door to the room opens, and a few children enter, hesitant at first, for fear of being shewed away. Nicolaus sees them, and beckons them inside. They see he is clean and shaven. Immediately, they are happy to be warm.

Nicolaus offers them more crackers, and bread. This time, the children stay with him. At first, sitting on the floor, then gradually, moving to the chair, and the bed. They touch Manfred's hands, and observe him, as he seems gigantic to them.

One of the children beckons others through the window, and soon more pitter patter of small feet can be heard climbing the stairs. Soon there are ten children in the room, some joining Nicolaus on the bed. Then more children file in, little by little, until there are about thirty children in the room. Manfred notices how Nicolaus has perked up.

"I know, I know, we need food," Manfred tells them. "I'll be right back."

As the elevator doors open, Dr. Pearson steps inside the room, as he'd heard noises on the stairs and is there to investigate. When he sees all the children sitting with Nicolaus, some tugging on him, he can see the positive change about Nicolaus.

"I'm so sorry. Children seem to gravitate towards him. He's like a pied piper, or something," Manfred chuckles with Dr. Pearson.

"Oh, of course. I remember now that he was actually doing some work with children," Dr. Pearson put his hand to his chin in thought. "Hmm. You know something, I think I know of a place that you and Nicolaus may be interested in."

"I promise we will pay you for your kindness. In fact, I'm about to call his father now to get some funds."

Dr. Pearson nods. "Very well. This place is a large house that has been up for sale for a while now, and no one has purchased it. I think you two might be interested. Let me contact the realtor. It is not far from here."

"Realtor?"

Dr. Pearson spread his arms out about all the children, nodding.

After speaking in more detail with Dr. Pearson, and seeing the property online, Manfred made the call to Nigel. "Nigel, I finally got Nicolaus the medical care he needs. He has an infection and is on bedrest for two weeks. He will need surgery though, on his leg. The physician had mercy on us and gave us a room above the clinic. Thank God, it's freezing outside. Nigel, we need to pay him. And there are three dozen children who have found their way to Nicolaus, and now we need to take care of them."

"Say no more, how much money shall I send you?"

"Twenty-five thousand."

"How much?" Nigel frowns at the figure.

"Nigel, there is also a very large property that I think Nicolaus will want to purchase once we see it. The roof needs repair and it needs a clean-up. The realtor recognized Nicolaus' name and is willing to discount it if we do the repairs and if it is to take care of children."

"Oh, I see. My son is still doing good work, then?"

"Even on bedrest, Nigel. I can hardly understand it."

"Manfred, what you ask for is not enough if you will be taking care of those children. They will need things. I'll send you one hundred thousand, ... wait, no, two hundred thousand, and then tell Nicolaus to call me if he needs more. Okay?"

"Nigel!"

The surgery on Nicolaus' leg is successful and he recovers quickly due to his agility and physically fit health. Nicolaus uses proper crutches to keep pressure off his leg. Three weeks later, Manfred and Nicolaus assist the children out of the room in order to go see the property. Manfred orders a taxi for them.

"The realtor took this place off the market, and is holding it for us to look at," Manfred explains, just now popping this excursion from the room on him.

Nicolaus looks at Manfred as they approach the property. "Why do they only want ten thousand for this place?" The twelve room house is somewhat expansive, even has stairs and a side ramp up to the door. "Must be something wrong with it, like electrical wiring, or piping, or something."

"I know the roof needs replacing. Let's go check it out."

The realtor met them at the front door. He shakes both of their hands, and acknowledges Nicolaus' crutches. As they slowly walk into the house, they immediately see the sunlight, through the tarps that cover the roof. A few birds fly around the massive eighteen foot high ceilings. The floors are sandy, the house is very dated. "Look, there is an operative elevator."

The men go to the second floor, and are surprised to see that the bedrooms and bathrooms are all in good condition. Each bedroom has a distinct characteristic. One has round windows, one has built-in shelves, one window seats, one wall shelves, the main bedroom has ceiling windows so that one can gaze at the sky when falling asleep.

Both Manfred and Nicolaus are impressed. "Okay, give us the bad news. What's wrong with this place? Why is the price so low?"

"I promise you Nicolaus, the owner knows of your work and he knows Dr. Pearson. He wants to help. Now granted, this place does need some remodeling. He says if you replace the roof, and be sure abandoned children live here, he will sell it to you for ten thousand. We can get an inspection before you buy, and you'll see that the roof, a clean-up job, maybe some redecorating to your taste, will be all that is needed."

Nicolaus looks at Manfred. "What do you think, Manfred?"

"I think Dottie and my family will love this place! And so will those kids! Are you kidding?"

Nicolaus chuckles, understanding that Manfred seems to have decided to be all in with him. "Okay, let's get the inspection first, and if all checks out, we'll take it."

Chapter One Hundred Three

THREE MONTHS LATER

"Nicolaus! Good to hear from you. I saw on the news that you and your family were missing. Is everything okay?" Cecil asks, as he had quickly answered the phone, seeing a strange number.

"Mr. Omari, it's true, we were taken hostage by my ex-sister-in-law. We are okay."

"What? Sounds like serious family troubles."

"Yes Sir. I assure you, she will not be a trouble to us or anyone else. Justice has been served."

"My goodness, Nicolaus. I've been trying to keep this information away from Abigail. She seems very concerned about you, though. It is as if she senses something is wrong. And especially, lately. Are you okay?"

"Yes Sir. I just wanted to touch base with you, so you would have my new number, and let you know I'm still on the case to clear your name."

"Nicolaus, I appreciate that. Where are you calling me from?"

"I live in Switzerland now, Sir."

"Your family has moved to Switzerland?"

"Just me, Sir."

"Oh, I see. Well ... I think you should come see about Abigail. At least talk to her. I can get her."

"Oh, Sir, no. Umh ... I'll think about it. Okay?"

"Sure." This of course does not sit well with Cecil. He does not want to see Abigail heartbroken.

• • • •

TWO WEEKS LATER

· · · ·

ABIGAIL PACES HER HOME in South Africa with the intense worry that she has had for over a month now. "Dominique, why haven't we heard anything from Nicolaus? It has been over three months now."

Dominique is at a loss of explanation. "Maybe his intentions were not sincere. He is not who we thought he was."

Abigail turns sharply to face Dominique. "That cannot be true!" She defends Nicolaus. "Why would he have flown all that way to see us?"

Dominique shrugs, "Why do men do what they do? Perhaps he thought he could get something from you, Abby. Who knows?"

"Nicolaus is not like that. He would never do something like that!"

"Abby, really, we don't know Nicolaus Ravenell. We have met him one time and ..."

"And he truly loved my sister! You saw his tears, Dominique! He would never hurt father." She twirls on her heel, with a finger to her mouth in thought. "No, I think something has happened."

Abigail sits down to drink her coffee. She finds that her hands are trembling with anxiousness over Nicolaus, so much so, that she clangs a song with the ceramic cup and saucer with her jitter movements. She puts it down. "I just know it. Something has happened. Something is wrong."

"Well, have you called him?"

"Several times. His phone is not even working. Why would the phone of Nicolaus Ravenell not be working? Why hasn't he called us?"

Just then, the doorbell to their home rings. Abigail rises to answer the door. She opens the door, and there stands ... Nicolaus.

"Nicolaus!" Abigail rush jumps him, with hysterical laughter. She lands in his arms with a painful thud coming from him. His ribs are still a little tender and he has dropped his crutches on the ground to catch her. She steps back, "Oh my God, are you okay?"

Nicolaus chuckles and pulls her into a tight engulfing hug. Dominique watches as Abigail and Nicolaus hug each other tightly for a few minutes, as if they are old friends, or lovers who have not seen each other for a long time and who miss each other. She sees Nicolaus get emotional, as he pulls away to look at Abigail.

They touch foreheads. "I couldn't sleep ... thinking about you," he softly tells her, near a whisper.

Abigail smiles, and takes Nicolaus into another hug.

Cecil appears, and smiles at what he sees. He picks up Nicolaus' crutches. "Nicolaus! You made it. Come in, come in."

Abigail looks at his leg. "What's happened?"

Nicolaus nods, "It's a long story."

"You must tell me everything!" Abigail's reporter's voice sounds like she is ready to take notes of an adventure. She and Dominique assist Nicolaus inside.

Cecil prepares a meal while Nicolaus updates Abigail and Dominique on everything.

When he's done talking, Abigail comments, "So, you are taking care of fifty orphan children in Switzerland now? My goodness. That sounds like quite an undertaking, yet very important, Nicolaus."

"Nicky? Right? I understand you are called Nicky. I've seen it in news reports," Dominique asks him.

Nicolaus nods, as he sits between the two ladies. "Either is fine."

"What did my sister call you?"

"Usually, Nicky," Nicolaus chuckles, "unless she was reprimanding me, then she called me Nicolaus." The ladies chuckle with him. He notices that Abigail has that tight hold on his hand again. Nicolaus is not sure he is comfortable with where he sees this going, out of concern for Abigail's safety.

Cecil calls Abigail to the kitchen to help him, leaving Nicolaus with Dominique. Dominique smiles at him. "Nicky and Abby, hmm, has a sweet ring to it."

"No, let's not go there," he tells her gently.

"What do you mean? Abby was so worried about you. She's been out of her mind. She hasn't slept properly for at least two weeks. You're all she thinks about! She doesn't even go to work, Nicky." Dominique frowns at the look of surprise on his face. She shakes her head. "Don't try to pretend that you don't feel it, Nicolaus. I know you do! I see it when you look at her."

Nicolaus shakes his head and opens his mouth, yet says nothing.

"Don't you break her heart!" Dominique demands of him. "Don't you dare!"

Nicolaus sighs. "I'm not trying to hurt anybody. I don't want to hurt anyone. There's just ..."

"Just what?" Dominique snaps at him, ready to knock down any excuse he may come up with.

"There's a lot of complications. And dangers."

"Love conquers all! When I look at the two of you, I'm sure there is not anything you cannot overcome together."

"I used to think like that. And what I have found is that is not necessarily true. Usually, it takes more than love. It takes wisdom, courage, money, and experience to conquer most things. And sometimes, it takes the wisdom of avoidance to keep people safe. So I will ask of you, Dominique, whatever it is that you think you see, or whatever you think may be, please do not encourage Abigail towards it. I implore you, to warn her away from it."

Dominique looks surprisingly upon Nicolaus Ravenell, the unassuming, handsome, supposed prince or righteous knight, of many women's fairytale romantic fantasy, heir to the Ravenell empire, who only wants to exist in a small corner of the world and care for children. Her impression of him suddenly changed drastically. She now understands he is the real deal, and she has a terrible feeling Abigail is in for a tough time. "So you want to try to totally deny what you know in fact is happening?"

"Hey, you two," Cecil calls to them, "let's get this meal."

Dominique's worry grows two-fold when she notices that Nicolaus and Abigail fell silent. They had been left alone to talk with each other after dinner. Dominque peaks around the corner into the living room to see that they have fallen asleep, Abigail curled onto Nicolaus, her head and hand on his strong chest, his arm around her in a protective stance. She knew they were probably both exhausted, and the meal with wine most likely put them to sleep. Though Dominique did notice how comfortable they seemed with each other, as if they'd known each other for years.

When Cecil came around the corner and saw them, he chuckles, seeks out a blanket and covers them. He ushers Dominique upstairs.

In the morning, when Nicolaus finds himself curled up to Abigail, holding her tightly in his arms, he panics. His panic is mostly because he doesn't want to let go of her. He decides he'd better leave, not wanting to set anything more in motion.

After getting freshened up, changing clothes, and a quick breakfast, Abigail lingeringly walks Nicolaus to the waiting taxi. She has a tight grasp on his arm. Dominique follows close behind, her hand on Nicolaus' back.

"So, when will I see you again?" Abigail pressures him. "We cannot let so much time go by without contact, ever again, Nicky."

Nicolaus nods, "You're right."

"Maybe we can make a trip to Switzerland to see you and those lovely children," Dominique happily provides this idea.

Abigail perks up, "That would be wonderful!"

"Abby, you could even get a story on the orphanage," Dominique adds as a good friend would.

Abigail giggles and wiggles with excitement. Nicolaus looks at Dominique, understanding that she is not in his corner on his relationship with Abigail. He chuckles at Abigail's reaction, looking at her sparkling eyes, "Sure, why not?"

Abigail jump hugs him again. Then, without thinking, she smacks his lips, surprising both herself and Nicolaus. And then, she looks at the delicious lips of Nicolaus Ravenell, and she goes for the kiss, the real kiss. Nicolaus lightly responds, then Abigail is pulled away from him by Dominique.

"Girl, let the man get into the taxi, he's going to miss his flight!" Dominique pulls Abigail to the front door.

Nicolaus chuckles and waves goodbye to Abigail's air kisses. He grumbles to himself as he gets into the taxi, "What am I doing?" knowing he is all over the place with Abigail. He fears his avoidance tactics may not work.

Chapter One Hundred Four

The following month, Abigail and Dominique make the trip to Switzerland to see Nicolaus. Abigail got her news media employer to let her do this human interest story. It is Friday afternoon when they arrive. This is one of many trips they will be making to see Nicolaus, as well as Nicolaus returning to Johannesburg to see them. Abigail and Nicolaus have also been speaking by phone a few times a week, at Abigail's insistence. She is adamant about developing her relationship with Nicolaus.

"Oh my God, look at this place!" Dominique remarks. "This beautiful, huge house is for children?" She rings the doorbell while Abigail snaps photos of the outside of the house and the beautifully manicured lawn.

Dottie is Manfred's Native American wife, and House Mother to the children, providing them guidance and directives. She is also in charge of the staff and the cleaning ladies for which Nicolaus insists on paying her for her work. Dottie has brought their own children to live with everyone, and they have let these Swiss children experience some of their Native American culture, values, and norms.

Dottie opens the front door and receives a shock, as Abigail is now standing next to Dominique. "Oh my good Lord! Ladies, I think you had better come in!" Dottie pulls in Abigail by the hand, and Dominique follows. "You must be related to Deirdre Ravenell!" Dottie feels as if she is looking at the woman in the painting in Nicolaus' office.

Suddenly, Abigail and Dominique see a fabulously dressed woman with a fashionable afro appear before them with stretched out arms, as they are looking around the beautiful open air room with an eighteen foot ceiling, and winding staircase. "Oh my

God!" Francesca approaches them. "You must be Abigail, Deirdre's sister."

Abigail nods.

"I can hardly believe it. You look just like her, and yet you don't." Francesca takes her hands. "I'm Francesca, Nicolaus' sister."

"Oh! And this is my dear, dear friend, Dominique."

Francesca hugs Abigail. "Welcome." She hugs Dominique. "Welcome." She steps back and takes Abigail's hands again. "When Nicky told me about you, and that you would be arriving, I just had to be here to meet you."

"Abby!" Nicolaus' voice is heard from around the way, as he appears using a cane with a soft boot on his leg, Manfred behind him. He kisses Abby's face, as she has a huge smile for him. "Dominique." Nicolaus gives her the same courtesy, taking her hands and kissing her face. "This is Manfred, my good friend and business partner, and his wife Dottie. And I see you've met my famous sister, Francesca Olivia Kiviste, the anthropologist and department lead at Cambridge."

Francesca laughs, "Famous? Nicky! You're the famous one!"

Abigail chuckles, "He's always talking about you, and always reminds me of your position at Cambridge. He's so proud of you!"

"He tells us and everyone else, I suspect," Dominique jokes.

Nicolaus chuckles, "Yep!"

Suddenly, a rush of children surround the two ladies.

Several children react to both ladies, "Oh! Oh! You're pretty!".

"You're that lady in the painting in Papa Nicky's office."

Abigail chuckles, and looks to Nicolaus, "Papa Nicky? You didn't tell me about that!"

He shakes his head. "The kids refer to me like that, seems everywhere I am. I don't know why?"

The children are each vying for attention and full of excited questions for the guests.

"Will you read to us?"

"Are you staying for dinner?"

Dominique is also surrounded by the children and being pulled in several directions by her hands, and arms. "Want to see my toy collection?"

"No silly, she wants to see my dolls. Proper ladies don't care about your dumb trucks."

"Can I get you some soda, Miss?"

"Will you help me color?"

"Will you help me with my homework?"

Nicolaus claps his hands to try to get some order. "Okay, now children. These lovely ladies have just arrived. I promise they will visit with you. Let's let them get inside and get refreshed."

"Okay Papa Nicky," is heard from several children. The staff helpers usher the children out of the hallway. Suddenly, the large crowd of children dissipates to one or two very young children. One holds her arms to be lifted by Nicolaus, and he obliges her, placing her on his hip. She lays on his shoulder, tired from the day.

Abigail gently pats the little one on her back. "Nicky, this place is amazing."

"Sorry about that, they get excited when we have visitors. How was your flight?"

"Great! Took us twelve hours. Dominique slept most of the way."

Nicolaus chuckles. "Well, I hope you know you are staying here. The house is full of children, but we do have two guest suites. Francesca is in one, and I hope you won't mind sharing the other."

Abigail kisses Nicolaus on the cheek. "We prefer it that way. Otherwise, one of us will be sneaking into the other's room anyway, to be talking and asking questions." The ladies giggle.

After dinner, bedtime stories, and the staff have all the children tucked away, including the older children, Nicolaus and Abigail walk the grounds. He shows her the gardens of vegetables and flowers, the outside play area for the children, and the beautifully decorated porch with a swing, which they are now sitting in. Abigail plans to take plenty of photos for the story, tomorrow, in the daylight.

"So are you just never going back home? I mean, not at all? It's so hard for me to imagine you walking away from your family empire."

Nicolaus sighs, "Well, I don't see myself going back. My life is here now, with these children. When they turn eighteen, they choose college or work, and we help with that. It rotates a bed open, so if there are others out on the street, they can be welcomed in."

"And you don't feel like you might be running away from something, Nicky?"

Nicolaus looks at Abigail, surprised at her insight. "Maybe."

She touches Nicolaus on the arm. "I don't mean to offend you, Nicky. It just seems to me like you're hiding yourself away from the world. I understand you went through a terrible trauma with your family, but the world hasn't heard from you in months, and here you are, quietly working."

"Don't I deserve some quiet? I think I do. It's a nice change, is all."

"Oh yeah, sure, it's just ... Nicky, it's easy to get lost when you're hiding. And whether or not you realize it, the world actually needs you." She looks in his searching eyes. Nicolaus is surprised at her internal wisdom. "What about church, do you still go to church, and believe in God?"

"Oh yes! I'll never give up my faith! We have a whole section at the local church." Nicolaus laughs at Abigail's laughter at his statement.

Later, as Nicolaus, Manfred, and Dottie entertain Dominique, Francesca and Abigail have time to talk.

"Abby, I want you to know you can call me anytime. I know you'll be around for some time, as I can see that Nicolaus is in love with you. He's trying to hide it, but I can see how he looks at you, much like he used to look at Deirdre."

Abigail smiles, her heart warmed. "Thank you for that, Francesca. I love Nicky too. I don't even understand how all this happened so fast. We're still getting to know each other."

"Yes you do know how," she tells her softly.

"You're right. I do know. I've seen all seven of my children in my dreams, and Nicky has the face of my children. For years, I wondered who they looked like."

"Seven? DeeDee Mari, our ancestor, who you and Deirdre resemble had seven children!"

"Yes, I know. My father told me all about DeeDee."

"Abby ... then you know ... "

"About the curse? Yes, my father told me all about that too. He thinks that is what happened to Deirdre."

"So then, you understand Nicky's hesitation. Especially since he's in love with you."

"Yes."

"Promise me right now, that you won't hold that against him. He still struggles with the loss of Deirdre."

"I promise, Francesca." She sighs, "He really loved my sister, didn't he?"

Francesca nods, "With all he had."

"So, being our closest expert with your anthropology knowledge, what do we do about that darn curse?"

"I already told Nicky from what I know about curses, is that he has to be present at the time the tragedy is beginning to happen, stop it from happening, and that will break the curse."

"Jesus! That sounds like a riddle!"

Francesca chuckles, "That's what Nicky said!"

"Hmm, be there at the time it begins to happen, and stop it from happening. Hmm, so can a construct be the conduit of this thing?"

Francesca chuckles again, "What? Now you sound like a riddle!"

"You know, like set a scene to make something happen, for him to be able to stop it. Will that break the curse? Or does it have to be a spontaneous happening?"

"Well, that shouldn't matter. The action of stopping it happening is what will break the curse. It's the action."

"Hmm."

"What do you have in mind?"

"I'm not sure yet. I'm going to think of something!"

Chapter One Hundred Five

. . . .

"CEIL?"

"Constance, I'm sorry to drop by. Nigel gave me your address. Please, may I come in?"

Constance is extremely surprised. In all her years, not once has Ceil Ravenell ever appeared at the doorstep to the home Deirdre bought so many years ago. "Sure!" Constance stands back so Ceil can enter. She looks behind her and has another shock when no one else is present forcing Ceil inside. "Well, this is quite a surprise!" She leads Ceil to the living room.

"I know. I'm sorry I've never visited before."

Constance bids Ceil to sit down, while noticing how much she's changed since her captivity. She had of course noticed this before, however, now, inside the house she shared with Deirdre, Ceil seems very small and timid. A shell of her former self. The cold stare, gone. Her haughty attitude, gone. The feeling of high superiority, gone. She even sports a grey haired bob these days, whereas in the past, Ceil would have never let even one grey hair show. "Coffee? Water? Cookies?"

"Oh, no, thank you, I'm fine. I just need to talk to you."

Constance sits across from Ceil. "Talk? To me?"

"Well ...," she begins slowly, "I know that I certainly owe you an apology. I know I was a terrible person, and I must have offended you so many times, Constance. I'm so sorry about all that. Truly, I am sorry."

Constance looks at her with a raised eyebrow. "Ceil, what is this about?" Constance knew she would never get the real apology she is owed, for when Ceil ran off her husband so many decades ago.

Ceil takes a breath, feeling nervous. "Well … it's Nicolaus. I understand you speak with him frequently."

Constance nods. "Yes, we speak weekly. In fact, I just spoke with him this morning. He is doing very well, taking care of many children. He looks well, his leg is all healed, and he sounds well."

Ceil nods. "That's good." She falls quiet. Since the change has been brought over her, she has difficulty confronting herself about Nicolaus.

"What about it, Ceil?" Constance prods her gently.

"Well, Constance, Nigel is ill. I want Nicolaus to see about his father … before it's too late."

"Oh Ceil!" Constance moves to sit next to her, seeing that she is about to cry. She side hugs her to support her.

"He has lung cancer. We don't know why or how, and … he doesn't have much time left. He can't work anymore. He has trouble walking any distance, and … he has a terrible cough."

"Oh Ceil, of course Nicolaus would want to see his father. You should call him and tell him."

"No! I can't … I … I… I wouldn't know what to say. Please, will you tell him? Nigel doesn't want to bother him, and I don't agree with that, and …"

"Oh my! Nicolaus would want to know this information, so that he can make the decision on whether or not to see Nigel. And Ceil, knowing Nicky as I do, despite all that's happened, I'm sure he'll make the trip right over to see his father."

"You think so?"

"I know so. I'm glad you told me. Why don't we call him together?"

"No!" Ceil shakes her head. "I can't. I wouldn't know what to say. And I don't want to make him uncomfortable."

"Ceil, if Nicky does arrive to see his father, you will be talking to him, right?"

Ceil nods, "Of course. I know I have to face him, eventually."

Constance chuckles. "Oddly, it is Nicky who feels he cannot face you! Ever since Latvia, he has been ..."

"Devastated, I know."

"Not devastated. Marred, and emotionally injured. The worst you've ever done to him, Ceil. He's marred by the magnitude of your action of not wanting him around. I'm fairly certain he may never get over that, Ceil, though he won't really talk about it. So when you see him, don't expect too much."

Constance is again surprised by the hurt look on Ceil's face, something she's never seen before. Ceil seems timid and ashamed.

"It will take a lot for Nicolaus to make the journey back here," Constance tells Ceil, "and I believe he will, for Nigel, Nicolaus will do anything."

Chapter One Hundred Six

Nicolaus and Manfred sit in the library, that doubles as an office, inside the twelve bedroom mansion in the city of Lausanne, Switzerland. The coastal town is beautiful with lovely views of Lake Geneva. The people speak French as well as English.

The men have their desks side by side in the massive room, that has a twelve foot ceiling, three chandeliers, floor to ceiling bookshelves filled with books and artifacts on the top shelves. The room laments cherrywood coloring throughout. And there is a life size painting of Deirdre on the wall, directly in front of Nicolaus' desk; a painting that Nigel commissioned.

Nicolaus had decided to maintain weekend video contact with the children in the homes he and Deirdre created in the United States. Currently, he is working on the finance books for this children's home, as the children are arriving from school. Manfred is working on staff items and verifying payroll. Both men are dressed professionally, as usual, modeling and demonstrating work ethics for the children, especially the older children.

Nicolaus sighs at the interruption of the ringing of the phone on his desk, however, he always answers it.

"Nicolaus, this is Constance."

"Oh, hello Mom. Everything okay?" He asks, not stopping his work, nor looking up.

"Nicolaus, hon, are you sitting down?"

Nicolaus stops at her words. He frowns, "Mom, what's happening?"

"It's your father, Nicolaus. He's sick. Ceil says you need to see about him."

"Ceil?"

"Nicolaus, take it seriously. Please, you need to see your father. The sooner, the better."

"How sick is he?"

"Nicolaus, you need to get here."

The realization of what Constance is saying strikes Nicolaus. He nods, "Okay. I'll get there."

As soon as Nicolaus is done with the call from Constance, his phone rings again.

"Nicolaus, so glad I reached you, I know we have a time gap. This is Juan from the law office. I've got good news about Cecil Omari."

"Juan! I haven't heard from you in a while."

"I know. The wheels of justice move very slowly, my friend. After several requests and string pulls for the district attorney's office, we finally got them to reopen the Omari case. And guess what, my friend? We got all charges dropped!"

"For real?"

"Yes. There was no concrete evidence of embezzlement for those arrest warrants. And there actually appears to be collusion between Ceil and the then mayor's office. And that former mayor is now under investigation for corruption, though that may not go far, Nicolaus, because he's in his nineties. However, we got a judge to drop all the charges. Cecil Omari has been completely cleared. And, my friend, because I know you, I got the DA to write us a letter saying so. I'll email it to you right now."

"That is really great, Juan! Thanks so much for that hard work, and for getting to the bottom of all this. Mr. Omari will be so happy to know his name is now cleared."

"I'm sending this to you now."

"Thank you Juan. Thank the team for me."

"You got it!"

"Looks like I need to make some travel plans," Nicolaus tells Manfred. "Mr. Omari's name has been completely cleared, and my father is ill."

"Nigel is ill? Oh no!" Manfred grabs Nicolaus by the shoulder, "Do not worry about any of this, my man. Dottie and I will take care of everything. Family and country first! We both know it would be the right thing to do, and is how it should be."

The following day, Manfred gives Nicolaus a most encouraging hug, in sending him off for his travels. Nicolaus meets with the children before leaving. Many of the children are alarmed that their sweet Papa is going away from them. Nicolaus hushes them with kisses and hugs, kisses the little ones' tears, as he holds them close, then gifts them with one last story until his return.

Nicolaus first takes a flight to Johannesburg to see Cecil and Abigail. Upon arriving to their home, after hugging the ladies, Nicolaus gives Cecil the paper that clears his name.

"Whoo-hoo!" Cecil is ecstatic. "You did it, Nicolaus! You did it!" Cecil grabs Nicolaus' face, and kisses it. "You really came through!"

Nicolaus chuckles at his excitement. "I know it took a while. Worth the wait though, cuz now your name is completely cleared."

Abigail also gives Nicolaus a hug and a kiss. "Nicolaus!"

"It was just as I thought, no evidence. It took them time to get the case reopened, and re-examined. They found no evidence, and are looking at investigating that former mayor."

Cecil waves the paper in the air. "Do you know what this means?" He asks everyone with joy in his voice. "It means I can travel without fear. I can see my wife now! My Constance!" Cecil is suddenly gripped with emotion. He sits himself down, tears running from his eyes. Abigail is quick to be next to her father, hugging him. "My Constance! After all these years."

Abigail pops up before Nicolaus, and Dominique tends to Cecil. She touches Nicolaus shoulders. "Will you help us go see my mother? Oh my goodness! It is so strange to hear myself say that I have a mother!"

Nicolaus frowns, "Of course! Let's call her right now!"

"No." Abigail stops him getting his phone. "That would be so awkward. And we can't really just pop up, it might frighten her. I mean … it's been so many years. Nicky, I must ask this … for my dad … please, you have to take us to her. Please!"

"Well, I guess I see what you are saying. I am going back anyway; my father has fallen ill."

Cecil stands at hearing this. "Oh no, Nigel is ill? Please let us all make the journey together. I can see my Constance, and Nigel as well. And I have a few choice words for Ceil."

Abigail has Nicolaus hands, as he nods in agreement. "Only, Nicky, my dad doesn't fly."

"Oh yeah, right. How 'bout if I meet you once you land, or embark, or whatever they call it? I'll pick you up and take you to Mom's."

Abigail giggles. "When the ship docks!"

"Oh, docks."

"Nicky, it would mean the world to me if you would travel with us. I know you have told me many things about … my mother, but I want to hear it again! Oh my God! I'm going to meet my mother." She puts her hand to her cheek, "I can't even believe it. Finally!"

Nicolaus sees the dazed look about Abigail. This really is a big deal. He smiles at her and nods, "Sure, okay, we'll all go together."

Chapter One Hundred Seven

Cecil arranged for them to travel in style. However, Nicolaus immediately noticed the absolute fear and terror about Abigail. He assisted getting her onto the ship, lifting her in his arms and carrying her over the bridge, as Dominique ran across, not daring to look into the deep sea below.

Cecil was not fazed by any of this. He carried on like normal. He reserved a large suite for all of them to share, which had two beds. They travelled as the Omari family, and Nicolaus was grateful he seemed to not be recognized by random people, at least no one approached him. Their suite is on the same level as the captain's quarters.

Nicolaus is shocked at the colossal size of this particular cruise ship. All amenities are included, from a pool to a disco. He is amazed, as it is much larger than the previous ship he had boarded.

Abigail's fear of the ocean is visible, as she clang to Nicolaus, a privilege she never had before. They had a meal at one of many restaurants on the ship, saw a quick show, then decided to turn in for the night. It was intended for the ladies to share one bed, and the men to share the other.

Cecil had no trouble drifting to sleep, as his head is filled with excited dreams of reuniting with Constance. He dreamed of what she might look like, and the hope of his reception.

Dominique filled herself with alcoholic beverage. She is scared, as usual, of the thought of the ship going down into the icy waters, just like the Titanic. The several glasses of wine has her fast asleep, with her fuzzy eye mask in place.

It is Abigail and Nicolaus who cannot sleep. Abigail wasted no time in grabbing Nicolaus' hands. "Shall we?"

He nods to her. Just as they sit on the couch in the suite, across from the beds, the ship hits rough waters with rolling waves.

Abigails squeaks as the turbulent motion of the ship throws her against Nicolaus. His arms gently go around her, and she holds onto him for dear life.

"Oh God! Please help us," she prays aloud.

Nicolaus chuckles. "It will be okay, Abby." He holds her tighter to him. The waves rock the ship, with unease. "I've got you," he tells her, looking into her eyes.

The look on her face at his words is priceless to him, making him smile brightly at her.

"I am terrified of bodies of water, swimming pools, creeks, lakes and more so of the sea. I do not swim, and I have the most horrid fear of drowning."

"You don't have to worry, I will not let anything happen to you, Abby." Nicolaus' charm and confidence negates the fearful possibilities of the huge ocean and this large ship.

Abigail giggles, "Wow! I have always wanted to hear a man say that to me. And here you are, like a prince or a knight or something." She looks at his lips and realizes she is against his body. She can feel his taunt muscular frame against her. Suddenly, a magical moment seems to be presenting itself to them. Perhaps it is the rocking motion, or perhaps it is the warmth of his body against hers, or the warmth of his arms around her, or the engulfing easy embrace she is in. "And you know, the way you say it, I completely believe you!"

Their eyes lock on each other, and his hold remains steady.

"Maybe you should learn to swim," he tells her sweetly.

"Maybe I should," she answers just as sweetly. She is captivated by the feel of him against her.

They have been talking, and flirting, and planning, and discussing, and observing, and laughing, and debating for the last three years. However, Abigail has never actually been in Nicolaus' arms as she is now. She has a feeling of nervous joy.

Abigail knows she is destined to this man. She tries to sense why her twin loved him enough to marry him, even with all the chaos of his life. Perhaps she also felt destined to him.

The sensual aroma of Abigail engulfs Nicolaus' nostrils. The feel of her soft body against his is overwhelming for him. Her dainty hands rest on his chest, and she has a determined look about her, beyond her fear, and beyond her beauty. Slowly, he embraces her, remembering what it is like to hold a woman. To hold the soft, warmness of a woman's body next to his. He sees her fragile frame laced with feistiness, which reminds him of Deirdre.

It has been many years since Nicolaus let any woman touch him. He does not understand this phenomenon that is Abigail. Her trembling has subsided in his arms. He knows he makes her feel safe. He is glad for it, feeling it is what he should do.

The rocking of the ship continues, as she moves in for that magical kiss. Nicolaus is very hesitant at first, and then frowns with the realization that he cannot resist her. This kiss is more involved, and more meaningful than any other kiss they've had, as Nicolaus tastes Abigail. Abigail lets out a slight moan, as she does not want to part from Nicolaus, confirming to herself that he is indeed to be her husband.

Abigail's mind becomes consumed with how to go about getting Nicolaus, not realizing he is already hers, as he pulls her even closer to him, before parting that passionate, scorching kiss.

Breathless, she looks into his eyes. He seems to have a sad expression on his face, a look of loss. Even so, Abigail feels beholden to Nicolaus, as though it is her place to be next to him. She delights in him, and wants to be close to him.

"You have no idea how grateful I am to you. My father is very happy." Abigail smiles as she looks upon her father, who is peacefully resting. She finally caught her breath. "I'm so grateful for what you have done for us, and so glad you are here with us, Nicky."

His hands on her waist. "I'd do anything for you, ... and Mom," he tells her sincerely.

Abigail pulls him into a hug again. Then she turns her body, and she sits back against him and relaxes a little, as the waves seemed to have calmed. She holds onto both of Nicolaus' hands, as his arms wrap around her. "Please, tell me more about Mom. I want to know all about her."

Chapter One Hundred Eight

The sea journey took about ten days. Nicolaus eventually coaxed Abigail and Dominique out to the deck, though away from the railing, to experience the fresh sea air, and the beautiful scenic passages. Brazil has beautiful mountains, which one should not miss for being locked away scared inside the cruise ship suite. However, when the ocean waves grew choppy, Abigail found her way back into the arms of Nicolaus. Nicolaus had no complaints about this. He gallantly, and happily held Abigail whenever she wanted.

They dock in the Gulf of Mexico, in Texas. Nicolaus rents a nice car to drive them the rest of the way to Austin. Cecil takes to the back seat with Dominique, after Abigail jumps into the front passenger side to be close to Nicolaus.

"Do you notice the same that I am seeing, Mr. Omari," Dominique says in a whisper, nodding to the two in the front seats. Nicolaus and Abigail haven't stopped talking to each other since docking.

Cecil nods, sighing. "I do not want to encourage it, nor discourage it. My daughter has a mind of her own. Though I must say, she has always been a good judge of character. It is obvious that she and Nicolaus have a strong bond. Nicolaus has definitely impressed her."

"With those looks, he would impress any woman. I'm more concerned about his intentions."

"Well now, look at what he has done for us already. If we are looking at intentions, I believe he has clearly and easily proved himself to be a man of his word. And to be a man's man, trying to make improvements for people. You saw his operations in Switzerland firsthand. So, you tell me." Cecil touches Dominique's hand, "Don't let jealousy rule your heart, Dominique."

She scoffs, "You think I'm jealous?"

Cecil nods with a chuckle, "That tone! Yes, I think you might just be jealous. Don't worry, Abigail has more than enough love for everyone."

The drive took two and a half hours. Nicolaus pulls into the driveway of Constance's home with excitement. He is so glad to be delivering on the promise he'd made her years ago.

"This is the house that Deirdre bought. It's Mom's now. She is going to be so excited to see you!" He jumps out the vehicle, and first helps Abigail out, opens the door for Cecil, then goes around and helps Dominique out. They gather on the porch. "Okay, she doesn't even know that we are here, so this is going to be a real surprise. Why don't you wait here. First I'll bring in Mr. Omari." Everyone nods in agreement.

Nicolaus uses his key to open the door. Dominique and Abigail are surprised that he has a key.

"Mom!" He calls for Constance. "Mom!"

Constance appears from a back room. "Nicky! You didn't tell me you would be here today!" They hug tightly. "It's so good to see you. In person!" They trade kisses.

"Mom, you are beautiful! As always," he compliments her to reassure her.

Constance chuckles, waiving his words away. "Oh Nicky! Did you go see about your father, yet?"

"Not yet. I just arrived. I have a surprise for you, Mom."

"Nicolaus, you need to go see your father."

"I will, Mom, I will, I promise. First, I have a surprise for you." He leads her by the hand to the nearby couch. "Here Mom, sit down."

"Okay, okay."

"Now, wait right here." Nicolaus gives Constance another kiss to her forehead, then goes to the door, and brings Cecil inside. "Mom, look who I found."

Cecil steps forward, with tears in his eyes.

Constance gasps, her hand to her chest, eyes wide. "Oh my dear Lord! Cecil?" Constance cannot believe her eyes. "Cecil?"

Cecil goes to her nodding. He gets on one knee to hug his wife to him. "My love," he cries and holds her tightly, "you are still as beautiful as ever." With heartfelt joy, they hug, and cry, and hug, and finally kiss.

Constance looks around. "And Abigail? How is she? Is she here with you?"

At her question, Nicolaus brings Abigail forward to her mother. Constance gasps again, and stands. "Oh my God!" She reaches for Abigail, who takes her hand, "My God, my baby!" She hugs Abigail close to her. "Oh, look at you!" She looks Abigail over, touching her face and her hair. "So beautiful!" She hugs her again, "My baby," she repeats, and hugs her as a mother should. Everyone in the room is in tears at this moving moment, even Nicolaus.

Abigail sobs in the arms of the mother she had always longed for. "Mother," she cries. She is beyond words, although no words are needed. Cecil holds onto both of them. After several minutes, Abigail reaches for Dominique. "Mom, this is Dominique. She's like a sister to me." Constance enfolds Dominique in the circle hug.

Constance breaks the hugs, "Are they safe? How did you ..." she asks Nicolaus.

Nicolaus wipes his face. "I got his name clear. I told you I would work on that."

Cecil pulls Nicolaus to him by his neck in a man hug. "This young man here, is quite something. He's the reason we are here. I'm totally free now, Constance. Totally free!"

Nicolaus is pulled into the family group hug.

Nicolaus wipes his tears again, as he quietly backs away from the Omaris. He wants to give them time, and knows he must also go see about his own father.

Abigail runs to him before he is out of the door. She looks at him and hugs him. His arms go around her. "Nicky, I know all this must be difficult for you. I cannot thank you enough for all you've done for us, to reunite us. Thank you so much for making this possible, it means the world." She holds onto his hands.

Nicolaus nods, "Of course! You don't need to thank me. An injustice was done, and I was able to erase it, with the help of others."

"Nicky, it's more than that. You have given my mother to me. That's priceless, Nicky! Thank you so much!" She tells him through her tears.

They hug each other tightly. "I'm going to check on my father, and I'll be back around later. Okay?" He looks at Constance who is overjoyed.

Abigail giggles, "Oh, I'm going with you!"

"Abby, you've got some catching up to do with Mom."

"I want to meet your family."

Cecil agrees, "Let's all go!"

Constance agrees, entwining her arm with her husband's. She nods, "I'm sure you can use some support, Nicky."

Nicolaus is a little surprised. "Okay. Mr. Omari, you sure you're up for this?"

Cecil nods, "Yes. If Nigel is ill, I want to see him."

"Okay, well, let's go!"

Chapter One Hundred Nine

"Oh my goodness! Look at the size of this place," Abigail says as Nicolaus drives the car down the half mile cobble stone road. The Ravenell mansion is ahead of them.

"Just as I remember," Cecil comments. He feels a little nervous about seeing Ceil and Nigel after all these years. However, after what Nicolaus has done for him, he sees Nicolaus as a protector.

As Nicolaus pulls up to the front of the house, in the circle driveway, anxiety fills his brain. His grip on the steering wheel tightens, even though the vehicle is in park, and everyone is getting out. The closing of the vehicle doors gives him the nudge to get out as well. Nicolaus steps out and looks up at the house. He feels frozen.

Constance goes to him. "Nicky, you okay?"

"I ... ah ... hmmm." Nothing appears in his mind to get him out of this situation. He stares up at the house. Everyone is looking at him, waiting for his move forward. Anxiety grips his guts. "I ... I don't think I can go in there," he says with a frown.

Constance touches his arm. "Nicky, it's all right." She tells him this, though almost feels the same as he does.

Abigail is immediately by his side. "I know this can't be easy for you. Not after all you've been through," she tells him. "Nicky, your dad is in there. You have to go in," she states logically.

He looks at Abigail, her words striking him. Her beauty striking him, as her light brown skin glistens in the sun, her curly hair blows in the light breeze, her hands take his. He nods, "Yes, you're right, of course."

"Just breathe, Nicky. We'll all go in together," Constance whispers to him.

Gathering his warrior courage, he leads the family to the front door. When the door opens, Ms. Mary greets them. "Mr.

Nicolaus!" She takes his hands to shake them, but then throwing all professional protocol aside, she hugs him, then greets Constance and the others she does not know.

At the sound of Nicolaus' name, several staff members appear to welcome him home.

And then stands Ceil, Elsa, and Niall.

Ceil is the first to step forward. "Nicolaus," she gently says his name, so very glad to see him. "I'm so glad you are here," she tells him uncharacteristically. She ignores the look on his face at her words. "Your father will be glad to see you." Nicolaus doesn't respond to her, as she has never spoken to him in such a nice manner. He just sort of looks at her strangely. Ceil touches his shoulder, then greets Constance.

"And Ceil, you remember Cecil," Constance tells her, wanting to dig into her. Ceil's look of greeting turns into a surprised shocked look. "Nicolaus assisted in clearing his name from those fraudulent charges you helped concoct so long ago."

"Hello Ceil," Cecil says, pulling Abigail next to him, "And this is our daughter, Abigail."

"Oh! My goodness!" Abigail looks much like Deirdre, except with a stronger stance and a thicker fuller head of hair. "Cecil, I don't know what to say, honestly. I'm sorry for ...,"

"Ah, Ceil, don't," he interrupts her. "An apology cannot be accepted for such life changing damages."

Ceil nods at Cecil's words, then moves towards Abigail. "Abigail, very nice to meet you. You are as beautiful as your sister."

"Mrs. Ravenell," Abigail says, as they gently shake hands. "This is my dear friend, Dominique."

"Nicolaus!" Elsa hugs tightly to Nicolaus. She has tears. "It's been so long. I wasn't sure we'd ever see you again." Elsa pulls her young daughters forward. They are bashfully hiding behind her legs. "Elaine, you remember your Uncle Nicky? Emily?"

Nicolaus bends to five year old Elaine. "Wow, you have grown!" She shakes her head, and shyly hugs Nicolaus around the neck, remembering him. "You ready for kindergarten?" Elaine nods with a big smile, and without words. Not to be left out, four year old Emily hugs onto Nicolaus too.

When Nicolaus stands, Abigail is by his side. He greets Niall. Niall offers his hand, awkwardly, Nicolaus accepts his brother's hand. However, Nicolaus does notice that Niall acts strangely towards Abigail. He doesn't want to look at her, or acknowledge her. He moves himself next to Ceil.

Niall feels nervous, and fear seems to grip him. Abigail's eyes follow him. He cannot look at her. He cannot look into her eyes. He feels and sees Deirdre. "Excuse me," he quickly leaves the room.

Nicolaus frowns to Elsa as she hugs Abigail and greets Dominique and Cecil. "What's with him?"

Ceil watches her younger son run from Abigail. She knows what the issue is. Abigail is a much stronger version of Deirdre.

Ceil touches Nicolaus on the shoulder again. "Nicolaus, can we talk? Please?"

Nicolaus sighs, not really wanting to be alone with Ceil. He gathers his warrior strength and mind, and follows her to the other side of the room.

"Please, let's you and I talk later. For now, I'm sure you wish to know about your father."

Nicolaus nods, feeling as if he is in a movie or something. The last time he interacted with Ceil, she was crying and not talking much. He wondered if the captivity and a three year time span could have changed her much. As she speaks to him, he feels that he does not know this woman before him.

"I want to be honest with you. Your father ... he hasn't much time."

"What do you mean? He's that sick?"

Ceil nods. "Lung cancer."

"What?"

"They are keeping him comfortable, but he has trouble breathing, and he tires easily. So when you speak with him, try not to get him too excited, and forgive him if he drifts to sleep while you are speaking."

"My God! If I had known ... I would have been here sooner."

"No, you are right on time. In your time. And it's fine. He will be very glad to see you."

Ceil leads the way, Nicolaus follows, and gestures to Cecil, who has Constance hand, who has Abigail's hand.

The whole of the small clan follow Ceil to the bedroom, where Nigel is half sitting up, supported by pillows, and coughing, though on oxygen. He is being tended by a nurse. Ceil leans and kisses her dying husband on the forehead, "Look whose here to see you."

Nicolaus kisses Nigel on his head. "Hello father," he frowns with a smile, sitting next to him.

"Nicolaus. Oh Nicolaus." Nigel hugs Nicolaus tightly to him. He cries hoarsely, "Nicolaus!" His breathing is labored.

"I know we talk every now and then father, just the same, I have missed you," Nicolaus tells him softly, through his own tears. He is greatly saddened by the looks of Nigel. Dark circles are around his eyes. His skin looks ashen. His breathing is labored. His skin is clammy and sweaty, yet he is covered with blankets, while the window is open to provide the fresh air of nature. "I am so sorry I wasn't already here for you. I didn't know you were sick like this."

"The most important thing is that you are here now. By my side, towards the end." Nigel wipes the tear he sees on Nicolaus' face. "We must be honest about all this. I grow worse every day. Cancer eats at my lungs. I breathe less and less every day. I will not be better." Nigel pauses to breathe. "Who is this?" He looks to Cecil as if he recognizes his face. "Cecil? Old friend, is that you?"

Cecil steps forward and takes Nigel's hand. He smiles. "Nigel. Yes, it's me, Cecil. It has been so long since I've seen you last."

"Cecil!" Nigel gestures for him to sit on the bed. "My son has found you, and now you have generously come to see about me," Nigel muses with him. Nigel wheezes a little. "Such bad blood between us." He squeezes Cecil's hand lovingly. "Your beautiful wife there has kept all of us on our toes."

Cecil chuckles. "Yes, I understand she cares for Nicolaus. He loves her very much, so he has shown us."

"Yes, yes."

Nicolaus touches Nigel's shoulders, just as Niall appears and sits in a chair next to Nigel's bed. Niall wants to understand all that is happening. "Father, I was able to get Mr. Omari's name cleared."

Nigel looks at Nicolaus in amazement for doing something he hadn't the fortitude to do himself. He nods. "Well done, my son." He looks to Cecil. "I hope you can forgive all the ... mess that occurred so long ago."

Cecil frowns, and chuckles. "Now Nigel, that's not fair to ask for such a thing at a time like this." The old friends chuckle together, making Nigel cough terribly. "We can talk about that later. Though I must say, you must be very proud of your son, Nigel. He even helped us in getting here. Getting me back to my Constance."

Nigel squeezes his hand in kindness, and nods. "Perhaps that can make up for some of the bad feelings." He looks over to Abigail. "And this is your other lovely daughter?" He keeps hold of Cecil's hand and reaches for Abigail with the other hand. She grasps it with a smile. Weakly, Nigel raises her hand to kiss it. He gestures for her to sit on the bed, next to Nicolaus.

"It is a pleasure to meet you Mr. Ravenell," Abigail states.

"What is your name, beautiful young lady?"

Abigail's near presence makes Niall uncomfortable again. He shifts in the chair and tries to avoid her eyes.

"Abigail."

"Abigail. You look just like your sister. I am sure you are as determined and stubborn as she." Cecil nods, and Abigail chuckles. Nigel looks to her wedding finger, gently lifting her hand, and seeing no ring there. "I see you are without a husband."

"That's correct," she smiles, "I don't have one." Her eyes look straight at Nicolaus, just as Nigel wanted to see if she would.

He nods. "Good! Perhaps you will find one amongst our people, who are your people." Nicolaus meets Abigail's gaze, that familiar look of love about him. He feels all eyes on him, and retreats his gaze, looking to his lap, knowing Nigel is speaking of their ancestry. He does not want to encourage such a notion.

"Perhaps," Abigail agrees, still looking at Nicolaus. "Perhaps one is closer than one might think." Nicolaus looks to her again, then to his father, feeling quite uneasy. He sees Nigel smiling because Abigail understands his meaning. Nicolaus says nothing and worries about what Constance might be thinking.

"Now everyone must let me have time alone with my son." Nigel crosses Abigail's hand to that of her father. "I will see you again, before my end," he assures them.

Abigail and Cecil leave the bedroom together. Constance gives Nigel a kiss to his cheek before leaving. Niall follows out, taking Elsa and the children with him.

Nigel chuckles at Nicolaus, and his laughter turns into another awful and labored cough. The nurse tends to him.

"You don't need to fuss over me," he tells her. Nigel reaches for Nicolaus' hand. "Son, have you known Abigail long?"

Nicolaus nods. "It's been three years since I've made her acquaintance. That's how long it's taken to get Mr. Omari's name cleared."

Nigel scoffs at his words, with a slight laugh. "Made her acquaintance? That girl is in love with you. She looked right at you, in front of everyone, when I asked her about a husband."

"Father, don't, please."

"Well, son, I have some hard asks of you. As your dying father … there are three things that must be settled." Nigel goes into a coughing fit, unable to get a breath. The nurse is by him, assisting him. She adjusts the oxygen machine, and he is able to breathe better.

"Father, I think you need to rest right now." Nicolaus stands, feeling panicked at Nigel's condition. He knows there is nothing he can do to make things better.

"No, we need to talk. I don't have much time." Nigel reaches for Nicolaus. He breathes relief when Nicolaus rejoins him on the bed.

"You didn't come back. After we were rescued, you didn't come back!"

"How could I? It is obvious that Ceil doesn't want me around. And anyway, after what I chose to do … hard to come back from that."

"What you chose to do? Nicolaus, you chose to save us. To get us released and back home. It's heroic when one sacrifices their very life to save another. Son, you know this, and have the medals of valor to prove it." Nigel frowns to Nicolaus shaking his head in disagreement. Nigel touches his shoulder. "You're thinking about this all wrong, Nicolaus. Look, I know that Ceil was against you. You were both in battle with each other over your lifetime. Your actions to save her life changed her. God works in mysterious ways, son. Being locked in that cell, behind those bars, and her life threatened, changed her. And that change came about when you saved her, without qualms, you just did it."

Nicolaus looks at Nigel doubtfully.

"I'm telling you, she's different," he half yells at Nicolaus. "She cried for three days straight when you didn't return. She is sorry for what she did to you, and she wants to apologize and make things right." Nigel went into a coughing fit from yelling. The nurse assists him.

"Father, you're getting yourself all worked up. Please, rest. We can talk more later."

"And Abigail." Nigel begins to wheeze as he speaks. "God has presented you with a last chance at love."

"Father!" Nicolaus frowns, not liking where this is all going.

Nigel eyes him. "I will bet you have had no one since the day you left here. No woman friend, no relations, ... nothing. Am I right?"

Nicolaus sighs, not wanting to discuss this. Nigel grabs hold of his arm, wanting an answer. Nicolaus sighs again. "No, father. Of course there has been no one. There's a curse on me. So please let's not speak about Abigail. I need to protect her from all this. Anyway, how would I pursue anyone after that choice I made?"

"You're thinking all wrong, man! The choice you made was to save us!" Nigel gives another ugly, straining cough.

"Father please, you are upsetting yourself!"

Nigel lays back and relaxes himself to receive air. "I am getting upset over my fool son!" he yells at Nicolaus. "Admit it! Admit it now."

"Okay!" Nicolaus frowns with concern over his father's distress. "What do you want me to admit?"

"Admit that you made that choice to save us."

Nigel is shocked at the emotional release from Nicolaus at his words and his demand. Though he tries to stop it happening, a flow of tears fall from Nicolaus' eyes. Nigel knew the self-exile and shame had taken a toll on Nicolaus. "You will admit it to me and yourself, right now, damn it!" Nigel yells. "Admit it before I drop dead of anger!"

"All right! All right. I admit it."

"Say it!" Nigel yells at him, coughing, fighting to get air.

"Father, please!"

Nigel yells louder, "Say it!"

Nicolaus does what Nigel wants. He wipes his tears. "The choice I made was to save us."

Nigel nods, "And I am grateful to you beyond words. We all are."

Nicolaus' tears are back, as he cannot fight them. He'd thought he'd put this pain of his shame away. His shame of the willingness to give himself over to a man. It stung him fiercely, because his warrior masculinity had been wounded. He wipes the tears away with a smoldering anger, and just tries to concentrate on his father. His father, who is now kissing his hand in gratefulness.

"I ... we love you, Nicolaus. I want you to know that we all understand that day. We think so much of you. You have given so much of yourself. You are not a shame to our family. You are a hero. None of us knew our fate that day. It's possible that if you had not gone with Baird, which by the way you could have refused to do so, we might still be in captivity, or worse. We know you surrendered yourself to save us all." Nigel looks at his son as a precious jewel, as a gift born from him.

Nicolaus nods, appreciating his father, especially during a time like this. He receives his father's words and sentiment.

Nigel lays back with labored breathing, despite the oxygen. He wheezes and begins to drift to sleep. "No more tears over this," he says lightly. "No more heartache. No more, my son! Please." Nicolaus nods at his father's words, and plants a gentle kiss on his forehead. "I have missed you so much." Nigel's hand drops. "I'm tired right now. You must let me rest. We will talk more, before you sleep tonight." Nigel is asleep with labored breathing before Nicolaus can stand.

Ceil sees Nicolaus appear around the corner in the hallway, leaving Nigel's bed, looking upset. She notices that Abigail goes directly to him.

"Please, stay for lunch," Ceil tells Cecil and Constance. "Francesca is on her way from the airport now. I believe her plane has just landed. Please stay. I'll have the chef make us something special."

Cecil nods, looking to Constance, his arm around her. "That would be nice, Ceil, thank you."

Chapter One Hundred Ten

Niall, Nicolaus, and Francesca are closest to Nigel's bed. The rest of the family and friends are standing and sitting throughout the large luxury bedroom. Nigel smiles as he sees everyone present. Francesca kisses Nigel on the cheek. The hospice nurse had just let them all enter as she cared for Nigel, and refreshed him after his nap. His breathing is still very labored, and now he drifts in and out of sleep.

As Niall sees Abigail enter the room, he grows frightful, and very uncomfortable. He rises to leave. Nicolaus frowns at his swift departure.

The room is bright with evening sunshine. The breeze from outside blows through the opened window, giving the room a smell of flowers from the garden below. Nicolaus touches Nigel's hand. "I am here, father, as is Francesca. And everyone."

Nigel opens his eyes at the sound of the voice of his eldest son. A smile appears across his face. "I had a wonderful dream about you. I dreamed that you were leading our company again, with a curly headed woman by your side. And that riches did not matter to you, but love, mercy, and justice is what concerned you." Nigel sighs. "Do you know what that means?"

"No. What does it mean?"

"It means your time has come. It is your time to be head of this family." The heaviness of that statement hits Nicolaus.

Francesca knocks her brother on the arm. "Well, of course!" She says loudly. "Of course it's you, Nicky!"

"I also saw Deirdre and Rachel in my dreams!"

Nicolaus smiles. "I've seen Deirdre in my dreams before, too. Once we were in some place, it was dark, except for this great beaming light. She kept telling me to go back."

"Ah, when you were unconscious?" Nigel asks.

"I don't know. Maybe."

"Well, you know, when one is dying, one hears things and sees things that others cannot. I can see the two of them as clearly as I see all of you."

Constance and Cecil step forward, Constance giving Nigel a kiss to his face. "I'm so glad my daughter is with you."

Nigel nods. "She says she and Rachel will be escorting me on the next leg of my journey. She says there are many angels."

Constance clasps her hands together, "Oh my God. That's wonderful."

"And she says babies are waiting to be born."

Constance chuckles. "Babies? That's what Rachel used to say to Nicky." She and Nigel hold hands in a sweet moment in remembrance of Deirdre.

Nigel begins to struggle with breathing, despite the oxygen. Everyone steps a little closer with great concern. He begins to cough, and struggles even more. The nurse assists him, and he coughs up much blood. Once he's settled again, after several minutes, he is wheezing as he speaks.

"This darn cancer. It's eating my lungs!"

Nicolaus is next to Nigel, touching his chest. "Father, take it easy. I think you need to rest."

Nigel chuckles and coughs, "Rest. I'll be resting plenty soon enough." Nicolaus helps to readjust his pillows so he can lay back. Nigel breathes in the cool air that is flowing through the room. "Please, everyone, I thank you for being here, but I need to speak to my son, and Francesca, and Abigail."

Abigail looks surprised at Cecil and Dominique. She nods, and takes Nigel's outstretched hand. He gestures for her to sit to his left, across from Nicolaus on his right, and Francesca is in a chair to the left of Abigail. Everyone else quietly leaves.

Nigel breathes in the air, gathering strength for this talk. He continues to hold Abigail's hand. "You're so beautiful," he quietly tells her, as he breathes the air.

"Son, I told you I have three things to ask of you."

Nicolaus nods. "Yes, father."

"The first is as head of the family, I need you to ... no, I want you to step back into the helm and run the company. I saw Dwight yesterday, and he agrees. We need you back, Nicolaus."

"Well, of course he will," Francesca chimes in, happily.

"I need to hear from Nicolaus. Son, we cannot recreate the wealth, nor what you did for morale and culture at the company. It's sorely lacking without you. You know it is impossible for me to leave the business in Niall's hands. It would be utterly destroyed within a matter of weeks. Will you lead again?"

Ceil is outside the door of the bedroom, listening to the conversation. This does not sit well with Constance, so she goes to Ceil and takes her arm to get her away from the door. "Ceil, Cecil and I would like to speak with you."

Ceil moves with Constance and looks to Cecil. "Oh yes! Cecil, I know I owe you an apology for my horrid behavior towards you all those years ago. As you have said, an apology hardly seems fitting."

Cecil nods in surprise. "I could have gone to jail, Ceil."

In the bedroom with Nigel, Nicolaus sighs in thought, knowing he'd have to give up his life in Switzerland. He nods, "Yes, I will do that for you."

Nigel nods with relief, "Thank you. Before you did about half of everything, and now you'll have all of it. All our assets, all investments, all finances, inside and outside the company." Nicolaus nods in understanding. "I have put your name to every document I could think of."

"Thank you father, that will make things easier. Don't worry about it, I'll take care of everything."

"And you'll need backing, love and support. You must have a good woman with morals and courage at your side to listen to you, to help you, to support you, and most of all, to love you, son." Nigel gently shakes Abigail's hand. "That is where you come in my dear."

Abigail sits straight and smiles.

"Abigail, do you think, in time, you could grow to love my son, and be a support to him now, if he needs it?"

"Father! You cannot ask that of Abigail!"

"It's all right, Nicky." She turns to Nigel, "Yes, Sir." She looks at Nicolaus. "I do love him, and I will support him."

Nigel sighs relief at Abigail's answer. He knew he was right about what he saw about her. He knew she was in love with Nicolaus. He is very glad about this. "And Nicolaus, do you believe that in time, you can grow to love Abigail?"

Nicolaus looks at Abigail. Francesca sees that look of love that he'd usually reserved for Deirdre. "Yes," he says softly, "I do love you, Abigail."

"Enough to marry her?" Nigel pushes.

Nicolaus nods, "Yes. Some day."

"No, tomorrow," Nigel tells them forcefully. "I only have a few days of life left in me, and I need to know that you have a wife and will be cared for."

"Father!"

"No, it's okay. I'm willing. I'm willing to marry you, Nicolaus. I want to do it."

Francesca feels tears flow from her eyes at this very romantic moment. She sees that Nicolaus is flabbergasted at Abigail's response. "Extraordinary!"

Abigail giggles while her heart is pounding with love, and she takes Francesca's hand with her free one.

"Tomorrow, then," Nigel demands. "Tomorrow."

Both Abigail and Nicolaus nod in agreement.

"Okay, now just one more thing." All attention is back on Nigel. "Nicolaus, I want you to make amends with Ceil. You cannot be head of the family with such a huge rift. She wants to apologize to you, and you should let her do it. However, the hard part will be accepting the apology and moving forward. This you must do. Take Abigail with you for support."

"Yes, father."

"Okay you two, leave me with my daughter. I need alone time with her. Please don't disappoint me tomorrow." He reaches for Francesca.

She rises and kisses her father on the cheek. "Oh dad, I've missed you so much."

Outside the door, Nicolaus speaks to Abigail, away from everyone. "I'm sorry about that," he tells her. "I certainly didn't expect my father to have such demands."

Abigail gladly touches Nicolaus' chest with a smile. "It's fine. I'm perfectly willing to marry you."

"Abby, you can't just decide this on a whim! There is so much about me that you don't even know."

"Who says it's on a whim? I think your father is wise. He sees something between us." She steps closer to him. "I mean ... there is something between us ... right?" She looks up at Nicolaus in his gorgeous brown eyes.

"Abby, we should discuss this more, first."

"It's okay, we'll have time to discuss it all later. Unless you are saying that you are not willing to go through with the marriage tomorrow. Were you just talking to pacify your father?"

"Well, no ..."

"So you truly do have love for me?" She steps even closer to him, placing her hands to his shoulders. She feels his arms go around her.

Nicolaus nods, his insides feeling fuzzy and jumbled at her touch and her closeness. "Yes."

"Okay then honey, it's settled. Only Nicky, since we're to be wed tomorrow, you'll need to speak to my father about it tonight. I don't want us to be rude or him to think you're being disrespectful."

Nicolaus nods and sighs. "Right."

"My dad really likes you, and he respects you, so I don't think it will be a problem, just the formality of it, you know."

"Of course. I'll come by tonight."

Chapter One Hundred Eleven

Nicolaus sits alone and watches the majestic opulence of God's magnificently created sunset, as he had hundreds of times before. Only today, he sits on the grassy slope on the side of the Ravenell mansion.

He is trying to come to grips with the reality of his father's illness and impending death. He knows it is just a matter of time before he will have to take over as leader of the family, indeed, leader of the Ravenell empire.

Nicolaus lays back upon the grass, and stares at the God created open sky and celestial stars, thinking about all the things his father has been telling him.

And then he thinks about Abigail. Is it a coincidence that God had created two beautiful, special people, Deirdre and Abigail, of the same family? Is it just coincidence that his relationship with Abigail blossomed into love and deep compassion at this particular time of his father's illness? Why had they been brought together? The more he thinks about it, the more he knows it could not possibly be coincidental.

Nicolaus knows he is but a small grain of salt or a small grain of sand in God's humongous creation called humanity. He knows he must have God's help to get him through all that is about to occur.

Nicolaus phones Bishop Leighton. "Hello Bishop Leighton, it's Nicolaus Ravenell."

"Nicolaus! How are things? I imagine you are here for your father."

"Yeah, you know he is ill."

"Mrs. Omari told me so, yes. How is Nigel doing?"

"I think he's near the end, Bishop. I was wondering if you would please be with us for the next couple of days, perhaps a week, until his passing. I'll pay your fee, or whatever you need. And we can make accommodations for you here at the house."

"Nicolaus, of course I'll be there for Nigel, you and your family. I'm glad you called me. I can make my way over right now."

"Thank you Bishop Leighton. My father needs your prayers, and we need God's blessings on our household."

"Of course, Nicolaus, of course."

"And Bishop, my father has asked that I marry Deirdre's sister, Abigail, tomorrow as well. I've known her for a while, and we are in agreement to the marriage."

"Really? Sounds like your father is trying to ensure you have a wife to help you."

Nicolaus chuckles, "Yes, I believe that is his intention."

Bishop Leighton chuckles at Nicolaus' laugh, and this very Ravenell situation. "Nicolaus, all of us at the church, we have all missed you."

"Thank you, Bishop Leighton."

"Oh, and Nicolaus, ... I want you to know that Ceil and I had a very lengthy discussion a few years ago, about what happened in Latvia. She is very repentant about it, and ... I want you to hear from me, that she has changed. Her attitude, her demeanor, her behavior has all changed. I don't know if anyone has told you, but I want you to know that the change you see about her is real."

"Well ... yes, my father told me she said she was sorry. Thank you ... for the input, and ... for helping her. I hope you are right, that she really has changed," Nicolaus understandably has skepticism in his voice.

"Okay, well, I just wanted you to hear it directly from me. Let me grab my things, and I'll arrive to your house soon."

"Thank you, Bishop Leighton."

Nicolaus then calls Xavier, his uncle, Nigel's brother.

"Nicolaus! Thanks for calling me. Ceil had Elsa call us to let me know about Nigel. How is he doing?"

"Uncle Xavier, he is not doing well, and feels he will not recover. Will you be making your way here? I'll fly you out if needed."

"Yes, okay, please. I want to be there for Nigel."

"No problem, I'll make the arrangements."

Nicolaus stands and goes inside to go see about his father. As he enters the house, Abigail walks up to him, placing her hand on him, having been worried for not seeing him for a few hours.

"Nicky, you okay?"

Nicolaus looks into her green eyes, he nods, feeling emotional, he frowns, "Yeah. This is all ... a lot to take in."

Abigail nods. "I'm sure it is."

Ceil steps up to both of them. She touches Nicolaus' other arm and bids him to walk with her, towards the library. "Your leg, does it pain you?" she asks, as they walk slowly.

Nicolaus notices the library is unchanged as he walks through the doors with Abigail holding his hand. The library holds many memories for Nicolaus, both good and bad.

"It always has some pain, though it is healed. I feel it a little more so if the weather is cold or rainy. I can manage it all right."

"Please," Ceil bids them to sit on the small sofa, as she closes the doors to the library. She gives no objection to Abigail staying. "Pain is something you have always handled well, even as a child," she compliments him, reaching back to the pain she caused him when he was young.

Ceil can see a worried look about Nicolaus as he watches her. She knows he is unsure of what to expect from her. She keeps talking anyway. She wants to cleanse herself of her wrongdoings. As Nigel lay dying, Ceil also feels her mortality, and nowadays, she appears aged. "In your lifetime, I have inflicted much pain upon you. Your leg, for instance, it was me who first broke your leg, because I ..."

"Ceil," Nicolaus interrupts her, not sure that he wants to know the specific details behind her mean spirited behaviors towards him. He already knows she despises him because Rachel is his mother due to his father's infidelity in their marriage. "I ...," he is not sure what to say to her.

"Please, let me say it," she says softly, then continues. "I had hatred for you, even when you were a child. Not because of anything you did. I was very angry at your father. And you, to me, were a reflection of the cause of my anger. So I took all my anger out on you. I admit that I broke your leg, when you were a child. I do not know if you remember."

Nicolaus nods. "I remember. And I remember being terrified of you."

"Yes, yes you were. And then when I saw you had hopes for something, for anything, I dashed it, whatever you hoped for. And when I saw that Deirdre made you happy, and you wanted to be with her, I did my best to crush the love you had for each other, or to make you run off and leave the family." Tears stream from Ceil's eyes as she spoke, facing up to what she'd done to Nicolaus. "You were stronger than I ever imagined," she says softly, "loyal to your father. Always loyal. Even now."

Ceil admitting what she had done, also made tears stream from Nicolaus' eyes. Abigail clanged to his arm, as she listened and watched in silence. She felt the emotions between them. "Ceil, you do not have to do this," he says softly.

"Please, please let me. I have waited three years to tell you what everyone already knew. Please, I owe this to you. I owe it to Deirdre." Nicolaus nods, and Ceil continues. "No matter how much I made you miserable, Deirdre would not leave you. No matter what, she stayed by your side. She loved you … with all her heart. She loved you.

"And when you went away to rescue ambassadors, you asked me to watch over Marguerite. I could not believe it …," her words wane as she cries. "I knew you were trying to reach me. And when you were away, I did watch over her. And then we had terrible times." She sighed, bearing her ugly deeds, cleaning her soul. "You were right about Gwen. It was my doing. And after that, when you and Deirdre found that one moment, the two of you ceased it, and got married before I could stop you. And then when you left to rescue Jonathan, I knew Deirdre loved you with every fiber of her being. I knew because when the letter you sent arrived from Spain, she asked me to open it and read it to her. And I know she was doing that for you. To help make things better between you and me.

"And when Deirdre died … I could not believe that she died. I could not believe it! I held your stillborn son in my arms." She looks upon him, "We did not know how to tell you. Oh Nicolaus, those were awful times.

"And when you had turned to Helena, I was so angry at you because she had been mine. I knew she was in love with you, but I wanted to crush that love. It was easy for me to blame you for her death." She shakes her head. "Of course it was not your fault. You tried to save her out of that fire!

"When I look back on everything, I know I was a horrible mother to you, I know I was ugly to you. I do not know how you stood it.

"And then I did my most malicious act against you when I tried to trade you away to the Drone family. Nicolaus, your father knew nothing of my plans. I wanted to be rid of you, so that I could have Niall in your place permanently. All went awry."

Nicolaus stands, crying, wiping his tears, unable to take much more. He wants to leave out the library.

"Please," Ceil begs him. He stands away from her, by the window. He sits on the large windowsill, "Your father hated me for what I had done, I saw it in his face. Penelope tricked us into going to that old castle, locked us away in the dungeon, then waited, knowing you would save us. And how many times did you save my life when you could have let them kill me for all I had done to you?

"And then you went with Jonathan falling into his dubious trap, for all of us, in spite of myself and what I had done to you," Ceil shrieked with pain and tears. She took breaths, calming herself to finish what she had to say, "that is when I, ...we, truly understood the span of your love for all of us. Nicolaus, you are so noble."

Ceil stands and walks to Nicolaus. She sees he is still crying as if her words have devastated him. She wants to put her arms around him, and hold him tightly, but she has never done such a thing for him. She doesn't know how to begin to give him a hug, so she holds onto both of his forearms. "I am so sorry for all the horrible things I have ever done to you, and for all the horrible things I have said to you over your lifetime. You didn't deserve any of it. Everyone loves and respects you, and I should have also. Could you ever ... ever find a way for us to move forward? Could you ever forgive me?"

Nicolaus nods through his tears. They both make a move, and he just pulls Ceil into a hug. His arms embrace Ceil, whom he has been unable to truly know all his life because of the wall of hatred she had built between them. He felt as though he were dreaming as he hugged her. So many times in his life he had wanted to hug Ceil to either comfort her or to try to make things better.

They held each other tightly for a long time, as if to make up for all the missed opportunities. Nicolaus knows it is God who is moving through them at this very moment.

Ceil breaks the hug and looks into Nicolaus' face. The handsome face of the man she should have loved as if he were her own son. She wipes his tears, only for them to be replaced by other tears.

"I should have loved you, and respected you," she says in a loud whisper.

"What you've said, and have done right now, is enough to make up for all that, Ceil. I want you to know that ...," he frowns, "that I believe what you're telling me. And I'm willing to move forward, if you are."

Ceil smiles at him, shaking her head in unbelief of his forgiveness. She feels the power of it in her heart. "I promise ... things will be different between us. I promise to be here to help you, and support you, and love you as I should have done in the past. And I know that it is you who should, rightly so, inherit your father's seat as head of the family and leader of the company. I promise I will support you in every way I can."

Ceil hugs Nicolaus to her again, without hesitation this time, knowing the hug will be returned. She feels so relieved.

Abigail is surprised at all she has just witnessed and has to wipe her own tears away. She gravitates towards Nicolaus as he reaches for her. She knows this reconciliation is important and will make Nicolaus' life easier.

The three of them sit and talk for a while of Nicolaus' life since he's been away. They also talk about Abigail's upbringing and her career.

Afterwards, Nicolaus makes arrangements to fly Xavier to Austin to be with Nigel.

Chapter One Hundred Twelve

After their talk with Ceil, Nicolaus goes to see about Nigel. As he did so, Elsa escorts Abigail through Nicolaus' wing of the mansion, a part of the mansion Abigail had not seen.

"Your husband is very unfriendly towards me," Abigail states as they go through the doors into the west wing of the mansion.

"My husband is afraid of you," Elsa corrects her.

"Afraid? Why?"

"I do not know," Elsa lies, feeling it is not her place to say, nor does she want to be the one who tells. "Pops gave Nicolaus this whole side of the mansion."

"Really?"

"Yes." When they entered the living room area, Abigail sees the large, life sized portrait of Nicolaus and Deirdre on their wedding day, the Saint Nicholas church behind them. She sees that they look overjoyed. Abigail steps up to the large photo and studies the image of her sister. This image reminds her of the painting in Nicolaus' house in Switzerland.

Elsa leads Abigail upstairs and stops them before a door. "Nicolaus was married a few times, and he never used the same bedroom." Elsa touches the door before them. "This is the bedroom he shared with Deirdre." Elsa opens the unlocked door and they step inside. "This is the only room that Nicolaus never had changed. It's been untouched since ...." Elsa let her words fall off.

"Elsa, will you take me to Deirdre's grave? I'd like to see it. I understand it is here on the property."

"Yes, of course."

Abigail looks around the bedroom. Abigail likes the light-heartedness of the room. She walks around the large space, observing and touching things.

"When Deirdre ... left us, Nicolaus ordered the room to be locked, and her things left untouched." Abigail listens as she touches a brush that lay on the vanity table. "And it has stayed untouched for years. Only dusted and cleaned by the house maids."

Abigail sits on the bed, knowing Nicolaus had made love to her sister here. She feels strong emotion. "For years?"

"Yes, I don't think even Nicolaus has stepped foot in here since then. I am sure it is too painful for him.

"Mother Ceil brought these." Elsa hands a large wooden box to Abigail. Abigail opens the box and finds two bundles of letters. "These are the letters they wrote to each other when Nicolaus was away," Elsa explains.

Abigail carefully picks up one bundle, as if they are precious documents. She frowns, "Why are some of these letters scorched?"

"Mother Ceil tried to burn them all in one of her rages against Nicolaus. Pops saved them."

"How awful!"

"She used to be very mean spirited towards Nicolaus."

"So Mr. Ravenell understood the love between Nicolaus and my sister?"

"Oh yes," Elsa steps closer to Abigail. "Abigail, you can believe whatever Pops says to you about Nicolaus. I am not saying that he has never made mistakes, but in all the years I've known him, he has never been wrong about Nicolaus. If you want to get to know Nicolaus, I think these letters are a good start. And they will tell you about your sister too. She loved Nicolaus very much. Even when he was married to others, she always stood by Nicolaus. We all knew that Deirdre was special."

Abigail touches Elsa's arm, "I can tell that you loved her too."

Elsa nods, "She was like a sister to me. More than my own sister was. And I miss her."

"You have a sister, too?"

Elsa nods. "Yes, had, ... but that is a long story. We shall talk about it later. For now, I leave you with the letters." Elsa kisses Abigail's cheek, and leaves the room.

Chapter One Hundred Thirteen

A bigail tucked the letters into her purse bag, as Nicolaus led her by the hand to the vehicle to take her home. She had not yet finished reading the letters, and decided to wait until after they were married, not wanting her thoughts or her mind to be tainted against him for any past actions.

He smiled at her the whole ten minute drive to Constance's home. He glanced at her often without words, her beauty striking him again. No words passed between them, only thoughts of their future together.

Ceil had their driver bring Constance and Cecil home earlier. As Nicolaus and Abigail enter the home, Abigail goes right to her parents and hugs them.

"Mr. Omari, may I speak with you?" Nicolaus asks.

Cecil looks at Nicolaus with a smile, knowing what he wants. However, Constance stops him. She steps up to Nicolaus.

"Nicky, dear, it's late. We'll talk more tomorrow," she tries to halt his actions, also knowing what he wants.

"Mom, I just need to talk to Mr. Omari."

"No!" She tells him. She touches his arm, feeling awful about the look of surprise on his face. She sighs, and tries to soften her demeanor. "Honey, look, it's late and ..."

"Mom, it will just take one minute."

"I said no!" She tells him unusually, insolently.

"Mom, Nicolaus and I are going to get married tomorrow," Abigail blurts out, seeing that Nicolaus is getting nowhere with her parents. Constance looks at Abigail with a frown of anger, so Abigail moves herself to stand next to Nicolaus. They take each other's hand in a stance of unity.

"Mom, look, we've known each other for a few years now and ..."

"No!" Constance cuts off Nicolaus words, not wanting to hear any of it.

"Mom, his father understands that we should be married and..."

"How many times do I have to say no? Now Nicolaus, you know I think of you as my son. And I thank you for all you have ever done for me, including bringing my Abigail back to me." She shakes her head, feeling that she may fly off the handle at any moment. "I know you, Nicolaus, and I have seen how you have been looking at Abigail. I stood by you when you chose to love Deirdre ..., this is different. Please, I beg you, do not take Abigail from me," she says through angry tears. "I beg you to leave her be, please do not let the curse claim her too. I beg you!"

Constance grabs Abigail's other hand, and pulls her over to stand next to her, away from Nicolaus. She addresses Abigail, wiping away her own tears, "I will not have you fall prey to that Kiviste family curse! Because of it, we lost Deirdre and I will not lose you too."

Cecil chimes in, "Constance dear, Abigail loves him."

Constance scoffs, "She can love him from afar."

"Wait a minute, now Constance, Abigail is a grown woman and she can make up her own mind about who she wants to love," Cecil defends his daughter.

"I don't care! I said no!" She tightens her grip on Abigail and looks her in her eyes, "You stay away from Nicolaus. You hear me, Abby? You stay away from him."

Abigail chuckles at her mother for the unreasonable demand, and glances to Nicolaus. "I thought you loved Nicky, Mom."

"Well, I do, ... and I love you much more. Your my child, my daughter. Whose only now been returned to me."

"Mom ...." Nicolaus is amused by all this and not sure what to do at this point.

"No," Constance tells him sternly, almost yelling at him.

"Constance dear, you do know Abby is just as stubborn as you are."

Nicolaus steps forward to touch Constance, and she rebuffs him, pushing at his chest. She shoves at him, pushing him back towards the door.

"Mom ...," Nicolaus tries again.

"No, Nicolaus! Just go now, please. Just go!"

"Mom!" Nicolaus is very surprised at Constance's actions against him. This has never happened. Nicolaus attempts to push his way past Constance, and is reprimanded with a hard slap to his face, as Constance strikes out at him in desperation, as if to protect Abigail from an unseen force. Nicolaus looks at Constance with shock and disbelief.

Constance shouts at him in her upset, "You will not take my Abby from me! You cannot have her! You will not have my Abby!"

Nicolaus steps away from Constance's attack on him, and steps out the door. Out of character, Constance slams the door on him.

"Mom, what did you just do?" Abigail asks Constance, also feeling shocked at her abusive attack on Nicolaus. She leaves out the front door, closing it. "Nicky," she sees him sitting on the porch swing, while inside Cecil hugs Constance to him, trying to console her.

"He can't have her!" Constance cries against Cecil, "He can't have her!"

"Abby, maybe we should call this off. I've never seen your mom so upset like that before. And certainly, she's never stricken me." Nicolaus rubs the sting to the side of his face.

Abigail sighs, "She's really worried about that curse."

"May Jesus please protect you! I'm really worried about the curse."

"We are not calling off the marriage. We just have to find a way to break the curse."

"Abby!" Nicolaus is exasperated, not sure what to do. "And there are other things about me that you don't even know about."

"And I don't want to know, Nicky."

"Abby, you should know. You might change your mind."

"No, Nicolaus!" He frowns at her, having heard the word 'no' tonight more than enough to last his lifetime. "I want us to go into this marriage fresh. I don't care about what may have happened in the past. I'm looking to build a strong future with you."

They lovingly clasp hands.

"I've never seen Mom like that. And I've never disobeyed her or gone against anything she's told me."

Abigail chuckles at him. "Well, she is wrong about this. And if you want to marry me, you'll have to go against what she is saying."

Nicolaus sighs heavily. Today has been a bit much.

Abigail frowns at his silence and uncertainty. "You do still want to marry me, Nicky, don't you?"

Nicolaus nods, and looks into her soft green eyes. "Yes."

"Okay then!" She smiles at him, "I'll see you in the morning." She puts her complete trust in him.

Gently, and passionately, they kiss a lover's kiss.

Chapter One Hundred Fourteen

The following morning, Abigail waited for Nicolaus by the Ravenell mansion pool. She'd texted him to meet her and her parents there. The morning is cloudless, with the sun beaming on them. Abigail feels happy in her soul, on this day, her wedding day.

Even though Abigail knew everything would be informal, she dressed fashionably in her light blue heart shaped bodice dress, which gave a peak at her beautiful cleavage. The knee length design has dramatic sleeves, with a matching flowy, chiffon material train. The chiffon train has sensational embroidered flowers stitched around the edges.

Dominique sat Abigail on the stools, next to the bar counter, while they waited on Nicolaus. "Elsa and I went shopping yesterday, and I got this for you."

Abigail smiles at Dominique, "So sweet of you. When did you go shopping?" They laugh together. Abigail wastes no time in opening the golden wrapped box. Inside, she finds a frilly, flimsy frock. Abigail giggles, "Oh my!" She holds it up to the daylight and can see right through it.

Dominique giggles with her, "There is a matching robe there, as well."

"Dominique! Very thoughtful! Thank you."

"Well, you've got to have something! This can be your something new, anyway."

Abigail nods, "Yes, yes it is! I'm sure Nicolaus will appreciate this!" The ladies giggle more.

Constance is in a foul mood, not agreeing with any of Abigail's wishes. "Abby, why are we out here? What's going on?"

"Oh, I asked Nicolaus to meet us out here. I want to speak with him before we go inside."

"Well, why are we out here, by the pool?" Constance questions her.

Abigail quickly puts the gift down, and positions herself close to the pool, knowing that Nicolaus would be arriving at any moment. Her plan is to break that darn curse for all time. She knows that if she appears to be falling into the water, Nicolaus will immediately catch her and save her from falling, especially dressed as she is. Thus, she believes that his action of keeping her from falling into the water, since she cannot swim, should break the curse. "Just be patient Mom, he should be here any moment."

Suddenly, they can hear Nicolaus' voice as the back door opens. He seems to be speaking to someone inside. He steps out, and is dressed handsomely in a dark French suit.

The site of Nicolaus makes Abigail's heart beat much faster. Just seeing him approaching, as he walks with his usual confidence, looking fine, makes her realize her true love for him, as she cannot picture herself with any other man.

"See, there he is now!" She says excitedly, as she feels full of life. After all, this is her wedding day.

With her enthusiasm on full display, Abigail has a huge smile for Nicolaus and she waves at him as he begins to stroll the distance of the long walkway. Only, the heel of Abigail's fashion shoe, gets tangled on the leg of the pool furniture. In a fraction of a second, her body twists, and ... "Whulp!" She screams as she falls hard, right into the pool water.

"Abigail!" Nicolaus frantically calls to her as he sees her fall into the pool. "Abigail!" Nicolaus' stroll has become crisis running.

Abigail struggles. This is not what she intended. She feels herself gulping lots of water, which hurts her chest and fills her lungs. However, she doesn't know how to stop swallowing the water. She feels herself violently jolting a few times, then she stops.

She can hear actions above ground, while she sees scenes of her life flash before her eyes. She can no longer move.

"Oh no! Abby!" Cecil yells, and begins to take off his shoes to jump in to get his daughter, as she never came up from the depths of the pool. However, before he could even get one shoe off, in another fraction of a second, Nicolaus dives into the pool water, fully dressed.

Constance shriek screams, "Oh my God! My Abigail!" Dominque takes Constance into her arms, as they all three watch.

Abigail feels her person floating away from the pool. She is soaking wet and water is dripping from her as she is lifted away. She cannot understand how she is floating, while she sees Nicolaus trying to save her. She sees her parents in a frantic panic. She sees Dominique crying, and holding onto Constance.

Suddenly, Abigail finds herself in a dark place, only a beautiful bright, large beam of white sparkling light illuminates from above, seemingly going on forever. She looks around and all she sees is darkness, the immaculate and majestic beauty of heaven cloaked from her human eyes.

When she focuses front and center, she sees a being, dressed in a bright white robe. They gravitate towards each other and as she gets closer, she sees herself. She realizes it is not herself, but that she is seeing Deirdre, her twin sister. Without hesitation, Deirdre gives Abigail the warmest most special hug she has ever received. Deirdre kisses her cheek. Abigail feels as if she is dreaming.

Deirdre smiles at her twin. "Abigail, you will not be staying here. You must go back," she immediately puts that thought of going back into her mind. The angels have tasked Deirdre to assist with the breaking of the curse, as Nicolaus and Abigail are bound to each other by destiny.

"Deirdre!"

"Take care of Nicolaus for me. He needs you. He needs your love and your happiness. He adores you already. Don't worry about his hesitation. You are meant for him."

"But ... your love for him ..."

Deirdre nods. "I was the placeholder for you." Deirdre points to the right of her, where a brief image of sleeping babies are floating in the air. "Your children are waiting to be born."

"Those are my babies?" Abigail seems a little shocked.

Back on Earth, Nicolaus pops up for air without Abigail, and he dives back down. Under the water, Abigail is already suspended and not breathing, as she has fully taken water into her lungs. Nicolaus struggles to get her dress out of the enormous pool fan, which has caught her. He rips the material, releasing her, bringing her unconscious body to the surface in his arms.

Quickly, Nicolaus lays Abigail on the pool surface, climbs out and sees that she seems to not be breathing. Though he is panting and Out of breath, Nicolaus immediately begins cardiopulmonary resuscitation on Abigail. He breathes for her, pumps her chest, pushes on her stomach, and repeats this actions several times. "Abigail," he calls to her with great panic. "Oh God, please!"

All Constance can do is watch and pray. "My God! Please save my Abigail! Please save her!" She cries, "Abigail!"

Within that heavenly space, Abigail feels a tear fall from her eye, as she realizes that all this time, her dreams were actually premonitions. She is thankful. She knew she'd be birthing seven babies.

Deirdre hugs her again. "Nicolaus is already yours. It is written in the stars, so don't ever be afraid. Your actions today have broken the curse, Abigail. There is to be no more worry about it." Abigail smiles with relief. "Nicolaus is a good man, with a religious heart. He will love you and the children. He is loyal. Together, you will do great things on Earth. Your children are destined for greatness as well."

Nicolaus breathes for Abigail, then lifts her arms, one at a time, then together. "Come on, Abigail! Please, Abigail!" He pushes on her stomach and water gushes out of her mouth. He turns her on her side and presses his knee against her stomach, trying to release water. He shakes her on her side, as more water gushes out of her mouth.

Deirdre hugs Abigail again, and kisses her face once more. "Tell Nicolaus what you have seen, he will understand. Tell mother I love her and give her many kisses for me. I wish we could have had more time together. You must go back now." Deirdre gives Abigail a soft push backwards. "I love you, my sister."

Abigail feels herself float backwards, away from this place, just as easily as she floated there. She feels herself drifting, and she sees the huge beam of light gets smaller and smaller. In a suddenly distorted, blurry distance, she can see Deirdre waving to her. Suddenly, in a different reality, Abigail feels the love that Nicolaus has for her, as she sees he is working to save her life.

Abigail's eyes pop open as she coughs and gags on the water. Nicolaus physically supports Abigail as she half sits up, and more water gushes from her mouth. Abigail realizes she is back as she feels herself in Nicolaus' hands. Nicolaus pushes on her stomach again, and she coughs more, spitting out more water.

"Oh Abigail! Oh thank God, Abigail! Are you all right, darling?" Nicolaus hugs this precious jewel that is Abigail. She fits right in that special cut of his chest, close to his heart, that space which previously belonged to Deirdre. His arms engulf her with a kindhearted affection.

Abigail clings onto Nicolaus, nodding, laughing, and crying at the same time, while still coughing. "My love, you saved me!" Her words are strangled by coughing. "You did it! You broke the curse!"

She looks upon his dripping wet face. She lovingly holds his face; the coughing has finally subsided. "You did it, Nicky!"

Nicolaus hugs Abigail tightly to him, then looks to her parents. "I think she is all right," he tells them. "She's talking. She can think and reason," he looks at her with a chuckle and tears, knowing this is a miraculous moment, "I think she is all right."

"I saw Deirdre!" Abigail hugs onto Nicolaus around his neck. "She gives her blessings for us. I saw our babies!" Abigail reaches for Constance. "Deirdre sends her love to you, Mom. It's for real! Heaven really exists! I saw Deirdre! She touched me and hugged me and kissed me, and we talked!"

Intense emotion escapes Nicolaus through more tears at Abigail's words. He holds Abigail even tighter to him. "Thank you, sweet Lord," he gives reverence to God.

Speechless, Constance kneels to hug them both to her, despite them being soaking wet. With tears of gratefulness to God, and gratefulness for Nicolaus, she kisses Nicolaus' face, where earlier she had struck him.

Chapter One Hundred Fifteen

After Abigail receives an all clear from the emergency department at the hospital, they rush back to the Ravenell mansion. Abigail changes clothes and joins Nicolaus to enter Nigel's bedroom for their wedding ceremony. Only the family, Dominique, some of the staff, and Bishop Leighton are present.

Nigel's breathing has turned very ragged. He is tired and ready to face death. This marriage assures him that everything will be as it should be, and the future will be as it is written in the heavens. Xavier sits next to Nigel, and touches his shoulder with a smile, while watching all the happenings with great surprise. As he looks upon Abigail and her beauty, he is very happy for his nephew.

Bishop Leighton officiates the simple ceremony. Nicolaus and Abigail exchange the usual vows, knowing they can have a special celebration at a later time.

They hold hands between their chests, standing closely to each other, "I take you this day to be my lawfully wedded wife/husband. I promise to love, honor, and cherish you, for richer or poorer, in sickness and in health, only in death will we part."

The couple does not even have wedding bands at this time. Nicolaus sweetly and quickly kisses Abigail to seal their love.

Holding onto Abigail, Nicolaus hugs Xavier, then he bends to kiss Nigel's head. "Thank you father. I love you," Nicolaus whispers to him, fearing it may be the last time Nigel would hear this from him. "Thank you for everything you've ever done for me." Nigel grabs Nicolaus' hand, and in a vertical position, he shakes it, showing his joy.

Constance joins them and receives a kiss from Nicolaus as well. "Thank you, Mom," he tells her softly.

Abigail and Nicolaus want no party and no celebration at this time. They just wanted to give Nigel his wish, as well as fulfil their own destinies by being married to each other.

This very night, Nigel grew worse. As the dutiful son, Nicolaus stays by his father's side. Abigail watches as Nicolaus prays over Nigel, laying hands on him, praying for his release of pain and suffering. She watches as he prays in Latin, then in English, with fervor and intense authenticity.

Abigail is glad for the privilege to wipe the tears from her husband's eyes, she kisses him, and then leaves him with the men of Nigel's circle, as they stay with Nigel.

In the wee hours of the morning, Nigel's breathing grows shallow, almost non-existent. Nicolaus holds onto his father's hand, and prays, in a low soft tone. He quotes scripture to his father's smiling face. Bishop Leighton also prays over him; Niall and Xavier are present. Just past four in the morning, Nigel slips away.

Nicolaus kisses Nigel's hand, the hand that created the family's wealth and good nature to do for others. "Father!" Nicolaus then kisses his father's forehead, tears streaming down his face. He lays on Nigel to hug him, "Father."

The physician is present and officially pronounces the passing. As he does so, Nicolaus sits in the chair, next to the bed. He looks upon his father as Niall silently watches the scene, motionless. Nicolaus observes his brother, not sure he is moved by any of this at all. He is not sure what to think.

"You know what this means, Nicolaus? Now, right now, in this moment of time, you brother, are now head of the Ravenell family," Niall tells him, reiterating his relief that it is Nicolaus who will lead the family and not him.

Nicolaus sits back in the chair, laying his head back, letting reality hit him. Tears of the loss of his father continue to stream down his face.

Nicolaus' new role, as leader of the Ravenell family feels different to him, different than his previous responsibilities. He suddenly is aware of being inextricably strapped to the heavy burden of the Ravenell Empire, with the overwhelming perception of hundreds of things to do; thousands of people to take care of; and thousands of decisions to make. Nicolaus sighs, wipes his eyes, looking upon his father.

He then gazes at Niall, "First, we must tell your mother of his passing."

Chapter One Hundred Sixteen

So many people attend Nigel's funeral, there is standing room only, with people lining the walls of the interior of the large church. Several press outlets attend, knowing they will get valuable photos of Nicolaus and his new wife, which they had just been made aware of.

This breaking news of Deirdre having a twin sister, who happens to be reporter Abigail Omari, marrying Nicolaus Ravenell, the widowed husband, is Abigail's first time being the main story of international headline news. Abigail personally knows many reporters who are present at the funeral. Those she knows certainly hope she will pick them to be the one to get exclusive rights to tell this fascinating human interest story.

After the funeral, leaving the church, Nicolaus protects Abigail from the large and never-ending mob of reporters with his own body, which she appreciates. Not only did she see this as sexy, she also loves that Nicolaus thinks of her in this manner.

The burial service is held at the Ravenell Family cemetery site, located a quarter mile from the back of the Ravenell mansion. Abigail observes Deirdre's grave and the beautiful headstone. It moves her to tears, Dominique hugging her and comforting her. Constance is a comfort to Nicolaus and Ceil, while Elsa comforts Francesca.

The repass inside the mansion is coordinated by Ms. Mary. Many guests are present, including Nigel's extended family, which means they met even more cousins. Cato, Bobby, and Ned are present, as well as Ceil's sisters, Zoe and Janelle. Zoe puts her arms around Ceil in a warm hug and escorts her to sit down. She loves the change that came over her sister. Ceil has morphed into the type of sister Zoe has always wanted.

The reading of the will is to take place two weeks after the funeral, at the mansion. In waiting for this event, Nicolaus and Abigail go back to Switzerland for a weekend to see the children and Manfred. The children are so happy to see their Papa Nicky, and then saddened to learn he would be returning to the United States, permanently with the woman that looks like the lady in the painting in his office. Nicolaus promises visits, and lots of video calls to curb their sadness.

Several children beg to go with him, and the youngest children demand to be held by their Papa. Nicolaus obliges, accepting the loving hugs of their little arms.

Later that night, Manfred and Dottie inform Nicolaus and Abigail that they want to stay on and raise the children. Nicolaus is very happy about this decision, as he knows Manfred has settled into this new role. The children really look up to him as a father figure as well.

"Nicky, that beautiful portrait of Deirdre. I'd like for us to have it in our home," Abigail tells him with a smile.

Nicolaus hugs his wife, "Of course Abby, anything you want."

Nicolaus signs anything he can over to Manfred. This is such a burden lifted off him, and he is very glad for it. Nicolaus knows the children are in good hands.

The following week, at the reading of the will, the family learns that Nigel has left eighty percent of the estate to Nicolaus, including his VMC stocks, company ownership shares, and his insurance.

Nigel specifically states in the will reading that "Nicolaus is my firstborn son, and heir to my fortune. I thank you, my son, for your loyal support to our country, to the family, and to the business. You have grown our business beyond any measure I could have ever imagined. You demonstrated your loyalty to all of us, even willing to give your life, and actually giving your limbs to demonstrate your love for us."

The will also notes that anyone disputing this gift to Nicolaus will forever lose their portion of the estate.

Nigel provides a large investment trust for each of his current grandchildren, Elaine and Emily, which cannot be touched until they reach adulthood. Nigel provides one percent of the estate to Xavier and his family, two percent to Francesca, two percent to Elsa, and five percent to Niall. Ceil receives ten percent of the estate, and also retains ownership of the Ravenell mansion. Nigel's estate is worth one hundred seventy-seven million dollars.

Nicolaus is amazed, not knowing how his father was going to set this all up. He stands, with Abigail by his side, holding her hand, demonstrating that she is part of him now, his wife. Nicolaus puts his hand to his heart with a frown, feeling touched by his father's belief in him. "I feel stunned right now." He looks to Ceil. "Is everyone okay with this arrangement?" His eyes search the looks and demeanor of his family members.

Ceil nods, then stands next to Nicolaus and takes his free hand. "We are all okay, happy, and comfortable with this arrangement. No one is going to challenge you. We will all respect you as head of this family now," she says loudly for all to hear. Ceil pulls Nicolaus into a hug, and Francesca joins them.

The following week, Nicolaus quietly adds to Francesca's estate, he provides a large sum of funds for Constance and Cecil, and he promptly sets his wife up with a free access account of ten million dollars, to ensure her autonomy.

Chapter One Hundred Seventeen

After three weeks of marriage to Nicolaus, Abigail delights in Nicolaus' arms as he holds her, and lovingly kisses her. She chuckles as he kisses her neck, giving her feelings of love, raising her passion mood. However, she knows this is fleeting.

Abigail stops him and looks at him, as they lay upon the bed he once shared with Deirdre. Abigail insisted they use this room for their marriage as well. She looks at this handsome man who is now her husband.

Nicolaus smiles at Abigail, and holds her close. He sweetly kisses her soft lips, as he loves to do. She smells gorgeous. And as usual, he stops short of taking the next step.

Abigail lovingly reaches up to hold his face in her hand. "And ... tell me again, why we are waiting to consummate?"

"Abby, ... I'm sorry. I know this is not what you expect. I thank you for choosing to be by my side ... otherwise I'd be completely alone."

She smiles patiently. "Umhum, and the consummation part?"

Nicolaus sighs. "I just need to stay focused right now. There is so much that needs to be done." Abigail lets him have that excuse. She flips herself in his arms so that they are face to face. With a smile, she touches his lips with her fingers. "If I make love to you now, that's all I'm going to be thinking about."

Abigail chuckles, "That's all I am thinking about now!"

Nicolaus kisses her lips. "Thank you for being patient with me."

"Of course, honey."

The following day, Abigail and Dominique are in the sitting room, reading through the stack of love letters between Nicolaus and Deirdre. Indeed, the letters help Abigail get a grip on the strong love bond that held Nicolaus to Deirdre. She wonders if it may still be holding him. Abigail discovered the heart of the man, and from that moment on, she saw Nicolaus Ravenell in a different light.

"This must be why he is so reluctant to touch me," Abigail reasons aloud to Dominique.

"No. These letters clearly show that Nicolaus has deep passion, and that he is an independent thinker. I'm sure he does love Deirdre, and Abby, I'm very certain he also loves you just as much, if not more."

"Having some trouble, ladies?" The voice of Ceil interrupts them. She enters the sitting room with a smile.

"Oh hello! We were just discussing these letters."

Ceil touches the letters, recognizing them. "Oh, I see. Abigail, you have questions? You must have questions." Ceil sits herself without an invitation. She wants to help with this transition, as much as she can.

Abigail chuckles. "Well, yes, actually. Uhm, ... what would you have me call you?"

The question hurt Ceil. "Oh," she sounds as if she'd been physically hurt. She puts her hand to her chest.

"I'm sorry," Abigail pops up and goes over to sit next to Ceil. "What did I say? I didn't mean to upset you."

Ceil looks upon Abigail. Her perfumed aroma enhances her beauty and her charm. "You are lovely, dear," Ceil tells her quietly, taking her hand. "That question. Nicolaus asked me that exact question once, after we had a tiff about Niall."

Abigail looks at Dominique who shrugs, then to Ceil. "I'm sorry, I don't understand."

"I used to be ... harsh, ... cruel, ... and mean to Nicolaus. You see he is not my son. And there was a time I demanded he stop calling me his mother. That is why he calls me by my name now. He's never gone back on that."

"Oh." Abigail frowns, not having known this information. "Well, who is his mother?"

"My sister, Rachel, Francesca's mother."

"Oh, I didn't know."

Ceil pats her hand gently. "She has passed on, years ago."

"So what do I call you?"

"Well, Deirdre used to call me Mother Ceil. You can call me that, or just Ceil."

Abigail smiles to her. "Then we shall call you Mother Ceil, as well." She gently pats Ceil's hand, following her lead, finding this amusing. "Mother Ceil, will you tell me about Nicolaus? I want to know all I can."

"Oh, right now?" Abigail happily nods. "Oh, well, where should I begin?"

"From the beginning!"

Ceil talked to Abigail and Dominique about Nicolaus for hours that day, answering any question the ladies had for her. "And so that is why I want to be fully supportive of Nicolaus now. He is the rightful heir."

Abigail nods. Ceil had mentioned a few things that peaked Abigail's curiosity, and she knew she'd need to get a different perspective on her questions.

Abigail's sleuthing mind demanded more information. She went to Elsa, "Tell me exactly what happened during the captivity. I want to know why Nicolaus is so ... different than before."

Elsa feels pained at the thought of reliving the horrible days. The thought of telling anyone what her own father had required of Nicolaus for their freedom, including her own, pained her, as she has not spoken to her father since then. Elsa looks at Abigail and Dominique with wide eyes. She sighs deeply, deciding she would tell all to help Nicolaus.

Elsa takes both of Abigail's hands, pulling her to the sofa just inside her bedroom. "Best you sit down. This is a long story." Elsa pulls Dominique inside, motions to the nanny to take her children to play, then closes the heavy door to protect her children from hearing the ugly truth. She sits next to Abigail and begins.

After speaking with Elsa, and having heard the Ravenell story from Ceil, Abigail feels she much better understands Nicolaus. However, one glaring piece of information was missing for Abigail. She had a bleak understanding that Niall was the last unseen person with her sister before she went into early labor. So now the question is, what actually happened to Deirdre?

Chapter One Hundred Eighteen

Abigail entered the church of which the Ravenells are members. Immediately, she went looking for Niall. Elsa informed her that Niall had been spending much time hiding out at the church, especially since her arrival, and more so since Nigel's funeral. If he was not at the office, then he could now be found at the church. Although neither Elsa, nor Abigail thought of Niall as devout in his religion, Abigail chose to look for him at the church first.

Abigail decided she must venture this fact finding mission on her own, leaving Dominique at the mansion with Elsa.

As Abigail begins to walk the long aisle of the church, she has the understanding that this church holds some of the history of her sister. As she moves down the aisle, the hand of a young priest stops her.

"May I help ..." he freezes at the sight of Abigail. "You are the sister of Mrs. Deirdre Ravenell," he beams a smile at her.

"Yes, I am." Abigail returns the smile.

"I knew your sister. She helped me through Ms. Helena's orphanage, where I lived for a short time. Ms. Deirdre was very kind to me. To all the kids, really. I have just stepped into my calling at the church, here."

"I am very glad she was able to help you."

"Are you here to see the bishop? He was called away and has not come back yet."

"Really? What a shame! I would have loved to speak with him. Right now, though, I am looking for Niall Ravenell." Abigail looks beyond the young priest and sees Niall sitting on a pew at the front of the church. Abigail smiles to the priest, "Excuse me please."

Abigail slowly makes her way to where Niall is sitting. She stands over him, waiting for him to notice her.

When Niall looks up, he jumps with startle to see Abigail.

"Niall, I would like to talk with you."

Niall balks, wanting to run away. He has a hard time looking at Abigail. "I have nothing to say to you," he says awkwardly. He briefly shies his eyes away from her face. When he looks up, Abigail's fiery eyes of Deirdre are looking back at him.

Niall feels frozen in place in his seat at the church. He wants to get up and run, yet does not seem to have the nerve to do so. "Oh God!" he shrieks. "Please," he burst out crying, "those eyes!"

Niall had thought his ugly deeds were buried with Deirdre, never to be brought up again, except to complete his penance. However now, Deirdre's very eyes harshly stare at him, inside the church, as if she were getting her revenge on him.

"What's wrong, Niall? You seem afraid of something." Abigail demands to know, her voice echoing throughout the empty church.

"Those eyes!" Niall finally turns away from her.

"My eyes remind you of my sister," she states knowledgeably. Niall nods. "Why should you be afraid? Unless ... you have something to do with her death, Niall. Tell me," she steps closer to him. "What happened with my sister, Niall? You had words?" She questions him, feeling the situation was much worse than just having words. "What happened with my sister?" she demands, touching Niall's shoulder.

Niall flinches away from her touch, out of fear, feeling freaked out. This is too much for him, and he does not want to tell lies inside the church, already feeling tormented, so he tells the truth. "I did not mean to harm her, I swear!" The burden of guilt engulfs him.

Abigail grows angry, knowing justice has escaped her sister. "Tell me what you did to Deirdre," she says more forcefully, not caring that the young priest is watching. "Tell me, Niall," she grabs his shoulder again, "What did you do?"

"I touched her when I should not have. I ... touched her."

Abigail went closer to him, her eyes blazed on him, "Explain yourself," she pressures him.

Niall breaks down in tears. "I loved Deirdre. I did ... I loved her, too much. She would not have me, even when Nicolaus was married to another. And when Nicolaus did marry her, I was enraged, ... insanely jealous. And then ... Nicolaus went off, as he always did, to save ... my father-in-law, and ... I ..."

"You what?"

"I touched her, I ... I did not mean to hurt her ... I just wanted to have her ... to ...."

Abigail stood away from Niall, putting what he said together. Her hand momentarily went over her mouth from shock, and then she confronted him. "You raped her?" She half shouted. "You raped Deirdre to get revenge against Nicolaus?"

"I did not mean to ..."

"Oh my dear God!" her hand went to her mouth again, shaking her head in revulsion as tears trickled from her eyes.

"I have changed Abigail. I swear to you, I have repented my sins before God. Her death changed me. When my father told me she had died ... I ... changed."

"You were the cause of her death," Abigail angrily accuses Niall. More importantly, she wanted him to know that she understood the significant part to all of this. "Nicolaus doesn't know, does he?"

Through his own tears, Niall answers softly, "No, he does not know. And I beg you, please, do not tell him. He will hate me. He will kill me and leave Elsa with no father to our children."

"You disgust me!" she says in an even tone. Abigail walks down the aisle of the beautiful church, leaving with a determined mandate.

Abigail asks the driver to go slowly. She wants to think about things, as she now has all the pieces of the puzzle. She has to resolve how she is going to break this tragic news to Nicolaus. She wonders if her mother knows the truth.

Abigail decides she wants to tell Nicolaus right away.

Chapter One Hundred Nineteen (TW)

A bigail is not sure what type of first time reception she will receive showing up unannounced at Nicolaus' office. She is impressed with the glass tower that holds the VMC empire.

As she steps into the elevator, she wonders if Nicolaus is even present in the building. She tried to time her entrance at the last hour of the workday. She receives warm and welcoming nods from many people as the elevator slowly climbs to the twelfth floor, where the VMC executive offices are housed.

Suddenly, she feels a little apprehensive, hating to break such news to Nicolaus, here at his office. As she steps off the elevator, she sees Nicolaus' office some paces before her, just to the left. It is quiet on the floor, though she does see other offices and many people working and talking.

Taking a breath, Abigail knocks twice, then tries the knob to Nicolaus' office. The door opens, and she is relieved to see him alone, at his desk, though there are piles of papers.

"Come on in," Nicolaus says loudly without looking up from the papers. The noisy hinge lets him know someone has entered. "Yes, what is it?"

"Honey, sorry to bother you, ... we must talk!"

At the sound of her voice, Nicolaus looks up. A surprised look and smile greets her. She is more relieved and gives a big smile right back to him.

"Abigail! I didn't expect you to be here!"

She sees him drop what he is doing, and stands, walking to her. Gently, he kisses her forehead.

She uses one hand to brush his suit, sighing from the sweet kiss. "I've scarcely seen you for three weeks now Nicolaus. Not a way to make your bride very happy."

Nicolaus chuckles. "I know. I'm sorry." He spreads his hands about. "It has been so busy. And by the time I make it home ..."

"I know, you're exhausted. Honey, we need to talk about a serious matter."

Nicolaus takes her hands. "Okay. Well ..." Nicolaus looks at his watch. "I'm about to go into a meeting. I'm sure they are setting up the call, should be in about two minutes." He touches her shoulder. "Hey, you want to join the meeting?"

"Me?"

"Sure! It's with our partner in Africa. There is a crisis there, and ..."

"Nicolaus, you do sound busy. I just thought you could break away early so we can talk. I should let you get to your work."

"I'd love for you to join the meeting!" He kisses her hand to coax her. He ushers her into the conference room.

Nicolaus stands with Abigail by his side, smiling at her. He gestures for everyone to calm down, as Ibrahim, their Africa partner joins by video. "Thank you everyone. Hello Ibrahim, my friend."

"Nicolaus! My very good friend, welcome back. How are you?"

"I am fine. We have a special guest joining us today, and I'd like to introduce everyone to my beautiful wife, Abigail."

Abigail blushes as she receives claps.

"Hello Ms. Abigail. May I say, you are indeed beautiful, and must be very related to our dear, dear, Deirdre, ma'am."

Abigail giggles and nods. "Yes, I am her twin sister."

"Twin sister? Well, that is amazing!" Ibrahim chuckles, "the good Lord blessed this messed up world with two of the same wonderful people! And Nicolaus, my friend, you seem to be doubly blessed there."

"Yes, for certain! And Abby, I'd like you to meet Daniel Araceli, our Vice President." Abigail shakes hands with each of the four people she is also introduced to. Nicolaus sits her next to him at the oblong conference table. "So Ibrahim, tell us, how are things?"

"Well, thank you all for this meeting, I know it is short notice. I have to let you know that things are getting very cramped in the camp here, as there has been an easing between the warring factions, and many more thousands of people have crossed the border into Eritrea. Might there be additional assistance we can provide these people, such as additional passage, or food resources?"

Nicolaus points to Daniel. "Ibrahim, I'm not sure on additional passage. Our government worked with us to house eight hundred, so I'm not sure they will increase that number. Let me work with my legal team to see what we can do."

"Ibrahim, I can have my team work on food resources with our Egyptian partners," Nicolaus nods to another staff member who begins taking notes, "to see how they can help. And ... hmm ... maybe we can reach out to other countries to see if they may be willing to take some additional refugees, like Egypt and Canada, comes to mind. I can't promise anything, but let us check on this for you. Just give us about two days to get back to you on this."

"Nicolaus, as always, my friend, you are quite amazing."

As the video call ends, the staff exit the room with chattering, ready to get to work. Nicolaus smiles at Abigail who is looking at him with admiration. She likes the way he handles the staff. He stands, reaching out for her hand, and escorts Abigail the short distance to his office, and closes the door. Abigail turns to touch her husband, "Nicky, we must talk, but honey, not here."

Nicolaus nods. He escorts his wife to his vehicle, and they drive in silence at first, as he wonders what this is about. It worries him a little.

"So, tell me how are you doing? You and Dominique get settled in?"

"Well, besides missing a husband, I think I'm settled. The house is lovely, of course. And, well, I've never had staff before, so that takes a little getting used to."

Nicolaus chuckles. "I'm sure it won't take long to get used to them. They are very nice people. And let me know if any of them causes you any trouble. I absolutely won't tolerate that."

"So, how are you feeling?"

Nicolaus' smile makes Abigail a little nervous. She clears her throat. He nods. "I definitely miss my father."

Nicolaus pulls the vehicle into a space overlooking the Hippy Hollow public lake. They are in a shaded space, with few patrons around them.

Abigail frowns, "What is this place?"

"Deirdre and I used to swim here often. You see that ledge on the other side," he points across the way, "there is a less used shoreline by some large rocks, and we'd swim in the water over there."

"Really? Deirdre could swim?"

Nicolaus chuckles. "Yes! And we are getting you swimming lessons. You must know how to swim, my dear."

Abigail chuckles with Nicolaus. "Okay. Okay."

"So," he takes her hand, "what is it we must talk about?"

"Oh, Nicky. I'm not sure how to tell you this. It's about Deirdre."

"Okay," he says softly.

Abigail sighs. "I talked with Mother Ceil this morning for hours, and then I talked with Elsa. You see, I wanted to find out everything I can about you." Nicolaus nods in understanding. "And then my questions seemed to lead to Deirdre. And I found out that Niall was the last person with Deirdre before she went into early labor. A fact that Mother Ceil suspiciously did not tell me. Anyways, it seems that he was behind a locked door with my sister."

"Abby, what are you saying?"

"I'm saying that he was the last person with her when she was found. Your father had to bust open the door, and Deirdre was found in a ... terrible state. And Niall was somehow not in the room with her. So, I went looking for Niall, because I wanted answers. I found Niall at the church. And Nicky, he confessed to me that he raped Deirdre."

"Abby!"

"He confessed it, Nicky." She felt herself get emotional again. She holds back her tears.

Nicolaus looks away from Abigail in thought. She touches him, and he looks at her again. The look on his face was different. Abigail can see hurt, disappointment, and anger written in his face.

"Nicolaus, I don't want you going to jail over this, honey. You had to know, because ... apparently, no one told you."

In silence, Nicolaus slowly nods, his anger creeping up.

"Promise me you won't do anything crazy. Niall is very afraid of you, Nicky."

"He should be! He did that to Deirdre? She was my wife! My wife! And nine months pregnant!" Anger ceases Nicolaus. He gets out of the vehicle, slamming the door. He is not sure what to do with his anger. He jumps back into the vehicle, and drives them down to the church.

"Nicky," Abigail tries to calm him down, however, she made no inroads. She can feel his wrath through his muscular arms.

"You stay right here." Nicolaus gets out of the vehicle and enters the church. Immediately he sees Niall on the front bench, close to the altar.

Niall looks back, sees Nicolaus, quickly gets up and runs to the back of the church. Nicolaus chases him, and catches him, slamming him against a wall. "Why are you running from me, brother?"

Niall is caught in Nicolaus' hands. He does not try to run again, or try to get away. He turns his head from Nicolaus eyes, afraid of his wrath after all these years.

Nicolaus harshly shakes his brother. "Tell me it's not true, that you did not rape Deirdre." Nicolaus feels enraged.

"I cannot tell you that," Niall states.

Angrily, Nicolaus mercilessly strikes Niall hard across the face, then severely backhands him across the other cheek, his ring cutting Niall's face. Niall cannot get out of Nicolaus' grip. Nicolaus wants to hurt him more, however, he jerks Niall free of his grip.

Through gritted teeth, Nicolaus says, "My God, Niall! I never thought you had it in you to actually ... go that far."

"I will not lie to you Nicolaus, not here in the church." Niall touches his cut face. "I was in love with her. I wanted her so much. Too much."

"So much that you would rape her?" Nicolaus asks angrily, grabbing Niall up again. He wants to hit him once more, instead he slams him against the wall.

"Yes, that much Nicolaus! I was angry at you,... at her." He shakes his head, "I swear to you, I never meant to hurt Deirdre."

Nicolaus angrily yells at Niall, feeling his rage, wanting to punch him. "Oh and raping her was somehow not hurting her?" Instead of punching Niall, Nicolaus harshly throws him across the room. Items get broken, falling to the floor, while other items go flying. Nicolaus clinches his jaw. "For God's sake man, she was my wife!" He yells at Niall.

Bishop Leighton and the young priest can hear what is happening in the back room. When the young priest tries to go to stop the fight, Bishop Leighton holds him back with a hand. The bishop knows this must play out.

Niall touches his cut face while getting up. The cut is dripping blood and burns. "I was sick in the head with love for her. I am sorry."

"Sorry?" Nicolaus grabs Niall up again and slams him against the wall, ready to beat on him, as Niall's words continue to grow his anger.

Niall catches his fist, and tries to move out of the striking path. "I am not the same person, Nicolaus! I am not! I have changed," he says loudly. "I've changed! Her death changed me," his words are broken as tears spill from his eyes. "I have repented my sins to God. I asked Elsa to forgive me. And now it is time I ask you to forgive me." He grabs onto both of Nicolaus' wrists. He knows he deserves more pain then what Nicolaus has barely begun to inflict upon him.

Nicolaus sighs, and harshly jerks his wrists free from Niall.

Niall slides down the wall, and drops to his knees before his brother, feeling like an empty person. He takes Nicolaus hand, "I beg you Nicolaus, forgive me my sin against you and Deirdre, please forgive me. I disrespected Deirdre, and I also disrespected you. Please forgive me."

Nicolaus is speechless at Niall's actions. He is shocked that he seems sincere. Niall bows his head, placing Nicolaus' hand to his forehead, humbly waiting for an answer. "I do not want you to hate me for the rest of our lives. I need you brother. I need your guidance. Please forgive me," Niall adds.

Nicolaus sighs again, his heart broken. He feels sick in his gut over this. Niall has never been humbled. His actions are not anything Nicolaus could have ever imagined.

"So many years have passed, ... there is nothing I can do to bring her back. Hating you is not the answer, Niall," Nicolaus says sadly, in his mature wisdom. "No, I do not hate you." He pulls Niall to his feet, and turns to leave.

"But do you forgive me?" Niall yells after him, stopping him in his tracks.

Nicolaus turns to face his brother, again shocked at him. He steps up to Niall, his anger returning. "You want my forgiveness for raping my wife?" He shakes his head. "You have some nerve! I'll have to think about that one," he says sarcastically. Nicolaus turns to leave again.

Niall drops onto his knees once more, and scoots himself to grab Nicolaus around his legs, stopping him going. "Please, brother, please," Niall has genuine tears, "I beg your forgiveness! Please!" Niall wants his penance over with so that God can forgive him. He feels his sin like a heavy weight around his neck. A weight that will never go away if he cannot be forgiven. He knows if Nicolaus does not forgive him, that weight will be on him for the rest of his life, bringing him hardship with his own daughters.

Niall's begging brings grief to the surface for Nicolaus. He feels the magnitude of the ask in God's house. Scripture plays in his mind. Nicolaus takes breaths to calm himself as he looks at the walls of the church. He looks at the arched ceiling, which has a sky window, where he can see the starry heavens above. He feels the pull of Niall around his legs, as he begs him again. He feels Niall's tears, bringing tears to his own eyes.

Nicolaus scrapes Niall off him, pushing him away, making him fall to the floor of the church. He steps away from his younger brother and looks at him, then clearly, yet sternly, he yells at Niall, "You have no right to ask my forgiveness. After what you've done, you have no right to ask anything of me."

Niall watches as Nicolaus exits the room, leaving him on the floor. "Wait," he reaches for his brother, as he sees him walk away, "Wait! Please!" Niall curls himself on the floor of the church and cries. He believes that for sure he's lost Nicolaus, and that Nicolaus might never forgive him.

Chapter One Hundred Twenty

As months progress, Abigail enjoys being Mrs. Nicolaus Ravenell. She often accompanies her husband to events, galas, openings, ribbon cuttings, parades, children's fundraiser causes, parties, dinners, and many art events. She and Nicolaus attend high school graduation ceremonies in several states for the children in the children's homes.

Abigail appreciates that Nicolaus involves her in his life, and she enjoys these new adventures. She met the Darfurian refugees and saw the operation of the shelter. Nicolaus took Abigail to their home in Denver, which Abigail loves spending time there. She can see Nicolaus literally relax in this space. She perceives that he loves this home. Peace is here.

They have found their marriage to be very agreeable and loving. They seem to be the perfect match for each other. As a couple, their spiritual lives also thrive as they are both active in the church, in both cities. Nicolaus has resumed mentoring young men, and Abigail has taken to this new supportive role for the young women.

Sometimes Abigail goes into the VMC office, like today, to see if she can be helpful.

"Actually, darling, I need something to do. I don't want to just sit around all day. I'm used to working."

Nicolaus smiles at the comment. "Hmm. Well, what would you like to do?"

"I was thinking about us starting a school."

Nicolaus is surprised. "A school?" He thinks for a moment. "Abby, a school might be a bit much. I mean it's too much red tape, too much liability, and very expensive. Though funny you should mention schooling. I do have work that I cannot get to in scholarship awards. I have two million to endow it from my business grants project, and I literally have no time to develop it. Would you be interested in taking this on?"

"Nicky, are you serious?"

Nicolaus nods. "You set the criteria, the awarding schedule, the amounts, the topics, everything. Would be great to form a partnership with a couple of colleges, as well. I assume you'd like to lean towards journalism or reporting or something?" He chuckles as Abigail nods excitedly, wide-eyed. "I'd love to give endowments to see our name, ... your name ... on a college hall. Abigail Deirdre Omari-Ravenell Hall. I already know the students would call it Abby Hall."

Abigail puts her loving arms around her loving husband, who is holding her at the small of her back. She smiles at his vision. She is amazed at him. She'd never had an inkling of a thought of anyone offering her such a gift; a gift that actually helps others, especially young people.

"And maybe some of our foster kids will be interested. And you can run two tracks, one for journalism and one generally, if you want. It's your department, you set it up how you want it. It would be a job of the foundation, so I will pay you, reasonably, but yes, I can pay you."

As he kept talking, Abigail looked upon the light caramel skin of her husband, his soft curly hair, his strong, muscular frame, and those very inviting lips. She planted a kiss on those lips, making him chuckle.

"And you can have the office next door, which used to be Deirdre's office."

"Nicky!"

"I haven't let anyone else in that office, but it's yours if you want it. You set your hours. It would be your department, and if you think you need assistance, you can hire someone."

"Or have Dominique?"

Nicolaus smiles with a nod, "If that's what you want. This would really help me out."

Abigail pulls Nicolaus in a tight, loving hug. She is in awe of the wonderful kind of man her husband is. She looks into his eyes, feeling mesmerized, then goes in for another kiss.

Chapter One Hundred Twenty-One

Another three long months have passed and Nicolaus has not consummated his marriage to Abigail. Abigail took this to heart. For all the sharing they do, fun with events, dinners, parties, and talking, he has not touched her sexually.

Her normal routine after their loving kissing session each night, is to turn on her side and cry silent tears, wondering why her husband just does not want her.

Nicolaus and Abigail are in bed. As usual, Nicolaus lovingly and respectfully kisses Abigail's sweet lips. Kissing her is something he cannot resist. Abigail is hopeful that he will finally make love to her. She feels his hand on her stomach. His kiss is long and deep, passionate and involved. His kiss sends all kinds of messages to her body, getting her ready for him. She has been ready for him every night for the last five months of their marriage.

Breathless, Nicolaus breaks the kiss. He looks at Abigail and can read the want for him in her face, in her deeply searching eyes. Her hands are on his strong shoulders, as she pulls him closer to her. She wants more kissing, and he gently obliges. In a rare move, her hand moves his hand to her bosom, fully letting him know that she wants him to keep going.

Nicolaus keeps the kiss going, while giving in to her demand and gently caresses her soft bosom. The feel of her makes him moan with desire for her. He needs his most lovely wife, his beautiful wife, his Abigail.

Desire for her increases throughout his body. Nicolaus pulls Abigail into his arms. Her hand pulls at his and places it on her groin, as his scorching kiss melds her to him. She feels her body hot with desire, and damp with want for him. She is ready, she is so ready, and ....

Abigail opens her eyes as Nicolaus tears himself away from her with a groan and heated breathing. She is panting with want for him, they were so close this time. So close.

"Oh God!" She says aloud, no longer wanting to hide her frustration of getting heated only for him to run from her. Abigail sits up and is right on him, not willing to let him get away this time. "Nicky, what is it darling?" She chuckles, as she straddles his lap, his back against the pillows, against the headboard. Nicolaus has nowhere to go to get away from her, unless he gets out of the bed.

"Abby, don't ..., please."

Abigail can feel him through her sleek negligee. She doesn't know what else to do, short of grabbing him in her hands, which her mind has fantasized about doing. She rubs herself right on him, making him moan. His hands on her hips, lifting her off him. She forces her weight right on him, and slowly moves herself, grasping his lips. She wants him. And ... "Oh!" He's out of the bed!

Nicolaus retreats to the beautifully shaped window of their bedroom. His hand is on the frame as he's trying to cool himself down. He takes long breaths.

However, Abigail is not willing to let him get away so easily tonight. She wants her man! She is right on him, her arms around his bare torso. "Nicolaus, honey ... come back to bed." She runs her hands through his curly soft hair. She lays her face to his back, hugging him to her.

The feel of Abigail's torso against his back makes his passion rise again. Nicolaus removes her hands and retreats from her, sitting on the bed. He moans as Abigail is right on him. She sits on his lap, lady like this time, crossing her legs, and puts her arms around his shoulders.

"My love. My sweet, sweet, extremely handsome husband, what is it going to take for us to have sex?" She directly asks him. She touches his face and lifts his chin to her. "So what is it, then? You're not attracted to me?"

Nicolaus knows he must respond as she is waiting for his answer. His hands go around her waist. "Abby, you're very attractive! You are more than beautiful, so much so, there isn't a word for how beautiful you are."

She chuckles. "Oh my goodness! Thank you, darling. Okay, well, then, you just don't want me?"

"No, no. I do want you." He sighs, "You have no idea how much." He receives a kiss to his forehead from her, which fires him up again. He breathes it out, trying to stay calm, not wanting that kiss or the fact that she is sitting right on him to activate his loins.

"Well, there is something you are not telling me then. You're not capable of doing it?"

Nicolaus gently moves Abigail off his lap, and stands away from her. He looks at her, grabs his neck in frustration, sighs, then looks out the window.

"Nicolaus!" Abigail stands, exasperated. "We can't go on like this!" Abigail walks into the luxurious bathroom and slams the door in frustration. Normally, she just turns away from him in bed and cries herself to sleep in need of him. Tonight she has a strong determination to make things different between them. She paces the floor, thinking of what to do, and what to say. What can she try?

Abigail stays in the bathroom for a few minutes. She washes the tears from her face. She brushes her hair, and applies additional fragrance which sits on her vanity table.

As she exits the bathroom, she sees Nicolaus in the same place by the window. He turns to face her.

"Abby, I'm so sorry," he goes to her, and hugs her, praying she will not feel rejected. "You're right, of course." He brings her to the bed, and pulls her to sit on his lap again. "I know this is not what you expect in a marriage. I'm failing to take care of your needs, and I'm so sorry for that."

Abigail searches his eyes, and sees that he is being honest. She hugs Nicolaus. "Darling, what is the matter? Talk to me. We've been married a little over five months now. I feel like we have great communication, that we can talk to each other about anything."

He nods. "You're right. I … I am … terrified to touch you, Abby." He shakes his head, looking in her eyes. "I'm terrified! I can't even touch you. I can't even do it. I get shaky, and …"

"Nicolaus! Is it the curse?" She asks him frowning, wanting to understand.

He nods, "Yes, that, and … other things."

"Other things?"

"Abby, I tried to tell you, … before we married."

"Okay, well, honey, tell me now."

"My family was taken hostage," he sighs, "really because of me." He takes full blame of being sold into captivity by Ceil. "And … I … "

"Nicky, what is it? Did they hurt you? What did they do to you, Nicky?"

His face flashed emotional pain, then a frown of anger. "They tried to destroy me!"

"Oh Nicky!" She touched his chest to try to comfort him. She thought for a moment. "So they made you incapable of doing it?"

"No, not that. I … ah … I did some things that I'm not very proud of." He pauses with a sigh and a face that shows emotional pain. "I was forced to make a choice to have my family rescued, and …"

She touches his face, putting her forehead to his. "Nicolaus, that sounds very courageous, not something to be ashamed of."

"Abby, I was willing to give myself over … to a man."

Abigail touches his face. "To save your family. Nicolaus that is admirable. You risked your person for them." Abigail sits up straighter, nodding in understanding. "So, they sexually abused you? You went through that too, like my sister did?"

Nicolaus shakes his head. "Well, no ... only by the grace of God. Sadly, it was Elsa's father. He couldn't bring himself to ... take me. He left, without touching me."

Abigail nods without judgement, having known part of this information. "Wow, that is a blessing!" She says sounding relieved. "So you have post-traumatic stress over all this. Sex brings back those horrid feelings, and your terrified of the curse. The curse you have broken."

"Abigail, what if I didn't break the curse? If it's not broken, I'd be putting your life in danger."

"You did break it, Nicolaus. When you saved me, it was broken."

Anxiously, "What if it's not?"

Abigail sighs, fully understanding that she has to pull Nicolaus past all this. She kisses his forehead again. "Okay, Love. My sweet, sweet husband, whom I love dearly. Tell me, then. How exactly is this supposed to work? We keep a sexless marriage?"

"Abigail, I know it's not what you expect, nor what you want."

"No it's not! What I want, Nicky, is to bring our seven children into the world! The first is supposed to be born next year, darling."

"Seven?"

"Yes, seven. My Lord, is that biblical enough for you?"

Nicolaus frowns at her. "How do you know that?"

"I've seen them! I've seen them in my dreams ... or a vision, ... or a premonition, whatever you want to call it. And remember, Deirdre showed me our babies! The first is Nicolai ..."

"Nicolai?"

"Yes, he's named after you, but also has his own identity."

"Deirdre named our son Nicolai. And ... she told me something just like what you just said." He is amazed.

Abigail giggles, "Well ... we are twins!" She continues, "Nicolai, Nathanial, and Matthew will take after you and be involved in the business."

Nicolaus frowns in amusement, "You know their names? And what they will be doing with their lives?"

Abigail chuckles and nods with certainty. "Then we have Natalia."

"Natalia?"

Abigail nods. "Natalia Deirdre Grace. She must keep the Deirdre name going. She will be some kind of teacher or professor."

Nicolaus chuckles, "What? A professor? Like Francesca?"

Abigail nods again, with raised eyebrows. "And then our other three sons will do their own thing. Corey will sing, or act, or something. I'm not exactly sure, though I see him on a stage. Ian does something with buildings. And our youngest, Djordje Jovan, will have a Greek name, and will be a runner, ... I think."

Nicolaus takes her hands, "You are truly an amazing woman."

Abigail chuckles. "I've been seeing my children for years, and before I met you, I never understood who they look like. And of course, now we know, Love, they look like you."

Nicolaus is in awe, her words having calmed him. "My mother used to tell me that my babies were waiting to be born."

"It's true! And it's me who will be their mother. It's like your father said, our finding each other is not a coincidence. It's our destiny."

"Abigail, you're so amazing!"

Abigail shakes her head, "No, love, it is you who is amazing. You are a gift to this world, and you don't even realize it. I know you are hurt from things past, Nicky, I can feel it and I can see it.

Oh darling, this is a new time for us. A new life, together, with our seven children."

Abigail kisses his forehead again. "So you see, Nicky darling, the only way to get our children born is we must have sex. Wonderful, glorious, feel good sex! That is what I want for us! Together!" Abigail giggles, "You've got to believe that I'll be around at least until our seventh child is born, though I have to say, I have seen visions of myself as an elderly lady, with grandchildren as well. Now, the grandchildren count and names, I'm not sure of that just yet."

Nicolaus nods, "I love you, Abigail. I don't know what I'd do without you."

Abigail puts a sweet peck on her husband's lips. "Nicolaus, you have helped so many children around the world. And I am very sure you will continue this work to help even more children. And now it's time for us to create our own children, who I'm very sure will continue your work, and probably do even more than we can imagine.

"Nicky, darling, you broke the curse. There's to be no more sorrow, darling. You must understand now, my sweet husband, that you are a gift, my love, to me, and to the world. Only good days ahead for us." She kisses Nicolaus again, and he responds to her genuineness.

They wrap themselves in the bedcovers, and he holds his God given wife, appreciative of her. In each other's arms, they drift to sleep.

Chapter One Hundred Twenty-Two

A bigail full on hugs her mother, and her father, as she enters their home.

"So how are you, my sweet daughter?"

"Mom, I'm good! Nicky and I are getting closer to where we should be. We are working together at the office now, and we do lots of events. I've met so many people, and we help so many children and families. Our work is remarkable! Only we are having some intimacy issues, and ... well, I just don't know how to push him. You know what I mean?"

Constance chuckles and nods. With a grin, she beckons Abigail to a different room, closing the door, away from the hearing of Cecil. "Let's have some woman talk."

Abigail giggles. "Okay Mom. I'm all ears!"

They sit next to each other, Constance taking Abigail's hands. "So if I read between the lines, when you say having intimacy issues, I'm assuming you are talking about sex."

Abigail nods. "I literally had a talk with Nicky when he ran from me, again. I told him about our children that I've seen in my visions. And he did finally admit that he's terrified, is the word he used, terrified to touch me. He's not convinced the curse is broken."

Constance nods, "That is understandable. Nicolaus is the type of man that protects his loved ones."

"I just don't know what to do to push him. I feel like when we are so close to something happening, he bolts from me. Although after we talked, we did have a really sweet night of holding each other. Mom, that's all we do. Hold each other!"

"Hmmm. Well, you know honey, Nicolaus can endure much. Deirdre had him waiting for ten years."

Abigail chuckles. "Wow! That is incredible. I also think the house may be a problem. He acts like he may have PTSD after all that's happened."

Constance nods again. "That is very possible. You need to get him out of that house. You know, you two haven't even taken a honeymoon. I think you should demand he take you somewhere."

"You're so right. He just works so much. I mean I'm sure there is much for him to do, and he hasn't taken a break."

"I'm sure he needs a break. You should have him take you to the castle, since you haven't been there together."

"I love that place!"

"And gosh, maybe the two of you have your wedding there, at the Saint Nicholas church, like Deirdre did. That would be wonderful!"

"Mom! I even bought the same dress Deirdre bought."

"What? You have the same wedding dress?"

Abigail nods, "Yes, though I think I'll want to get something different ... for Nicky."

"Sounds like a shopping trip for you and Dominique. Or why don't you buy it in Estonia?"

"I like that idea too!"

"Bishop Moratey is still there. I just heard from him last week. He actually called to check in on you and Nicolaus."

"He did?"

Constance nods. "So as you can see, all these opportunities are present for you to use your charms against Nicolaus. I think if you continue to make strong demands about it, he won't be able to resist you much longer."

"Strong demands about it? What do you mean, Mom?"

"Like be in his face about it. Lay it on thick. So for instance, instead of kissing him two times, you kiss him seven times. In fact

..." Constance pulls closer to her daughter, "I have just thought of a plan that would be certain to work."

Abigail listens to her mother intently, with excitement.

"So honey, you demand Nicolaus take you on your honeymoon tomorrow. Don't let him wiggle out of it. You see, Nicolaus is a person who is very structured, so spontaneousness will be good for him. And ... it will be better if we get to Estonia in the morning time, remember, that place is eight hours ahead of us."

"Okay. Why is that important?"

"To throw Nicolaus off schedule, get him out of his routine. Now here's the action part. You have the staff make you a meal. Before going down to eat, you put on something frilly and flimsy, something he hasn't seen you in. You have something like that?"

"Actually, yes, I do! Dominique bought it as a wedding gift."

"Okay, so you put that on. And just before the food is ready, somehow, you have him wait for you at the bottom of the staircase. Probably get the house staff to help you with this. Okay, and then, you dramatically glide down the stairs ... like you're in a telenovela."

Abigail cracks up with laughter at her mother's suggestion. She playfully acts as though the wind is blowing her hair back. Constance laughs, "Yes! Just like that! Dramatic! You glide down the stairs. Of course he won't be able to take his eyes from you. You take his hands and pull him to the table to eat. And as he sits down, you sit in his lap. And then, my dear, the most important part! You feed him. A little at a time. And between each bite of food, you kiss him."

"Oh my gosh! Mother!" She says with excitement.

"Get it? You feed him, then kiss him, then feed him, then kiss him. And honey ... before long, just the wonderful atmosphere of that castle will have you in his arms making those babies in no time."

"Oh Mom!" Abigail clasps her hands together with excitement. "Do you think it will really work?"

Constance chuckles. "Oh yes, dear. Well, such actions worked to get you and Deirdre born!"

They giggle, then Abigail hugs her mother to her, with gratefulness in her heart.

Chapter One Hundred Twenty-Three

The following morning, Abigail stopped Nicolaus from leaving for work. She helps him dry off as he steps out of the shower. As he wraps himself in the towel, she stands behind him and puts her arms around him. "Love, if you want to stay married to me, you will cancel everything today, and fly me to Estonia, so that we can be officially wedded in that beautiful historic church where our ancestors lay."

"Abby! You know I can't do that! I've got ..."

Before he can finish his sentence, Abigail kisses his shoulder blade, then his neck. He stops talking. "I'm not kidding, darling. You will cancel everything, and fly us for our honeymoon, or I'm marching down to the courthouse and getting our marriage annulled today."

Nicolaus turns and takes his wife into his arms. He kisses her lips. "Okay," he gives into her, not sure if she is bluffing since she sounds very serious. "You're right! We need a honeymoon. How about two weeks?"

Abigail kisses Nicolaus, then slips out of his arms. "That sounds more like it, honey!" Excitement is in her voice as she exits the bathroom.

Chapter One Hundred Twenty-Four

Nicolaus and Abigail have a small wedding ceremony at the historic church in Estonia. Abigail did not want any fanfare or reporters, only wanting this between her and Nicolaus. Present at the church are Ceil, Constance, Dominique, and Cecil, happy to walk his daughter down the aisle.

Abigail has a beautiful, glittery white waist wrap wedding dress. The dress bodice has spaghetti straps over the shoulders, and elegant material hugs tightly to her bosom and her hips. Nicolaus is sharply dressed in a light blue suit. Cecil walks his daughter down the aisle to the song *Evergreen Love*, and then midway, to the religious song *Oh Perfect Love*, both sang by an Estonian songstress. Abigail carries a beautiful wedding bouquet with red and white roses.

Nicolaus bought Abigail a beautiful diamond wedding band, with small diamonds encircling a gold band, and seven large, rounded diamonds set into the ring. One round diamond for each of their foretold children. Abigail loves it. And Nicolaus has a matching band with the seven round diamonds in his men's golden band.

As Bishop Moratey happily performs their marriage ceremony, they exchange vows and these beautiful rings.

Lovingly, Nicolaus kisses Abigail's hand, then places that wedding ring upon Abigail's finger, watching her with romance in the air and love for her in his heart, as her face lights up to his action. Then carefully, Abigail removes the wedding band that binds Nicolaus to Deirdre, she hands it to her father, then places the wedding ring that binds him to her upon his finger. Their eyes meet in a gaze of pure love for each other.

"Nicolaus, for years now, I've had a foreshadow of you, seeing your face in that of my yet to be born children. I'm so happy that we've found each other and that we have Deirdre's blessing to wed. I promise to love you with all my heart, to take care of you, and respect you. I look forward to building a life with you and nurturing our children. Together." Abigail wipes away the tear of joy that streams from her eye.

Nicolaus takes a deep breath, to clear his emotion and to be present in the moment. His hold on her hand tightens a little. "Abigail, I love you and honor you, and I also look forward to building a life with you. Sometimes I'm shocked that we found each other and that we have each other, and I thank God for you, every day. I promise to love you, and cherish you, and respect you, and honor you each day that I live. I truly love you, and never want to be separated from you."

Married in the eyes of God in the church, they accept the Eucharist and prayers said over their lives and their persons. Once Bishop Moratey anoints their foreheads with holy oil, both Nicolaus and Abigail fall back onto the ground, wrapped in God's love, their hands still clasped together.

As Constance has already seen this scene with Nicolaus at his wedding with Deirdre, she comforts Cecil, Dominique, and Ceil, explaining what is happening, as the Bishop remains calm and continues to pray over the couple.

Cecil watches with fascination, as the couple endure God's divine love. After a few minutes, Nicolaus pops up on his feet, in awe of this happening to him again. He helps his wife up, their hands never leaving each other. Abigail is amazed at what she has just experienced.

Romantically, they kiss to seal their destined love, to the claps and happy banter of the family.

Later, back at the Ravenell castle in Tallin, Abigail disappears while the kitchen staff prepare their light dinner. Constance had everyone out to give the couple privacy, and let them feel more comfortable. Constance had Ceil book them rooms at a lively hotel, so they could be entertained and enjoy a meal, while seeing the beautiful sunset, and appreciate the moon, all in the same night.

The castle staff ask Nicolaus to wait at the bottom of the stairs for Abigail. Within minutes, Abigail sashays down the stairs in her flimsy frock with a solid matching robe, allowing a tease to Nicolaus, with flashes of that ankle length frock, as the robe flows behind her. As her mother said, Nicolaus could not take his eyes off her.

Descending the last stair, she takes him by the hand, and guides him to the small dining table. They sit close to the fire. Abigail sits herself on Nicolaus' lap. Immediately, his hands go around her waist and he does not object to her actions.

Then slowly, she puts the soup spoon in his mouth, then she kisses him. Nicolaus seems a little stunned at this action, and gives a light chuckle. When she does it again, she feels his hands tighten around her waist, and move along her hips.

Soup spoon number three, their kiss is deep and hot, making Abigail giggle. That giggle seemed to be the thing to do it, as he gently takes the spoon from her, and full on kisses her. Nicolaus holds Abigail in his arms, pulling her close to him. He feels his passion rise, and his desire for her is immense. Her soft body against him is more than inviting.

Nicolaus stands, lifting Abigail in his arms. Quickly, he romantically carries Abigail up those stairs, and into their bedroom, the same bedroom that he once shared with Deirdre, which once belonged to Nicohls and DeeDee, their ancestors.

Gently, Nicolaus lays Abigail upon the bed. He is next to her, admiring her lovingly. "You are so beautiful. Everything about you is absolutely beautiful. Your hair, your face, your body, your brain, your thoughts, your voice, your gestures. Even your strut."

Abigail giggles, "That's so sweet, honey, but I don't have a strut."

"Yes you do. You have an elegant, sexy walk, yet lady like. And those beautiful lips." He gently grasps her lips, one, two, three times. "The lips I love kissing. Merely kissing you gets me going. I've been suffering for five, no six months."

Abigail giggles again, "Oh my love, well suffer no more."

"I love you Abby. I thought love was over for me. That I would never be able to love again. You saved me. You know that? You restored me." He kisses her lips again, so grateful to have Abigail in his life. He is grateful every day that his father pushed them to be together.

"I'm here for you, my sweet, sweet love."

"You are such a blessing to my life. I love you Abigail Deirdre Omari-Ravenell. Promise you'll never leave me."

"I promise, Nicky. You're my sweet love."

Nicolaus took to kissing Abigail even more and all over her body, making her moan with desire for him. Her frock is gone, and their smooth, nude skin is upon each other.

As Nicolaus finally enters his wife, he receives a surprise. "Abby, darling, you're a virgin?" Her barrier stopping him momentarily.

"Yes, honey. Is that awkward?"

"My love, it's a wonderful gift." He grasps her lips, "Thank you."

Finally inside the sweet vaginal walls of his love, the feel of her warm flesh against his own flesh perplexes him beyond understanding. Nicolaus moans loudly at the feel of her as he robustly thrusts her with passion.

His love passion takes over his body, pushing him deeper and deeper inside of Abigail, stroking her soul, evoking pleasure utterances from her lips, until he reaches the height of intensive pulsation inside of her, making him cleave tightly to his wife. Their breathing is erratically elevated.

Abigail feels unbelievably happy. She takes Nicolaus' face into her hands, "Mr. Nicolaus Ravenell?"

"Yes, Mrs. Ravenell," he smiles at her with playfulness.

"You are truly my husband now."

"Yes, my love. I'm all yours."

"And we'll make babies, now?"

"Yes Love, we'll make all the babies you want," he kisses her irresistible lips.

"You promise, Love?"

"Yes, my love, I promise." He kisses her lips again, ready for another round of lovemaking. "You'll have to bear with me if I get nervous about the babies, though."

"Only good days ahead for us."

Chapter One Hundred Twenty-Five

Together, Nicolaus and Abigail decide to plant their roots and begin their family at their home in Colorado. They both enjoy and appreciate the atmosphere of the capitol city, the never-ending glorious and beautifully picturesque surroundings of nature, the endless hiking trails throughout, and the opportunity to learn the new sport of skiing, which Nicolaus easily masters.

Nicolaus moves the whole of the VMC company operations to Colorado, with approval of the board members. Nicolaus feels this will be fresh beginnings and a way to get innovative for the company, as well as having the advantage of the open-minded governmental leadership. He was delighted to find offices in the city, towards the top of a lovely glass skyscraper, which has a beautiful view of the Rocky Mountains. The building has all the amenities he wants for his staff, as well as state of the art technology.

Nicolaus offers relocation funds to any staff who want to move with the company, and six months' severance pay for those who don't. He is thrilled that Daniel Araceli, his Vice President, and most of the leadership team join them in Colorado. Eighty percent of the staff decided to take the new adventure. Within six months of the move, Nicolaus throws in a raise for everyone in appreciation of their loyalty to VMC.

Ceil seems sad as Nicolaus and Abigail finish packing the last of the belongings they want to take with them to Colorado. They stack the boxes for the movers to easily grab.

Constance and Cecil will be joining them in Colorado, keeping Deirdre's home for winter months to avoid living in the cold snowy weather.

Nicolaus and Abigail hug onto Ceil, Nicolaus wiping her tears. "Don't worry, we're just moving, not leaving forever," he chuckles.

"Anyway, once the kids start arriving, we'll be forced to visit. I promise you spring break and Christmas, right honey?"

Abigail nods with happy laughter and agreement. "Mother Ceil, you know you are welcomed to visit us at any time. There is plenty of room for all of us. Anyway, Nicky and I want to make a few holidays official family holidays, especially Thanksgiving and New Years."

Nicolaus picks up Elaine, and she gives him a very tight hug around his neck. He kisses her, and gives a kiss to Emily, who is in Elsa's arms.

"Yes, Mother Ceil, anyway, I have my own place in Colorado, and there is plenty of room for you at my place as well. I can imagine, eventually, Nicky and Abby's place will be crowded with lots of children."

Abigail laughs, "That's the plan! Seven children! Right, darling?" She lifts her head and gets on her tippy toes for a kiss from Nicolaus, and is not disappointed.

Abigail loved setting up their home in Colorado. She loved the house, felt that it fit them and their personalities perfectly. The area of town had wonderful schools for their future children as well. Both Abigail and Nicolaus loved having Constance and Cecil with them.

At first Constance and Cecil stayed in the house with Nicolaus and Abigail, until Nicolaus asked his wife to look for a house for them close by. Abigail surprised them with a house of their own. Constance absolutely adores the new house. Both she and Cecil cried at the generosity of Nicolaus.

Chapter One Hundred Twenty-Six

Nicolaus kept his promise to Abigail. Their children were born one year after the other, just as Abigail had envisioned. First Nicolai, then Nathanial, Matthew, Natalia, Corey, Ian, and Djordje, most recently arrived.

Nicolaus places intense prayers and blessings upon each child as they are born from Abigail's womb and when placed in his arms at the hospital. Each child also receives God's blessings as well, in the church, as each child is baptized.

By the age of five, the children get the treat of going for morning runs with their father. At first Abigail resisted this idea, and then realized that Nicolaus wanted his children to be strong, healthy, and to have the mental ability to rise up to a challenge. Once she realized this, she relented, and loved how Nicolaus included the children in most aspects of their lives.

"He really is a wonderful father," Abigail tells Ceil as she puts Djordje Jovan in her arms at the Ravenell mansion. Little Djordje is all of two months old, wrapped in a blanket. He looks up at Ceil, and she thinks she sees a smile.

"Oh my goodness! He's gorgeous! And with such a name!"

Abigail nods, "Yes, he's destined for greatness!"

"Grandma! Grandma! Watch this!" Nicolai excitedly calls to Ceil.

"Yeah, Granny, watch us get our dad!" Nathanial reiterates.

Ceil watches as the children work together as a team to climb up the muscular body of their giant father, each getting onto a particular spot. Then together, as a unit, they lean forward with the intent of pulling him down to the floor. Nicolaus goes with their intention and brings himself down with overly dramatic acting, for which the children giggle and laugh. Nicolaus laughs with them, as he ensures none of his children get hurt. When they have him on the floor, they each take to tickling and pinching him, making him laugh hardily, until he gives up and tells them they have won.

Ceil and Abigail laugh with the children as they perform their victory dance for their grandmother, then they help their father off the floor.

"We won grandma! We won!"

Ceil chuckles, loving the joy the children bring, no matter where they go. She appreciates how they all get along with each other, and how they look out for each other. She can see that they clearly understand that they are privileged children.

"Well, you sure did! You're all champions! Each and every one of you! You are Ravenell champions!" Ceil tells them.

Nicolaus grabs a football and he chases the children outside to play, grabbing his toddler, Ian, in his arms, carrying him out. Immediately, she can hear happy banter as the children play on the front lawn with their father.

Ceil sits down with the baby, holding him as if he is a precious jewel. Abigail sits with her. "My word, I have never seen Nicolaus so animated." She looks towards the door. "I've never seen him so happy." She touches Abigail, "You make him happy, dear. You've done that for him."

Abigail waves at her comment. "Oh, he's like that all the time." She touches Ceil's arm with sincerity, "You are due to pay us a visit at our Colorado home again. At least for Thanksgiving!"

Ceil nods slowly, "Perhaps I will." She has not been feeling well lately, though she did not tell this to anyone. She knows it is her time to go.

After about an hour, Nicolaus re-enters the Ravenell mansion with the children. The house staff and nannies are more than happy to assist the children to get cleaned up and clothes changed for mealtime, as does Nicolaus.

Nicolaus refreshes himself, changes quickly, and is downstairs. He sits with Ceil and Abigail, giving each a kiss to the head.

Ceil is quick to take Nicolaus' hand. "Nicolaus, I want to speak with you."

"Of course!"

"Would you please walk me to my room?"

Nicolaus nods, "Sure." He frowns with a little worry, as Ceil has never asked this of him. She puts her arm around Nicolaus' arm, as they slowly walk up the stairs and towards Ceil's bedroom.

Away from the joyful noise of children laughing and playing, Ceil tells him, "I am not surprised that you are such a wonderful father," she says proudly.

Her comment surprises Nicolaus, "Thank you," he says humbly, as he helps her up the stairs. "I just do the best I can for each of my children." Gentlemanly, he opens the door to the bedroom for her.

"No, it's more than that." She touches his shoulder. "I mean it Nicolaus, you are wonderful at everything you do; being a father, a CEO, a husband, a brother ... and a son." She hugs him to her. "I am very proud of what you have accomplished with your life. I apologize for so many wasted years between us, and I am so glad it is all worked out now."

Nicolaus kisses Ceil on the cheek. "Thank you, Ceil." The way she is saying these things worries him a little. He looks at her with an uncertain slight frown, "Are you feeling all right?"

"Oh yes. I am just a little tired, and am going to get some mandated rest now," she chuckles at her own words. "Remember always, ... that I love you, Nicolaus. My grandchildren are wonderful. I'm very proud of you. Your father would be very proud of you."

Nicolaus nods, "Thank you," and he turns to leave. Something makes him stop. He turns around to face Ceil, as she is still watching him walk from her. He steps up to her and takes her hands. "I love you, too ... mother," he tells her.

Ceil beams with a motherly smile to her face, and tears drop from her eyes. He has not called her 'mother' since the spat they had years ago when she told him not to call her 'mother'. For Ceil, this is a realization of true forgiveness that he is giving her. And what a time to give it!

Nicolaus hugs Ceil tightly, for a long while, in his warm, strong arms. Mixed emotions flood his brain and his heart. He kisses Ceil's cheek again, before leaving her.

Later that night, Ceil dies in her sleep.

Chapter One Hundred Twenty-Seven

SEVEN YEARS LATER

• • • •

NICOLAUS REMAINS AT the helm of VMC, and has expanded indigent care services with additional clinics. VMC continues to earn record multi-billion dollar profits and continues to receive generous community donations each year. The VMC children's homes are thriving in rescuing hundreds of children from foster care; and the VMC foundation and the educational scholarships have expanded. Nicolaus and Abigail continue their mentorship work for young people in the church, and their mentoring for start-up business owners. Nicolaus and VMC has received several awards and highlighted recognition from many professional organizations, both locally and nationally.

Nicolaus and Abigail's marriage is also quite a success, as they complement each other, and they truly have strong love for each other. They work as a team in everything: raising their children, the business, their volunteer work, and as mentoring leaders in their community. Abigail is thrilled and satisfied with Nicolaus, and Nicolaus enjoys being Abigail's husband.

Nicolaus is grateful that Abigail is the mother of his children, and they are both very grateful for their family. Nicolaus has provided a generous trust fund with trickle affects for each child to ensure their future. He has also fortified his inheritance for future generations of Ravenells.

Nicolaus keeps the romance in their marriage alive, as their attraction to each other ensures passionate lovemaking. Mother's Day is a massive celebration of importance in their family. Additionally, Nicolaus and Abigail take time to be away from the children to discover the world together and to strengthen their marriage.

Nicolaus takes Abigail on romantic getaways to France, the Alps, Egypt, Jamaica, the Bahamas, and anywhere else Abigail chooses to go. During the summer months, they vacation with the children, always to Greece to see Abigail's family; they spend time in Estonia; and Nicolaus travels to Morocco in discovery of his North African Moorish ancestors on his father's side.

Nicolaus learns his direct African ancestors were vital to the development of Morocco and Spain, and he learns he may have ancestral ties to well-known warriors in the ancient Mauritanian army of that region.

Abigail and Nicolaus continue their new annual family tradition of hosting a weeklong Thanksgiving celebration, and their festive New Years' party. Their guests are all of their family, including many cousins and their children, and several of their friends, in addition to Roddy, Sanchez, and Washington, and their wives and children, and Ishani and Maggie, and their husbands. They maintain these connections throughout their lifetimes.

Niall was reluctant to be included with family activities, now living divorced and alone at the Ravenell mansion in Austin. The mansion keeps him aggrieved of his sins, having not received the prescribed forgiveness from anyone. The weight of his sins is heavy on him, giving him a bitter spirit, and a loss of the zeal he once had for conquering women. Niall also now has a serious heart condition, which interferes with his proper manly functions.

Niall is often tormented by thoughts of Deirdre when he walks the halls of the mansion. His mind constantly sees images of her, and sleep has eluded him for years. Niall tries to atone for his sins by working in the church. Nicolaus has charged him with upkeep of the mansion and grounds, and he continues to work for the company, though remotely, and without ambition. Niall is a former shell of himself, barely visiting his daughters.

Even though Niall does not want to be around the family, Nicolaus insisted that he join all family gatherings to have some contact with the children, and so he begrudgingly attends. Niall has never really gotten comfortable being around Abigail, and it is apparent to everyone that she does not trust him. Nicolaus ensures Niall is always accompanied by another adult, as Abigail does not give him one speck of peace of mind regarding Deirdre.

During the Thanksgiving season, the men take two or three days for bonding on the ski slopes, away from their wives and children. They return in time to assist with any meal and holiday preparations and to attend other sporting events.

All year long, the Ravenell house in Colorado, is filled with love, joy, happy banter, and happy times. The only thing missing was a dog, until Djordje insisted on this, wanting them all to have a running partner. Finally, one Christmas, he is gifted an English Border Collie puppy. The children love this dog, and they name him Buddy. Buddy happily runs and plays with the Ravenell children.

Nicolaus corrals his healthy, happy, tall sons, all who resemble him: face, caramel skin color, hair texture, and frame. He gathers them around Abigail for their yearly portrait. He has the boys stand behind their mother, with the two tallest boys on each end. Nicolaus stands behind everyone, the only adult standing. With true joy in his heart, and gratefulness to God, he has his arms surrounding his children.

Djordje Jovan is now seven years old, and Nicolai is entering his teenage years. Emily and Elaine stand mixed in with the other children as normal, as their Uncle Nicky is their father figure. These two girls stand in with Nicolai, Nathanial, Matthew, Corey, Ian, and Djordje, who stand behind a seated Abigail. Natalia, who resembles her mother, sits on Abigail's lap. On either side of Abigail sits Constance and Cecil, both touching her shoulders, with Dominique next to Cecil. Elsa and Niall sit on the opposite line end of Francesca and Alan, her husband, newly added to their clan. Buddy sits at Abigail's feet.

The photographer speaks, "Okay now children, and everyone, be still, and smile at the camera! Ready? One, two, three!"

The photographer squeezes the flash bulb and freezes the moment in time of the prestigious, diverse, and celebrated family members of the prominent Ravenell Dynasty.

END OF BOOK THREE

Don't miss out!

Visit the website below and you can sign up to receive emails whenever Kamrynn Bellary publishes a new book. There's no charge and no obligation.

https://books2read.com/r/B-A-FNSCB-TLXMF

BOOKS 2 READ

Connecting independent readers to independent writers.